IN
GOD
WE
TRUST

—

A THRILLER

ADAM P.
GROSS

SETH K.
GROSS

IN GOD WE TRUST
East Channel Press

First Edition. First printed in the United States of America

ISBN: 978-0-9984622-0-2

10 9 8 7 6 5 4 3 2 1

DEDICATION

For Dad

AUTHOR'S NOTE

IN THE LATE 1970S, the Shah of Iran, with tacit US approval, purchased intaglio printing presses identical to those used by the US Bureau of Engraving and Printing. The presses were to be used by the Shah to print perfect counterfeit $100 bills to prop up his regime. Within months, Iran was wracked by revolution, the Shah had fled the country and the presses had fallen into the hands of the Ayatollah Khomeini and the newly created Islamic Republic of Iran. Despite credible expert witness testimony on the subject before a congressional committee, neither the United States government nor the Islamic Republic of Iran has admitted to the existence of the currency presses.

By the mid-1990s, so many perfect $100 counterfeits, known as Supernotes, were appearing in the Middle East and Russia that Interpol had set up a special unit just to track them. Interpol was convinced the source of the Supernotes was Iran. Expert witness testimony before the US Congress suggested that either Iran or Syria were behind the Supernote. The Iranian government called the accusations "wild hallucinations." The US government continued to officially deny the existence of the Supernote.

As a matter of public record, in 1996, the US Treasury reversed a long-standing policy, issuing a redesign of currency, which had not happened since 1929. The redesign added additional security features to US paper currency that are still being used today.

As a matter of public record, Supernotes, mimicking the $100 bill's redesign and security features, continue to appear throughout the Middle East. And Iran, despite a population explosion and a weak economy wholly dependant on the price of oil, has managed to spend hundreds of millions of dollars supporting Islamic groups, which engage in terrorist attacks against Israel and Western interests in the Middle East. The US government, though not the Islamic Republic of Iran, freely admits this last fact.

CHAPTER ONE

FARRAGUT WAS a dead man but he felt like a million bucks.

That was the strange thing. The thing he couldn't get his mind around. John Beckwith Farragut, PhD, Gene Garthwaite chair of Persian studies at Dartmouth College, once short-listed for the National Book Award, dues-paying member of Mensa, and an avid *Times* crossword player, was, by all accounts, a very intelligent man. He couldn't quite fathom how his own much-celebrated brain was being eaten away by the tumor.

As Farragut stared at his reflection in a bathroom mirror at New York's LaGuardia airport, the picture of health stared back. A full head of sandy blond hair was just starting to gray at the temples; he was one of the lucky ones whose hair resisted the ravages of chemotherapy.

Farragut looked closer at his reflection. *How appropriate*, he thought. *A covert cancer*. The tumor, like his time working for the Central Intelligence Agency, was hidden deep from view and known only to a select few. Although he'd retired from the CIA ten years ago, Farragut believed the tumor was cosmic payback for the terrible things he had done in the service of his country. And maybe, he reasoned, it was a gift. If the tumor could eat away his brain, perhaps it could devour those monstrous memories?

"United Airlines Washington Shuttle 715 will begin boarding in fifteen minutes, we will be asking our first class and special need passengers to begin boarding at that time."

The amplified voice of the boarding agent got Farragut's attention. Flight 715 was his father's flight. He knew better than to keep his father waiting. He splashed water on his face and then exited the restroom.

When Farragut entered the waiting area, he saw Rand Farragut, a silver fox in a Saville Row suit, sitting alone in a row of seats at the shuttle boarding gate. Farragut sat next to his father. Rand did not look up from the cell phone he was dialing.

"No need to stick around, son. The flight boards in five minutes."

"No problem," replied Farragut. "My flight doesn't leave for two hours and we're never in New York together. I just wish I wasn't here to see my oncologist. Greenblatt says I'm —"

"Greenblatt's top-notch. Top notch," said Rand, cutting his son off. "Heath Perkins from my board said Greenblatt did great work when his wife came down with breast cancer."

It was true. Dr. Benjamin Greenblatt was one of the top oncologists in the country, and thanks to his father's influence Farragut had bypassed his lengthy waiting list. Farragut, however, would have traded the inside access for a heart-to-heart talk with his father; they had never actually discussed the cancer and Farragut's prognosis. But Rand Farragut did not believe in probing human weakness unless it involved inveighing against a deficient employee.

"Dad, I never got to thank you for getting me in to see Dr. Greenblatt."

Rand held up a hand as his call went through. "Tim? Tell Senator Dulin that I can't make drinks tonight. I've got to meet with that idiot Miller over at Energy. And make sure the company jet is at National for my return. You know how I hate to wait in airports…"

As Rand gave a lengthy list of instructions to his assistant, Farragut rubbed his temples. His head hurt. Maybe it was the tumor.

Maybe it was his father. Or maybe it was the no longer easily suppressed acknowledgement that he was more like his father than he cared to admit. Farragut knew that he, too, was capable of cutting off his emotions. His preternatural detachment well served him in his Agency work, at least in the beginning but now he was seated a foot away from his father on possibly the last day he would ever see him. And he felt like there was nothing more to say.

Farragut heard someone clear his throat to get his attention. He looked up to notice a man in a blue pastel sweater standing next to a boy in a wheelchair. The boy had a plaster cast extending from his right leg to his hip. The man and the boy both wore black yarmulkes and a dark handsomeness. The boy looked to be around 12 or 13-years old and wore *Tefillin* strapped to his head and upper right arm. Farragut, who had traveled extensively in Israel, recognized the small cubic leather boxes worn by the boy. He knew they contained scrolls of parchment inscribed with Torah verses and were worn by observant Jews during weekday morning prayers.

The man said with a Middle-Eastern accent, "Excuse me, sir. My name is Asher Doron. This is my son Barak. May I trouble you please with a question?"

Farragut smiled. "How can I help you, Mr. Doron?"

"Barak's traveling alone to Washington. I myself was supposed to be traveling with him but the ticketing agent booked me on a later flight and I cannot find anyone who will switch. Barak is a polite boy but he is afraid to fly. Would it be too much trouble for you to look out for him on the plane? His uncle will meet him at the gate in Washington."

"Normally it would be my pleasure but I'm not going to Washington. I'm just waiting here with my father until he boards." Farragut gestured towards Rand, who had his face buried in The *Financial Times*.

"Yes. Well. Thank you much," Doron muttered in his uneven English. He anxiously glanced around the boarding area in search of a chaperone for his son. Farragut, feeling guilty, did the same. It was a typical Washington Shuttle crowd, people with power and prestige, arrogance and attitude, their faces buried in iPads or their ears pressed to cell phones, too self-absorbed for anyone but themselves.

Farragut turned his attention back to Doron, who was still scanning the boarding area. "Mr. Doron, I'm sure my father would have no problem looking out for Barak."

Rand Farragut peered out from under his paper.

"Now see here," barked Rand, glaring at Doron and Barak, this crippled boy with the odd black leather boxes strapped to his head and arm. "I'm a businessman, not a babysitter."

"Sir, Barak is a well-behaved boy who will be no trouble," pressed Doron. "All I ask is that you remind him to say his prayers and alert the flight attendants for him if there is trouble. You see, he is a shy boy and afraid to fly." Doron squeezed Barak's arm just below where the *Tefillin* was attached with black leather straps. The straps ran down the length of Barak's arm.

Rand Farragut rolled his eyes. "Really, this is most inconvenient —"

"Dammit, Dad," Farragut snapped. "Just look out for the boy, okay? For once in your life do something nice, for someone else's son if not your own."

Rand regarded his own son with shock. He was not used to being snapped at. He mumbled, "Okay," and buried his head back in the *Financial Times*.

Farragut took a calming breath. When he had learned about the tumor, he had made a promise to stop judging his father, but Rand's lack of grace never failed to rankle. His anger abated as he watched Doron tenderly kiss Barak goodbye. Barak was sweating and trembling, biting his lower lip in a futile effort to control his fear. Doron handed Barak's first-class ticket to Farragut.

"Thank you. And God bless you," Doron told Farragut. He turned and walked away.

Barak watched with tears in his eyes as his father disappeared into the crowded terminal. He was sweating so heavily that the head *Tefillin* began sliding down his forehead. The straps unwound and the prayer box landed on the floor with a soft *thump*. Barak practically jumped out of his wheelchair, alarmed by this transgression against God. He stared at the *Tefillin*, too terrified to pick it up.

Farragut picked up the little box with its attached leather straps and placed it in Barak's lap. "It's okay. God won't punish you for being nervous. When I was your age I hated to fly, too."

The boy gave Farragut a brave smile and suddenly Farragut felt an overwhelming, irrational love for him. The intensity of his emotion shocked Farragut. His tortured relationship with his own father had extinguished any paternal longing he might have felt. He now realized that he desperately wanted a child. Of course, the tumor made fatherhood impossible.

A voice over the loudspeaker announced, *"United Airlines Washington Shuttle 715 will now begin boarding our first class and special need passengers."*

Farragut wheeled Barak to the gate and checked his tickets with the flight attendant. Unexpectedly, Barak gave Farragut a hug. Farragut returned the gesture. He felt a tug at his sleeve and turned to see his father.

-:::::-

"You can beat this, John," Rand mumbled. "This cancer..." His words trailed off.

Farragut knew his father's concern was not insubstantial, in light of the strain between them. He understood this truth; his father wanted to feel but no one had ever shown him how. Oil was meant to rise from the depths; feelings were not.

Farragut shook his father's hand. He watched as his father grabbed the handles of Barak's wheelchair, pushing the boy down the gangway and disappearing from view.

Farragut stood still for several minutes, thinking about nothing in particular, especially not his own mortality. As he began to walk back towards the main terminal, he saw it on the floor, Barak's *Tefillin*. Apparently, the *Tefillin* had fallen from Barak's lap when he had hugged Farragut. The boarding gate was now closed. No sense returning the religious artifact to its owner now. He picked up the small black leather box containing the most sacred verses of a religion he did not believe in and thrust it into the pocket of his tattered Harris Tweed. "I could use some luck," he thought.

-:::::-

Twenty minutes later, Farragut was eating French fries at an airport McDonald's and on the cell phone with his health insurance company. The customer service rep on the phone had the unique ability to make dying of cancer an even more miserable experience than it already was.

"I'm sorry but it's more than a problem with the paperwork," she warned him. "The doctor you saw in New York is not a part of our network and we can't reimburse for the visit."

Farragut shoved a French fry in his mouth. "But Dr. Greenblatt was listed as part of the network in the directory."

"Yes. But he had opted out after the printing of the directory. If you had checked the up-to-date, online directory, you would've known this."

"Then what was the point of the printed directory if you only go by the online version?" She put him on hold before offering an answer. An instrumental Muzak version of The Carpenters' "Superstar" droned through the phone. Farragut considered a Muzak version of any Carpenters' song to be redundant, but he had to admit the hook was catchy.

Farragut sang the first verse. Through the plate glass windows of the terminal, he watched the plane carrying his father and Barak taxi towards the runway. He was singing the part about the guitar sounding sweet and clear when the plane exploded on the tarmac.

CHAPTER TWO

I AM FACE FIRST on the floor. The floor is red. That must be blood. My blood. My nose is bleeding. I can hear a whooshing noise. The wind is blowing up a gale. I thought I was inside? But outside is now inside. The explosion has torn a huge hole in the side of the terminal.

The plane is outside on the tarmac. The cabin has been blasted into two parts. The front half is destroyed, belching fire. The rear half sits on the runway. I can see people sitting in the split cabin as if they were miniature people in that ride I used to love at Disneyland. Father took me there when I was a boy.

The boy. Barak. My father. Are they alive or dead?

The blast has blown the windows out of the terminal. Bodies everywhere. That woman lying next to me has her leg twisted behind her head. The bone jutting from her thigh seems more yellow than a bone should look.

Who is that crawling out from the remains of the boarding gate? It's Asher Doron. His blue sweater is covered with gray dust. That pastel blue sweater. Didn't the Agency train me that pastels deflect suspicion?

Doron has a briefcase. He didn't have a briefcase before when he dropped off Barak. Now he is walking away calmly down the corridor.

Doron is walking away with the briefcase that he didn't have before.

Farragut hoisted himself to his feet. His legs were weak, his balance off. Through the hole where the terminal windows had been, he now saw the plane burning on the tarmac more clearly. His initial impression had been correct; the plane had been cleaved in two. The explosion had consumed the front half, first class and business class, including the cockpit and the wings. His father and Barak would have been sitting in first class. Only the tail section of the plane was fairly intact and not on fire. Emergency vehicles were descending on the wreckage and dousing the flames. Survivors were spilling out of the rear emergency exits on large inflatable chutes.

In the terminal, Farragut saw a wave of humanity rushing away from the point of the explosion. Yet Doron continued to walk away with conspicuously unhurried strides. Farragut stumbled after Doron.

As he began to recover from the shock of the explosion, Farragut noticed the terminal area affected by the blast was limited. Twenty yards from the boarding gate there was no damage and no bodies. If the plane had been closer to the terminal, the carnage would have been much worse.

Farragut quickly caught up to Doron. His body and brain not yet in full sync due to shock, he grabbed Doron by the shoulder. Doron turned to face him. For a moment, each man stared in the other's eyes, contemplating a next move, brains still scrambled by the blast. Doron slammed the briefcase into Farragut's ribs, knocking the wind from his lungs.

Farragut collapsed to the floor. Doron stumbled forward, still holding the briefcase. Farragut lay on the floor trying to catch his breath. The air in the terminal was hot, filled with dust and seemed to lack oxygen. From the floor, he saw Doron break into an unsteady run down the terminal corridor along with several dozen frightened souls. Farragut pulled himself to his feet and staggered after Doron.

Down the corridor, Doron sprinted past a female Port Authority officer who was futilely trying to stop the stampede. She didn't notice Doron as he ran past. He, like the dozens of other panicked people, ignored her command to remain calm. Farragut arrived seconds later. The officer's nametag identified her as Tattivito.

"There's a man who just ran past. He's wearing a blue sweater, a yarmulke, and holding a briefcase. I think he's the one responsible for this."

"Relax, sir. Remain calm," commanded Tattivito.

Farragut noticed she looked young. She had schoolgirl's acne and had done a poor job plucking her eyebrows. She was experimenting with looking older. The thought occurred to him that this time last year, she was probably picking out a prom dress.

"Dammit. Call it in and alert the others."

Farragut pulled her radio from her belt, pressed it into her hands, and stumbled after Doron.

Down the corridor, Doron's instinct for self-preservation was kicking in. He used the briefcase like a club to cut a channel through the gridlock caused by terrified travelers. The people here had heard the explosion but had no idea the perpetrator was among them.

Doron approached the ticketing agent at the American Airlines gate. His lips pulled back into a smile that leaked desperation.

"I have a ticket to Chicago. When do we board?"

The ticketing agent took in the sight of the bloody, manic man in the blue sweater. She was a ten-year veteran. She had dealt with VIPs on angel dust and two attempted kidnappings. She was frosty then. She was frostier now.

"Sir, there's been an explosion on the tarmac," she said to the man who had obviously just lived through it. "We are pulling passengers off the plane who have already boarded."

"I must leave now. I have a ticket."

Doron reached into his pocket and handed her his ticket. It was covered with blood from a jagged cut he had near his thigh that had not yet registered with his brain.

"The flight has been cancelled, sir. Now if you'll just sit down and relax I will see that you get medical attention."

"I have money. I will pay money for the flight not to be cancelled."

Doron slammed the briefcase on the counter. He fumbled for the locks. The "click" of the briefcase lock was echoed by the "click" of the safety on a 9mm Beretta.

"Put your hands in the air where I can see them."

Officer Ted Hartney, his gun drawn into a professional two-handed stance, stood five feet behind Doron's back. He had been on the job for eight years — seven longer than Tattivito — but this was the first time he had ever pulled his gun.

"Officer, what have I done wrong?" pleaded Doron while turning to face Hartney.

Doron immediately saw an advantage. The cop was holding him too close. Doron edged closer.

"Drop to your knees and lie on the ground," ordered Hartney.

Doron kicked with his right leg and caught Hartney in the groin. Hartney dropped his gun. Doron grabbed Hartney's Beretta and fired two shots. The kick to the balls had hurt Hartney more than the two bullets to the head, but it was the bullets that killed him.

Just twenty yards away Farragut heard the shots and the ensuing screams. As people dropped to the floor, cowering with their hands over their heads, Farragut dropped with them. Officer Tattivito did not. She had been running ahead of Farragut to back up her fellow officer. Doron shot her dead with two more shots from his Beretta.

Doron swept the revolver back and forth. "I will shoot you all! I will! I will shoot you all!"

"If you're going to shoot anyone, shoot me," said Farragut. He was already standing up again, now not twenty feet away, walking cautiously toward the fallen body of Officer Tattivito.

Doron whipped the gun around and aimed at Farragut. "Stand back or I will kill you!"

Doron searched the ground. The ticketing agent cowered and cried at his feet. He yanked her up and stuck his gun against her head. But his eyes were on Farragut.

"You," he screamed at Farragut. "You get down now. Or I will shoot her."

Farragut lay down by the body of Officer Tattivito. He had hoped to have been ordered to lie down there all along.

Using the ticketing agent as a shield, Doron backed up towards the walkway that led outside to the American 767 waiting on the tarmac. His right hand held the gun to her head. His left hand held the briefcase.

"I want this plane and a crew to fly me to wherever I want or I will shoot this woman."

With a motion so surreptitious as to suggest no movement at all, Farragut slid his right hand over Officer Tattivito's holster and felt the comforting contours of the 9mm Beretta secured within. He was well acquainted with this weapon. A short recoil. A fast cycle time. As Doron repeated his demands, Farragut pulled Tattivito's gun from the holster and sighted it at Doron.

Farragut fired. The bullet tore through Doron's left hand, forcing him to drop the briefcase. Instinctively, he brought his right hand down over his wounded left, dropping his gun.

The ticketing agent was unhurt. In fact, she ran off down the corridor with such speed that it appeared a superhuman act, given she was wearing three inch heels.

Farragut stood and aimed his gun at Doron, who was staring at the bloody claw that had once been his left hand. It took a Herculean effort of self-control for Farragut not to shoot dead this man who had just murdered so many. He grabbed Doron and shook him violently.

"Why, you son-of-a-bitch? Why?"

Doron said nothing. He didn't need to. The answer had spilled from his briefcase onto the blood-soaked terminal floor.

The answer was one million dollars' worth of $100 bills.

CHAPTER THREE

TWENTY HOURS later, $990,000 of that $1 million sat on the table of the interrogation room of the FBI offices in lower Manhattan. A random sample of $10,000 was being analyzed at the US Secret Service Forensic Analysis Lab in Washington, DC.

Kareem Shuqueiri, aka Asher Doron, sat stone-faced in his chair, fighting the urge to sleep. Towering above him on the opposite side of the table stood FBI Special Agent Doug Alson. Alson stood 6' 5" and was built like an Olympic wrestler gone to seed. When he spoke, the gut straining over his belt jiggled with each syllable.

"I'm boring you, aren't I, Kareem. I'm boring you because we've gone over this a thousand times. Let's make it 1,001 just for fun. So here's what we know, amigo. You blew up the plane to kill Dov Lowenstein, an Israeli arms dealer with strong ties to the Israeli Defense Force and the US Congress. You also got his bodyguard, Misha Gochman, an ex-Mossad agent known as the "Gargoyle of Gaza." Two Jews for the price of one. And if you had to waste a planeload of innocent people to do it? Fuck it. Hey! Open your fucking eyes!"

Alson jabbed a meaty finger into Shuqueiri's forehead. Shuqueiri's eyes fluttered open. He had been under interrogation for hours. The doctor had bandaged his hand and pumped him full of codeine for the pain. He couldn't remember whether they had offered him a lawyer. The codeine made it hard to concentrate. He concentrated instead on his tormentor. Alson's bald head was covered with beads of sweat. His breath stank from the bacon burger he had devoured earlier.

"Smart," said Alson as he tapped his nose with a ketchup-stained finger. "You and the kid posing as a couple of Israelis. Hey, I see those news reports on the TV of the Jews killing the Palestinians and even I can't tell them apart. Then molding the bomb with C4 into a cast on the kid's leg? Brilliant. But here's the dumb part. I'll bet the bomb wasn't set to go off until the plane was over the Potomac. Except your kid – what's his name? Not Barak. His real name."

Shuqueiri said nothing. Alson pulled a scrap of paper out of his shirt pocket, read whatever was scrawled on it, then tossed it over his shoulder.

"Yasir. That how you pronounce it? Okay, Yasir is sitting there minding his own business, nervous, waiting for the plane to take off. And that's when he notices. He lost one of the detonators. It must have slipped off back at the terminal. Luckily, somebody found it."

Alson pulled something from his pants pocket and placed it on the table in front of Shuqueiri, Yasir's *Tefillin*. The one found by Farragut at the airport.

"I ain't gonna try to pronounce the word for this thing. *Putz* and *schmuck* is the extent of my ethnic vocabulary. But we know this is an Orthodox Jewish prayer box. The ritual involves strapping this doohickie to your head and arm. What it does not involve is soaking the straps in potassium nitrate and turning them into fuses. Or treating the parchment verses inside the box with potassium chlorate, red phosphorous, and Elmer's glue, turning them into matches to light the fuses. Or glazing the prayer box with mercury fulminate, turning it into a detonator when attached to the C4 and set off by the fuse. And you knew that the TSA would not check your prayer boxes closely, not after those poor *schmucks* got into trouble praying with these thingamajigs on that Alaskan Airlines flight a while back.

There was plenty of fallout from the Jewish Community for 'religious insensitivity' after that little fuckup. But hey, you know that. In fact, you were counting on it."

Shuqueiri stared at the *Tefillin* on the table. He felt groggy from the codeine but wanted desperately to think clearly.

"Where did you get that?"

"I told you. Yasir misplaced it back at the terminal. A concerned citizen found it but by then the plane had boarded. No doubt Yasir realized pretty quickly that the backup detonator was gone. So he panicked. He decided to take care of business right then and there. So he got a flight attendant to help him into the restroom. Then he strapped the detonator box around his cast, lit the fuse strap with the homemade parchment match, and then Ka-Blam-Ka-Fucking-Boom!"

The last word erupted from Alson's chest like a gunshot. Shuqueiri jerked in his seat.

"So one last question," said Alson as he picked up a roll of hundreds. "The $64,000 question. Christ, let's correct that. It's the $1 million question…"

Alson picked up a roll of hundreds. His face flash-cracked rage.

"What kind of sick fuck kills his own kid for a million bucks?!"

Alson smashed the roll of bills across Shuqueiri's face. Shuqueiri showed no reaction. He wanted to talk but talking was what his benefactors in Beirut had told him he must never do. And if Shuqueiri did talk, would Alson even believe him? How to explain to this imperialist puppet that Yasir had volunteered – yes, *volunteered* — to become a martyr?

Alson had referred to Yasir as a "kid." That was incorrect. Yasir, although only eleven, had never experienced a real childhood growing up in the poverty and soul-destroying captivity of the Rashidiyeh refugee camp. He knew that he could pass through security with his leg cast bomb without drawing the attention of the authorities the way an adult like Shuqueiri would. Even then, Yasir had agonized over the decision; not because he was afraid but because the Quran forbids suicide even while Allah had decreed *jihad* as legitimate to

IN GOD WE TRUST

deliver believers from those infidels who would enslave them. What true "kid" had ever struggled with such thoughts?

There was a knock from the other side of the one-way observation mirror. Alson got up and left the room. Shuqueiri closed his eyes and let the codeine caress him. Alson entered the observation room to find Treasury Agent Mia Kelly hanging up the phone.

"That was forensics lab in Washington. They confirmed that the bills in Shuqueiri's suitcase were Supernotes."

"Supernotes. Fucking Yippee-kay-A!"

"The Attorney General is passing the ball from FBI to Treasury. I'm authorized to deal in exchange for Shuqueiri's cooperation on the cash."

"Deal what? This mook wasted a whole bunch of taxpayers!"

Alson already knew what the deal would involve and he hated dealing with dirt bags like Shuqueiri. But what could he do? He and Kelly were both assigned to the Joint Terrorism Task Force, but Supernotes were a Secret Service sacred cow — Kelly's turf. Alson was a Bureau boy — plots and plans and people, living and dead — the meat and potatoes stuff.

Mia handed Alson a thick manila file folder. "CIA sent this over. A present from their friends in Israeli Intelligence. Seems the late Mr. Lowenstein had powerful friends in Tel Aviv and Washington so this thing's gone global."

Alson couldn't read the Hebrew on the file folder or the funny little look Mia's eye.

"Terrific. What am I supposed to do with this?" he said.

"That's our ace in the hole. When I need it, knock on the window and I'll come back here and get it."

"Why don't you just signal me when you'll need it?"

"No. It's gotta come from you. He doesn't like you. Me, he's gonna love."

"For Chrissakes, Kelly. I'm a special agent, not a psychic. How am I supposed to know when you'll need this file?"

"You'll know. And by the way, call me Mia."

Alson had just met Kelly last month and he couldn't get a handle on her. He recalled what his buddy Weglarz at Treasury had told him about her. She was a too intense for Weggie's taste but an excellent agent, smart, political, and methodical. Her father had been a state Supreme Court judge. A grandfather had been a congressman. She probably should have been doing the Beltway Waltz with the Brahmins at State rather than busting her hump with the law enforcement grunts in New York. But Weglarz said she never made anyone feel like she was slumming it. She was always the first to buy beers for the team even if she only drank single malt Scotch.

Alson watched Mia walk into the interrogation room. He had to admit that she looked a damn sight finer in her sleek designer suit than he did in his off-the-rack suit.

That fuck face Kareem was going to eat her alive.

CHAPTER FOUR

S HUQUEIRI WATCHED the woman stride into the interrogation room and take her place behind the desk. She was
much smaller than the brutish Alson. Luckily, she didn't look
as venomous. She looked…blank. He couldn't read her. And that
scared him even more.

"Mr. Shuqueiri, I'm Special Agent Mia Kelly of the United States
Secret Service. I don't care how or why you blew up the plane so save
that for the FBI. What I do care about, very much, is how you were
paid. Specifically, the bills you were paid with."

Mia picked up the roll of bills with which Alson had hit Shuqueiri.
She examined the roll as if it were a rare orchid she had traveled a
thousand miles to touch.

"We've confirmed that the bills in your suitcase are Supernotes."

And so there it was, thought Shuqueiri. *The Supernote.*

For as sure as every pilgrim's road led to Mecca, every Treasury
agent's trail led to that Holy Grail. Every fighter at every point in the
interweaving webs of resistance knew that the Americans were ob-
sessed with finding the source of the Supernote. Well, the location
of the Supernote facility was the most valuable secret Shuqueiri's
benefactors had. He would never betray it.

Mia's eyes drilled into Shuqueiri's. "Not familiar with the Supernote? Okay. I will not insult you and assume that you are a liar. Let me explain. The Supernote is the world's finest counterfeit American currency. It passes right through our scanners here at the Federal Reserve. It's printed on the same paper as real US legal tender. Same ink and same process on the same type of press. But instead of buying baseball, hot dogs, apple pies and Chevrolets, these dollars buy terrorism."

Terrorism. Mia let the word hang in the air like dead smoke. She could have gone on about how the Supernote had been linked to funding terrorism against American interests abroad. These included countless hijackings, the bombing of the Marine barracks in Beirut in the 1980s, the attack on the USS Cole in the 1990s and the US embassy bombings in Kenya and Tanzania but Shuqueiri would have shrugged and said nothing. No, Mia was here to make a human connection. She would appeal to his heart rather than his hate.

Mia placed a photo on the table and slid it across to him. Shuqueiri twitched in his chair. He recognized these were just typical interrogation theatrics as taught to him by his masters. *Don't even look at the photo*, he told himself. But through tired eyes he did look because he didn't know when he'd ever get to look at this photo again. It was a photo, his photo, of the twins at 10-years-old. Laughing on the beach in Lebanon. This picture had occupied a place of honor by his bed in his apartment in Brooklyn. That meant that these people had been there in his home. It was an outrage. Shuqueiri felt like screaming but he said nothing.

Mia looked at Shuqueiri looking at the picture.

"Your twin boys, Marwan and Jawad, were murdered by an Israeli booby trap in Gaza 10 years ago. They were what? Eleven?"

They had been ten but he said nothing.

"They were beautiful boys, Kareem. Can I call you Kareem, Mr. Shuqueiri?"

Kareem said nothing, then nodded. What did it matter what she called him? What mattered was that he was the father of the twin boys: Marwan and Jawad. Or rather, *had been* their father.

Mia handed him some tissues to dry his eyes. Why? He was not crying. Yes, his eyes were tired, watering from lack of sleep, but he was not crying. The tissues she gave him smelled nice. Like a flower. Like a woman. His wife's perfume, jasmine and orange blossom, seeped from his memory, even as he had trouble recalling her face.

"We didn't find a picture of your wife, Kareem. But we know that she died from the cholera epidemic that swept through the Rashidiyeh camp seven years back. We also know that your brother died —"

Murdered. He was murdered. But he would not tell her that. And to his surprise, he didn't have to.

"Correction: was murdered by the Israelis during the Gaza War in 2009." continued Mia. "His son was Yasir, the poor lamb on the plane. He was your nephew, right? You don't have to answer. Canada's Immigration authorities have sent over all the paperwork. Yasir immigrated to Toronto last year to live with your cousin. Admittedly, their immigration laws are more lenient and liberal than our own, particularly in light of recent events. The Canadians are already cooperating and have questioned your cousin. We know he helped you smuggle Yasir into America but we have no reason to believe that he had anything to do with this regrettable incident at the airport today. I assure you, he will not be charged. And the guys at the garage in Jersey City where you work? They won't be charged either. They are very disappointed, shocked really, at what has happened. But they say you were a nice guy and a terrific mechanic. Here, you need to blow your nose."

Mia handed him another tissue as his eyes were really watering a great deal. Shuqueiri dabbed his cheeks with the tissues that smelled like his wife.

"Kareem. Please believe me. I know the will it must have taken for you to sacrifice your nephew after all you've lost. Some might think you a coward but I do not. To live on after a loved one dies? That pain is worse than death. Death would be deliverance. To lose a child is to feel as if your insides have been torn out."

"You cannot know how I feel," whispered Shuqueiri.

Mia reached out and put her hand over Shuqueiri's left hand, which was clenched into a tight fist. Her touch shot through his body like morphine, dulling everything, pulling the pain and tightness and tension from his body and soul.

"Oh. But I can know how you feel, Kareem. You see I, too, lost a child. My only child. My son."

Mia pulled out her wallet and put a photo of an adorable blond boy in front of him. Shuqueiri stared at the photo. The boy sat in a backyard swing. His smile revealed two missing front teeth. He wore a "Harry Potter" T-shirt. Yasir had loved those movies and watched them many times. His twins had never seen them but he was sure they would have loved them, too.

Shuqueiri looked up at Mia but she was not looking at him. Her eyes were far away, looking beyond the observation mirror, as if the boy in the swing who loved "Harry Potter" was somewhere out there.

"My son, my baby, died not as a martyr, not as your nephew did. He died because another man had too much to drink. And that man ran over my son with his car, killed my baby, as he played in the street in front of our home."

For the first time, Shuqueiri wanted to say something. To make contact with her like a man. Instead, he spoke like a *mullah*. He wished he had said nothing at all.

"The Quran forbids alcohol. Allah has forbidden everything that harms the body and saps the strength."

"I know. Allah wisely forbids everything that is harmful to a person. But the man who murdered my son had not read the Quran. He was not a man of God like you. What this man was, was my husband."

Shuqueiri looked up at Mia who was still staring sadly at the ghost of her son in the mirror beyond.

There was a knock from outside. Shuqueiri watched Mia take her son's photo and place it back in her wallet. Then she walked out of the room. She had left him the photo of his twins. He slipped it into his pocket. He didn't want to look at photos of dead children anymore.

Shuqueiri listened to the faint electrical hum from the overhead lights. He could not hear what Mia and Alson were saying behind the observation mirror. The room smelled like Alson's bacon burger. Puddles of congealed grease defiled the tabletop. Shuqueiri sniffed one of the tissues Mia had given him. He smelled his wife's perfume again.

Shuqueiri opened his eyes as Mia entered the room. She held a manila folder in her hand. She sat across from him and put the folder down on the table.

"How strong is your belief in God, Kareem?"

It was a question that seemed to have come from a strange place. The answer came straight from his heart.

"God is great. Muhammad is his one and only prophet." Okay, he was talking now. But what harm was there in talking about God?

Mia said, "Forgive me, it's been years since I studied it at university, but you, as a Muslim, believe in Divine Predestination, right?"

Shuqueiri nodded. "*Al-Qadar*. God knows everything. He knows what has happened and what will happen. God has recorded all that has happened and all that will happen. Whatever God wills to happen, happens, and whatever God wills not to happen, does not happen. God is the creator of all things."

"But Muslims also believe in free will? A man can still choose right from wrong and is responsible for his actions?"

"Correct," said Shuqueiri. This was a woman he would have liked to have known in a different time and place. She was not like most of her countrymen. Not like that infidel Alson.

"So you can choose, Kareem. And whatever you choose, God has willed it. So if you choose to tell us where this Supernote Press is, well, God has willed that, too."

Shuqueiri considered this. She was back to the Supernote. He preferred talking about God. He raised his injured hand. The pain was getting more intense.

"If I could get another shot..."

"Soon, Kareem. God knows I don't want you to suffer anymore. But about the Supernote Press? I must know where it is and who is running it. If you tell me these things, if you help me, I will be able to help you. And I do want to help you. I think you know that."

"I told you. I don't know about the Supernote Press or the Supernote."

Mia nodded and reached for the manila folder. She pulled out a photograph.

Shuqueiri looked at the photo without being asked. He saw the description of the photo was written in both Hebrew, which he could recognize but not read, as well as English, which he read with difficulty. But he recognized the neighborhood in the aerial photograph with no difficulty. It was a certain Gaza City block circled once with red marker and a certain house on that block circled twice in red marker. His sister shared that house with her husband and three daughters. They were not freedom fighters. They were simply his family. The only surviving family he had left.

Mia said, "Israeli intelligence sent this over to aid in our investigation. The photo was taken from an Israeli gunship. Our people got to them just in time, kept the missiles from going off. They were ready to level the whole block. Dov Lowenstein was a much beloved favorite son. An eye for an eye with those people, right?"

Shuqueiri closed his eyes. He saw the Israeli gunship hovering a few thousand feet in the gray Gaza sky. He saw his sister's house squatting below in the dusty street. He saw the rockets from the helicopter crashing into the house and the house collapsing to the ground and the heap of flame and dust and death. He saw all these things.

Mia saw it was all over.

"I'll play their game, Kareem. Because it's my job and you must pay for what you did. Twenty-four people died on that plane. Including Yasir. It would have been more if it had been airborne. My government wants your blood. The Israeli government wants your family's blood. But I don't want to see anyone else die. Including you. You give me the Supernote Press and I will give you my word. The death penalty comes off the table. The Israelis back off and you remain alive along with what's left of your family. You'll be in prison for a long time. Life, probably. But maybe you'll live long enough to see the creation of the Palestinian State so many have already died for. Because it will happen, Kareem. A wind of change is blowing in the Middle East. Look at Egypt. Look at Libya."

Mia walked around the table and leaned close to Shuqueiri. She whispered in his ear the way his wife had whispered to the twins when his wife and the twins were still alive.

"Don't blame yourself. You are doing the decent thing by helping us. Allah understands. Allah has willed it. So it is written."

She was right, of course. He hadn't wanted to talk but Allah, the Almighty, the Creator, the Sovereign and the Sustainer of everything in the universe, had known all along that he was going to tell her what she wanted to know.

CHAPTER FIVE

OUR HOURS later, Kareem Shuqueiri had talked, blabbed, conversed, and confessed with the lie detector both off and on. Tired and twisted into a thousand knots, he had thanked Mia profusely when it was over, then got another codeine shot and a warm bed in the Federal holding cell. But most important, he got peace of mind and a reason to live. Mia had given him that and he had given Mia the Supernote.

Mia and Alson did the post-game analysis at a nearby Chinese restaurant, Madame Wong's Four Rivers. Mia sipped club soda because the liquor list had not looked promising. The favored drinks at Madame Wong's tended toward the lethally alcoholic garnished with chunks of canned fruit. Photographs of famous Taiwanese actors — she assumed they were famous — looked down from the red walls. They had chosen this place because they wanted to avoid the local watering holes filled with DAs, cops, and defense lawyers. Like a couple on the downside of an illicit affair, Mia and Alson needed a place to pout and shout in privacy.

"Bullshit. Crap. Zip. Nada. A fucking waste of time," moaned Alson after devouring the cherry atop his Fog Cutter.

"I disagree," said Mia. "Shuqueiri gave us the location of the Supernote Press. Three basic rules of real estate. Location. Location. Location."

"He gave us the *general* location. That's still like looking for a needle in a haystack."

"But at least we know the haystack is in Tehran, not Lebanon or Syria."

"Iran or Lebanon or Syria or Timbuktu, they're all the Agency's business, not ours."

Mia thought of John Farragut and the fact that the Agency had already taken care of business right here in New York. But Farragut's past and her past with Farragut was not Alson's business. Not yet.

"It's our business, too. Look at it this way, Doug. The idea behind the Department of Homeland Security is for all of us to share information and ideas and strategy. FBI. CIA. NSA. DIA. Treasury. The whole alphabet soup is supposed to get mixed up and made into something better. You know, like a delicious bouillabaisse."

"What's bouillabaisse?"

"It's a French fish soup. More like a stew, actually. Delicious."

Alson sipped his Fog Cutter. His stomach was empty and he was feeling the buzz.

"Fact is, I was happy to have you in there today with Kareem," he said. "You cracked him good."

Mia sipped her club soda. Alson was still calling him Kareem; Shuqueiri being just too difficult to pronounce, especially after a few drinks.

Mia said, "I think there may be an opportunity to act on the information Shuqueiri gave us in a unique and creative fashion. Let's go over it again."

"To recap," said Alson wearily. "Our boy Kareem enters this country legally five years ago on a student visa and then goes to ground. Gets a job in a Jersey City garage where he works hard and hardly makes a peep about being paid less than minimum wage which endears him to his employer — an Egyptian with a soft spot for slavery. Kareem keeps a low profile. Never late. Never sick. Never complains. Nice to old folks and animals. He goes to Church …"

"Mosque. He goes to a mosque," interjected Mia.

Alson pulled a chunk of pineapple from his drink and wolfed it down.

"A mosque. Whatever. He's an average Joe, excuse me, an average Kareem, when one day, a mystery guy at the mosque approaches him and tells him that he can get even for all the shit that happened to has family back in Palestine. Kareem is a willing recruit and this mystery guy makes it easy by taking care of everything. Arranges for little Yasir to get a Canadian visa on a hardship, humanitarian beef. Works with Kareem's cousin to slip the kid across the border into the USA and right into Uncle Kareem's loving arms. Picks the target, buys the plane tickets, engineers, the explosives — very clever that cast bomb set-up. Then mosque man puts the cherry on the sundae, $1 million in Supernotes for future operations to be dispensed by Kareem who, by the way, should take a little taste for himself to supplement his slave wages at the garage. All Kareem has to do is convince his nephew and make sure he gets on the plane. Kareem does this. Mystery guy drops the money in the men's room at LaGuardia on D-Day and then disappears on a domestic flight, no doubt to a port city, where he is then probably smuggled out of the country on a merchant marine vessel. Wouldn't surprise me if that were how he got into the country in the first place. Easiest way. All those billions for Homeland Defense and it's nothing more than a Band-Aid on brain surgery. But I digress."

Alson took a long pull on his Fog Cutter because his throat was very dry from talking and his emotions very raw from recounting the crime.

"So Kareem picks up the cash from the trash in the men's room," continued Alson. "Kareem has a ticket for Chicago that lets him into the departure terminal in the first place and will allow him an easier international departure point after the shit hits the fan. But the bomb goes off too soon and then it's a dead end and 24 dead people on the Washington Shuttle. Not to mention two Port Authority cops in the terminal. We're just damn lucky that Farragut was around to make like a hero or we wouldn't be having this lovely bonding experience. By the way, maybe you and I should both have another word with Farragut. You seemed to rush through that one."

He was right. She had and she didn't want to talk about it. Mia changed the subject.

"Shuqueiri mentioned his contact was Hezbollah. That's something new, Hezbollah operating in the United States."

"That could be smoke. That could've been a cover story just to take the heat off *Al Qaeda*. We've never had any reports of Hezbollah operating in the US. Raising money? Yes. But they run southern Lebanon like an independent state and their area of operations has always been there and Israel."

"Exactly. Hezbollah's main gripe is with Israel. That's why they targeted Dov Lowenstein — one of Israeli's biggest arms dealers."

"So whack him in Israel. Why take the risk and run an operation here?"

"The competition for terrorism's dollars is fierce. *Al Qaeda* still gets most of the press coverage. Maybe Hezbollah's just trying to keep up with the Joneses?"

"You mean the Bin-Ladens."

She smiled at that one. She raised her club soda for a toast and they touched glasses.

"May he rot in hell," she said.

They drank. Alson raised his glass again.

"And to Professor John Farragut for pulling our fat from the fryer. How lucky was that?"

Not lucky. *A sign*, thought Mia. But she drank to it anyway.

"Hezbollah's main backers are Syria and Iran," continued Mia, happy to get off the subject of Farragut and back on track. "We used to think the Supernote Press was hidden in Lebanon's Beqaa Valley. The Syrians control that. Since the Iranians had the Supernote press to begin with, maybe they arranged to take it back from Lebanon for safety's sake. Tehran's a lot farther from Tel Aviv then Lebanon or Syria and any possible commando strike by the Israelis. Either way, Syria and Iran are under international pressure to curtail their sponsorship of terrorism, especially with democracy growing in places like Egypt and Tunisia. It makes sense that Iran would take measures to protect an unlimited source of funding that can't be traced. And it follows that Hezbollah felt they had to do something bold to keep the flow of dollars coming."

Alson pulled a wedge of pineapple from his drink and sucked on it. The sourness made him wince. Or was it Mia's line of thought?

"That's a lot of speculation."

"The Israelis want to talk to Shuqueiri. They have better intelligence on Hezbollah's operatives. If Shuqueiri picks out the cash courier from their files and links him definitively to Hezbollah or any number of these Iranian funded groups, well, it's a whole lot less speculation."

Alson considered this. He didn't like where it was going. He tossed Mia the menu.

"Fuck it. I'm getting the sweet and sour pork. Unless you'd like to go somewhere else?"

"I'd like to go to Iran. To Tehran," she said.

"Long way to go for dinner."

"It's the only place to go to destroy the Supernote Press."

Alson nodded, not really listening. He signaled for the waitress. Mia stared at the menu. The design on the faded, red leather cover showed four rivers flowing into one. The image crystallized something deep inside Mia's subconscious. A plan she had she had casually been playing with for years started to come into sharper focus.

Four rivers. Four men. She would need four men.

Farragut would be one. The second man was one the Secret Service had been watching for a while. The Israelis could provide the third; they had good people on the ground in Tehran. Alson and the FBI would provide the fourth man. She couldn't remember his name, just the details of his case from long ago. He would be perfect.

The waitress arrived wearing a tight, tattered, red silk dress. Mia wore a look of utter determination. Something had clicked inside of her. This was going to happen.

"Doug, I'm gonna need you to do some heavy lifting with the Bureau if we are really going to do this."

"Do what?"

"Put together an operation and take out the Press."

The waitress looked at both of them and tapped her pad. Alson waved her away. She did not look happy and neither did Alson.

"You're serious about this?" he said.

Mia looked ecstatic as she drained the last of her club soda. She stood up and put a hand on his shoulder.

"Not me. *We.* Doug, can you track me down some information on a guy the Bureau put away a few years back? He's a real hot potato. A hard case. Political. There'll be racial and religious overtones. I need you to start setting the groundwork with the Bureau because he's your collar and we're gonna catch hell when we spring him from prison.""

Alson might have been a little drunk but he wasn't so drunk that he hadn't heard right.

"Spring him from —? What? What the hell are talking about?"

"I told you. We're gonna destroy the Supernote Press. Exactly how, I'm not yet sure. But we'll have to spring this guy from prison to do it. He's gonna blow it up."

"What's his name?"

"Shareef Salaam. His name is Shareef Salaam."

Mia shook Alson's hand before he could offer it. He felt like Mia was operating in a different dimension, moving at Mach speed while he dawdled in slow motion. Mia marched for the door, leaving him at the bar. Alson signaled for the bar tab. The check was $10. Alson only had twenties. He hesitated. He needed to wait for change but he also had to catch up with Mia. But hell, $10 was a big tip on a $10 check. Alson was a bureaucrat, not a billionaire. He had to worry about money; his own and now the funny money being printed in Iran by a special press that Treasury Agent Mia Kelly had decided they were going to blow up.

It was at that moment that Alson felt like throwing up. He was glad he hadn't ordered the sweet and sour pork after all.

Mia felt relief as she entered her large, two-bedroom apartment on 57th Street right near Carnegie Hall. It was neat and elegant with killer views of the park. She'd had a nice alimony settlement. Her husband had been a prosperous bond trader and a preposterous drunk. He had been many things but he hadn't been a bastard when it came to the divorce or money. Then again, he didn't have much use for money now. He was serving eight years at Ossining Correctional Facility for the vehicular manslaughter of their child.

Mia took a shower and washed the cop off her. She put on a robe and poured herself a glass of St. Emilion. The cupboard was bare. She hadn't shopped in weeks. She should've eaten with Alson when she had the chance. She promised herself that tomorrow night she'd go out and eat a proper meal, even if she ate alone, just to make the effort.

She poured herself another glass of wine and got in bed. She sipped her wine and thought of her plan. It could work. They could stop the Supernote. But it would be a hard sell, not only to her bosses in Washington but to the one man whose participation she absolutely had to have.

And she would have to convince that man quickly, because he had a time bomb ticking away inside his head.

CHAPTER SIX

JOHN FARRAGUT touched the granite of his mother's tombstone and tried to remember what she looked like. Jane Macintosh Farragut was tall and lean; he remembered that. She smoked too much and ate too little and always had a drink in her hand. When he was younger, Farragut thought it was water. When he was older, maybe ten, he realized it was gin. He remembered half-empty gin bottles stashed around the house: under the couch, behind the enormous Webster's dictionary in the library, inside the red rain boots she never wore at the back of the closet.

Farragut laid some yellow gladiolas on his mother's grave. He recalled his mother loved the color yellow. He remembered a white dress she used to wear — clinched flatteringly over her slender waist — with yellow bananas printed on it. She called it her Carmen Miranda dress. Farragut remembered her dancing the conga in that dress. She would put on a Tito Puente record and thrust her hips back-and-forth as if she were trying to dislodge a clutching monkey. Her dance would make Farragut laugh – he was still a boy — and he would laugh harder still when she made him dance with her. Farragut recalled even his father would grind out a smile at that one.

But Farragut could not remember many smiles growing up. As much as his father loathed Iran his mother loved it. She looked at the country not through the distorted prism of politics or religion, but through the unblinking eye of an expatriate woman with a generous heart, trapped in an unhappy marriage. Farragut recalled that when he was a boy he and his mother were close. She would drag her son on long day trips, pulling him out of school so they could travel the country together. Through their shared experiences she instilled in him her passion for their adopted homeland, a passion devoid of prejudice or judgment. Jane Farragut had loved the spiritual vibrancy and dark beauty of the Persian people. She loved the pink sunsets over the Karaj Mountains. She loved the thick, meaty steam produced by a hot vat of *kaleh-pacheh*, the Iranian breakfast stew. She loved haggling with the merchants in the Grand Bazaar. She loved the bizarre rock formations lining the Karaj-Chalous highway. She loved Iran's heat, its exoticism, its sad, ancient beauty.

She also loved one of its men, a geology professor at Tehran University. Farragut did not discover the affair until after the family had moved back to the States. He found the man's letters stashed along with another half-empty gin bottle inside his mother's old Radcliffe sweatshirt. She had asked Farragut to donate the sweatshirt along with some other tattered clothes to Goodwill. Farragut had read the letters and been amazed to discover that his mother, who had shared her love of everything with him, had not shared this.

After he had finished reading, Farragut had hidden the letters under the half-empty gin bottle behind the canned yams in the pantry. He never mentioned the letters to his mother. He never forgave her because there was nothing to forgive. He loved her and wanted her to be happy. He supposed there were things married people did in order to stay married despite their unhappiness. He did not dwell on it. He was young, talented, and had just graduated from college. The welcoming warm heat of life's possibilities burned just over the horizon and that was the direction Farragut was heading.

Farragut's mother had been drinking the night she crashed her Volvo wagon into the back of a stalled Grand Union tractor-trailer on Christmas Eve 1981. She was driving home on Interstate 684 from a party in Bedford to their home in Rye. The road was slick, but the five Tanqueray Martinis she had sucked down that night didn't help driving conditions. Jane Macintosh Farragut had never specified what she wanted done with her remains and her husband had buried them in the graveyard in Rye. His parents were barely speaking by that point – Rand Farragut had a mistress, a young litigator at Benton Oil who would become his second wife – and Farragut had fought with his father. Farragut's mother detested suburbia and the thought of her body spending eternity there infuriated him. He had wanted his mother cremated and her ashes spread over the Alborz Mountains in Iran. That, of course, was impossible. His father had won.

Farragut stood. A glance at the dates on the tombstone confirmed what he already knew: he was the same age as his mother when she died.

Farragut checked his watch. It was 3:34. He had been expected at his father's house at 3:00. Rand Farragut had miraculously survived the bomb blast that destroyed his flight and took the lives of 24 people. He had suffered a broken leg and second-degree burns over 15 percent of his body. He was recuperating at home under the care of a private nurse, his lovely wife, and his three pugs. Farragut still had some time off before classes began so he had called and told his father he would drive down and see how the old man was doing. Rand had told him not to bother. He was fine, never better; but Farragut had made the trip anyway.

Truthfully, Farragut had wanted to visit his mother's grave and his father's proximity made it easier. Besides, he couldn't blame his father for surviving, could he? Just because the old man had fobbed off the Palestinian boy posing as an Israeli with a broken leg to some Ghanaian diplomat? Just because he had traded his first class seats for the coach seats of some mortgage industry lobbyist? No, Farragut couldn't blame his father for that. How could Rand Farragut know his casual act of indifference would save his life? It was the luck of the draw. Survival of the fittest. The American Way.

Farragut left the graveyard. He got in his car, got on Interstate 95, and drove the seven hours back to Hanover without stopping. He was in bed by midnight and dreamed violent dreams of strange cities that deep down he felt he knew.

CHAPTER SEVEN

MIA KELLY MADE her pitch two days later in a windowless conference room at the FBI's Hoover Building in Washington, DC. Her audience was known unofficially as the Supernote Committee because officially, the Supernote Committee didn't exist. When mention of the Supernote came up in public testimony, which was not often, the venue was before the spectacularly banal sounding Congressional Subcommittee on General Oversight and Investigations of the Committee on Banking and Financial Services. Hiding the government's embarrassment behind such a stolid, bureaucratic brick wall ensured that only the most ardent C-SPAN junkies would catch a whiff. But Mia had more than a whiff; she had a taste for blood.

She took in the scene around the conference table. Her boss, Frank Finley, Deputy Director of the Secret Service, offered an avuncular smile. Calvin Bowles, Assistant Secretary of State for Near Eastern Affairs, adjusted a cufflink and coughed discreetly into a monogrammed handkerchief. Harry Carruthers, Special Consultant to the National Security Agency, nodded his head from side to side and worked a kink out of his neck. Alan Myers, Assistant Secretary of Defense for Special Operations and Low Intensity Conflict, had made a pyramid with his fingers behind which he hid a mouth that was either frowning or smiling — his eyes gave nothing away. Steve Van Asselt, Deputy Director of the FBI's Counter-terrorism command, chewed on a hangnail that was of much more urgent interest to him than Mia's plan. It was left to David Whedon, head of the CIA's Directorate of Operations, to start the counter-attack. Short and boyish-looking with an undernourished mustache, Whedon threw his palms up in mock surrender and drawled on in a voice that was as sweet as the peaches from his home state of Georgia.

"Interesting idea, Agent Kelly. But can if I can be so bold as to ask just one question it would be this: Why go after the Supernote Press right now? Wouldn't it be better to have all our ducks in a row before we act?"

Mia, who had been sitting, stood. Whedon was in charge of making sure the Agency's multi-billion dollar annual budgets brought home terrorist bacon. She needed him on her side.

"Sir, the Press is a sitting duck right now. We know it's in Tehran. In the last two weeks, the Israelis, acting upon our information, have confirmed our suspicions and identified a man in Tehran they believe is the master printer employed by the Iranians to print the Supernote. The Israelis have been tailing this man in hopes he'll lead them to the Press but so far no luck —"

"That's all well and good but this committee needs more time," interjected Whedon.

"This committee has wasted too much time. We've dithered and blathered for over 20 years. Meanwhile, the number of Supernotes in circulation grows exponentially as will the number of innocents who die because of Supernote funded terrorism."

Whedon shook his head. "Pardon my French, but you're making a tit out of a nipple. Since 9/11 the IMF, World Bank, and G-20 nations have all cracked down hard on the flow of money to terrorist groups and their supporters."

"Director Whedon, with all due respect, tightening banking regulations and restricting Muslim charities is the easiest but most ineffective way to stop the flow of terrorist money. The hardest money to track is cash, especially counterfeit cash that moves from hand to hand through informal Middle Eastern money transfer points known as *hawalas*. The *hawala* system operates on trust and leaves no paper trail. The *hawala* system can transfer counterfeit dollars into another currency, perhaps Euros, or convert them into clean money, gems, cigarettes, whatever. But my plan stops the flow of counterfeit money at its source."

Mia was pleased to see the members of the committee consulting the background books she had prepared. Diverting from their disinterest at the beginning of her pitch, the committee members now took notice of Mia's obsessive attention to detail and unbridled passion. Maybe, just maybe, she was on to something.

-:::::-

"Gentlemen, now is the time to act. The Supernote represents one of the greatest threats to our national security since Bin Laden. Bin Laden's bank accounts have limits but the production of Supernotes knows no limits. We can't cut this flow of funds off with an army of accountants armed with MBAs. Supernotes are immune to real world economic downturns and investigative techniques. Tens of millions have been printed over the last decades and hundreds of millions will be printed in the years to come. They're already out on the street and in the hands of killers. They're hidden under mattresses and passed from palm to palm. And they're not just in the Middle East. Supernotes have found a home from Beijing to Brussels. They grease the palms of every gung-ho gun broker, nuclear proficient nutball, and gone-bad biological weapons brain. Gentleman, the Supernote is the very lifeblood of the worldwide terrorist body. To kill the body, we've got to bleed it dry. Terrorism's soldiers are willing to sacrifice their lives, their children's lives, in the belief that God will reward them as martyrs. And the only way to fight against men who have nothing to lose is to find our own men with nothing to lose."

"Lose the attitude, Kelly," said Whedon. "There isn't a man on this committee who wouldn't give his own life to save one innocent life. But no one's gonna be saved by your cockamamie plan."

Whedon's attempt at intimidation drew a smile from Finley. Both he and Whedon were Southerners, but the man's lack of that region's fabled courtesy and charm rankled. Finley decided to come to Mia's defense.

"The plan is not 'cockamamie,' David, much as I like that word. The plan is the result of Agent Kelly's extensive knowledge of undercover and clandestine police work. It is a good plan. With the information supplied by our suspect, Kareem Shuqueiri, it is a doable plan. With the current political climate, it is a necessary plan. The only thing it's not, is an Agency plan."

"Thank God for that," blustered Whedon.

Harry Carruthers stirred in his seat. Like most of the men at the NSA, Carruthers preferred technology to talking, but felt obliged to move things along before lunch.

"Agent Kelly. You believe Kareem Shuqueiri's information is credible?"

"I do. And so do the Israelis. On our request, Mossad's been going back through their taped Hezbollah chatter. They have found coded messages that they now believe directly link Hezbollah to the recruitment of Shuqueiri stateside. Further, they interpret conversations between Hasan Shehabi, a Lebanese based Hezbollah operative, and his Iranian contacts, to confirm that the Supernote Press has been moved from Lebanon to Tehran, just as Shuqueiri suggested."

"How did they miss this before?"

"How did we miss the warnings of 9/11?"

There was collective squirming from around the table but Carruthers kept his cool.

"So Shuqueiri tells us the Press is in Tehran and the Israelis believe it, too. I want to believe it. But the NRO has had a bird watching that city 24/7 and we haven't seen or heard shit. Not even a decent place to get lamb kebab. Sorry, Kelly, but we think the signal intelligence is smoke and mirrors. And until that data is definitively proved to be more than deceptive chatter, I still think the Press is in the Beqaa Valley, guarded by Hezbollah."

Mia shook her head. "I strongly disagree. I don't have the data but we have these decrypted conversations. The Press is in Tehran, guarded by the Revolutionary Guards. Just as interesting is that Shehabi's Hezbollah cell and his Revolutionary Guards contact in Iran appear to be operating independently of their superiors. We're talking about rogue elements within two rogue organizations. That makes them doubly dangerous."

Tense silence filled the room. The idea of rogue elements within rogue organizations was too real and too terrible to contemplate. This made more unpredictable the already unfathomable calculus of terrorism. Mia continued, trying to bolster the room's confidence.

"We should look at this schism as a good sign. It means we are having an effect on the forces of terror. This will sow the seeds of their destruction, with a little help from us, of course. While it appears that both the LaGuardia bombing and the movement of the Supernote Press were the work of unpredictable rogue elements, one thing is predictable; once the Press was moved to Tehran, it was probably buried beneath a civilian building to provide a human shield in case of attack."

'Which is why Defense won't send a cruise missile in to blow it up," bellowed Myers, his voice having more impact than any bunker blasting bomb. "Hell, we did that in the Sudan in '99 and all we did was kill a few janitors, crush a whole lot of aspirin, and get CNN so damn cock-eyed that they damn near crucified us."

Whedon welcomed a fellow agnostic. He smiled warmly at Myers even while he aimed his condescending comments at Mia.

"Now if we can't use cruise missiles, we certainly can't consider your creative, undercover scenarios, Kelly. As I said to you before, we need time to digest this information. And given enough time, I'm sure the Pentagon powers that be might even map out a professional scenario in which we send in ground troops."

Whedon turned to Myers and found a smile under his mustache.

"What do you think, Alan? Perhaps Delta Force could handle this down the line."

Whedon's mention of the Army's elite, counter-terrorist unit drew an enthusiastic nod from Myers.

"Oh, I plan to send in the Delta Force alright. But only against CNN."

Everyone laughed except Whedon who wore the pained look of a man discovering a parking ticket on his windshield. Myers milked the moment; his brown skin flushed red at the cheeks as the laughter died down.

"I'll be candid," Myers continued. "No one at the Pentagon has the stomach for close work. Our special ops boys fought like gangbusters in Baghdad, but that was as part of a larger military force. Now imagine fighting in the middle of a hostile, metropolitan area like Tehran? Tehran will be a hundred times worse. The Revolutionary Guards are much more professional than Iraq's Republican Guard."

Myers did not mention, nor did he need to, what had happened the last time America had tried a military operation on Iranian soil. The disaster in the desert of 1980 had left soldiers dead and President Carter's re-election hopes dashed. But Mia sensed something in Myers' tone that was sympathetic to her strategy. She needed the Pentagon on her team even if the role they would play was purely fictional.

"But the Pentagon's cooperation is essential, Director Myers. And I absolutely couldn't proceed unless you could create a believable scenario for getting Delta Force in and out. I trust that such scenarios exist, at least in theory."

"I can see that's part of your plan and my answer is affirmative. It is imperative that your operatives train with Delta Force and believe that Delta Force will extract them. But in reality, even if we could get Delta Force in, and I think we could, I doubt we could ever get them out alive."

"I understand. But as you see, we will only need them for the training of our operatives, not the actual operation. That's the beauty of the plan. It preserves our valuable assets like Delta Force by keeping them out of it. Plus, it offers minimal government exposure. That spells deniability."

All eyes turned to Whedon, a virtuoso at the Washington game of covering one's own ass. "I'm the first to admit. Our human intelligence ain't shit. We've got few officers that speak fluent Farsi. Even fewer that can assimilate into Tehran. Hell, the only time most of our people are around anything Iranian is when they go out to dinner at some hot new place that's been written up in the *Post*."

That got Whedon some laughs of his own. He waited for it to die down before continuing. "Yes, the Directorate of Operations has been in decline for years. But let me tell you that I have gone on record in arguing that more money and resources are provided for clandestine operations. And now, with the new mood in the government and the country, I believe it will happen." Whedon sat down, adding, "I'm on your side, Agent Kelly. But you can't be too careful."

Mia felt conciliatory. She threw Whedon a bone along with a tactical flash of her well-toned thighs.

"Director Whedon, I understand that this type of operation is not normally the Secret Service's domain. We have only a few dozen agents abroad. We need the Agency and my plan provides for complete cooperation with the CIA as well as an integrated command structure. Most importantly, a CIA operative will be in charge in the field."

Whedon made a show of looking in his briefing book. But only after having looked at her legs, which he found infinitely more interesting.

"Technically, he's an ex-CIA operative."

"An ex-CIA operative we can trust. His record speaks for itself. And he was there in New York last month. At LaGuardia. He performed brilliantly."

"If we do this, CIA comes on board with tactical authority, Kelly."

Whedon was coming around but Mia wanted it on her terms.

"No. It's a Joint Terrorism Task Force operation. And we'll have to negotiate how Mossad's asset fits in. But it's my plan and I have tactical authority."

Whedon looked at Finley who nodded his agreement. Whedon shrugged.

"The Israelis could be a problem. I can't make a promise but I could make the calls. But if the shit hits the fan, you burn for this, Kelly."

Bowles from State, who had sat silently and stiffly throughout the proceedings like some Boston Brahmin preserved in aspic, allowed his tobacco-stained teeth to form a tight smile.

"I knew your man's father, Agent Kelly. Rand Farragut and I were at Princeton together. He was a good sport even though we black-balled him for Ivy. He was more of a Tiger Inn man. Very athletic. And one tough sonofabitch, judging by how he survived that bomb blast. Although I know a few folks on the Benton board who wished he hadn't."

Bowles chuckled at his irreverence. A few of the other men in the room checked their watches, anticipating the New York strip steaks and martinis that awaited them at the Palm. The meeting was winding down. Finley caught Mia's eye and offered an encouraging wink.

Van Asselt, the FBI counter-terrorism expert, stopped gnawing on his hangnail long enough to clear his throat. He had kept his opinions to himself because he was on board from the get go. Special Agent Alson had filled him in on the plan beforehand and spoke highly of Mia.

"Everyone knows how the Bureau took shit for 9/11," Van Asselt said. "We had some of the hijackers in our sights but field agents couldn't get Washington to take their reports seriously. The bureaucracy bungled it. People slipped through the cracks. And then this bombing last month at LaGuardia. This Shuqueiri character didn't slip through the cracks; we plain didn't even know this crackpot existed. This despite the fact that we have a state of the art, computer database containing information on over 200,000 individuals and over 3000 organizations with possible links to terrorist groups. Two hundred thousand individuals and 3000 organizations but there's only one plan, one, that I've heard in the last six months that makes me think we can really do something pro-active here. That's Agent Kelly's plan. And I think it's just crazy enough to work. And I think we all ought to think long and hard about what's more important: protecting our bureaucracies or showing some balls?"

Van Asselt gave Mia a smile and then turned his attention back to his hangnail. At that moment, Mia felt like kissing him and making it better.

Mia caught Finley's eye. He rapped his knuckles on the table. Then he spoke.

"To sum up the situation, gentleman. If we continue to do nothing, the Iranians will continue to print old issue Supernotes. Despite the currency redesign, these old bills, both genuine and counterfeit, will be in circulation, particularly overseas, for years to come. Given the Iranians have the means to recreate the paper and ink and the plates for the old bills, we are looking at another decade of problems, a decade in which the Iranians will have, despite their promises, developed their own nuclear bomb. The Stuxnet computer virus that sabotaged their uranium enrichment facility at Natanz bought us some time, but may also have increased the Iranians urgency to go out and buy centrifuges on the black market or, perhaps, share counterfeiting technology with the North Koreans in exchange for nuclear technology. But if we act now, albeit with the risks associated with this plan, we stand to stop this counterfeiting in its tracks. Maybe we stop the development of the Iranian bomb. And if not, maybe they'll think twice about using it if they know we can infiltrate them at the very heart of their security apparatus."

The room was silent. All eyes were on Finley. He continued.

"So, I say we finish this thing," he said to the room while looking at Whedon. "David, I suppose ultimately this is your sort of game on your type of turf and you have to get the Israelis on board. Any last thoughts?"

Whedon kept his thoughts to himself. He knew the Iranians had used the Supernotes to buy everything from North Korean SCUDS to Russian SU-30 Fighters. He knew they gave upwards of $200 million per year, most of that probably Supernotes, to Hezbollah as well as to Hamas, Islamic Jihad and other groups not yet on their radar. And in Iran, the political situation seemed more unstable than ever. Reformers were more vocal in their demands but seemingly incapable of achieving real change vis-à-vis the conservative clerics, as the failure of the Green Revolution had shown. Maybe Mia's plan would tip the balance in favor of the reformers by breaking the reactionaries' piggy bank.

Everyone watched Whedon stand and fix his gaze on Mia. "Fuck it. You wore me out, Kelly. Let's do it.'"

The room erupted in applause. Yes, in the flush of success immediately following the fall of Saddam, there had been talk of taking on Tehran with American troops. Now, such a mission had to be undertaken in a dramatically different fashion. Mia's plan had that appeal. It would have to clear the Secretary of Homeland Security and then the President himself but both were a mere formality. The Committee had the juice and the administration had the desire.

The room cleared with only Finley lingering behind. He acknowledged Mia's victory with a proper handshake. He offered to buy her lunch. She declined. She offered to walk him back to the Secret Service headquarters a few blocks away. He accepted.

As Mia and Finley walked the rainy Washington streets, past the K Street lobbyists in their Gucci shoes and the secretaries in their sneakers, Finley made small talk. His son had just started at St. Albans and his daughter was a freshman at Wesleyan. The freight was murder for a civil servant but Finley had some offers from private security firms and was weighing them seriously. Finley's wife was recovering from her hysterectomy and really appreciated the beautiful flowers Mia had sent. Was she interested in meeting his wife's brother? He was a very successful orthodontist in Scarsdale.

Mia tuned out her boss to stare at the gray sky. It looked like snow but the weather was still a touch too warm. New Hampshire was sure to be colder and probably snowing. She thought of New Hampshire and seeing Farragut again. The thought of seeing him again made her smile. And then it made her shiver.

CHAPTER EIGHT

HE SOFT *shush* of Farragut's cross-country skis was barely audible above his measured breathing. It was ridiculous, this early freak snow. Peak leaf season wouldn't be for another week or two. Halloween was weeks away, yet the Dartmouth golf course lay covered under a foot of icy, White Mountain white stuff. Of course, Farragut did not care. Time had lost importance for him. All that mattered now was the tumor.

Farragut had nicknamed it the "tumor with a sense of humor" because of the cruel joke it now played upon him. Unlike Farragut, the tumor had decided to stop moving in any direction. The doctors had told him the tumor was neither growing nor shrinking. There was hope. They were pleased. Farragut was not pleased. He had already accepted the reality of his imminent demise. He hated this limbo. He only understood movement, backwards or forwards. Farragut continued skiing at a slow but steady pace, relishing the cold air and dramatic landscape and heavy silence all around him. He had learned to ski in Zurich; Benton Oil kept a chalet there, a reward doled out to those executives who had surpassed their quotas. His father had taken the family there every Christmas. Rand Farragut had preferred the more glamorous Alpine skiing, letting gravity dictate his movement. But Farragut had always preferred Nordic. He liked to fight gravity, pushing against the planet's immutable desire to make him stop. And then, of course, Nordic offered more than skiing. Nordic offered the biathlon and guns.

Farragut liked guns. His father collected guns and passed his love of them onto his son, a son he appeared not to love at all. Farragut had learned to shoot first and ski second. Skiing and shooting seemed to him a glorious marriage. The skiing pleasantly drained the tension from his body and then the shooting offered a thrilling release at the height of exhaustion. The comparison to sex was obvious, although not the pedestrian type practiced by the boys at Farragut's prep school. The Tehran American School, where American boys were boys and the Iranian sheep were scared. But Farragut didn't want to think of the past. There was only the present.

Farragut spotted the shooting target in front of a crooked evergreen, its branches straining under the weight of snow. He had set up the target yesterday before the storm, and its crimson bulls-eye looked like a blood clot against the landscape's deathly pale veneer. He pulled his .22 caliber bolt action rifle from his back and lay flat down on his stomach. The snow crunched under his weight but held firm. He sighted. His mind was a blank but the bullets were real.

Crack. Crack. Crack. Crack. Crack. Five shots. Five bulls-eyes. The blanket of snow muffled the rifle's report but Farragut's heart beat like a drum and sent waves of blood up to the tumor that was neither growing nor shrinking. Like Farragut, it was waiting for the next move.

Farragut skied back to the main campus in 20 minutes. The Dartmouth green seemed a misnomer, for it too lay covered beneath a mountain of white. Farragut slung his skis over his shoulder and entered the imposing Dartmouth Hall on the east side of the green. He ducked into his cramped office long enough to lock his gun up in the closet, pull off his ski shell, and throw his favorite Harris tweed over his sweaty Red Sox T-shirt. He checked his watch, saw he was running late, and darted down the stairs to his ancient history survey class.

Farragut barreled into the overheated, overfilled classroom. He smelled like sweat and snow and damp wool. His hair was matted to his brow. The students greeted him with catcalls. If he was going to be late for his own class, he had to expect some grief. He took a seat on the edge of his desk and got to work.

"History. Why care about history? Why make an effort to remember the past when you're just trying to forget how many beers you shotgunned last night?"

There was laughter from the packed classroom. Even the students forced to stand sullenly against the back wall chimed in. Farragut didn't flatter himself that the class was filled because he was such a great teacher, although that was indeed the main reason. Rather, he allowed that Introduction to Ancient History was a painless way to a Gentleman's B for the future lawyers, doctors, bankers, and sitcom writers that made the class oversubscribed every fall term.

"Well, I'll tell you why you should care about the past. Because as Faulkner said, 'The past is not dead. It's not even past.' History matters because you are all, in your own ways, sometimes sublime and sometimes absurd, repeating the events of history in the present. For example, Pamela…"

Pamela Dymes, a pretty sophomore sitting in the front row looked up from her notebook. Raven-haired and blue-eyed, she wore a short plaid skirt, tights, and elegant leather boots that showed off her shapely legs.

"…Sweet, suddenly studious Pamela," continued Farragut. "Most days you come in here dressed in sweats and skulk around in the back with the rest of the Kappas. But today you're sitting up front and — I don't think the PC police could arrest me for this — and you look, well, quite fetching."

Catcalls came from the males in the class. The radiator clanged loudly as more heat pumped in. Pamela's painted lips parted to show off an expensive, toothy smile.

"Thank you, Professor. I'm glad you noticed."

"Oh, I'm sure all the multicellular male organisms in the room noticed. As I have also noticed that today is the 23rd which, if memory serves, means we have an appointment to discuss your long overdue term paper."

"I have a good excuse," she promised, although she didn't offer one.

"I'm sure you do. But save it for later. For now, I single you out simply to demonstrate a point. There is historical precedent in your actions. Yours is neither the first nor the most brazen attempt to seduce the enemy through such methods. In fact, the Greeks used the same strategy in their war with the Trojans over 4,000 years ago. But instead of hiding behind short skirts, they hid inside a huge, wooden horse. Which brings us to today's lesson: The Trojan Horse."

Farragut sat up from the desk and began to walk amongst the rows of students. It was easier for him to conjure the past while moving. For history to Farragut was an immutable force of the universe, to be felt and fought with like gravity when he skied.

"Our story begins with a woman. A woman whose exquisite face could launch a thousand ships and, unfortunately, a million cheesy clichés. But Helen of Troy was such a woman. Helen of Troy was the real McCoy."

Ted Pearson, a lanky freshman wearing a tense expression and an expensive cashmere sweater, raised his hand even while cutting in before he was called upon.

"What dates exactly are we talking about, Professor?"

"Dates? The war between Greece and Troy raged roughly around 1200 B.C. But don't write that down. I don't care about dates. This story is timeless. Dates won't be on the exam."

"Is that a promise? No dates for sure?" asked Pearson, writing down the date anyway.

Farragut nodded but couldn't avoid rolling his eyes. The boy was the heir to some mini-mall fortune in the southwest yet he worried as if his next meal depended upon his grade point being perfect. They all did. Such misplaced passion depressed Farragut.

"The only date that matters is the first date between Helen, wife of the King of Sparta, and Paris, son of the King of Troy. That date led to one of history's greatest love affairs as well as nastiest wars.

Now, I suppose a cynic might say that Helen, though beautiful, was just your basic trophy wife who cheated on her husband. And Paris? Well, he was just your basic spoiled rich kid who took what he wanted. I'm sure you all know the type."

Farragut cast an accusing look at Pearson but the arrow missed its mark. He, like all the students, was scribbling notes too furiously to notice. Farragut glanced through the steamed-up windows out onto the green. The sun bounced off a janitor's snow shovel and reflected light into his eyes. For an instant he saw the plane exploding on the tarmac at LaGuardia. He blinked to flush image from his memory.

"And so, the King of Sparta attacked Troy in order to get his wife back," Farragut resumed, turning back to the class. "He thought it would be a cinch. The Spartans were the best fighters in the world. But the war didn't go according to plan. For 10 years it raged but the Spartans could not break down the walls of Troy. At the end of the decade, exhausted and demoralized, they were desperate. They realized they had to outwit the Trojans to win the day. So in order to fool the Trojans into thinking they were quitting the fight, they offered their enemy a gift of infinite beauty and incalculable value. A sort of 'sorry about last night' token of their contrition. The ancient history equivalent of a dozen roses, or, in the case of some of you, a week in Cozumel on daddy's dime. The gift was, of course, the Trojan Horse."

Pearson's hand shot up again as he shot off his mouth.

"Why did the Spartans pick a horse? What specific value did a horse have to the Trojans? Did the horse play an important part in their religious ideals?"

"I'm not sure," shrugged Farragut after a theatrical pause and knitting of his brow. "Perhaps the Greeks realized that the story of the Trojan Cockroach wouldn't resonate throughout history with quite so much power."

The class laughed, even Pearson. Farragut gave him a wink to let him know the ribbing was nothing personal although, in fact, it was.

"So the Spartans built a huge wooden horse, secretly filled it with soldiers, stood it up at the gates of Troy and sailed for home. And the Trojans, well, at first they couldn't believe it. The Spartans had never quit at war before, yet here was a magnificent peace offering. And because the war had been long and bloody, and they had prayed for peace, the Trojans finally believed what they wanted to believe even though it was unbelievable. But don't we all? Isn't blind belief in the unbelievable the only way to get through the day?"

It was unbelievable, his doctors had told him, but he was in re-mission. Like the tumor, he was waiting for his next move. So was the class as Farragut walked back to his desk and pulled a bottle of Evian from the top drawer. He opened it and took a long drink. The room was quiet. Pam, the pretty co-ed, was shocked to see that Farragut's face, which she had always regarded as handsome, looked haggard and pale. She gasped quickly and covered her concern with a question.

"And then what happened, Professor?"

Farragut put down the water bottle and looked at Pamela. It took him a second to remember where he was. He had to keep moving. He walked back among the rows of students and plunged back into the past.

"Then what? The Trojans partied, of course. By nightfall, the whole city was in a drunken uproar. And why not? The Trojans were clearly blessed by their Gods. How else to explain their upset victory and this gorgeous gift of a horse and their handsome Prince Paris and their ravishing Queen-to-be Helen? So the city went to sleep, intoxicated by wine and winning the war. And then in the middle of the night, when all of Troy was asleep, the Greeks climbed out of the belly of the horse, pulled out their knives and — *Shwip!*"

Farragut had sneaked up behind an unsuspecting junior named Mark Silverman and pantomimed slitting his throat. The boy was a thick-necked football player with an athlete's easy confidence, and he played a horrendous death scene to the back rows.

But no one laughed, as they normally would have. The students were taking their cues only from Farragut now. And something in his tensed body and weary eyes suggested that he was not so much recounting past events but witnessing them in the present. He helped Silverman to his feet and continued after the boy had taken his seat.

"Death. Destruction. Catastrophe. The Greeks flung open the Troy's city gates and their comrades, who had only pretended to sail for home, stormed inside and the slaughter began. Blood flooded the streets mingling with spilled wine. Dogs, who hours before had slept soundly at the feet of their drunken masters, now gorged themselves on their masters' entrails. The sky turned black from a thousand fires as the Greeks torched every standing structure. Death. Destruction. Catastrophe. And for what?"

It was not a rhetorical question but the class didn't have an answer. They hadn't even heard the question. They only heard the screams of the dying and the crackling of the fires and the growling of dogs fighting over scraps of human flesh.

Farragut heard a rustling by the doorway and looked over. How long had Mia Kelly been standing there? Not long. He would've sensed her presence. That was the spy in him. And she was no doubt here because he had been a spy and was still a friend. He didn't need to ask. But he asked his class the question one more time.

"What was it all for? Well, I told you. For the love of a beautiful woman. For the love of Helen of Troy."

All eyes followed Farragut as he returned to the front of the room.

"What would you be willing to die for? People throughout history have given their lives for many things. Love. Country. God. Money. And that is the subject of your next paper. Choose a historical figure from ancient history who died for a cause and tell me whether you think their cause was worth dying for."

"How about an 'A' on this paper?" whined Pearson. "That would be worth dying for."

The class laughed again. That was fine with Farragut. He liked to laugh. He was going to miss the sound of laughter after he was gone. And he was certain that the appearance of Mia Kelly in his classroom meant that day was approaching sooner than he anticipated.

CHAPTER NINE

THEY MADE love slowly and with great tenderness. Farragut remembered that she liked to be nibbled on the nape of the neck and have her bottom stroked. Mia remembered that he liked to mix up positions and didn't like to talk too much. They both wound up laughing, though. They were both a bit drunk and embarrassed. They had been lovers half a dozen times over the last 20 years but not for almost three. Not since her son died.

They came together. They were both athletes. Timing was instinctive to them.

Mia kissed him on the top of the head and got out of the mahogany four-poster bed. She padded over toward the room service cart by the fireplace in which a fire dutifully roared. Their room at the Hanover Inn was elegant and warm. The candles on the bedside tables illuminated the floral pattern wallpaper and red, overstuffed couch. Mia's superiors would balk at the bill when she expensed it, but she was going to ask Farragut to pay a much higher price.

At the room service cart she grabbed the half-finished tin of caviar and the second bottle of Krug from the ice bucket. Like the caviar tin, the Champagne bottle was half full. She carried it back to the bed and slid underneath the covers. She gave him the bottle. He took a swig. He handed it back to her. She didn't drink, just stared at the label.

"How long do the doctors say?"

"A year. Eighteen months, maximum."

"You haven't lost your hair."

"Nope. Guess I'm just lucky."

Mia took a sip of Champagne. "Are you in pain?"

"Only when I think."

Mia did not smile but Farragut did. "Actually, I don't feel anything. Even when I think about the tumor. I'm in remission, you know. Just the same, I keep waiting for the headaches. The searing bolts of lightning behind my eyes. But I don't feel anything. Nothing at all."

He lied about the headaches. He didn't want her pity. She slid her hand between his legs. He swelled at her touch.

"Nothing at all? You could've fooled me."

They kissed. Farragut stroked Mia's hair. "I'm still skiing. My stamina's terrific."

He grabbed the bottle from her and took another sip. He played the Champagne on his tongue and swallowed. Then he handed the bottle back to her.

"Let's talk about the plane that exploded on the tarmac in New York. That's why you're here, isn't it?"

Mia took a sip of Champagne to steel herself. She turned to face him.

"Supernotes funded the LaGuardia bombing, John. They've funded numerous terrorist acts both here and abroad, always directed against Israel and the United States. But we're going to put an end to the money pipeline. We have reason to believe the Supernote Press is back in Iran. We're going to Tehran to destroy it and we want you to lead the team."

Farragut said nothing for a moment, then laughed. Mia's balls never failed to impress him. "If you're going after the Press, you need a field man. I was an analyst."

"But you were a field man first."

"That was a long time ago and for a very short time."

"But you were very good."

"If I was very good, I would never have had to kill people."

"You were given orders. You followed them. It wasn't your fault. You are, in fact, still admired by more than a few people for your efficient methods and unflinching discipline."

"She said as he got shitfaced."

Farragut drained a glass of Champagne and felt lightheaded. It was infinitely more pleasurable than the sensation of Mia's eyes burning into him.

"I need you, John. You can operate in Iran without arousing suspicion. You've done it before. You've got excellent contacts in Iran. You're viewed as sympathetic by the regime, thanks to your research and published positions. It will be no problem getting you in on a long-term visa. And once you're there, your friends are reformers who will expedite your mission and cover your ass should it come to that. But, of course, it won't come to that."

Farragut pulled back the window curtain. He looked down on the college green. He saw a couple of students, a boy and a girl, lying in the snow side-by-side making snow angels. He couldn't remember the last time he had made a snow angel and realized he never would again.

Farragut said, "Okay, I'm just drunk enough to play along. Tell me about the other men."

Mia pulled a thick, manila folder from her briefcase on the floor by her side of the bed. She handed him the folder but he hesitated taking it. When he finally did, he carefully pulled out the first dossier as if half-expecting it to explode. He stared at the police mug shot of a handsome Iranian man in his thirties. He had thick hair and high cheekbones. His wide smile revealed teeth that looked capped and expensive.

Farragut let Mia do the talking.

"Number one is a printer to infiltrate the Supernote Press. Omar Azadi is an Iranian-American whose family got out just before the Revolution. He works for the family printing business in LA but makes his real living as a master counterfeiter. He's expert on standard intaglio presses or the latest photocopiers. He did a juvie stretch for shoplifting when he was fourteen; six months became three years because of fighting and disciplinary problems. He did not adjust well to prison back then and there's no way he's gonna want to go back now. We've had him under surveillance for over a year and this bust will be his first as an adult. Counterfeiting is a major felony. He'll do serious time —"

"— Or he can accept your offer," cut in Farragut. "Take this mission or take 10 years at Terminal Island."

"Right," she continued with a nod. "We'll concoct a hate-crime cover story. Torch the family business, you know the drill. Not too much of a fiction in these times. That will increase his sympathetic profile with the Iranians and expedite his emigration."

Mia looked for a reaction from Farragut but his expression was blank. He examined the second dossier. This was a Bureau of Prisons' mug shot. An African-American identified as Shareef Salaam stared back at Farragut with intense eyes and a dignified face framed by a neat salt-and-pepper beard. He wore an embroidered Muslim skullcap and a con's institutional glower. Farragut sensed the man had a mind that was brilliant and beyond easy comprehension.

Mia said, "Number two, the explosives expert. Shareef Salaam's doing life at Terminal Island for murder. His past support for radical causes plus his devout Muslim faith, discovered in prison by the way, will give him credibility with Islamic extremist groups. We'll fake his escape and use the Israelis to plug him into Lebanon where he'll infiltrate Hezbollah. Once connected to the Supernote pipeline, we'll use him to blow up the Press."

"I remember him," nodded Farragut. "His story was all over the news 20 years back. He was a chemistry professor at Berkeley when he got mixed up with some radical group past its prime. He blew up some Federal courthouse."

"He's an expert on the explosive quality of chemicals. Teaches basic science to cons who care enough to get their equivalency exams. He's done some consulting for the FBI on occasion in return for favors — extra copies of the Quran, prayer rugs — that sort of thing. He's been on ice for a while but he has full access to the Internet and the latest texts on his subject of expertise. He's as brilliant as he was before he got himself incarcerated."

"If he's so brilliant he wouldn't be incarcerated," Farragut said.

He hadn't meant it sarcastically. He was dead serious and already making his calculations. Mia was happy to see it and even happier that she had a good answer.

"Salaam was fingered by some associates wishing to cut a deal for themselves. He took the fall and never talked himself. He's very clean, very credible, and very good."

Farragut nodded and pulled a third dossier from the envelope. On top was an Israeli intelligence file photo identifying Ari Jashni as a member of Israel's famed intelligence service, Mossad. Mia knew what Farragut was worried about and let him peruse the file in silence for a full minute. It felt like an eternity.

"You've got a problem with Jashni?"

Farragut reached for the caviar on his bedside table.

"I never met a Mossad man who didn't want to run the show."

"If you come on, you'll be in charge."

"If I come on, the first thing I'll do is dump this guy."

"Not an option. Jashni's essential and so is Israeli cooperation. They have much better intelligence on the ground in the Middle East than we do. And no one's better than Jashni. He's Mossad's top operative in Iran. He'll act as liaison and provide on-site intelligence. He'll be the link between all of you. You see, John, the team must never be seen to be together. You will be cutouts. Compartmentalized. The Iranians will become suspicious if the see any connection between the three of you."

Farragut sniffed the caviar and made a face. The caviar smelled fine but he wasn't so sure about Mia's plan.

"The Iranians will already be suspicious of any Americans in Iran. Especially since we named them charter members of the 'Axis of Evil.'"

"Yes. They'll be suspicious at first. But that's the beauty of this plan. Each of you brings a special skill to their side. Each of you represents, in your own way, the failure of the American Dream. They will believe in you because they will want to believe in you. You three are a gift they won't refuse. A modern day Trojan Horse, if you will."

Mia instantly regretted having thrown his lesson back in his face. It was ham-fisted and over the top. Farragut gave her a wry smile that confirmed as much. He settled back against the pillows and closed his eyes. He was tired. He hoped it was the lovemaking and not the cancer.

"So you use sleepers, hidden, human time bombs, just like they use on us. Sleepers that arrive in the country under legitimate pretenses and blend into their culture. Sleepers that live their lives amongst supposed friends. Friends they must betray."

"It's the only way," she pleaded softly. "We can't afford another disaster in the desert like in 1980. Can you imagine if we sent regular troops and had another hostage crisis? Or another slow slog like Iraq? No. The nation can't bear it. This way, when you succeed, Americans will never know but the Iranians certainly will. And the damage you cause will extend far beyond destroying the Press. What will really be destroyed is the government's confidence that their closed society can protect them. Maybe they will think twice about that nuclear program of theirs. Certainly they will think twice about funding more terrorists with bogus dollars."

And with that Mia stroked Farragut's hair and gave his arm a little squeeze. Her touch repelled him but he didn't show it. He would have to lie with his full body and soul if he did this and he wasn't sure he was going to do it yet. But the plan did pull at something deep inside of him. A patriotic desire to strike back at terrorists? Yes, of course. A chance to tip the balance in Iran from the conservatives to the reformers. Definitely. But maybe it was just the chance to keep moving. Fighting gravity. Feeling alive even while the tumor tried to trap him in limbo.

Mia was normally a patient woman but the Champagne was wearing off and her patience was wearing thin.

"John, this is not about hurting the Iranian people; it's about helping them. It is about taking out a money source run by an un-elected group of *mullahs* that wield dictatorial power. The things a small minority within this small minority does with the money are not even supported by the large majority of the people. The Supernote Press preserves the power of the Revolutionary Guards, not the new guard. This could be the reformer's Boston Tea Party. Their storming of the Bastille. Their Battleship Potemkin. We just have to light the spark. Dammit, John. You're from a free country. You have the right to say 'yes' or 'no.' But know this: we're going in with you or without you."

The fire crackled. Farragut saw it reflected in the black of Mia's eyes. Who was this woman, he thought? Had she ever really been a wife and mother? Did she really have no better way of spending her day than concocting such schemes and dreaming such dreams? For the first time since he had known her, Farragut felt like Mia and he were complete strangers.

"If I come on board with these men, how do you intend to get us out?"

Mia took a sip of Champagne straight from the bottle.

"We don't get you out. There will be no extraction."

Farragut felt his stomach drop but he kept his voice even.

"So this is a suicide mission?"

"As I said, there will be no extraction."

Farragut bit his lip to tamp down his anger. He hated Mia at that moment.

"Extraction? We're talking about men, not teeth, Mia. Finding a man to be a martyr is not easy. These men are not the type."

"Agreed. Azadi and Salaam will be told there's an extraction plan. They will train with Special Forces practicing that extraction plan. It is imperative that Azadi and Salaam believe up until the end that the extraction plan works and that they have a decent chance to get out alive."

"And I'll have the job of executing them to make sure that they don't."

The words hung there. Farragut picked up the caviar. He spooned the last dollop into his mouth and concentrated on the taste, the salty sensation of these unborn baby sturgeons. He thought of Mia's dead kid and it made him not want to spit the caviar in her face.

"You know the drill, John. We use men like these because they're not known operatives. They're sleepers. They can fly in under the radar."

"As I recall, the term is mission self-destruct."

"That's right. No loose ends."

"And what about me, Mia. Am I a loose end?"

Mia didn't answer the question and in truth he was glad she didn't. But she was asking Farragut to kill and now he had to ask himself: Does a man become less concerned with other lives as the end of his own approaches?

He didn't know. He wasn't sure he ever would. He reached for the bottle but the Champagne was gone. He looked into the empty jar of caviar; he'd finished it off. He was dying of thirst and hunger. He got out of bed and walked bare ass naked to the minibar.

"You will receive $10 million," Mia said to his retreating behind. "That's tax free and under the table. Azadi and Salaam will receive the same. The government appreciates your sacrifices. We're not monsters."

Farragut managed not to laugh at the lie. "And Jashni? He's getting paid, too?"

"Jashni is the Israelis' asset and is not covered by the same terms and conditions. He lives to do or die another day. But we don't have to pay him a dime."

Farragut opened the minibar. The cool blast of air caused his skin to sprout goose bumps. Or was it the bureaucratic ice in Mia's voice that made him feel so chilled? He grabbed two small bottles of Grey Goose vodka and returned to the bed with his booty. He handed Mia one of the vodka bottles after twisting off its top.

"You can use the money any way you want, John. I remember you telling me that your father had cut you out of his will."

"I never wanted his goddamn money, Mia. You know that."

She did. But she was obviously running out of things to say because she sat silently, staring at the fire through the prism of the vodka bottle, as if that would somehow inspire her salesmanship. Farragut took a long pull on his vodka and felt fire rise in his throat.

"The old man's gonna outlive me, Mia. He was supposed to be sitting next to Barak – excuse me. I mean Yasir. I was the one who made him watch the boy. If he had listened to me, he'd be dead. But once he got on the plane he traded his first class seat and dumped Yasir off on someone else. He took a seat in the rear of the plane. Coach. Can you believe it? And it saved his damn life. The damn tail section of the plane is the only part that was spared. My father barely got a scratch. But all those other people…and poor Yasir, well…"

Farragut finished off his vodka. Mia made a show of sipping hers.

"You almost sound disappointed your father lived, John."

Farragut shrugged. He knew she was testing him, angling to ignite the anger that would be so necessary if he was to carry out this mission. She wanted to see that old fire crackling in his eyes. Farragut just stared at the fire crackling in the hearth.

"I know the money won't mean much, John. But wouldn't it be nice to leave something behind to be remembered by? Wouldn't it be nice to make history instead of just teaching it?"

Not a bad question, thought Farragut. Eloquent and playing to what little vanity he had left. But he wasn't thinking about history now; he was thinking about the dead.

I will do this for Yasir.

I will do this for all the children who will become bombs and will be killed by bombs. And I will do this, even if that means I must kill one mother's child to save another's.

I will do this for my mother.

I will do this for a woman who loved Iran and despised politics. Who taught me to love the country in which I was born. Who, if the Revolution had not happened, would no doubt have stayed and kept me with her. Who no doubt would have lived a longer and happier life with her son and a man she adored in a land that touched her soul.

But that's not what Mia wanted to hear and he wouldn't disappoint her. She needed a killer. She needed a patriot. She needed a professor of Persian studies who wanted to set Iran back on track to a golden future even if he had no future himself. If he had to be, he could and would be all those things for Mia. But it was for Yasir and his mother that he decided to accept the mission. Really, what else was he going to do with his last days on earth? Flirt with clueless co-eds and teach the future bankers, lawyers, and doctors of the world about an ancient culture that would recede from their memories as quickly as an icicle melting in the spring thaw?

He raised his vodka in a toast. "To the Jane Macintosh Farragut Chair in Persian Studies. In honor of his mother, ten million dollars from the estate of the late Dartmouth professor who died abroad after a long illness..."

And then he said it, because saying it would convince him he was actually going to do it.

"The deceased left no survivors."

CHAPTER TEN

OMAR AZADI had the top down on his silver Mercedes S600 as he drove west on the Marina Freeway. The Santa Ana wind was at his back, God's blow dryer, blistering hot and dry, pushing him faster towards his beachfront condo and the ocean which was as flat and still as a mirror.

Azadi wore a chic, pale green linen suit. He wore thin, Gucci loafers with no socks, stylish and practical in this searing heat. It was past midnight and more than 90 degrees yet neither heat nor wind could ruffle his expensively styled, thick black hair. But Amber, Azadi's "date" for the evening, was ruffling his feathers with her inane chatter.

"Did you know that Marina Del Rey used to be a really big oil field, Omar? All those condos around where you live? That whole area used to be oil derricks. You don't believe me? Rent the movie 'Touch of Evil' sometime. A lot of it was shot in Venice and around the Marina, you know, near the Grand Canal and all. It was supposed to be Mexico but I guess Mexico looked more like Marina Del Rey back in the '50's. It's a great movie. Have you seen it?"

Azadi turned up the volume on the stereo. Hard, aggressive gangster rap from Genocyanide, his favorite band, blared from the speakers. Amber didn't get the hint.

"It's got that fat, old guy in it. Orson Welles. He gets shot at the end of movie and dies in the field of oil wells. Hey! Orson Welles and oil wells. That's a pun, right? I love old movies. I used to watch them all the time when I was a kid and worked in this video store down in Redondo. It didn't pay as much as stripping at Bare Elegance but it was a blast."

Azadi pulled onto Speedway. The last road before the beach ran parallel to the Pacific. Million dollar condos sandwiched Speedway on either side. The condos of Marina Del Rey were a lot like Amber: overpriced, overbuilt, and tacky. Azadi's home was at the end of the Speedway, jutting up against the channel from which the yachts of LA's rich and famous made their way into the Pacific from berths in the Marina. Azadi drove towards home, towards the channel, and saw one of those yachts heading towards the sea. It was lit-up like a Christmas tree. On the boat he could see a throng of people partying. Men in tailored suits like his own. Women in slinky dresses. It probably cost five grand in gas just to keep that tub afloat for an hour, not to mention the money for the booze and food to keep the guests happy. A midnight sail; that was living. That was class. Azadi thought of how he would kill to have a boat like that someday. If only he didn't get seasick. If only he wasn't scared of the water. If only he had the type of real friends it was worth buying such a boat for. But it wasn't a question of money. He knew how to make money. Literally.

Azadi pulled up to his condo and pressed the button on his garage door opener that was hooked to the sun visor. He pulled the Mercedes into the garage and parked it between his vintage, cherry 1965 Mustang convertible and his brand new Harley-Davidson VRSCA V-Rod. Both were sweet fucking rides. Cost him a fortune. Amber was yammering on about some friend of hers that had made a fortune by blowing the Sultan of Brunei. This fucking broad…

-:::::-

A half-hour and a half-dozen Patron Silver shots later, Azadi and Amber were spread out on the floor before the floor-to-ceiling windows, staring out at the aptly named Pacific and a black, moonless sky. It was a million-dollar view, well, technically, $2.1 million. The air conditioner quietly fed cold air into the condo but it wasn't the cold air that gave Azadi goose bumps. Something, some undeniable fear, tugged at him. He'd felt it since they'd exited the freeway onto the surface streets. The heat, the police, was on his ass. He just knew it. Or was it just the desert wind? Earthquake weather made everybody jumpy. He listened to the hot wind play the chimes hanging from the balcony. He began to relax. Then tensed again. He heard the clothes dryer going downstairs. He thought he'd turned it off. What if Amber heard it? Shit, she'd just think he was drying clothes. Besides, how could she hear the dryer above the din of her own chatter?

"So what do you think? Should I or shouldn't I, Omar?"

"Should you or shouldn't you what?"

"Haven't you been listening to me?"

Azadi listened to the wind chimes.

"Yeah. Uh. What were we talking about?"

"I was just asking you, should I have my boobs done?"

'I thought you already had."

"I had them done two years ago. If I get them done bigger I could double my tips."

"Your tits look great."

"Thanks. But they could look better. What do you think?"

Amber was very thin, naturally or courtesy of excessive dieting and fanatical exercising. Azadi didn't care. When she pulled down the top of her black, silk dress, her perfectly spherical, unnaturally large breasts were estimated by Azadi to be 34 DD's. He had a good eye for detail. He needed that in his business.

"Your tits look great, Amber."

"You already said that."

The conversation lagged after that so Azadi turned his attention from Amber's tits to his music collection. Azadi took his music seriously, and his toys even more seriously. He owned one of the most expensive MP3 players in the world, an iPod Touch designed by Stuart Hughes, the luxury gadget maker from Liverpool. He had bought it from some idiot nephew of the Sultan of Brunei, who he had met while playing the back nine at Pebble Beach. The MP3 player had been refitted with 125 grams of solid 24k gold and embellished with 124 flawless diamonds totaling 75 carats. The Apple logo was set with fifty-three diamonds, a border of diamonds around the face and a 2-carat diamond set in the center of the home button and surrounded by twenty-eight smaller diamonds. Sure, iPods were old school. In the age of smart phones who needed a dedicated music player? But that was not the point. The point was that he could afford it. The fucker had cost Azadi over $300,000 and he had paid in cash. Well, counterfeit cash, but why quibble?

Azadi selected a song by his favorite band. The four bad motherfuckers from Compton had formed Genocyanide only two years before. They had just signed a $30 million deal on the strength of their first album. He'd met the guys at a party thrown by some asshole A&R executive who owned the condo next door. Azadi and the band had hit it off immediately. Genocyanide, like Azadi, had earned their bones the real way by keeping it real. And their music, like all rap, with its relentless, pounding beat and defiant message, affected Azadi in a profound way. Rap articulated his life philosophy, money and women and power and cool toys. Rap was black music. Azadi wasn't black but he dealt with a lot of black guys in his work. He liked most of them. One of his best customers, a top-shelf banger from the smoggy badlands south of downtown, called Azadi his "sand nigger." Azadi had been called sand nigger before, years back, by the big men on campus at University High. The white boys had meant it as an insult. The banger had meant it as a compliment. *Words*, thought Azadi, *were imprecise things*.

Azadi inserted the CD and cranked the stereo.

"Dead Presidents in black and green/ Dead Presidents don't mean the money is clean."

These words were crystal clear. Counterfeit. Dirty money. Presidents pushed bills through Congress but their portraits never appeared on legal tender.

"Dead Presidents in black and green/ Dead Presidents don't mean the money is clean."

Genocyanide's lead singer, Kwaku, had written this song about him. The man was an artist and appreciated his artistry. As Azadi settled back and let the bass and beat get into his body and manipulate his moods, he became aware that Amber was talking to him. Again.

"I don't get why an Arab guy like you is so into this ghetto stuff, Omar."

"I'm not an Arab. I'm Iranian. I mean, I'm American. Do you fucking understand?"

"Huh?"

"I'm Persian. Persians aren't Arabs. Capice?"

Maybe Amber hadn't heard. Maybe the music was too loud and she was too drunk. In either case she was preoccupied with picking up the cigarette case on the coffee table. Amber opened the case and admired the contents: ten tightly rolled joints. Amber stuck one of the joints between her lips. She didn't ask for a light. She wasn't the type of girl that needed to.

"Dead Presidents make the world go 'round/ Dead Presidents make the booty go down."

Azadi torched the joint with his white gold cigarette lighter in which his initials had been monogrammed with diamonds. Amber inhaled. And then she put her lips on his and exhaled down his throat. Azadi grooved on the blowback, his lungs expanding and his brain flying away like a helium balloon. The Sinse was sweet, smooth shit.

Amber slipped down the spaghetti straps of her dress and exposed her silicone tits once again. He put his mouth between them. He went to work with his tongue. They tasted of talcum powder and were surprisingly cool. Amber reached between his legs.

"*Dead Presidents are a player's life blood/ Dead Presidents make a eunuch a stud.*"

The music was loud. So loud that Azadi couldn't hear the wind chimes singing in the hot breeze or the clothes dryer downstairs or the phalanx of cops breaking down the door and storming into the room.

CHAPTER ELEVEN

MARINA DEL REY was in an unincorporated part of the county and out of the Los Angeles Police Department's jurisdiction so the LA County Sheriff's Department had taken down the door. The Treasury Agents entered right behind the Sheriff's deputies. One Agent yanked Azadi away from Amber and pushed him face first into the pile carpet. With an economy of movement and effort, he then jammed his knee into the small of Azadi's back while handcuffing both wrists. Azadi, despite a mouthful of carpet, screamed obscenities to no effect. Another Treasury Agent appeared with the search warrant and politely held it up to Azadi's eyes should he care to read it. He did not, or, at least that's how his stream of invectives was interpreted.

Two more Treasury Agents took care of Amber. They were careful not to touch her breasts or in any way violate her civil liberties. The task was made even more difficult by the fact that Amber's dress was down around her ankles and she wore no underwear.

Mia strode into the condo just as Amber was being led off. The place was now occupied by more than a dozen treasury agents and sheriff's deputies. The sheriff's deputies had responsibility for checking the rooms and securing the scene and they did this quickly and efficiently. The house, like Azadi, had been under surveillance for weeks so Mia was not surprised when they told her that the three bedrooms, three bathrooms, den, playroom, and garage were all empty. Mia walked over to the platinum cigarette case which, far from being empty, was still filled with nine joints. She sniffed the joints and handed the case to a sheriff's deputy.

"Bag these. I know you're more liberal here on the left coast than we are back east but dope's still illegal, isn't it?"

The sheriff's deputy placed the pot in evidence bags. Azadi looked up from the floor, straining to catch sight of Mia's face but only able to see her stylish Jimmy Choo boots.

"Fuck you, bitch. You have nothing."

Azadi provided a fanfare of obscenities for his exit music as the cops pushed him out the door. Genocyanide's rap continued to pound from the speakers. Mia turned off the iPad, killing the music. After several seconds, she heard it, faint but unmistakable. Mia zeroed in on the sound and walked downstairs. Two treasury agents fell into lockstep behind her as she honed in on her quarry. She led them into the guest bedroom. The room was beautifully done in plantation style and was the only room in the house that showed any taste in her opinion. She pointed to the large, dark wood bureau opposite the bed and nodded at the two treasury agents.

"Move it away from the wall."

The two men shared a look. The bureau was huge and looked heavy — it took up fully one wall of the room. But to their surprise, they moved it with little difficulty. It was empty and made from balsa wood, like a model airplane. Where the bureau had stood was a door. The doorknob had been removed so as not to scratch against the bureau that had stood in front. All three treasury agents could hear the sound now...

The sound of a clothes dryer spinning.

Mia stuck her hand in the doorknob hole and pulled the door open towards her. The room just beyond was dark. Mia guessed right and flicked a light switch on the wall to her right. The illumination revealed the room's contents. A state-of-the-art offset press sat in one corner, a top of the line Canon copier in the other. Neatly stacked supplies of paper, toner, powder, dyes, plates — all the paraphernalia of counterfeiting — sat on sturdy metal shelves. A laundromat-sized dryer leaned against the far wall and hummed contentedly.

Mia walked to the dryer and turned it off. The air inside the dryer was as hot and dry as the Santa Ana wind blowing outside the condo. Mia pulled out a handful of bills and several poker chips. The brand new bills had been spinning with the poker chips for only a few hours but they looked as if they had been passed from hand to hand and wallet to wallet for years.

Azadi was hers.

Mia smiled. And then she did something that she didn't do very often, on the job or off: she laughed. Mia tossed the counterfeit $100 bills into the air.

They fluttered around her like birds.

CHAPTER TWELVE

"**DEAD DUCKS,**" said Farragut. "Hear me, Doc? The Yankees are dead ducks."

Farragut had come to New York to see his oncologist at Memorial Sloan-Kettering. Dr. Benjamin Greenblatt was fanatical about two things in life: the New York Yankees and astrocytomas, the type of malignancy growing inside Farragut's head. As usual, they chatted about baseball and brain tumors. Opening day was six months away but Greenblatt was already crowing about the Yankees formidable pitching. Farragut, a Red Sox fan, felt the Yankees' bullpen was thin. He asserted the Red Sox would be in first place by Labor Day. Greenblatt went slack-jawed and wondered if Farragut's tumor was starting to affect his sanity.

Farragut had reviewed his latest CAT scan with Greenblatt. The doctor had explained once again that there were low-grade astrocytomas and high-grade astrocytomas. Low-grade were slow growing and composed of the least aggressive cancer cells. High-grade were fast growing and highly malignant. The CAT scan had confirmed that Farragut had a high-grade astrocytoma. Farragut had smiled at the irony. A high-grade tumor would kill a teacher who had lived by the principle that a little grade inflation never hurt anyone.

Yes. Farragut was in remission, admitted Greenblatt. But it was only a matter of time before the inevitable. So Greenblatt wanted to be proactive. Greenblatt wanted to try surgery. They could cut out some of the cancer cells. Farragut's robustness and lack of symptoms gave Greenblatt confidence that he could prolong Farragut's life by a year, maybe two.

Farragut thanked Greenblatt for all he had done and told him he wanted to end his treatment and collect his files. Farragut knew he had made the right decision because Greenblatt, a man who became apoplectic over the dearth of good left-handed pitching in the Yankee farm system, had merely bit his lip and nodded.

-:::::-

Farragut walked back to the Carlyle Hotel from the hospital. A large man was waiting for him in the lobby. His off-the-rack suit and Brut aftershave screamed FBI. The Fed courier handed Farragut an encrypted laptop and left without saying a word.

Mia had told Farragut she was sending him the video of the Feds' interrogation of Omar Azadi. She had wanted Farragut to be in LA during the proceedings, to observe Azadi in person behind a one-way mirror. Mia knew Farragut had been a superb shakedown artist in his day; he could prove invaluable in case Azadi resisted the squeeze. But Farragut had told her he had to finish things up with his doctor in New York. If she was pissed off she didn't show it. She even got the government to pay for his night at the Carlyle, on the condition he catch an early flight to Los Angeles the next day. The Feds were going to make their pitch to the other member of the team, Shareef Salaam, and Farragut had used his one "get-out-of-jail-free" card.

Once in his suite, Farragut poured a Bushmills neat and popped a Vicodin. His head throbbed – headaches were so far the tumor's only symptoms. He turned on the laptop, typed in the password to "unlock" the encrypted video file, and began to watch Azadi's interrogation.

On the monitor Farragut saw a hotel room. He heard the drone of jets taking off and pegged it as a hotel room near the airport. He knew the CIA and FBI both kept rooms around the city with standing bugs and one-way mirrors because certain jobs required more privacy than the friendly confines of the Federal Building in Westwood. Mia was standing over a darkly handsome man sitting in a chair. That would be Azadi. The gorilla leaning against the wall with his arms folded above his gut would be Alson. Good cop/ Bad cop: the bedrock of the Fed playbook. Farragut watched Mia offer Azadi the deal.

"You go undercover in a Middle Eastern country. You gain employment as a printer at a small printing business. You win the trust of your employer and with our help you gain employment as a printer at a government-controlled printing business. Eventually, two other undercover operatives will assist you in destroying the business."

"And you can't tell me any more than that?"

"Not unless you agree to help us."

Azadi shrugged. "I must still be fucking stoned."

"Quality of the pot you smoke, it wouldn't surprise me. But it's the quality of your counterfeit that needs work."

Mia dangled a hundred-dollar bill in front of Azadi. "The front of your bills were superb, right down to the watermark and the non-consecutive serial numbers. The backs weren't bad. Except for one small but crucial detail. You used the same plate identification number on each bill, 82."

Mia crumpled the bill and tossed it in Azadi's face.

"You got careless, Omar. With the drug and counterfeiting charges, you're looking at hard time. Unless you take the deal."

Farragut watched Azadi stick a forkful of Pad Thai noodles into his mouth from a carton on the table. Azadi talked while he chewed.

"No deal. I'm calling Herb Glickman."

Farragut knew that name. Herb Glickman was a celebrity LA lawyer with a taste for high-profile clients and low-level tactics.

Mia handed Azadi her cellphone. "You want to call Glickman, go ahead. But you may find him less than willing to put his neck on the line for you. Seems he has another client, a big studio chief fighting his ex-wife for custody of their daughter. In a moment of poor judgment, the guy took his little girl to Hawaii for the week instead of returning her to her mother Sunday night as required by the visitation agreement. That's kidnapping. A Federal offense. Well, you can imagine the mother threw a hissy fit and wanted to press charges. Luckily the Bureau talked her out of it and Mr. Glickman's client has been spared any embarrassing publicity. As you know, Mr. Glickman has a strong sense of *quid pro quo* and has already indicated to us that he would encourage any hypothetical clients in your position to cooperate fully with the interests of the United States government."

Farragut could see the sweat peppering Azadi's brow. The iceman had begun to melt.

"Tell me more."

"We create a cover story and insert you into the country. Once you do the job, Special Forces gets you out. You'll train with them for two weeks. We have a detailed escape plan. It's risky but it can work."

Farragut watched Azadi smile. His grin said, "You can't bullshit me." Maybe Azadi doubted the escape plan would work. Maybe he guessed the truth — that there was no escape plan at all. Farragut couldn't tell.

"You got the wrong guy. I'm not the hero type."

Mia got right to it. "Then do it for the money. Ten million dollars tax-free in a numbered account in the Caymans."

Azadi laughed. Mia didn't.

"What's so funny?"

"Look, I like money. I like the cars it buys, the clothes it buys, the women it buys. Hell, I like money so much that yes, I've been known to print my own. But you are one dumb bitch if you think I like money so much I'd risk dying for it."

Mia sighed. "Guess I misjudged you."

Alson stepped in front of Azadi. He had been biding his time near the window, as inconspicuous as a battleship in a bathtub. He rabbit punched Azadi in the stomach. Azadi convulsed and puked Pad Thai noodles and pink lemonade. Alson jammed his thumb into Azadi's carotid artery. Azadi's eyes rolled back in his head.

"Listen up, fuckup. If you don't take this deal your ass is penitentiary prime rib. You understand me? We'll stick your dick in some godforsaken pit, put the word out that you're a snitch, then let the butch boys eat you alive. And you can kiss these fancy suits goodbye because you'll be wearing nothing but diapers from here on out. Trust me, your sphincters gonna be hanging like a hammock after you've been fucked up the ass for 20 years."

Alson shoved Azadi backwards. The chair with Azadi handcuffed to it hit the floor like a sack of cement.

Mia watched Azadi squirm face down on the floor. "Do we have a deal?"

Farragut could see the pool of piss collecting on the floor beneath Azadi. Azadi's voice sounded far away.

"Yes…I'm in…Christ…Stop…I'm in…"

Mia looked into the camera and signaled. The video went black.

Farragut turned off the computer. He looked out the window. The lights of the Upper West Side twinkled across the park. Traffic sounds vaulted up from Madison Avenue.

Farragut went downstairs to the Café, ordered a steak, drank three martinis, and listened to John Pizzarelli sing Cole Porter:

"What a glimpse of paradise/ Someone who's naughty/ Showed to someone who's nice…"

CHAPTER THIRTEEN

ABOUT 30 MILES down the coast from Azadi's luxurious condo sat the grim concrete monolith known as the Federal Correctional Institution at Terminal Island. Terminal Island was a medium security institution, rated for 478 men but populated by 1023. The buildings were rotting from the sea air and over 60 years of continuous use. But an inmate, looking north past the barbed wire and watchtowers, could admire the rapidly gentrifying San Pedro neighborhood and dream of one day walking its palm-lined streets. An inmate might hear the foghorns of ships pulling into and out of the nearby port of Los Angeles, giving promise of any number of exotic places that the inmate might one day visit when his debt to society had been paid. Yes, Terminal Island was a place that held out a modicum of hope to its inhabitants, hope for a better future and a more exciting life. That is, unless a man was doing life at TI. In that case, a man had to find other things to give him inner peace.

The inmate Gary Hastings found his inner peace when he found Allah. After that, he took the name Shareef Salaam, for "Salaam" means "peace" in Arabic.

Salaam's conversion to Islam, like his conversion to violence, had been gradual. The tenured Berkeley chemistry professor fell in with violent radicals, the People's Radical Front, in 1982 after more than a decade of non-violent protest. He attended meetings, gave some speeches, gave even more money and generally flirted with actually doing ... something.

In 1985 he sealed the deal with the bombing of the Federal Courthouse in Philadelphia. By design, the bombing had been carried out at night. The intent was not to kill but rather to make a political statement and show solidarity with Philadelphia's own black radical movement, known as MOVE. In May of that year, MOVE's house on Osage Avenue had come under attack by hundreds of Philadelphia police. Six adults and five children died under a hail of bullets and C4 military explosives. The whole surrounding neighborhood – 61 houses in all – had burned to the ground because, it was said, firefighters were ordered to let them burn. And for what? Because MOVE had refused to respect the values of Ronald Reagan's America? Because MOVE had exposed the city's politicians and police for the racist murderers they really were? So, reasoned then named Gary Hastings, blow up the Federal Courthouse in Philadelphia and make a statement to rival the crack in the Liberty Bell.

The charges were set to go off in the middle of the night. No one was supposed to die. But someone did.

Following the bombing, Gary Hastings went underground only to be caught six months later in a supposed safe house in Emeryville, California. He had been fingered by known associates who suspected him of having second doubts about the effectiveness of violent resistance. They were right. He did. But he wouldn't have talked. And he never did. He was sentenced and convicted in 1987.

Those were the years of isolation and despair. He had not yet started the inmate tutorial program that would become a model for the entire Federal system (and would earn him featured segments on "60 Minutes" and "Oprah.") He had not yet begun his tireless correspondence with progressive politicians and activists the world over upon which a book was compiled (and would earn him a glowing review in the New York *Times*). All this was to be in the future after Gary Hastings had found God.

He spent the next five years doing his time and waiting to die. Martin was dead. Bobby was dead. Malcolm was dead. The white kids that had marched with fists raised through the streets of Chicago were making fistfuls of money on Wall Street. Gary Hastings wanted to be left alone and, for the most part, he was. He had rebuffed the proselytizing efforts of the Black Muslims in the prison population. The same invectives and cold stares were paid out to the born again Christians. He had long since rejected the idea that any good could come from God or religion. He was not a Marxist but he agreed with King Karl on this. Religion was the opiate of the masses. Gary Hastings spent 1,707 days in prison waiting for day one of his new life.

September 29, 1992. Gary Hastings still remembered the day he found God. He was reading the Quran for the second time. This in and of itself was not a sign of any great interest or determination on his part. Gary Hastings had read almost every book in the library at least once and some three times. He was particularly fond of the poetry of Langston Hughes and the mystery novels of Ross MacDonald. But he had decided, for reasons he could not remember, to dip again into the Quran. As he read, a strong sensation began to grip him. It was not a sensation he immediately recognized but once he did, he luxuriated in its power.

Awe embraced Gary Hastings.

Awe in the awareness of God wherever he turned his eyes. Awe in the confluence of God with a material, mathematical world. Awe in the existence of and value placed upon his soul and the souls of others. Awe in Allah.

He was a scientist, a celebrated scientist, and he retained his critical eye. The Quran was a flawed work, filled with inconsistencies and some outright nastiness. But what religion wasn't? What person wasn't for that matter? And what of the scientific world and its own inconsistencies? Change one chemical bond and a harmless compound becomes a killer poison. Almonds have the same smell as cyanide.

As a scientist he valued logical reasoning. Islam exhorted men to reason and think for themselves. "He will not be rewarded but by the manner in which he has used and applied his reason," said the Prophet. Islam courted inquiry and rejected dogmatic thinking arrived at without reasoning. Gary Hastings reasoned thus; Science and God were not inconsistent but one and the same. Science was the expression of God's design of earth and math was the language in which He expressed it. The Quran was another type of math, the math to describe not God's relation to the physical world but God's relation to man. This powerful, compelling simplicity...

Islam also appealed to his hibernating radicalism. The Quran clearly stated that the uncultivated property of a rich man became *ipso facto* the property of the poor man if the poor man would cultivate it. Potentate and pauper had the same rights on the floor of the mosque, on their knees in worship.

It was a religion based not upon blind faith but a logical application of rules and daily worship. To do things rightly as prescribed in the Quran, to do them to the best of one's ability, was all that was asked. After that, you could trust in the Will of God.

Even if a young woman and her unborn baby had to die in a Philadelphia courthouse for Gary Hastings to become Shareef Salaam in a California prison. It was the Will of God.

Even if Shareef Salaam's soul was finally free but his body would never walk the streets a free man again. It was the Will of God.

Even if Shareef Salaam would never be given the chance to make even one second of his daughter's and grandson's lives a little better. It was the Will of God.

-:::::-

Billie Hastings sat across a table from her father in the visitors' room at the Federal Correctional Institution at Terminal Island. Her nose was running but she did not cry. When she was this angry the tears didn't flow, just the snot.

"I hate you, daddy. I hate you for everything you did to our family."

Salaam flashed Billie a smile that said he knew he deserved it. "Wipe your nose, baby."

Billie took a tissue from the box on the table and wiped her nose. Salaam watched his grandson Gary – six-years-old and as energetic as electricity — playing with a headless Iron Man action figure in the far corner of the room reserved for small children.

"Is that all you have for me, daddy? Wipe my nose?"

Salaam turned his attention back to Billie. "As the Prophet Muhammad said: Trust in God and tie your camel, baby."

"The Prophet Muhammad actually said *baby*?"

"Well, I might've made up the *baby* part," admitted Salaam. "But the camel part and the trust part? All true."

Billie kept the clamps on her smile, which normally she would have offered. She was 30 years old. Her skin was smooth, flawless, and cocoa brown. Unlike her namesake Billie Holiday, she couldn't sing a lick. But she knew a thing or two about pain.

"Nice try, daddy. But I'm not a Muslim."

Salaam heard the anger in her voice.

"We talked about you exploring the possibility."

"No. *You* talked about it. Then those Stepford Sisters with their perfect teeth you sent over to the house talked about it."

Salaam felt the ire rise like bile in his throat. "Give the Muslim Women's League more credit than that. If you'd listened to them you'd have discovered they are far from submissive help maidens. You'd have discovered that the Muslim Women's League protects an Islamic woman's designated rights."

"I don't care if they protect designated rights, designated hitters, or designated diddlysquat. I'm not converting to Islam and neither is Gary."

Billie clenched her jaw. So did Salaam. She had learned the gesture from him.

"Gary is my grandson. He carries my Christian name. But with me in here and his father God knows where, he needs a positive male influence. The Muslim community provides –"

"—Does it provide a living, daddy? 'Cause I had to close the store."

"What? Why?"

"Jesus, daddy. Are you really that naïve? I mean, who the hell's gonna buy kids' clothes from a woman whose father killed a...a..."

Billie swallowed her words and lowered her head. Salaam stared at his daughter and felt unmitigated shame that he could cause her such pain.

Billie said, "Sorry, daddy, I went too far."

She raised her head and met her father's gaze. Salaam gave her a wry smile.

"It runs in the family."

Then Salaam made a face. The type of face a father makes to get his baby girl to giggle. And despite the tension and the life-time that had passed since Billie's childhood, the smile worked its magic. Salaam leaned back in his chair and soaked in his daughter's laughter.

"I ever tell you that you look like your mother when you laugh?"

"Oh, just six, maybe seven thousand times."

"What a woman. I was off changing the world and she was home changing diapers."

"That's right. You wanted a revolution and she wanted a refrigerator."

Salaam chuckled. Victoria Lott Hastings was the love of his life and the most patient woman in the world. She was starting her Master's in Public Health at Boston University when he was just starting at MIT. He was a cocky kid off the mean streets of Oakland who was secretly terrified of being 3,000 miles from home. She was a preacher's daughter from nearby Roxbury, three years his senior and amused by this nappy-headed scarecrow that sat down next to her at the Harvard Coop Café and announced he was going to be the first black astronaut. He was a prodigy — only 16. It was 1969 and Armstrong had just walked on the moon and she was the foxiest woman he had ever seen and he couldn't think of anything else to say by way of an intro. They talked and discovered they both loved Billie Holiday's voice, the words of Langston Hughes, Eldridge Cleaver's attitude, and Willie Mays's everything. They were married the day after he graduated from MIT. He traveled a few blocks over to Harvard and picked up his Master's and Doctorate before he turned 25. They moved across country when he got an assistant professorship at Berkeley and stayed together through his early tenure, the birth of their daughter, the miscarriage of their son, his growing disillusionment with academia and attraction to political militancy. The aneurysm killed her three days before her 36th birthday and destroyed his innate belief that his life was blessed. Five years later he was in prison, but he missed her far more than he missed his freedom.

Salaam said, "You know, baby, if you don't want to become a Muslim, don't do it. I'm just trying to do what I can to look out for you."

"Aunt Lucille says she might be able to get me a job at her Nordstrom. They're looking for someone in women's shoes."

Salaam flexed his long fingers and squeezed out the panic that his voice did not betray.

"Your Aunt Lucille's in Seattle."

"So's the job. I'm really thinking of taking it. Uncle Jim loves Gary and he needs a positive male influence in his life. You said so yourself."

"How will you be able to visit me if you're in Seattle?"

"With great difficulty, to be honest."

Salaam told himself that if his daughter moved a thousand miles away with his grandson, then it was the Will of God.

"Daddy, I know you don't have any money and, if you did, you'd give it to me. I'm not asking for money. I'm just asking for you to understand."

Salaam stared out the barred window at the gray sky. The marine layer had socked in the coast for the past two weeks. He listened to the sounds of other conversations around him. He didn't focus on the words, just the sound of conversation that he likened to buzzing bees. And then Salaam found himself hearing his own words, unable to halt the flow of his confession even as his brain urged his mouth to stop.

"I'm working in the laundry now. Bad job. Nobody wants it. Me? I volunteered. Every day, I'm buried under dirty clothes and soiled sheets. The stench is overpowering. Not the stench of piss or blood or shit or sweat. You get used to those. No. What gets to cons, even the hardest, is the stench of hopelessness. It's in the clothes, the sheets, anything we touch. The stench of absolute, irredeemable hopelessness."

Salaam heard a choked sob. He turned from the window and saw Billie crying. There was no Plexiglas between him and his daughter. His good works had earned him the luxury of the low-security meeting. Although the guards prohibited physical contact between inmates and visitors, Salaam reached out and put his hands over Billie's.

"It's okay, baby, really. Because after you run those rags through the machines, a miracle happens, the smell of warm, clean clothes. Reminds me of your mother. Sometimes I imagine that smell rising up and floating over these walls. Maybe it does, maybe it doesn't. Don't know if I'll ever know. But I do know you have to do what's best for you and Gary."

Salaam couldn't bear to see Billie cry. He lifted her hands to his mouth and was about to kiss them when a guard put his hands on Salaam's shoulders. The guard's touch was hard and hostile, like his tone of voice.

"That's enough, Salaam. You know the rules."

Salaam pulled his hands from his daughter's. He continued to stare into her eyes.

"And besides," continued the guard. "The warden wants to see you. You have visitors."

CHAPTER FOURTEEN

COMPARTMENTALIZATION dictated Farragut stay hidden from Salaam's view so he stood in the warden's office closet, watching from behind a one-way mirror as Mia and Alson pitched the mission. The closet was five-by-seven, about as big as the cells that confined the pitiful souls who called this prison home. To Farragut, however, Shareef Salaam seemed far from pitiful. He looked like an ascending African prince. His skin was clear; his eyes were clearer still and, judging by his deliberate responses to the Feds' questions, his conscience was clearest of all. And that's what worried Farragut. He doubted he could have sustained his own physical and emotional well-being under such terrible strain. Jesus, he had a tumor eating away at his brain and for the last five years he had done nothing more stressful than reread Thucydides. He knew he'd have to keep a close eye on Salaam if he joined the mission.

"Do you have any more questions?" Alson asked Salaam after Salaam had said nothing for a while. Alson was sitting in the warden's worn leather chair, his feet up on the oak desk. Salaam was standing by the window, staring out at the gloomy marine layer socking in the coast. Mia was perusing the bookshelves at the far wall, as if she had better things to do than ask a man to go halfway around the world to die for a cause that seemed contrary to his very soul.

Salaam said, "I don't know what else to ask. I assume you've told me everything."

Well, not the part about this being a suicide mission, thought Farragut from behind the mirror. *That little morsel of bullshit we left out.*

"All you need to know is ten million dollars," said Alson. "Half up front and half when you complete the mission. Tax free in a numbered account in the Caymans."

Salaam watched a seagull float on the fog. Alson kept up the attack.

"Your family might not be so dismissive of the money. Your daughter lost her store. And you know how much college costs these days? You won a full scholarship to MIT but little Shareef may not be so lucky."

Salaam's voice was flat. "His name isn't Shareef. It's Gary. Gary Hastings."

The room got quiet and still. Farragut smelled a stalemate. Mia had pulled a book from the warden's bookshelf and appeared to be engrossed. Alson tied his shoes. Salaam focused on the view beyond the window, seagulls fluttering above the razor wire and concrete walls.

They had told him of the mission in as much detail as he needed to make a decision. They had told Salaam that he couldn't meet any of the members of the team until the day of the mission. Salaam had seemed to understand. He had been in the radical underground. He accepted the holy canon of compartmentalization. What else? The reward for his cooperation. The escape plan. All covered in believable detail.

Then Mia spoke up without looking up from her book.

"We're offering you a chance to do something positive with what remains of your life. It's risky, sure, but at least you'll be free. Or die working towards that freedom. But we don't have much time. We need your decision now."

And then Farragut saw it. It flashed across Salaam's face, an electro-chemical twitch that grazed the muscles of Salaam's mouth. Farragut knew its inspiration: the fear of death. Or was it the desire to live? Farragut had felt both more than a few times himself the past few months.

Salaam turned from the window and looked at Mia. "I won't kill anyone or anything. Not even a seagull. And certainly not a human being."

"You won't have to kill anyone," Alson said. "Just blow up what we tell you to blow up and then disappear. It's easy to disappear when you have $10 million."

Salaam ignored Alson and stared at Mia. "What are you reading?"

Mia held up the book so Salaam could read the cover. Farragut hadn't been able to read it from his angle but he saw Salaam smile, giving his approval to Mia's literary choice.

Then Salaam began to speak. He didn't speak to Mia and he certainly didn't speak to Alson. He seemed to speak to someone unseen outside the window, beyond the razor wire and concrete walls. His voice was soft, almost inaudible at first, but it grew with power and authority as he went on. Not even the squawking of the seagulls could diminish its impact.

"I've known rivers," began Salaam. "I've known rivers ancient as the world and older than the flow of human blood in the veins. My soul has grown deep like the rivers. I bathed in the Euphrates when dawns were young. I built my hut near the Congo and it lulled me to sleep. I looked upon the Nile and raised the pyramids above it. I heard the singing of the Mississippi when Abe Lincoln went down to New Orleans, and I've seen its muddy bosom turn all golden in the sunset. I've known rivers, ancient, dusky rivers. My soul has grown deep like the rivers…"

Farragut could see that Mia was touched and Alson, well, Alson was in awe. Perhaps not as in awe as Salaam was of God, but in awe nonetheless.

"Did you write that," asked Alson after a long silence.

"Langston Hughes wrote that," answered Mia, waving the book that she had taken off the shelf. She was staring at Salaam, a conspiratorial smile on her face.

"That's the only good thing about prison," Salaam said, more to himself than anyone else. "Time to read. Lots of time to read."

Salaam gestured for the book. Mia gave it to him. He casually flipped through its pages.

"I'm in," said Salaam.

And with those words Salaam, for the first time during the pitch, glanced at the one-way mirror. Mia and Alson didn't notice. But Farragut did, because somehow Salaam had, with a flick of his head towards a reflecting surface he had up to that moment pointedly ignored, managed to look Farragut dead in the eye.

CHAPTER FIFTEEN

OMAR AZADI sat in his Mercedes and stared at the nondescript storefront. "Azadi & Son Printers" was splashed in faded red paint across the tattered green awning. This Persian patch of the city normally bustled with commerce and college kids from nearby UCLA. But it was 3 a.m. on a Sunday night and nobody was around who could get hurt or witness what was about to go down.

Mia and Alson had parked their unmarked government Ford Taurus right behind Azadi's Mercedes S600 Sedan. They watched him as he watched two men, faces covered by baklavas, spray paint slogans on the sidewalk in front of the shop. The night before at Azadi's condo, now in escrow, Alson had shared the details with him over a pepperoni pizza.

"'Die Arab Motherfuckers,'" shouted Alson. "Do you like the sound of that, Omar?"

"I'm Persian, not Arab," said Azadi.

"But that's the beauty of it. This has to be authentic. That's just the type of mistake a bunch of ignorant, racist motherfuckers would make."

As would ignorant, fat fuck Federal Agents like you, thought Azadi. But it was the government's show. Azadi had swallowed his pride along with another slice of pizza.

The spray painting done, Azadi watched the two men in baklavas light their Molotov cocktails and toss them through the window. Fire consumed the interior of the shop. The two arsonists peeled off down the deserted boulevard in their stolen Ford van. The van, according to plan, would be found a week later burning off a freeway exit ramp near the desert city of Needles. Alson had hired the arsonists the week before; they were former snitches who had performed similar tasks back when Alson was LAPD. The fire had to be set by pros. It couldn't be allowed to spread to legitimate businesses or bear the signature of any known hate groups or arsonists.

Azadi had wanted to meet the men who would be responsible for the destruction of the family printing business that his father had started and he had disgraced. But Mia had refused Azadi's request three days earlier.

"What point would it serve?" she had asked him at the Hollywood infomercial production studio where she was prepping him for the news conferences that were sure to follow. "The men are professionals, bought and paid for just like you. Console yourself with the fact that your first $5 million is already in a numbered account in the Caymans."

Mia took particular pride in the way she had prepared the media side of things. Her favorite cousin was a senior vice-president at MSNBC. A week before the firebombing, she had planted the seed with him over drinks at the Rainbow Room.

"Hey, Tommy, I'm no Diane Sawyer but why not cover the rise in hate crimes against those of Middle Eastern descent? I have a hot story that'll scoop those flag-wavers at Fox. By the way, they're still killing you in the ratings, right?"

Cousin Tommy, knowing without being told that he couldn't be told the real reason for her sudden interest in news, sipped his Maker's Mark and signed on to be a co-conspirator in the game. He had flirted with the idea of joining the CIA after graduation from

Amherst and was enjoying the clandestine connotations – they were clandestine, right? – of his cousin Mia's request. MSNBC got the exclusive interview with Omar Azadi, a hard-working immigrant's son who had lived the American dream and was now being subjected to an Orwellian nightmare.

Farragut found it all unseemly as he watched from afar. He still had his students to teach and was stuck in Hanover. With his $5 million windfall, he had bought himself a brand new plasma screen TV to watch the brand new MSNBC special report on the plight of Omar Azadi. The picture was so clear and sharp that Farragut swore he could see smile lines curl up around Azadi's eyes as he tearfully spit out some slop about having to cancel his father's seventieth birthday celebration. They had been planning to go to the Statue of Liberty, said Azadi, as the lump built in his throat. Farragut could see that Azadi's father wasn't in on the joke. He wore the blank, battered look of a man who had been willing to settle for very little in his life and was now realizing that he was going to wind up settling for even less.

As Farragut watched the interview on TV he felt a growing respect for Mia's prep work with Azadi. Azadi looked right into the camera and whispered through trembling lips how he wanted to go back home, back to Iran. At least in Iran, he could hold his head up like a man. Then Azadi cried on cue. The full waterworks.

Farragut got on the phone to Mia to congratulate her on her creation.

"The Iranians are rushing Azadi's visa through their interests section at the Pakistani Embassy," reported Mia. "All according to plan, John. Hell, they've got kids rioting in the streets, calling for the death of the old regime and here they have an American who actually wants to return. Al-Jazeera picked up Azadi's interview and has been giving it major air play in the Middle East."

"No doubt about it, Mia," agreed Farragut, gulping down a couple Vicodin with a shot of Bushmills. "Azadi's a star. A white hot supernova."

-:::::-

Azadi was a star but, just as importantly, a master counterfeiter. That's why his tour of the highly secure Bureau of Engraving and Printing in Washington was unprecedented. Frank Finley almost had a coronary when Mia made the request but he pushed it through. The idea was to familiarize Azadi with the exact type of intaglio press and printing process that he would find in Tehran. Normally, the Bureau produced 8,000 sheets of bills per hour, 24 hours a day, 365 days a year. But on this day, for three hours starting at 3:00 a.m., the room was cleared and the presses were stopped. The pretext concocted was an anthrax scare that would later be quickly dismissed as a hoax. But Azadi was deadly serious as he went through the printing process, even though his disguise – hair dyed gray, blue contact lenses, twenty pounds of extra padding in his Hazmat suit – was comical.

Azadi had studied the training manual for the past two weeks. He was an expert at both photocopy printing and the intaglio method. But the presses at the BEP demanded a greater level of proficiency. He was rusty at first but he quickly found his rhythm and confidence. First he covered the meticulously engraved $100 printing plates with special Treasury ink and then gently wiped clean the surface of each plate, allowing the ink to remain in the design and letter grooves of the plates. Then he fed the currency paper, made especially for the BEP by Crane & Company, into the presses. Upon hitting the power switch, each sheet was then forced under 20 tons of pressure into the finely recessed lines of the printing plate to pick up the ink. It was a limited print run. Fifty thousand dollars in brand new $100 bills.

Mia watched Azadi hold a sample sheet to the light to search for visual flaws. Finding none, he closed his eyes and ran his fingers across the front and back of the sheets. He was making sure the bills' surface felt slightly raised, while the reverse side felt slightly indented.

"Intaglio printing, from the Italian meaning 'incise,'" said Azadi almost as an afterthought as he handed the sheet of bills to Mia.

"The feel makes it real," agreed Mia. "That stiffness, the crackle of the paper."

Mia felt the sheet of bills. Her fingertips confirmed it. The bills were perfect. She flashed Azadi a smile and then helped him shred the money into confetti.

They moved to the stuffy, glass enclosed supervisor's office overlooking the vast room. Azadi sat behind the metal desk, fingers tapping out a drum roll on the doodle-infested blotter. Mia stood by the slide projector. An image of the $100 bill illuminated the far wall. The $100 bill had been redesigned in 1996 to combat the spread of Supernotes and the ease in which currency could be replicated with the new, sophisticated color photocopiers. Design and security modifications had continued up through the present day. Most of the security measures were announced to the public to give the world confidence that the U.S. was way ahead of the counterfeiters.

But a few of the security measures were kept secret. Why give the crooks your entire playbook?

Any Treasury Agent can tell you," said Mia. It's impossible to create a bill that's 100 percent counterfeit-proof."

"Any counterfeiter could tell you that, too." Azadi countered with a cocky smile. "Are you going to tell me the secret, secret sauce?"

Mia smiled and shook her head. "No. But you're going to tell me yours."

And then for her benefit he repeated the litany of security features. The watermark of Franklin to the right side of the bill, optically variable ink that changed from green to black when viewed at different angles, a higher quality and enlarged portrait of Benjamin Franklin, and supposedly hard-to-reproduce fine line printing around Franklin's portrait and Independence Hall. Older security features such as interwoven red and blue silk fibers, microprinting, and a plastic security thread that glowed red under a black light. The individual Federal Reserve Bank Seal was changed to a unified

Federal Reserve Seal along with an additional prefix letter being added to the serial number.

And then he told her his tricks for replicating these features without the benefit of the government's equipment and standard operating practices. He spoke quickly, assuming she had knowledge of the trade that equaled his. Mia listened, asked a few questions when she wasn't quite sure of the technique. He noted her questions were good questions. Just a hair's width of expertise separated his knowledge from hers. Her talents were wasted on government work.

Azadi leaned back in his chair and put his hands behind his head. He was tired but happy to finally show off his professionalism. He had a feeling Kelly still considered him a moronic pothead.

"Any more questions, Agent Kelly?"

"Did you forget the newest security features?"

The smile slowly came off Azadi's face. He *had* forgotten them. They had been announced in 2010 and rolled out in 2011. He hadn't bothered to master them yet. Since plenty of the older issue hundreds were still in circulation and would be for years, it seemed like wasted effort.

"Right. Sure…Ahhhh…," Azadi found his train of thought. "Background color of pale blue. The 3-D blue security ribbon to the right of the portrait that contains "100s" and miniature liberty bells. The holographic shift effect of the "100s" to bells and back. Then the color-shifting inkwell inside the larger bell… "

"Here's how it's gonna go," she said cutting him off. "Many of those and the older security features are designed into the paper at Crane. We're going to make your job easier so you won't have to replicate them."

Azadi could feel anger well up. She didn't think he was good enough to pull off the toughest part of the job.

"I can do this. There's not a detail I can't replicate," he said.

"But you won't have to. We're going to supply the Iranians and you with the actual Crane & Company paper."

"The real paper? The top secret stuff?"

She nodded. Azadi rubbed his eyes.

"How?"

Mia smiled quickly. "Don't worry about that. That's not your problem. All you have to worry about is engraving new plates."

Another curve ball. Azadi exploded. "Are you fucking nuts? You're gonna have me engrave new plates? Portrait? Borders? Front and back? That could take me a year."

"Relax. When the time comes, the new plates, mostly completed, will be given to you. You will tell the people at the Press that you smuggled the plates into Iran in your Quran. Now it will take some work on your part but the Iranians must see you complete the plates. They must believe in your capability. We can't make it too easy for them, can we?"

"Too easy for them or too easy for me?" he said considering all the work ahead.

Mia looked at him like he'd asked the silliest question in the world. "Omar, by that point, *you* will be *them.*"

CHAPTER SIXTEEN

FIVE MINUTES after Mia and Azadi had departed Alson and Salaam stepped into the press room. Salaam, like Azadi, wore a Hazmat suit as a disguise. Salaam was officially a dangerous fugitive, star of six o'clock news reports and post office "most wanted" boards. For all he knew, best-selling books were going to be written and million dollar movie deals closed on the subject of his incredible escape from Terminal Island. Salaam would never see a dime of that money but he had seen the bank statement from Grand Cayman and the first $5 million collecting interest in his name.

"How will you be getting the explosives in?" asked Salaam after silently surveying the pressroom for several minutes.

"The less you know about that the better," said Alson. "Just tell me what you need."

"We'll go with plastic explosives. C4. M118 block demolition charges should do the trick. Military issue. They're real stable and malleable. They're particularly good as a cutting charge against steel targets. They come in half-pound sheets of flexible plastic so you can mold them to look like something else and bring them right under somebody's nose."

"Like I said. Don't worry about how we get the explosives in. Just worry about blowing this thing up."

"Fine. So, C4."

"I was thinking C4, too. I trained with it when I was in the Marines."

Salaam turned to Alson who was wearing a self-satisfied smile.

"So if you know all this shit what do you need me for?"

"Your scintillating wit, Salaam. Keep going. How much will you need?"

"Your man will have to bring in detonators, too. For every detonator he's carrying that means less C4 he can carry."

"Right. So how much will you need?"

"Depends on how much damage you want me to do?"

"For Chrissakes, Salaam, we've gone over this. The press has to be completely destroyed beyond repair. The paper and supplies, ink, etc., they gotta go, too. So how much fucking C4 will you need?"

Salaam had seen the technical specs for the press and knew by heart the formula for the weight of the charge required for destroying steel of that type and thickness. But there are the laws of science and then there is Murphy's Law. Anything that can go wrong will. So Salaam factored in an amount that gave him a large margin of security.

"Can your man bring in 20 pounds?"

"Twenty pounds of C4? That's doable."

"And the detonators. I'll need 10."

"Twenty plus the detonators. Sold to the man in the Hazmat suit."

Alson smiled like he'd just sold a lame pig for a fortune to a fool at the county fair.

-:::::-

From Washington, Alson drove Salaam south to Fort Bragg, North Carolina, where Salaam was scheduled to train for the fictional escape. As Alson drove, he fiddled with the car. Salaam stared out at the passing Virginia countryside. The gray dawn hung heavy over the gentle hills and their leafless trees. Salaam tried to ignore the smell of Alson's cheap aftershave and thought about the prison escape that the US government had so kindly facilitated for him.

Pills had been smuggled into his cell with directions for him to take three a day and damn the consequences. The consequences were conditions that mimicked a rare but potentially lethal strain of virus hereto isolated to some remote region of New Guinea. How an incarcerated inmate in Long Beach, California, should come into contact with such a strain, no one could say. No one, that is, save for a celebrated immunologist at the University of California at San Francisco Medical School. Dr. Ted Bennet, who had been on the Agency's payroll in a purely advisory capacity, had insisted on seeing the sick man and running some tests. Intense pressure filtered down from the Justice Department to the Bureau of Prisons. The plan had been Farragut's but it was the bureaucratic ballast of the Supernote Committee that had gotten results. The powers that be allowed for Shareef Salaam, an inmate in excellent standing to fly forthwith to Dr. Bennet's lab rather than undergo testing at Terminal Island's less than modern facility.

On the way to the airport, four armed gunmen had held up Salaam's ambulance and the US Marshals' car that escorted it. The Marshals inside were, in fact, briefed FBI counter-intelligence men who were more than cooperative in allowing the four armed gunmen, also undercover FBI, to spirit Salaam away to places unknown. The two paramedics in the ambulance were the real deal and as such unarmed and unwilling to die to save Shareef Salaam. A previously unknown radical group, Blacks United against Racist Nations, or BURN, was given credit for the escape. Farragut, a facility for acronyms being one of his many talents, had chosen the name. But it was left to the more creative types at Langley to handle the creation of phony social security numbers, doctored drivers licenses, backdated correspondences, coded e-mail messages and bank accounts hidden behind bogus businesses that gave a semblance of plausible reality to this purely fictitious organization and its members.

Since Salaam was a minor celebrity, the press chose to run with the story of his escape without any artificial prompting. The right wing media outlets had a field day as Salaam was not only black, well-educated and Muslim – hence a proxy for the President for those confused souls who still considered Obama "the other." Everyone agreed that the seeds were thus sown for Salaam to be welcomed back into the brotherhood of international terrorism.

-:::::-

Shareef Salaam and Omar Azadi were not to meet until the day of the mission or, more accurately, the day they found themselves together with Farragut inside whatever building housed the Supernote Press. The actual date – if they succeeded in finding the Press at all – was weeks, maybe months away. Yet both men might have been surprised to know they were training for their nonexistent escape at the same time, not five miles from one another.

Fort Bragg could easily accommodate both men and their respective handlers. Spread over hundreds of miles in the Cumberland County countryside, the base was home to tens of thousands of soldiers and their dependents. The Army's XVIII Airborne command called it home along with the 82nd Airborne and the Army's elite parachute unit, the Golden Knights. But it was the Delta Force, America's top-secret soldiers dedicated to anti-terrorism, who had the dubious honor of hosting the soon to be deceased duo. The soldiers were not told, of course, that the training was a sham. Nor were they told the why and who and what. Being in Delta Force meant trusting God and not asking questions. And when Alson and Mia asked some of their own, the soldiers answered with a smile.

"Both men are in perfect condition, Ma'am," said Staff Sergeant Hanson, entrusted with getting both men into fighting shape. "Salaam's in tip-top shape for a man his age. He can do 200 sit-ups and 100 push-ups without breaking a sweat."

Mia scanned Hanson's bland features. If the sergeant was aware that Salaam was a fugitive from justice – and how could he not be with all the attendant publicity of Salaam's escape? He did a damn good job hiding it. That's what Mia liked about Special Forces. They knew that sometimes playing stupid was smart.

"How about Azadi? Does he make the grade?"

"Affirmative. Stamina and strength to burn. Seems he was a real gym rat back in LA."

Not to mention a real peacock and a pain in the ass, thought Mia.

"Azadi's a natural," reported Captain Wilson who oversaw the fine art of jumping into and out of moving helicopters. "He would've made a helluva an airborne soldier."

"And Salaam?" inquired Mia, having trouble conjuring the image of a crew-cut Azadi in dress greens.

"Fearless, a quick study. Give him another week and he'll not only be rappelling up into helicopters, he'll be flying them solo." Captain Wilson paused to clear his throat. "However, both Salaam and Azadi have expressed the same concern to me. Independently, of course."

Mia was actually pleased that Salaam and Azadi, although they'd never met, we're both sufficiently on the same wavelength to actively engage their instructors. "What concern is that, Captain?"

"Both want to know who will call in the Delta Force. I keep telling them that it will be another team member they haven't met yet and not to worry about it."

"But they are worrying about it, aren't they?"

Captain Wilson nodded. "To tell you the truth, so am I."

"To tell you the truth, I can't tell you either, Captain. That man's identity is classified."

Mia smiled pleasantly. Farragut's identity being classified wasn't a lie. But the notion he would ever con Delta Force was. Captain Wilson continued. "They both understand the need to keep things compartmentalized but they continue to ask questions, especially Salaam."

"Such as?"

"Like how do we know the extraction will take place from a rooftop? How will the helicopters avoid hostile radar? How many birds do we have for back-up?"

"And you said?"

"We don't know for sure. Extraction points are fluid and will be communicated to us within 24 hours. We'll have Wild Weasels jamming the radar from their jets. We'll rely on a night snatch as well as the choppers' own built in stealth capability. As for back-up birds? If we really need them, we're fucked anyway so we'll have to do without."

"And what did Salaam say to that?"

"He said: 'Don't end a sentence with a preposition.'"

CHAPTER SEVENTEEN

THE ESCAPE training came to an end after two weeks. Salaam was scheduled to fly an Air Force C-130 transport to the Israeli base at Atlit, home of the crack naval commando unit, Shayetet 13. Israeli frogmen would then ferry Salaam up the coast and get him into Beirut, where he was to infiltrate Hezbollah, the Lebanese terrorist organization funded by the Iranians. Mia had had to fight her masters on letting the Israelis handle this part of the operation; Salaam was, after all, serving a life sentence in a US prison and the boys in Washington weren't thrilled with the prospect of him giving the Junior Varsity the slip. But Mia had argued that the Israelis had a lot more experience in the Mediterranean than the Americans. Besides, did anyone really want American sailors at risk for a mission that didn't officially exist in a part of the world where they weren't supposed to be? That shut up the skeptics real fast, Mia had told Alson.

On the day of Salaam's departure, Alson drove him from the remote Delta Force barracks to Pope Air Force Base, a closed base adjacent to Fort Bragg, and quizzed Salaam on his cover story. Salaam spit back the details between nibbles on his Krispy Kreme glazed donut – a going away gift from Alson who had put away most of the box himself. Salaam was to tell Hezbollah his escape from Terminal Island took him across the country in the trailer of an 18-wheeler driven by the brother of a BURN guerilla. The trucker's name was Vernon Doby who drove a big rig for Burke Transport Services based in Natchez, Mississippi. Doby delivered Salaam and four tons of unfinished steel sheets to the port of New Orleans. Salaam then stowed-away on *Mandingo*, a Liberian-flagged tanker bound for Cyprus. Two members of the African crew were sympathetic to Salaam and BURN and watched over him. Their names were Joe Chukwu and Christian Kanu. They were Nigerians listed on the ship's manifest. In Cyprus, Salaam rendezvoused with a Lebanese national, Abul Lateef, involved in the Cypriot arms-smuggling trade. Lateef was a friend of Rondell Payton, a BURN guerilla who had helped Salaam escape from the US Marshals. Lateef owed Payton a favor and smuggled Salaam into Beirut on his fishing boat, *Al Mina*.

Mia had left nothing to chance. All vehicle and ship registrations were legit, as were the names of the participants. She had written Salaam's cover story and various agencies in the US and Israel had financed it. Doby was an ex-bank robber on the FBI payroll. The CIA had bought Chukwu's and Kanu's cooperation with a year's salary. Lateef was a Mossad snitch. Rondell Payton was a FBI agent so deep underground that Hezbollah could dig to China and they'd still find jack shit.

When Hezbollah checked Salaam's story – and no one was under any illusions they wouldn't — they would get partial confirmation. Chukwu and Lateef would admit to helping Salaam; Doby and Kanu would deny it. That was the CIA plan. The counter-terrorism wonks in Langley knew that bad guys distrusted an airtight alibi even more than no alibi.

As Alson slowed at the gate to Pope, four soggy airmen clutching M16A2 rifles checked their papers and let them pass. Salaam stared out the window and made small talk about his daughter and his grandson. He missed them. That was the gist that Alson caught.

Alson did not tell Salaam the FBI had his daughter and grandson under 24/7 surveillance but he figured a man who in a former life he had been a Distinguished Professor of Chemical Engineering at the University of California was smart enough to figure out the hammer would come down hard on his family if he tried to bolt.

They pulled up to a single C-130 sitting on the rain-slicked tarmac. It was a big plane for one passenger, but in fact six Delta Force soldiers would be joining Salaam. Their job was to make sure Salaam didn't try to escape by jumping out of the plane at 35,000 feet above the Atlantic Ocean.

Alson stopped the car. He wished Salaam luck and shook his hand. He knew he would never see Salaam alive again and it made him sad because he liked the guy. He really did.

Salaam exited the car. Alson's handshake had smeared glazed sugar on his hand and he asked Alson for a napkin. Alson found one in the empty donut box and handed it to Salaam.

Alson said, "Hey, if you see Mia Kelly again, don't tell her I put away all these donuts, okay? She's always trying to get me to eat better and drop a few pounds."

Salaam nodded and gave Alson a crooked grin. He could keep a secret.

In fact, he had a few of his own.

-:::::-

Azadi demanded to dine with Mia in the Officer's Mess. Their last supper was held at 2:00 a.m. to afford them the necessary privacy. The cook whipped up a decent pot roast and potatoes but they had to serve themselves. Mia uncorked an unpretentious Bordeaux Margaux 98, a gift from the base commander. They went over the details again. And when they were done, Azadi pulled out an envelope and asked Mia to post it to his father.

"You shouldn't have sealed the envelope, Omar. We're gonna have to open it and read it just the same."

"Whatever. I've got nothing to hide."

But Mia noticed that he hid his mouth behind his hand when he said that.

-:::::-

An FBI courier delivered a copy of Azadi's letter to Farragut in Hanover. The cryptographers at Langley had gone over the original with a fine-tooth comb, checking for hidden messages and codes. They found nothing. Farragut found it strangely moving.

Dear Father,

A few last words that I could not find the courage to say to your face. Printing was your life. You brought honor to a profession I disgraced. You knew I made money but you never made me feel that I was beyond redemption. For this, I am most grateful.

It must sadden you that so much hate has been directed towards our family. I am glad that mother was not alive to see that. While you and I have never been close, I am proud of the way that this tragedy has brought us closer together. I do wish mother were alive to see that.

I know you don't fully understand why I am going back to Iran. You always said it was a country seduced first by the Shah, then sodomized by the mullahs. You chose America. You raised me to be American. You raised me to be a simple, decent man.

You always said it takes more courage to live as a simple, decent man, than die as a martyr. You have certainly been the former. I may prove to be the latter. I do not know yet. I do know that I have been a disappointment to you. So I have decided to go away. You were right about me. I am a coward. I always look for the easy way out. But there is a chance I will prove my worth someday. Trust me on that.

Your loving son, Omar

Farragut saw no reason not to allow the original to be sent to Azadi's father and e-mailed this opinion to Mia. Next, he burned Azadi's letter in his office fireplace and then wrote his own letter to friends in Iran, telling them he would be visiting soon. He thought of writing a letter to his father but the tumor was giving him a headache and he discarded the idea. Besides, in light of how he felt about his own father, he doubted he could do as good a job as Azadi.

Farragut gathered up his books. Tomorrow he would resign from the university, assign TAs to finish his lectures for the quarter, and start the journey back to his unlikely birthplace, the Islamic Republic of Iran. Like Azadi he, too, was going home to die.

CHAPTER EIGHTEEN

OMAR AZADI stepped out of the Iran Air Airbus 320 at Tehran's Mehrabad airport and felt as cool as the early winter air. He knew he had nothing to fear this first day. Mia Kelly had told him that the Iranian government would make his homecoming a public relations event and she had called it right. After all, the mullahs had been battling the bad PR unleashed from a thousand YouTube videos and Tweets as they brutally put down the so-called Green Revolution. And now here was Omar Azadi, a native son returning home from the land of the infidels to take his place in the cradle of Islam.

Some scrawny kid from the state-run Islamic Republic News Agency, IRNA, met Azadi at the gate, along with a somber-faced, bifocal wearing, bigwig bureaucrat from the Ministry of Foreign Affairs. They whisked him through customs. Guys with guns were everywhere but they barely checked his luggage. They did ask him if he had anything to declare. Yeah. He did.

"I'm just glad to be home. Allah be praised."

Everyone laughed, even the customs guy with the AK-47. Then they led him into a big room packed with reporters. He stood before a crush of cameras and answered questions. A reporter from the conservative *Kayhan* newspaper asked him what he thought about the traitorous students fomenting unrest against the courageous clergy who had rescued the country from the Shah. Azadi played it cool and said he wasn't a politician; he was a printer. A reporter from the reformist *Nowrooz* newspaper asked him what he thought about the brave students fomenting unrest against the corrupt clergy who had failed to bring economic and social reforms. Azadi said he wasn't a politician; he was a printer. The reporters grew bored of his platitudes, just as Mia Kelly had promised.

Two new bureaucrats, plus a fatigue-clad driver, took him into town in a new Mercedes SUV. The female bureaucrat wore a shapeless *chador* that concealed her curves and a headscarf that concealed her hair. She looked like a black potato — puffy, sad, and sexless. The male bureaucrat's balding head was badly served by a comb-over. The woman explained that she was from the *Vezarat-e Keshvar*, the Interior Ministry, and would assist him in getting his paperwork in order. She handed him his temporary ID and filled him on the variety of forms, cards, and visa extensions that would lead to his eventual Iranian citizenship. The man explained that he was also from the Interior Ministry and concerned with security. He didn't elaborate. He offered Azadi his business card and encouraged him to call if he wanted to talk.

"Talk about what, Payam?" asked Azadi, picking the man's name off the card.

Payam smiled vacantly and didn't elaborate.

They drove through the city proper. The stench of gasoline permeated the air. The city was modern and overbuilt. Shabby buildings elbowed for space everywhere, some were skyscrapers and others rose no more than a few stories. Most were the same color as the sky: milky beige brought on by years of neglect, dirt, and diesel fuel. Tehran was a city of over ten million and totally charmless, Kelly had warned.

Charmless, too, was the glowering face of the Ayatollah Khomeini staring out from countless billboards and building sites. Azadi wondered what the protestors of the recent unrest, many born long after the father of the Islamic revolution had died, thought of this archaic form of propaganda celebrating a man whose philosophy was rooted in the 7th century and whose experience born of the 20th century Cold War great game. They were the generation of YouTube, Facebook, Twitter, and cheap TV's built by formerly Communist Chinese capitalists.

Looking past the posters to the men on the streets. It was strange to be in a country where his dark, Middle Eastern looks didn't stand out. The women didn't stand out, either. More men than women walked the streets but the women were all covered up to some degree. Some wore dark, baggy, all-body *chadors*. Others, not as many, wore lighter, shorter coats. All wore scarves or veils, some high on their heads, others covering almost their entire faces.

They dropped him off at his state-issued home in North Tehran. Tall, leafless trees populated the pretty street. The buildings here were in better condition than those he had seen in the rest of Tehran – older, but less rundown and more elegant. Satellite TV dishes perched like gargoyles amongst the big balconies and roof gardens.

Payam and the woman whose name he couldn't remember escorted him into his building. The lobby was clean and bright. His apartment was on the third floor and they took the elevator up which was clean and compact and smelled like cooking – onions and lamb.

Azadi's apartment was small but nicer than he expected. Wood floors and a tasteful Persian carpet in the center. The smell of furniture polish and air freshener faintly lingered. A couch covered in green fabric, cheap but new, stood against one wall. A wood coffee table and two leather chairs stood opposite. The bedroom was spare, a single bed, a dresser with a mirror. Not a "fuck pad" but he wasn't expecting as much. Payam and the woman – he still couldn't remember her name — asked him if he would allow them to buy him dinner. He told them no thanks; he was exhausted. They bid him farewell and promised to see him tomorrow.

Azadi sat on the green couch and breathed in deep. He flashed on his beautiful condo in the Marina, now sold to a guy that owned a Mercedes dealership in Manhattan Beach. He tried to remember what the ocean looked like, what it smelled like. He couldn't. He stood and walked over to the window. He threw it open and looked out onto the street. It was dark now but the streetlights shined down on kids kicking around a ball and laughing like kids did everywhere. Late model Mercedes and BMWs parked on the curb. Men in suits were entering buildings and carrying briefcases, coming home from a day at work. He could have been in any prosperous neighborhood in any city anywhere in the world. He could have been in Chicago, Illinois. He could have been in Paris, France. But he wasn't.

He was in Tehran, Iran.

A chill went up his spine as the *adhan*, the Muslim call to prayer, blasted out from a thousand mosques across the city, filling the air with the sound of the faithful. Some of the *adhans* were mechanically recorded and broadcast from loudspeakers. Others erupted from the lungs of real *muezzins* standing atop minarets.

"*God is most great. God is most great. I testify that there is no god except God. I testify that there is no god except God. I testify that Muhammad is the messenger of God. I testify that Muhammad is the messenger of God. Come to prayer. Come to prayer.*"

But it was a messenger from Mia Kelly, not God, who occupied Azadi's thoughts as the call to prayer cascaded over the city. His stomach churned in nervous anticipation. For tomorrow he was scheduled to meet the mission liaison. Azadi knew him only as the cab driver.

CHAPTER NINETEEN

T HE FOLLOWING morning, Azadi shaved, showered, put on a tie and a $2,000 suit he had bought at Valentino in Beverly Hills. At 9.12 a.m., the same Mercedes SUV from the day before rolled up to his apartment. The woman in the *chador* was not there but Payam was. He offered Azadi a Styrofoam cup of tea and a sugar cube. Payam held his sugar cube between his teeth as he drank. Azadi let his sugar dissolve in the cup. The tea was excellent. Payam's mood was not. He remained quiet for a long time and when he finally spoke, his voice dripped with contempt.

"Your tie, Omar. Perhaps you should reconsider wearing it?"

Azadi turned his head from the window and yet another traffic jam. "What's wrong with my tie? This tie cost me $150 at Versace in Beverly Hills."

Payam smiled. He left the conversation hanging.

Azadi spent the morning at the Ministry of the Interior. He filled out countless forms. He posed for numerous pictures. He was given several official documents and IDs. At the end of the ordeal he was born again as an Iranian citizen and the bureaucracy was his birth mother. He had a celebratory lunch in the Ministry's cafeteria with the woman in *chador* from the day before. He sheepishly admitted he had forgotten her name and she said it was Mojgan. They ate an excellent *khoresh fesenjaan*, chicken and vegetables in a thick sauce tossed over rice. She said it was good but not nearly as good as her own.

"What's on the afternoon agenda?" asked Azadi, pulling a piece of chicken ligament from his teeth.

"You have an interview with the Tehran *Times*, an English language daily, and then with Al-Jazeera. They'll do the interview in English, too. Your Farsi is excellent, by the way."

"Thank you. And then what follows the interviews?"

Mojgan pushed away her empty plate and waved her hand over her mouth. Her round face glistened with sweat from the hot curry. Azadi offered her his water. She took it and their hands touched briefly. He noticed that she wasn't wearing a wedding ring — did they wear wedding rings in Iran? — and her nails were beautifully manicured. They hadn't been the day before.

"After the interviews, we talk about finding you a job," she said after draining the glass of water. "The government feels that a man of your skill and experience be given something substantial."

"If it's all the same to you, I'd prefer to look for my own job," countered Azadi, just as Kelly had told him to do. "I want to make my own way. I have some savings to take care of me until I do. I will be all right."

Azadi pushed away his half-eaten plate of *khoresht*. Mojgan gave him a funny look. He thought she was going to say something about what a great and impressive man he was for returning home. Instead, she asked him if she could finish off his plate of *khoresht*. That is, if he was done. Azadi said sure. She ate without looking up at him again.

-:::::-

The afternoon interviews with the Tehran *Times* and Al-Jazeera consisted of softball questions from them and simple, declarative answers from him. Azadi didn't get into Iran's chaotic political situation. He didn't bash America but he didn't condone what had happened to him either. He assumed a level of dignity and wounded pride combined with just the right amount of optimistic hope for the future. Azadi could make bogus bills that looked absolutely real. He found he had a criminal's cunning for creating the same impression about himself.

When the interviews were over, Payam and Mojgan offered to ride with him back home in the Mercedes. Azadi refused. He told them he wanted to walk a bit and then he would catch a cab. No special treatment, he repeated. All men are equal before God on the floor of the mosque, he reminded them.

Payam shook his hand and made some joke about the Iranian communist party and cabs. Mojgan didn't shake his hand, he knew that would have been improper, but she promised to cook him some of her own *khoresht*. He could call her anytime, day or night, if he wanted a home-cooked meal. Her generous smile didn't look like it got much use.

He knew it now. The dinner invite. The manicured nails. She was hitting on him.

Azadi hit the street. *No way*, he thought. *No way am I getting involved with this woman*. Not because she was unattractive. Azadi had been known to lower his standards every now and then. But because he was not allowed to date *any* women while in Tehran. Kelly had given him express orders to keep it in his pants. Sex was a distraction, and the ultra-conservative mores of the Islamic Republic made romantic involvement risky.

Azadi headed down Fatemi Avenue in the direction of Laleh Park just a few hundred yards away and smack dab in the center of Tehran. Businessmen and bureaucrats surged along on the sidewalk. People walked quicker than in LA but he walked slowly, his hands in his pockets. He hoped he exuded casual indifference, just an average man taking a walk in downtown Tehran. If they were following him, and Kelly assured him they probably were, they would have no reason to be suspicious.

He arrived at Laleh Park in ten minutes. The Laleh Hotel stood on the northeast corner of the park. Kelly said it was the most elegant in the city. Azadi thought it looked nice but he'd bet that he'd stayed in better. He crossed Fatemi Avenue over to the park side and continued heading west. It was cold and getting dark. The park was deserted. The trees were bare.

Azadi stopped in front of the Carpet Museum, a modern, low-lying structure that hugged the northwest corner of the park. Kelly said it was the most spectacular museum in the city. It was closing for the day and a crowd was spilling out. Azadi pushed to the front of the crowd. He raised his hand for a cab.

Immediately Azadi felt a strong hand grab his raised wrist and yank it down. A bearded man in fatigues, an AK-47 slung across his back, got right into Azadi's face. The man gestured towards Azadi's tie and grabbed it with his other hand. He tried to yank it off Azadi's neck. He barked at Azadi in rapid-fire Farsi.

Fear pulled at Azadi's stomach. He knew the bearded man with the gun was angry about his tie. Azadi went with his instinct and shoved the bearded man back with both arms. The bearded man stumbled and fell. He slipped trying to get up. His gun found its way from the sling around his back into his hands.

Azadi flashed on his own death.

A cab pulled up to the curb. The cab driver jumped out and helped the bearded man to his feet. Azadi squared his shoulders and held up his fists. He knew he looked ridiculous but he was ready to fight. Fuck them. Two on one. Whatever. All the anger and pent-up rage and terror he felt at being a pawn in this game suddenly came to the surface. Fuck this bearded asshole. Fuck Kelly. Fuck Alson. Fuck the Supernote. Fuck the world.

The cab driver whispered something in the bearded man's ear. The bearded man laughed. Azadi kept his fists up. Sweat dripped down his brow into his eyes but he wouldn't wipe it away; he wouldn't lower his hands. The bearded man smiled and offered his right hand to Azadi as if to shake. Azadi paused, thought about it, and then reached out to shake the bearded man's hand. The bearded man pulled back his hand and spit on Azadi's tie. Azadi saw red. He lunged for the bearded man but the cab driver came between them and grabbed Azadi. The cab driver was not a large man but his grip was like that of a Greco-Roman wrestler. Azadi could not move. The cab driver spoke in fractured, forced English and flashed Azadi a smile.

"I take you to that Turkish bath now, yes?"

The bearded man cackled, then took his beard and his gun and his attitude for a walk.

Azadi looked into the cab driver's face and felt the mission all coming back to him. He thought the man looked nothing like the photo Kelly had shown him back at Fort Bragg. This man was even sillier looking. No, the photo didn't capture the bright, squinty eyes or the fat cheeks or the upturned nose or the buckteeth that took attention away from the weak chin.

This goofball was the mission liaison? Azadi wanted to laugh. Leave it to Kelly and Alson to find the only spy in the world who looked like a goddamn chipmunk.

CHAPTER TWENTY

MOSSAD OPERATIVE Ari Jashni drove while Azadi sat in the back. This arrangement kept up the fiction of cabbie and customer even as the two strangers bickered like old friends.

"My Farsi's rusty but serviceable," grumbled Azadi. "You didn't have to tell that prick I was a faggot just because I like to dress nice."

Jashni replied with an English accent that had switched over from uneducated immigrant to pure Oxford debating society.

"I had to tell him something or he would have shot you. To some Iranians, a tie is a symbol of Western imperialism. I suggest that you dispose of it."

"Fuck that. This tie cost me $150 at Versace on Rodeo Dri —"

The words caught in Azadi's throat. Jashni had reached over the seat, grabbed Azadi by the tie, and yanked him forward.

"His hang-up might get you hanged. He is a member of the *Basij* militia, a fanatical, all-volunteer group pledged to defend the Islamic establishment and its achievements since the Revolution. They are little more than armed thugs brutalizing their own countrymen whose only crime is protesting peacefully for reform. I'll concede, however, that they showed exemplary courage while sacrificing themselves in human waves during the Iran-Iraq War. Violence has its place when used to inspire rather than oppress. Agreed?"

Azadi's response was a painful gurgle as the cabbie pulled the tie tighter.

"I thought you would," he continued.

Jashni released Azadi's tie. The American collapsed in his seat, struggling to breathe. He realized that the cab driver, though ostensibly there to keep him abreast of developments and supply information, was one tough son-of-bitch. Azadi decided to play nice.

"I'm sorry. It's been a long day, mister…Hell, no one's told me your name."

"Call me Ishmael," said Jashni. The name came from the Hebrew word meaning *God hears*. Jashni was the mission liaison, the eyes and ears on the ground.

"Fine. Ishmael. But I bet that's not your real name, right?"

Jashni ignored the question. The decorated Mossad agent was privy to Azadi's background but was wary of giving the common criminal too much information about himself. If Azadi were caught and taken into custody, he would be tortured and he would talk. Everybody talked. So Jashni decided to talk as little as possible with his co-conspirator. He turned on the cab's radio. Persian pop screeched from the blown speakers.

Azadi said, "Can't you play something with a little more, you know, soul?"

"Regrettably, no. American pop music is forbidden in this fundamentalist paradise."

"This fucking country. How do you stand it?"

Jashni ran his tongue over his buckteeth as he debated answering the question. There was no easy way to explain the life of a Jew, let alone an undercover Mossad agent, in the Islamic Republic of Iran. Iranian Jews could worship in freedom, produce wine for weddings and bar mitzvahs, and run their own butcher shops and nursing homes. Jews were, along with Christians, considered a legitimate religion, as they were people of the Book. At the same time, the *mullahs* restricted the teaching of Hebrew. Yes, the government guaranteed Jews representation in Parliament but it did not allow them to serve at the highest levels of government or the civil service. And while the government was vehemently anti-Israel and several Jews had been unfairly arrested in the past for allegedly spying for the Jewish state, others were celebrated and decorated for their service in the Iran-Iraq War. Jashni's family had left Iran in the 1950s following the CIA coup that put the Shah on the throne. He had returned ten years ago, albeit unofficially and undercover in his new role working for Israel. And now that he had returned, he was determined to stay, whether out of principle or spite, he wasn't sure.

"Let us talk about printing and your place of employment," Jashni said. He pointed outside the windshield as they passed a shabby printing shop squeezed between a shabby bakery and a shabby shoe store. "That is the Babajan Print Shop. Tomorrow, you will walk in there and secure employment. But be warned. The proprietor, Naghmen Babajan, is incompetent, stupid, and a drunk. Except when the black market in booze dries up. Then he is elevated to being merely incompetent and stupid."

"So I'm just supposed to walk in there and Baba Ganoush gives me a gig?"

"I'm afraid your scintillating personality and superior social skills would not be enough to garner employment in these tough economic times. But the dozen bottles of Johnnie Walker Black you will present to Mr. Babajan will secure you the desired position. And if you like *baba ganoush*, I know an outstanding little place near the Greek embassy."

"Pass. You sure my 15 years of printing experience will get them to bite?"

"One can never be sure. But Babajan's uncle, Amir Farjad, is a general in the Revolutionary Guards. They are the official muscle of the ruling *mullahs* and form the bridge between Iran and Hezbollah in Lebanon since the 1980s. Despite their fanaticism, some of the Guards are sympathetic to the winds of change sweeping the Middle East. General Farjad represents a particularly violent, fanatical reactionary faction that does not want to see peace and progress. He and his small cadre are quite dangerous, detested by the rank and file within the Guards, who can hardly be accused of being moderates."

"So in other words," said Azadi, "we're dealing with some crazy, bad-ass motherfuckers."

Jashni laughed. "Crazy, bad-ass motherfuckers. I like that."

Azadi's head was spinning from the pressure and pollution and jet lag. "Okay. Give me the connection between the Press and Farjad's nephew, Babajan, again?"

Jashni glanced at Azadi in the rear view mirror. "It's very linear. We know wherever the Press is located, the Revolutionary Guards will be guarding it. Your printing expertise will make you indispensable to Babajan's business. He will boast of you to his Uncle Farjad, tell him that you are a specialist in the injection of ink onto engraved plates, an essential skill in the art of printing money. He will also tell his Uncle Farjad that you let slip, quite innocently by way of coming clean to your new boss and best friend, that you were a counterfeiter back in the States. General Farjad will at that time become cognizant of a vacancy at the Press that, not coincidentally, requires your area of expertise. Recruiting your services at that point will be a mere formality."

Jashni turned off the radio to let Azadi think about all the connections without the distracting effect of Persian pop music blasting in his ears. He knew the American had been told all this information back in the States. Except for one crucial detail which Jashni could tell by the expression on Azadi's face, he was just now realizing.

"A vacancy?" asked Azadi. "Ishmael, you're talking about murder, right?"

Jashni sighed. The impending assassination of the Supernote Press printer had been kept from Azadi just in case he actually had a conscience about such things. Of course, by this time it was too late to do anything about it.

"I submit to you, Omar, you need not concern yourself with the details."

Jashni turned the radio back on and flooded the cab with the latest Persian disco hit. Azadi stared out the window and watched the dusty, dreary city slide into night.

-:::::-

The rest of the ride was uneventful. "Ishmael" dropped Azadi off at his apartment. He wished Azadi luck and drove off with a jaunty *honk* of his horn.

Azadi entered his apartment and walked right into his bedroom. He opened the window because the room was stuffy. He opened his closet because Ishmael had told him that's where he'd stashed the stuff while Azadi had been at the Interior Ministry.

Inside the closet, behind his still packed suitcases, Azadi found two large, cardboard boxes. Inside one box were ten small 1.75 ounce tins of fine Iranian Sevruga caviar. The small tins sat on top of 15 larger, 35.20 ounce tins. The 35.20 tins, unlike the smaller ones, were completely empty though they looked brand new.

The other box contained 13 bottles of Johnnie Walker Black. Azadi pulled out a bottle that had a note attached with Scotch tape. The note read: "This one's for you."

Azadi unscrewed the cap and toasted Kelly, Alson, Ishmael, and the man who would soon be murdered so that Azadi could take his place inside the Press.

Bottoms up, you bastards.

Azadi drank half the bottle. He staggered into bed and fell asleep in his clothes, adding a thousand new wrinkles to his $3,000 Armani suit.

CHAPTER TWENTY-ONE

AZADI ENTERED the Babajan Print Shop at 8:00 a.m. the next morning. He had a smile on his face and a cardboard box in his hands. His clothes were new but cheap. No expensive tie. No expensive suit. No arrogant attitude. Just a humble worker looking for work.

"Excuse me. I'm looking for a job," he said in Farsi to the man behind the counter.

Naghmen Babajan stood behind the counter. Azadi took in the puffy red eyes and unshaven jowls as well as the odor of cheap Georgian wine emanating from Babajan's puckered mouth, a mouth that offered no reply to Azadi's inquiry about work.

"My name is Omar Azadi," continued Azadi, still in Farsi. "I'm recently arrived from America. I'm a printer by trade. A very good one."

Babajan laughed and said in serviceable English, "My friend. You would need to show me the words of Muhammad printed in gold upon your ass before I could offer you a job."

Azadi put the cardboard box on the counter. Babajan continued to laugh while Azadi opened the top of the box to reveal the dozen bottles of Johnnie Walker Black. Babajan stopped laughing.

He grabbed one of the bottles and held it up to admire the color of the Scotch in the sunlight.

"You are aware that the eternal glory of the Islamic Republic depends upon the abstinence of its people?"

Azadi nodded. Babajan twisted off the top of the bottle and raised it in a toast, "To the glory of the Islamic Republic."

Babajan drank greedily, then offered the bottle to Azadi. Azadi took a small sip and handed the bottle back to Babajan, who took another long pull.

"I am recently arrived here from the United States," said Azadi, now in English.

"Yes. I saw your picture and read your story in the *Times*. Tragic. Most tragic."

Azadi had to give credit to Kelly. The fiction that she had created for him had caught the Iranian public's imagination. Even a wasted, old drunk like Babajan knew all the details.

"What did the papers say?" continued Babajan after another long drink. "Oh yes. Your family left Iran after the Shah's police tortured your father. Your father had been a most successful printer himself but also an outspoken critic of the old regime. In America, the two of you shared a printing business but it did not prosper. Then infidels, evil racists, perhaps Zionists, burned the business to the ground. And then..."

Babajan took another long pull on the bottle. The "and then..." hung there. Babajan had lost his train of thought but Azadi sensed that he had found a new friend.

"Mr. Babajan. I will work hard. I will not demand much in wages, the money is not important to me. Just the chance to prove myself to you."

"But why me, my friend? Of all the struggling printers in Tehran, why me?"

It was a good question. Azadi gave the answer that Kelly told him to. He pulled from his jacket pocket a reproduction of an extraordinarily detailed etching of the *Masjed –e Jome'eh*, the most famous mosque in Iran. Babajan stared at the etching. His expression was vacant.

Azadi said, "I saw this etching, the original, at an exhibition in the Victoria and Albert Museum in London. You did it when? As a student?"

Babajan blinked but his eyes were bone dry. "No. I had just graduated from Tehran University. I had a post-graduate fellowship in Paris. I did my best work there."

"It is magnificent work. It would be an honor to learn from you."

Babajan looked at Azadi, his brow pulled down by the ash-colored pouches beneath his eyes.

"And you really are an excellent printer?"

For the first time since he had arrived in Tehran, Omar Azadi did not have to lie.

-:::::-

As planned, Jashni retrieved Azadi ten hours later and five blocks away in front of the cinema. Azadi had completed his first day of work and then relaxed by watching a bloody Iranian action flick celebrating the heroic suicide bombers in Gaza bringing the war to the infidels in Israel.

"How was the movie?" breathed Jashni through foul smelling Turkish cigarette smoke.

"Kikes got the shit kicked out of them," said Azadi. He wasn't anti-Semitic but he suspected Ishmael just might be Jewish and hoped an angry reply from the man would confirm it. He was to be disappointed.

"Hooray for Hollywood," said Jashni with a wan smile. "Anyway good show, Omar. Well played."

Jashni seemed to sense that sounding like an extra in a bad BBC really irritated Azadi. Azadi chewed an ink-stained finger and swallowed his anger.

"Yeah. I got the job. Pays per week what my Mercedes burns in gas per second."

"Well, look at it this way, gas is much cheaper in Tehran than Los Angeles."

"But my fucking Mercedes ain't in Tehran, is it? I don't even own a car anymore."

Jashni picked up the brown bag in the seat next to him and handed it over to Azadi. Azadi pulled out the two partially completed currency plates for the redesigned $100 bill. He didn't need a printer's loupe to see that the portrait of Franklin on the front plate had been engraved in exquisite detail. Ditto for the Treasury building portrait on the back plate. Perhaps 80 percent of the necessary engraving was completed but he still had a lot of work to do.

"Whoever your man was did nice work," Azadi conceded.

"Of course, we used the best engraver."

"Second best," said Azadi. To his surprise Ishmael returned his smile.

-:::::-

In the two weeks that followed, Azadi went about proving his boast. By day, he worked the presses at Babajan's. By night, he engraved the currency plates at his apartment. Azadi welcomed the opportunity to work with his hands. Working with his hands gave his brain a rest from the fear he felt every moment he was not so occupied.

The capitalist in Azadi recognized that Babajan's business had great potential. Because of the man's connections, a critical mass of work orders always flowed in. But because of Babajan's alcoholism, a trickle of work product flowed out. The most lucrative part of the business included high-end wedding invitations for Tehran's top tier families as well as beautifully executed business cards for important bureaucrats and foreign businessman. Both products benefited from a skilled intaglio printer as well as a master engraver. Babajan had once been quite capable himself but now he reveled in his new role as Azadi's Iranian benefactor. Supervising Azadi suited him almost as well as consuming prodigious amounts of whiskey.

"Omar, did I tell you the time the Russian ambassador needed five hundred engraved invitations to his sixtieth birthday party and gave us only two days to complete the order?"

Babajan had told him that story three times in the last ten days.

"I don't think I've heard that one, Mr. Babajan."

So Babajan told it again as Azadi pushed the burin, a prism-shaped steel tool with a sharp point and a wood handle, along the metal plate. In doing so, Azadi created a furrow for the ink and dislodged a thin strip of metal. He was engraving invitations to the wedding of the Oil Minister's second daughter. He didn't listen to Babajan. He focused instead on digging out the words in the metal plate in a beautiful, flowing script. He made sure that the bur, or rough lip on the edge of the cut, was minimal. Time passed without making any impact on his consciousness.

"…Which is why I will never drink vodka again," said Babajan with a laugh.

It was the end of the Russian ambassador story. Babajan finished off the last drop of Johnnie Black from the last bottle Azadi had given him. He stumbled unsteadily towards the door. "I'm going home for the night, my friend. Will you lock up for me?"

"Of course. Goodnight."

Azadi had been in Tehran two weeks and he was already locking up for the man he would betray. Soon Babajan might trust him with the location of the Supernote Press.

Azadi finished the work order, running the engraved plates through the small but powerful intaglio presses. The plates pressed ink and shape onto the expensive paper and left a raised imprint. Azadi smiled as he surveyed the completed invitations. They were works of art. In two months' time, the invitations announced, a momentous event was to take place. The Oil Minister's daughter, Leila, was to be married. Azadi packed up the invitations and locked up the shop, not realizing that tomorrow an event even more momentous (at least in his life) than the future wedding of the Oil Minister's daughter was to take place.

John Farragut was flying home to Iran.

CHAPTER TWENTY-TWO

THE IRANIAN government didn't make a big deal about John Farragut's homecoming. Farragut had been back to Iran many times since the fall of the Shah. He returned at least once a year for research, sometimes for weeks at a time. His reputation was well known in respected circles for his enlightened view of Persian culture and laissez-faire attitude towards Iran's politics. Farragut lived in Iran's glorious past; he did not speculate on its troubled present or uncertain future. At least, not as far as the Iranian government knew.

Farragut had flown from New York to London. In London, he took two days to rest. The tumor behaved, limiting itself to a single headache that disappeared after a boozy lunch with an old colleague at his club, Boodles. Then. Farragut flew on to Tehran, refreshed and ready.

Ali Ardabili knew Farragut from way back. They had met as teenagers while standing in line to see "Star Wars" at its Tehran premiere. Ardabili met him now at customs.

"Hello, world traveler," said Ardabili. "You look like you've lost weight. Is it a woman? Are you in love again? Does she make you exercise and eat right so that you will never grow old?"

Farragut looked up from the customs officer who was inspecting his passport. Ardabili was still a handsome man, tall with a pencil-thin mustache, and expensively dressed in an Italian suit. His graceful movements matched the elegance of his mind. But his hair was going gray and smile lines – or perhaps they were worry lines – had deepened around his eyes and mouth.

"There's no woman, dear Ali. Just work. I'm always like this when I get to the end of a book. It eats me alive."

Farragut had not told Ardabili about the tumor. It would just complicate things. Besides, the man had enough to worry about as a westernized intellectual in the Islamic Republic.

"Well, then you will forget your book and remember your manners," said Ardabili as he and Farragut shook hands. "Meila has prepared you a special feast. We are here to spoil you rotten. You will let us. And you will enjoy it."

The custom's officer was still staring at Farragut's passport. Ardabili moved things along by flashing his ID to the customs officer. The man nodded, impressed, and waved Farragut through. Farragut and his friend pushed his luggage cart together through the airport, just as they used to push their bicycles along the paths of the Alborz Mountains when they were boys.

"Pushing me right through customs?" said Farragut with a wink. "Being head curator of the archaeological museum definitely has its perks."

"On the subject of perks? I've invited that special guest that you wanted to meet."

"Oh, is the wife of the German ambassador a perk? I thought she was a leggy redhead."

"She is more. A work of art. Now tell me more of this other work of art. The famous bull's head that brings you to Tehran."

Farragut waited until they were sitting in the privacy of Ardabili's new Range Rover as it plodded through traffic to tell Ardabili about the bull's head. At least he told him what he was allowed to tell him. The real reason Farragut wanted to bring the bull's head home was not for Ardabili's ears, no matter what a dear, old friend he was.

"I stopped over in London for a few days and got a good look at the piece," reported Farragut. "The bull's head is definitely the one lifted from the ruins of Xerxes' Palace. Specifically from the Gate of All Nations."

"Yes. But why is Lord Owen so willing to part with the piece? After all, it was his great-grandfather who took the bull, was it not?"

"Not took. Stole is the more accurate description of what Brigadier Owen did. Stole like a common criminal, even while he held the elevated position of the commander of the British regiment near Persepolis in the 1920s."

Ardabili braked to a stop. Traffic was at a standstill because a garbage truck had stalled in the middle lane. The smell of trash, sour milk, and rotten meat wafted through the car's vent.

"Indeed. So the Owen family stole the bull's head. But certainly the current Lord Owen is aware that the British government refuses to return even more famous pillaged treasures. So why sell this piece and why sell it now?

"Lord Owen's change of heart is not political but practical. He has an old, decaying castle to upkeep and a new, young wife to please. The current Lady Owen is 40 years younger and her artistic sensibility peaks at garden gnomes."

"For $12 million? I'm not surprised," said Aradbili.

The traffic started to move again. Farragut pushed the plan further along. And even though he and Ali were alone in the car, Farragut's voice was barely above a whisper.

"Ali, the antiquities world is a small one. Everyone knows that Iran has creative ways of financing these purchases."

Farragut kept his eyes on his friend. Ardabili sensed that he had to answer, and he did so after punching the gas and rocketing past a pick-up loaded with chickens.

"What exactly do you mean by 'creative,' dear friend?"

"Ali, please."

Ardabili let his gaze drift sideways and folded his lips into a wry smile.

"If by 'creative' you mean counterfeit, well, I can neither confirm nor deny."

But that confirmed it for Farragut. He already had confirmation from Mia that Azadi had secured employment at Babajan's shop. It was just a matter of time before the Iranians would allow him entry to the Supernote Press, where he would be in charge of printing the counterfeit money to buy the bull's head. Farragut allowed himself a grin. The plan was moving forward faster than the traffic outside which had once again slowed to a crawl.

"Ali. You're an honorable man. Lord Owen is not. His ancestors pillaged your country. Counterfeit cash is an appropriate payback."

Ardabili let out a long, slow breath as the garbage truck again pulled in front of them. "Give me ten days to get the money."

-:::::-

Ardabili drove Farragut to the Laleh International Hotel. Farragut checked in, showered, and changed into fresh clothes. Then, it was off to Ardabili's apartment, a large, elegant affair filled with fine antiques and graced by high ceilings. Ardabili's home stood across the street from the Norwegian Embassy in a stylish part of North Tehran. Omar Azadi's apartment, though not nearly as grand, was a ten-minute walk away.

Farragut and Ardabili lounged on the terrace, drinking martinis and munching pistachios.

"Ali, you still make the driest martinis known to mankind."

"A questionable skill for a nice Muslim boy. Happily, the government seems to tolerate a fair amount of liquor smuggling by the Armenian Christians. More so than I can remember."

"A release valve. People want revolution so they give them reform in dribs and drabs."

"Real change is coming, John. A wave of young Arabs and Iranians demand it. The internet and satellite TV have lifted the veil. They see what the West has to offer – freedom and democracy. Their own regimes, not Israel or the U.S., are the villains here — subjugating them and denying them their rights."

"It's a good thing, Ali. But the Mullahs won't go quietly."

"True. But if America doesn't stir up the pot and make the *mullahs* into martyrs, it will happen. The change that will come must, above all else, come from the Iranians themselves. Just as in Egypt."

Ardabili's pretty wife Meila walked out onto the balcony. In the privacy of her home, she felt no need to cover up or dress down. She wore a stylish black Gucci pants suit. Her heavy eyeliner brought out the gray-green of her irises.

"Dinner will be ready in an hour. Now John, as long as you will be shopping for antiquities in London, could you please pick me up some underwear at Marks and Spencer's? Oh look. You're not embarrassed are you?"

He wasn't but a frown had fallen across Farragut's face just the same. It wasn't the idea of buying Meila underwear but the fact that she knew about London, about the bull's head transaction, which caused Farragut to react. Meila squeezed his shoulder reading his mind.

"Ali told me about London, John. There are no secrets between a husband and wife as there should not be between good friends. You and I are good friends, are we not, John?"

"Of course, Meila."

Farragut managed a smile. Meila cast a look to Ardabili.

"And Ali is the finest bartender in Tehran. Now where's my martini, my love?"

"Gin or vodka, my dear?" asked Ardabili, taking the cue from Farragut's smile that his transgression had been forgiven.

"Vodka."

"Then, as I have told you before, that is not technically a martini."

Ardabili went inside to fix the "not technically a martini." Farragut fished out his olive and stared at this beautiful creature that had married his best friend. Of course, she wouldn't talk. Then again, he hadn't counted on Ardabili talking to her. Farragut had to be sure.

"I don't have to tell you that the London trip requires great discretion?" he said.

"Yes. Choosing underwear for a good friend's wife is not for the easily flustered. People would talk, so I won't."

So they understood each other. Artifacts and underwear. Farragut laughed but not Meila.

"You look thin and tired, John. Are you well?"

"Well, it was a long flight. But you look absolutely stunning. Love the new nose, too."

Meila blushed. "I know it's rather vain of me. But in a country where the most flesh a woman can show is on her nose, well, a nose job is a political statement."

Farragut laughed. They stared off at the snow-capped mountains.

"Things are difficult for you, my dear Meila?"

"Surprisingly no. Business has been good. With the economy such a shambles, the political process poisoned and social mores collapsing, there's never been a better time to be a marriage counselor."

"And with Ali?"

"Better there, too. We have accepted that we will never have children. Iran has too many children as it is. The government pushed big families after the clerics took over. Perhaps they feared they would run out of bodies to fight that blasted war with Iraq? And now, we have all these young people who want to overthrow the old men who had insisted they be born in the first place. Iran is nothing, if not ironic."

Ardabili arrived with a vodka "not technically a martini" Martini with a twist just as the doorbell rang. All three went inside. Ardabili answered the door and Ingrid Mader stepped inside the apartment.

Farragut had to admit it: he had chosen his fans very well indeed.

CHAPTER TWENTY-THREE

"SO YOU'RE THE John Beckwith Farragut?" Ingrid Mader said in English-accented English with only a suggestion of her Germanic origins. "You are not nearly as good-looking in person as your book jacket photo would suggest."

But Farragut thought the German ambassador's wife was very good looking. Her brilliant, green eyes demanded his attention. Her mouth, with full lips fronting perfect white teeth, smiled despite her sarcastic sentiments. Her strawberry blond hair was bobbed and framed her angular face and aquiline nose.

"That wasn't me; that was my body double," said Farragut. "Putting a sexy author shot on the jacket is supposed to stimulate sales. And as a matter of fact, sales have been so brisk that there is talk of turning it into a movie. Supposedly, Leonardo DiCaprio is interested in starring."

"He would play you?"

"An ancient stone statue, actually. Perfect for it because he's not Olivier, is he? No. George Clooney's more my type. Rugged. Funny. Nice ass. Or so I've been told. I've never actually seen it. Clooney's ass, that is."

Ingrid laughed and her lipstick-lined lips framed a luminous smile.

"And I thought Germans were supposed to have no sense of humor," Farragut said.

"They don't. That's why I laugh at bad jokes. But I read good books, and your book was outstanding. Rigorous research. Elegant prose. And, well, how do you say it…?"

Her English was excellent but she was searching for words that seemed to have slipped her mind. Farragut played along.

"Brilliant? Ground-breaking? Go on. I live for this stuff."

Ingrid sipped the gin martini Ardabili had mixed for her. "The word is profane. When you equated the British pillaging of Persian artifacts to the Iranians stealing the Queen of England's crown jewels, well, I could tell you were a man of a certain subversive sensibility."

Farragut was thankful that Meila and Ardabili had left him alone with Ingrid after making the initial introductions. His hosts were sitting on the couch in the living room, quietly conversing like the old married couple they were. He wondered if they still made each other feel the way Ingrid Mader was making him feel at this very moment.

"I appreciated your letter. It's not often that a boring, old academic receives such glowing praise, especially from a civilian."

"Oh? Is that all I am to you? A civilian?"

"Well, Ali and Meila have told me so little about you, save for the fact that you devote time and money to the National Museum."

Ingrid plucked the olive out of her martini. "What more would you like to know?"

"Do you have any other interests that I should be aware of? Do you play violent video games? Are you into collecting Hummel figurines? Are you an Elvis Presley fan?"

"Elvis Presley? No. Elvis Costello? Yes." She chewed and swallowed her olive. "But antiquities are my main passion though I also have a soft spot for the surrealists. So Darius the Great and Salvador Dali, I find both divine. Persian Kings and melting clocks. Iran's strength lies in the former, not the latter. Although one could say the clock is ticking for Iran."

Farragut liked the way her easy way with wordplay and politics. But talking about politics, in fact talking about anything, was the last thing he now wanted to do with this beautiful wife of the German ambassador.

"And your husband, the ambassador, is he an art lover, too?"

Ingrid stared at a slick of olive oil on top of her martini. "My husband, the ambassador, is not a lover of anything. Or anyone for that matter."

Ingrid peeled off the coat and scarf revealing a simple black cocktail dress seemed to have been painted on her broad-shouldered, thin-hipped frame.

Farragut took Ingrid's coat and scarf and watched her walk to a chair opposite the couch where Meila and Ardabili sat. He caught a whiff of her scent; it smelled clean and white like sailcloth in the summer sun. He held that smell in his mind as he saw her make some joke in Farsi to their hosts. Ardabili and Meila laughed. Farragut still felt a pang of sadness shoot through his body as he realized that she would be, no doubt, the last lover of his too short life.

CHAPTER TWENTY-FOUR

FARRAGUT WALKED home from Ardabili's under a half-moon and felt fully on top of things. Both the plan and his personal life were unfolding perfectly. He looked up to see if a light was on as he passed Azadi's apartment. Yes, one was. What was Azadi doing awake so late? Was he engraving the plate that would print the bogus Supernotes? Or was he engaged in something not scripted and, therefore, not allowed? Azadi was under orders not to take a lover. He fancied himself a ladies' man but a ladies' man in Tehran usually wound up in jail or worse. Farragut, on the other hand, was not under the same restrictions. In fact, Mia had concocted his seduction of Ingrid Mader as part of his cover in Iran. Ingrid knew nothing of this, but Farragut wasn't sure who was at a disadvantage, him or her?

Farragut walked to the cab parked across the street and got in the back seat. Jashni glared at him in the rear view mirror.

"You're late. Are you drunk? Are you aware they're probably watching you?"

Jashni passed an envelope across the seat to Farragut. As Jashni started driving, Farragut opened the envelope. He regarded the surveillance photo of Farhad Sepanlou, the printer at the Supernote Press.

"Did you take this yourself," Farragut asked.

"Yes, Professor, I did." Jashni said "professor" as if it were an expletive.

Farragut looked over the pages of notes written in Jashni's scrawl. Jashni had reported on the printer's daily movements over a month long period.

"You've been trailing Sepanlou for a month but you still haven't been able to trail him to the Supernote Press?" Farragut regretted the implied criticism the minute it was out of his mouth. He was merely thinking out loud but Jashni's hackles were up again.

"Professor Farragut, I'm sure you know it's rather difficult to trail a man to a secret location. If it were so easy, the Press would no longer be secret. The Revolutionary Guards are very careful when they take Sepanlou to the Press. They switch cars many times. Take circuitous routes…"

"I'll need two days. One to verify Sepanlou's itinerary, the other to terminate."

"I assure you. Verification is redundant. My observations are quite accurate."

"I'm sure they are but I still want to verify the itinerary myself. So, I'll need two days. And an M82A1A .50 rifle with a silencer –"

"—and an Unertl 10-power scope. Yes, yes. Both are already waiting for you in the room I have reserved for you. Securely hidden, I might add, in the usual place."

He's a pompous prick, thought Farragut. *But thorough. Very thorough.*

Farragut stuffed Jashni's notes back into the brown envelope. He dropped the envelope next to Jashni on the front seat.

"Drop me off here."

"But we are still several blocks from your hotel."

"I want to walk. Drop me off here."

The smell of falafel grease and the unpleasantness of the task at hand were squeezing Farragut's stomach. He felt like he was going to be sick and he did not want to do that in front of Jashni. The man was the type who flossed his teeth with human weakness.

Jashni pulled the car up to the curb. Traffic was light this time of night and the street was empty. As Farragut opened the door Jashni turned around to address him.

"Before you leave, I feel I would be remiss if I failed to mention that shooting deaths are quite rare in Iran."

"I'm well aware of that."

"Yes, well, to that end, may I suggest a more subtle means of termination?"

Farragut's grip on the door handle was as firm as the conviction in his voice. "No."

Farragut exited the cab. He slammed the door closed and walked down the sidewalk as the bile rose in his throat. He heard the screech of tires as Jashni's cab pulled away in the night.

He wondered if Ingrid Mader was free for dinner Tuesday evening.

CHAPTER TWENTY-FIVE

INGRID MADER lay awake beside John Farragut, listening to him snore. They had dined together that night. She had met him just three days ago. And here they were, in bed together at four in the morning, in a cheap but clean hotel, in South Tehran. It was all so very sophisticated. Or sleazy. Or delightful. Take your pick. But she had picked him and that made it all right. She had written him the letter because she admired his book, not because she wanted to get him into bed. But when Meila and Ali had told her that they knew Professor Farragut and that he was coming to town and wanted to meet her, she had agreed.

He was sleeping on his side, his back to her, the covers pulled down to his waist. She took her index finger ran it gently across his defined muscles from his broad shoulders to his narrow waist. He had the beautiful body of a boy athlete. So why was there the undeniable air of death about him?

She had sensed it upon first setting eyes upon him at Ardabili's. Was it because he spoke of long dead men like Darius I and Xerxes II as if they had been at the dinner table with them? Was it the matter-of-fact fashion he had related to her the story of his mother's death? It was her fault that the topic came up. She had playfully suggested that she would like to meet his mother because only a mother could teach a man to respect a woman's point of view as well as he seemed to. He had accepted the compliment and related the story of her death. Perhaps she was reading more into it all than she should. She could not deny her intuitive flashes but she had been wrong in the past. She had been wrong about her husband.

"Tell me about your husband," he'd asked her as they walked from the restaurant last night. She had been expecting the question.

"He's a brilliant, creative diplomat," she told him truthfully. "Before Iran, he was the chief political officer in our Turkish Embassy. He speaks five languages. He paints very respectable watercolors. He's a devoted father and reads to the children before bed. He makes me laugh. He makes his own sausage from an old family recipe that he swears will make us rich some day. Richer, I suppose, because his family is already rich. He thinks Led Zeppelin was the greatest band of all time."

"Jimmy Page is God. I think I would like your husband very much."

"You would. I know I do."

And if Farragut had picked up her confession of "liking," rather than "loving" her husband, he didn't reveal it. Not in his polite smile. Not in his questions which remained innocently off-point and harmless in their randomness.

"Where were you when the Wall came down?" he asked as if the Berlin Wall had fallen just the day before.

"That's a strange question."

"Is it? You claim to be enamored by history and what could be more important to a German of your age? Do you know that I was here in Tehran when the Shah fell? I never felt more alive. The convergence of energy and humanity and history? You feel part of something big and profound, like you will never die."

They were walking by the old US Embassy at that point. It had been converted into a museum called The Den of Spies. The armed guards out front were engaged in conversation and barely gave them a look as they walked by.

"Feel like you will never die? Do you fear death?" she'd asked him, as his hand found hers and held it firm, fingers interlocking.

"No. Not at all. But I'd like to live forever. Wouldn't everybody?"

"No. Of course, not. Who wants to outlive all your loved ones? But I suppose we live on through our children, don't you?"

"I don't know. I don't have children."

"Would you like to have children?"

She had regretted the words the moment they slipped from her mouth. She knew the night might turn sexual and she didn't want to confuse things.

"Maybe someday, if I get around to it. Sure. Why not?" he said, not flustered at all.

And that had been his last question to her as they walked in silence, savoring the moments before the seduction they both knew was inevitable. Ingrid waited for him to ask again about her husband, specifically why she was here with him now instead of home with the man who liked to read to the kids and listen to Led Zeppelin. But he didn't ask. Nor did he inquire if the rumor were true, a rumor known to be fact in the diplomatic and designer clothes wearing circles of Tehran, that her husband had two years ago come out to her about his homosexuality. True, yes true, their marriage was now political, not passionate. But he was still her very best friend and a wonderful father. And he was sorry but he was who he was. And she forgave him because that was her nature just as her husband was very safe and very discreet with his indiscretions because that was his nature. She had promised her husband to be just as discreet as he was.

John had flagged them a cab and they headed to South Tehran to check into a hotel where no one would know them and they could get to know one another intimately.

-:::::-

"I was in Munich when the Wall came down," she had confessed to him as they lay in bed and stared at the water stains on the hotel room ceiling. They hadn't made love yet. They had held one another and talked about making love until the moment had passed. He seemed very tired but not at all disappointed. She played with the fluffy down around his navel.

"You were in Munich? I've never been to Munich," he said, stifling a yawn.

"Advertising and insurance. You're not missing much. Anyway, I'd just been married and my husband and I were visiting his parents before our next posting. I watched the Wall fall down on television."

"I was writing a book and stuck in the stacks of the library doing research. I saw it on TV the next day, too."

"What exciting lives we lived in our youth, yes?"

He had laughed at that. A big, powerful laugh that pulled him from his fatigue and let her glimpse the life force within him. He ran his fingers across her lips and said nice things about her face. He kissed the back of her neck. She had no idea how he knew that drove her crazy. It had been a while since the last time for her and she appreciated his slow hand. He made a funny face when he came and she burst out laughing. He didn't mind at all. She set her watch alarm for 4:30 a.m. That gave her plenty of time to make it home to the kids to serve them breakfast before school.

The watch alarm went off as he snored and she reflected on their night. She shut it off so as not to wake him and dressed, pulling a bold Hermes scarf over her head and a baggy *rouposh* over her La Perla lingerie and Richard Tyler dress.

She kissed her hand and touched it to Farragut's sleeping head. She walked through the door and closed it softly so that she wouldn't wake him. She needn't have bothered.

Farragut was awake and ready to work.

CHAPTER TWENTY-SIX

Farragut's eyes opened as Ingrid closed the door. He lay in bed for five minutes and made sure that she didn't come back. She didn't.

He strode across the room to the cheap dresser and pushed it away from the wall. The wood floor underneath was filthy, covered with dust and dead roaches. It really was an awful hotel, not at all in the same league as the Laleh. But Farhad Sepanlou did not take his morning stroll near the Laleh, did he? No. Not according to Jashni's notes.

Farragut pulled a penknife from the pocket of his pants that lay on top of the dresser. He used the knife to pry up the floorboard that had been hidden under the dresser. The board came up easily and revealed the sniper's rifle underneath. A M82A1A .50 rifle. Beside it wrapped in chamois was the silencer and an Unertl 10-power scope.

Farragut assembled the gun.

-:::::-

Farhad Sepanlou exited his building, as was his habit, at 4:45 am. Tehran, a city he despised, projected an air of quiet dignity in these hours before dawn. Soon traffic would choke the streets and he would be fighting for sidewalk space and sucking on exhaust fumes with the rest of the citizens he anonymously served. But for now the city was his, and he found this solitude more precious than the bogus money he created at the Supernote Press. And it was to that Press that Sepanlou was traveling that morning. For he had been given a new assignment, the printing of $12 million in counterfeit to purchase, what was it again? Oh yes, some sort of antiquity…

As was his habit, Sepanlou walked quickly past the car repair shops and food warehouses towards the island of green just to the east of the massive railway terminal. Once inside the Be'sat Park, as was his habit, Sepanlou lit his first cigarette of the day and walked north. He passed the small lake, the still surface divided by a few islands of ice on this chilly morning. As was his habit, he bought a copy of the Tehran *Times* from the vendor at the northwest corner of the park. He chatted with the newspaper vendor, inquired about his ulcer and his fat wife who had taken to eating only grapes. Sepanlou remembered the little details, as details were the lifeblood of the counterfeiter. The talk of grapes made Sepanlou hungry and, as was his habit, he went to buy a kebab from the vendor across the park. As he crossed the street Sepanlou buried his head in the paper and glanced through the lead stories: The Sunni King of Bahrain again crushing the Shiite majorities brave protests against his criminal regime, Egypt taking baby steps toward elections after overthrowing the Zionist appeaser Mubarak, Government nuclear officials vowing the failure of the Japanese reactors could never happen in Iran…

Sepanlou strolled up to his favorite kebab stand on the sidewalk. It was a simple set-up. A few wood boards served as a stove-top while two exposed propane tanks underneath provided heat for the skillets. A log of succulent, spiced lamb rotated in a glass case also kept hot by the propane.

The vendor saw Sepanlou every morning but did not know what Sepanlou did for a living. He *did* sense Sepanlou was a man of importance, as Revolutionary Guards sometimes accompanied him to the humble kebab stand. The vendor affectionately called his customer "Balloon" because Sepanlou was a short man with a large gut and thin legs.

"Mr. Balloon. How are we this fine morning?" asked the vendor, holding out the first, though by no means the last lamb kebab that Sepanlou would consume for breakfast.

As was his habit, Sepanlou shook the man's hand before accepting his first kebab. "I am fine, my friend. Famished but feeling well."

Sepanlou, as was his habit, ate in silence but smiled knowingly as the vendor, as was his habit, vented his spleen about life in Tehran. The traffic. The pollution. The corruption. The cost of living.

-:::::-

Four stories above and 125 meters across the street from where Sepanlou devoured his breakfast, Farragut sighted his target through the Unertl scope. He could see grease running down Sepanlou's lips through his scope's crosshairs. He noticed that the target needed to trim his nasal hair. These human imperfections, if allowed to linger long enough in the mind, could discourage Farragut from the job at hand. His finger tightened on the sniper rifle's trigger...

Suddenly the pain pulsed through Farragut's head before he could get off a shot. Farragut's own imperfection, the tumor, was back with a vengeance. He dropped his eyes from the scope and shut them tight. His heartbeat boomed like a Beethoven symphony in his ears. Then the mosques erupted with the call to prayer, Farsi amplified into the chill morning air all across the city:

"God is most great. God is most great. I testify that there is no god except God. I testify that there is no god except God. I testify that Muhammad is the messenger of God. I testify that Muhammad is the messenger of God. Come to prayer. Come to prayer."

Farragut remembered the pills that had been prescribed by Dr. Greenblatt back in New York. He found the pills in his pants pocket and fumbled with the safety cap. He swallowed two pills to fight the pain of the tumor that was killing him and then he somehow managed to remember that Sepanlou was still alive.

Farragut picked up the gun and set himself at the window. Another blast of pain made him shut his eyes and he saw his mother's freckled face. He smelled Ingrid's fresh, clean scent. He heard Yasir's laugh and felt the heat as the plane exploded on the tarmac in New York.

I am on Yasir's side, he thought. *I am on my mother's side.*

With great effort Farragut looked through the scope. He saw Sepanlou was smiling as the vendor handed him another lamb kebab. Farragut swung the rifle down and sighted the propane tanks that had cooked Sepanlou's breakfast.

-:::::-

As was his habit, Sepanlou accepted the second kebab from the vendor. The call to prayer played out from mosques and minarets across the city. It drowned out the words coming from the vendor's mouth. Even if it hadn't, Sepanlou would never have heard the soft *phut* of a high-caliber, explosive bullet being shot from the window four stories up and 125 yards away. He might possibly have heard the bullet hitting the propane tank and piercing its metal skin.

The propane tank exploded upon impact with the bullet, igniting the second propane tank along with it. An orange blanket of flame swallowed up Sepanlou and his friend, the vendor.

The call to prayer rolled across the city like a runaway freight train. Even as sirens blared and smoke billowed, even as fire consumed flesh, the call to prayer urged the faithful to the mosque to pray.

The pain in Farragut's head subsided. Whether it was a miracle or the medicine, he couldn't say. He took apart the gun and stored it in a carrier bag from the National Museum. He dressed, grabbed the bag, and headed downstairs where the desk clerk, per Jashni's notes, had been asleep when Ingrid had slipped out onto the street minutes before. He would not be asleep now. He would be out on the street staring at the carnage. Farragut who had paid his bill the night before while checking in, walked by the empty desk and out onto the street. And yes, there was the desk clerk, his back to Farragut, watching the fire in fascination.

Farragut slipped away down the street in the opposite direction, towards his nicer hotel in the more elegant part of town. He saw Jashni's cab idling nearby; according to the plan he was to take this cab to the Laleh. But Farragut chose to keep on walking, past Jashni's angry gaze and against the crush of pedestrians streaming towards the scene of the accident.

As he walked, Farragut tried to pull Ingrid's smell, the scent of sailcloth in the sun, from his memory. It didn't come. Next he speculated on the sea and Salaam and the next phase. He did not know all the details but he did know that Salaam would not be sailing into action on some beautiful ship, rigged with clean sailcloth that brought back images of Ingrid. No. Salaam's insertion into Lebanon would not be quite so poetic. Not by a longshot.

CHAPTER TWENTY-SEVEN

SALAAM FELT his butt clench. He sat in the middle of the Zodiac inflatable boat and balanced chemical equations in his head. He did this to distract himself from the fact he was scared shitless. It was 4 o'clock in the morning and he was floating in a small fabric vessel with two Israeli frogmen, one fore and one aft. The three of them drifted approximately one mile off the coast of Beirut, Lebanon.

Science. Think science, thought Salaam. Science will soothe you.

The Law of the Conservation of Mass is the rationale for balancing a chemical equation.

Salaam thought about the rationale for why he was here. He was being ferried to Beirut to infiltrate Hezbollah, a Muslim terrorist group funded by Iran. Hezbollah was committed to the destruction of Israel and, indirectly, to the destruction of the United States.

Repeat: The Law of the Conservation of Mass is the rationale for balancing a chemical equation.

Salaam was a Muslim and a United States citizen. That to him was an unbalanced equation. Salaam did not know whether Hezbollah would receive him as a hero or a heathen. He did know, however, that Hezbollah had killed more than 200 United States citizens when guerillas drove trucks fitted with bombs into the US marine barracks in Beirut in 1983.

Salaam listened to water slosh against the side of the boat. Water was an easy equation to balance.

$H_2 + O_2 \rightarrow H_2O$. *This equation is unbalanced because there are unequal numbers of at least one atom on each end of the arrow.*

Salaam glanced at the Israeli frogmen on each end of the Zodiac. He had no idea what they looked like. They wore black wet suits and had yet to take off their waterproof infrared Night Vision Goggles. The frogman in the bow scanned the horizon. Salaam guessed he was looking for the Beirut skyline or Lebanese patrol boats. The frogman in the stern paddled the Zodiac, a necessity since the outboard engine had been disengaged so as not to alert those Lebanese patrol boats.

The frogman at the front of the boat turned and faced Salaam. Salaam recalled his name was Hadad. Salaam could only guess at the color of his eyes behind his monstrous NVG's.

"I can see the lights of Beirut. We'll take you to shore about three miles north of the St. George Marina. After that, you're on your own."

Salaam looked to his left. The frogman in the stern pulled his paddle out of the water and crab walked to the front of the Zodiac. Salaam flashed on his name, an unusual name: Regassa. It didn't sound Israeli to Salaam's ears.

"Let me have a look, Sergeant."

Regassa was in charge. He was an officer, a captain. He crammed into the front of the boat next to Hadad and scanned the horizon. Salaam heard the two Israelis whisper to each other in Hebrew. Salaam couldn't make out the meaning but their tense, strained voices told him they weren't discussing their golf games. They had Colt Commando assault rifles strapped to their hips. Regassa turned and faced Salaam. He lifted the NVG's from his head. Salaam felt his heart drop to his toes as he got his first look at the Israeli captain's face –

Regassa was black.

"Funny, but you don't look Jewish," Salaam said. An oldie but goodie. Fear was testing Salaam's ability to be funny.

Hadad pulled off his NVG's. He had blue eyes and freckles. He didn't look old enough to pick his nose, much less serve in the Israeli Navy.

"He's an Ethiopian Jew."

"I'm an Israeli captain, Sergeant," Regassa said, glaring at the freckles on Hadad's face.

Hadad put back on his NVG's and said, "Yes, sir."

Regassa splashed some seawater on his face. It was a beautiful face. Angular cheekbones cradled large brown eyes.

"Captain, I think I see something." Hadad's NVG's were focused off the starboard side.

Regassa flipped his NVG's back over his face. Salaam felt more regret than fear. He wanted to look at Regassa's marvelous African face. It helped him forget where he was.

"I see something, too. It may just be bio-luminescent algae," Regassa said.

"Swim ahead and check it out, Sergeant."

Hadad slipped into the dark water as quietly as a feather and disappeared into the night.

Salaam wondered why the Israelis had spoken English. Maybe they wanted to scare him, this black American cat wearing the crocheted Muslim skullcap who was responsible for dragging their asses out into the Mediterranean in the middle of the night. Or maybe they were just too terrified to remember to speak in Hebrew and keep Salaam in the dark.

Regassa watched the horizon, oblivious to Salaam. Salaam tried to think of chemical equations but the knot in his gut made it impossible to concentrate. He had to touch something to ease his fear. He ran his hand along the Zodiac's outboard engine. It felt cold and hard and powerful.

"Always loved boats, especially sailboats. As a kid growing up in Oakland, I used to watch the yachts on San Francisco Bay. I knew 'em all: Seafarer, Cape Dory, Hunter, and Catamaran. Told my momma I'd own a yacht of my own someday. She said, 'That's fine, child, but you best learn to sail first.'"

"Quiet. The less I know about you, the better," Regassa said, still with his back to Salaam.

Salaam stared at the black man in the black wet suit. In prison he had read dozens of books about African history. He knew something about the Ethiopian Jews. He knew their African neighbors called them *Falashas*, the alien ones, the invaders. He knew the Ethiopian government confiscated their land and forbade their religious practices. He knew Israeli operatives smuggled them into Israel, where they lived amidst crushing poverty and endemic discrimination.

"How'd you wind up in Israel? Operation Moses?" Salaam said. Operation Moses was an airlift campaign financed by the Israeli government and Jewish groups that brought 8,000 Ethiopian Jews into Israel via Sudan in the mid-1980s.

Regassa didn't answer Salaam. He kept his back turned and his eyes on the horizon.

"Come on, brother. I'm scared. And when I'm scared I talk. Besides, you're not asking about me. I'm asking about you."

Regassa pulled off his NVG's. He stuck his hand in the sea and splashed water on his face. Salaam could see the man was tense and trying to keep it together.

"I came to Israel in Operation Joshua."

Salaam nodded. He recalled Operation Joshua was a CIA sponsored follow-up mission to Operation Moses that brought an additional 800 Jews from Sudan to Israel.

"Then I guess we both got the CIA to thank for where we are now."

Regassa fixed Salaam with a very cold glare. "I told you not to tell me anything about you. My job is to get you to Beirut, not hear your life story."

"Sorry. I'm just fascinated we've got something in common besides the color of our skin. I mean, it's tough enough being a black man in America. Being a black man in Israel can't be an easy fit neither."

"I'm an Israeli commando, an officer. I'd say I fit in very well."

Salaam chuckled. "Hate to burst your bubble, brother. But when they look at you, they don't see an Israeli. They see a nigger."

Salaam was sitting in the stern. Regassa was standing in the bow. They were as far apart as you could be and the boat still felt too small for both of them.

"My countrymen see me as a nigger? Have you ever been to Israel?"

"No."

"Then how can you possibly know how my countrymen see me?"

"Same way you do. You know it when you're on a bus and grandma switches seats rather than sit next to you. Or when you can't give blood because the doctor is afraid all Africans have AIDS. Don't get me wrong, they'll let you spill your black blood on the battlefield, but they're not gonna pump it into the rabbi if his heart gives out. Sorry, Captain, but you're a nigger. That's the way of the world. Their world at least."

Regassa bit his lip. Salaam could see him trying to quell his anger. Whether Regassa was mad at Salaam or his situation or both, Salaam couldn't tell, but he respected Regassa's self-control. The man may have been born in the African heat but his nerves were made of ice.

Regassa said, "If you believe the world boils down to black against white, why are you here?"

"I thought you didn't want to know anything about me?"

Regassa smiled without showing his teeth. Salaam returned the smile.

"Well first off, I didn't say the world boils down to black against white. No. The reason my ass is in the Mediterranean? It's about one thing, plain and simple. Dead presidents."

Regassa furrowed his brow. "Dead presidents? I don't understand."

Salaam was about to respond when Regassa noticed Hadad floating off the stern. Regassa reached down and began to pull Hadad back into the boat.

"Did you see anything, Sergeant?"

Salaam saw the whites of Regassa's eyes. Hadad's body dropped into the Zodiac. His throat had been slashed from ear-to-ear.

Gunfire peppered the water around the Zodiac. Plumes of spray shot up into the fog. Salaam felt a hand shove him to the deck. He landed on top of Hadad's body. He felt the thickness of Hadad's leg muscles pressing against his chest. He smelled gasoline. He felt the Zodiac bounce along the water.

Salaam looked up. He saw Regassa working the Zodiac's engine with one hand and firing his Uzi with the other. He saw muzzle flashes. He saw a searchlight mounted on a Lebanese patrol boat about 150 meters aft. The bright beam of the searchlight danced across the water. The beam embraced the Zodiac. Gunfire erupted in Salaam's ears.

Salaam pressed his body down as low as it could go. He saw blood from Hadad's slashed throat mixing with seawater on the Zodiac's deck. He looked up again. Regassa was looking at him. His eyes flashed fear as he shouted above the roar of the engine.

"I'll lead them away from shore! You'll have to swim for it!"

Salaam tried to tell Regassa that no, he was not going to swim for it but the words collapsed in his mouth. He felt a hand pull him up by his collar. He thought of a cat carrying her kitten by the scruff of its neck. He felt Regassa's strength as Regassa heaved him over the side of the boat.

Salaam felt the cold, dark waters of the Mediterranean absorb him. He thought of rivers.

Rivers ancient as the world and older than the flow of human blood in human veins.

Salaam's head broke the surface of the sea. He heard more gunfire. He heard an explosion. He saw flames jump to the stars.

Salaam turned towards what he thought was the shore. He saw lights. He swam towards the lights. His body felt heavy. The moonlit water chilled his bones.

CHAPTER TWENTY-EIGHT

SALAAM SAT outdoors in a busy café and ate a dozen stuffed grape leaves for breakfast. He washed them down with a glass of iced *ahweh*. The coffee was strong and cold.

Salaam leaned back in his chair and closed his eyes. He let the morning sun warm his face. He listened to the café patrons around him. He heard snatches of conversation in French, English, and Arabic. For a moment he cherished his false reality: I am a man of the world; a free man enjoying his breakfast during a sunny morning in Beirut.

Salaam checked his watch. It was 9:31. Three hours and seventeen minutes ago he had awoken on an empty beach eight kilometers north of Beirut proper. He had stretched his sore muscles and thanked the sun for drying his clothes as he walked to the nearby village of *Harat al Ballanah*. In the village, he had hired a cab to take him to Beirut. The cab driver tried to chat to Salaam in English. Salaam knew there was an outside chance the cab driver was an undercover Syrian security officer. They often posed as cab drivers, the Israelis had told him so he curtailed the conversation by feigning a nap. Despite the official withdrawal of their armed forces, the Syrians had plenty of undercover agents and Lebanese allies keeping an eye on their interests.

Appearances are deceiving, the Israelis had told him.

Salaam, in fact, was counting on that.

The cab had come upon a Lebanese army checkpoint. A Lebanese soldier had looked at his papers and handed them back. He had smiled and waved Salaam and the cab driver on their way. Say what you will about their policy towards the Palestinians, but the Israelis knew how to forge papers. These documents identified Shareef Salaam, aka Gary Hastings, as Peter Mogale, a chemical engineer from South Africa employed by VTS Waste Management Systems. When the cab driver, still eager for conversation, had asked Salaam what VTS Waste Management Systems did, Salaam had told him he was involved in a project overhauling the sewage system of the southern Beirut suburbs. In less technical terms, he was a shit scientist, entrusted with removing human waste. Salaam suspected the Israelis saw this as an inside joke, but the cab driver/ Syrian spy didn't find it funny. He didn't even offer Salaam a smile when Salaam tipped him thirty Lebanese pounds after being dropped off in the Beirut Central District.

Salaam rose from his chair, dropped 20 Lebanese pounds on the table, and slipped into the pedestrian traffic. The ancient city – once so devastated by a violent, stupid war – now pulsated with renewed vigor, and for a moment Salaam contemplated getting lost in it. But he knew he was being watched. That man picking at his cheese pastry with the handgun bulge under his American University of Beirut T-shirt, he was probably Syrian Intelligence. The Israelis were watching him, too, but they possessed the decorum to melt into the background.

Salaam walked down the street and looked for landmarks that Mia Kelly had forced him to memorize. He passed the Maronite St. George Cathedral, walked up a side street, then another, and saw a lovely cream-colored building with a French-inspired façade. A sign above the wrought iron doors identified the establishment as Khalidi Booksellers. A fat calico cat slept on the doorstep. An Israeli agent posing as just-another-dark-skinned-guy-minding-his-own-business-and-walking-down-a-street-in-Beirut brushed past him and indicated with a too-polite "*pardonnez-moi*" that this was the place.

Salaam stepped over the cat and entered the store. It smelled of mold, dust, and lemon-scented disinfectant. There were no customers, which was not surprising since there weren't many books. A skinny youth sat behind a desk and read an Arabic newspaper. Salaam approached him.

"Good morning. I'm looking for Joseph Heller's *Catch-22*."

The boy looked up from his paper as if the Prophet Muhammad had walked in.

"Excuse me?"

"I said I'm looking for Joseph Heller's *Catch-22*."

The boy, shocked and speechless, stared open-mouthed at Salaam.

Salaam said, "Listen, sonny, I just said the password. So why don't you just bring me to your boss, okay?"

And the boy did, leading Salaam into the backroom to meet the mastermind behind the bombing at LaGuardia.

CHAPTER TWENTY-NINE

"**I AM NOT AN** anti-Semite," said Hasan Shehabi in his Oxford-inflected English marred by a slight lisp. "I am an anti-Zionist. You know the difference?"

Salaam sat in a chair in the stuffy back office of Khalidi Booksellers. The fat calico cat had made its way inside and was dozing in Salaam's lap. Two Hezbollah guerillas dressed in black uniforms stood behind Salaam and pointed AK-47's at his head.

Salaam nodded in reply to Shehabi's question. The cat yawned.

"Good. You see the popular misconception is that we Arabs hate the Jews. And especially that Hezbollah hates the Jews. No, I tell you. Not true! We merely want the Jews out of Palestine. They do not belong there. Just as they did not belong in Southern Lebanon. The Jews are Europeans. Let them go back to Europe. Or America. If they leave the Middle East, the Jews will find they have no better friends than the Arabs. No better friends, I tell you."

Salaam scratched his chin and nodded like he gave a shit. He had already made his pitch to Shehabi exactly like Mia Kelly had instructed him to. Shehabi, in typical Arab fashion, was going to give Salaam a lecture rather than a simple "yes" or "no."

Shehabi strolled to a desk. He opened a drawer and pulled out a Cuban cigar. He stuffed the cigar in his mouth and lit it with a Zippo imprinted with the Israeli flag. Salaam wondered if he had taken it off a dead Israeli soldier or bought it on the Internet.

"We heard of your escape on CNN. Most impressive. Oh, I'm forgetting my manners. Would you like a cigar?"

Salaam shook his head, glaring at Shehabi. "I'm a devout Muslim. I don't smoke."

It was true but Salaam said it to get a rise out of Shehabi. It didn't. The Hezbollah military leader just stood there enjoying his cigar and the subtle power game with Salaam.

"Yes. I would say your escape was most impressive. Remarkable, really. Almost as remarkable as my friend, Kareem Shuqueiri, telling you where to find me."

Actually, thought Salaam, *the Israelis told me that. They've been watching your ass for years; but we'll go with Mia Kelly's fictional stylings for now.*

"Kareem was a fellow con and a fellow Muslim. He made me see that Hezbollah and BURN had common goals. It's out of respect for him that I'm offering you this deal first."

"Ah, yes, the deal. Let me make sure I understand what it is you want. You said you're offering me your network of people to attack Hezbollah-approved targets in the United States in exchange for funding from our Iranian sponsors."

Salaam scratched the cat's ears. "Yes. That's the deal."

Shehabi blew a little smoke ring through a bigger smoke ring. "Very intriguing. But, alas, I have to think about it."

"Oh, okay. While you think about it, I'll mosey on over to Hamas or Hassad or Gamaa al Islamiya or any of the other nine hundred radical groups that'll jump at it."

Salaam stood. The cat hit the floor with a thud and raced out of the room. Salaam turned towards the door but Shehabi blocked his way. Salaam dug the desperation in his eyes.

"Please wait. You Americans always want an answer right away. You should learn to relax."

"Relax? Tell you what. You tell Butch and Sundance over there to pull their AK-47's out of my face, then I'll relax. Maybe I'll even take a nap, seeing as how I crossed ten time zones for you to treat me like Mossad's got their thumb up my ass."

Play the indignant bad-ass black radical, Kelly had told him. *They're insecure. With young people protesting across the Middle East inspired by Facebook and Western freedoms, not Islamic ideology, they're not sure where they fit in. They respond to confidence.*

Shehabi gestured to the two guerillas. They lowered their guns and, to Salaam's surprise, left the room. Shehabi smiled at Salaam.

"Are you thirsty? Would you like some water? Or maybe some juice?"

"Juice would be nice."

Shehabi hustled over to the desk. He opened a drawer and pulled out a small box of "juice" with a straw was taped to the box. Shehabi handed the box to Salaam. Salaam stuck the straw in the box and sipped warm sugar water.

Shehabi said nothing and smoked his cigar. Salaam glanced around the room and occasionally at Shehabi, but not at his face. He knew looking at his face was a mistake.

Hasan Shehabi had a harelip. It had been partially repaired by a village woman when he was a child, though not well. It was his affliction. It made him lisp. It made him a shy, loveless child. It made him swear to be smarter, stronger, cleverer and more ruthless than everyone else if God, in his eternal mercy, would just look out for him. It inspired him, the fourth son of a power fisherman, to study hard, to memorize the Quran, to win a scholarship to Lebanese Arab University, to learn to read and write in English and Farsi and Hebrew and graduate first in his class. It propelled him, with the help of a wealthy LAU alumnus, to pursue a graduate degree in Oriental Studies at Oxford. It made him cover his mouth in terror when a redheaded Jewish girl from Shaker Heights, Ohio, who was studying Arabic on a Rhodes scholarship, begged him to tutor her in his native tongue. It forced his virginity until he was twenty-three and the redheaded Jewish girl and he got drunk on Guinness and Gibran and finally did it. It smiled when she taught him about Joseph Heller and what a bagel with a *schmeer* was. It cried when she dumped him for a banker's son with a title, a trust fund, and a taste for hard drugs. It refused to be fixed permanently when, heartbroken, Hasan dropped out and returned to Lebanon and the wealthy alumnus offered to pay for the surgery. Hasan wanted a cross to bear, so to speak, and the harelip sufficed.

And so the harelip came along for the ride when the wealthy alumnus introduced Hasan to his friend, Sheikh Muhammad Husayn Fadlallah. It listened in rapture as Sheikh Fadlallah told Hasan about the primacy of Iran's Islamic rule and the purity of Ayatollah Sayyid Ruhollah Musavi Khomeini. It nodded in agreement when Sheikh Fadlallah told Hasan that the survival of Lebanon depended upon it embracing a fundamentalist regime modeled on that of Iran. It swelled with pride when Sheikh Fadlallah asked Hasan to join Hezbollah. It felt fear as Hasan led raids against the Israelis and the South Lebanon Army. It ceased being a congenital defect and became part of Hasan's fiction. It became a shrapnel wound suffered in a firefight against the SLA in Shama. It became a torture wound inflicted by Israeli commandos who briefly captured him in Metullah. It rose through the ranks as Hasan was promoted. It cheered the departure of the Israelis from southern Lebanon and vowed to keep fighting. The harelip was Hasan. It would die with him.

Salaam slurped the last of his juice.

"It's a matter of trust," lisped Shehabi. "Hezbollah has built a foundation of loyal supporters through years of delivering social services to our oppressed Shia population and spilling our blood against the better-armed Israeli aggressor. So when you come to me talking about an alliance, I am naturally hesitant. I don't know you or your motives."

Salaam waved cigar smoke out of his face. "I understand your paranoia but I come here out of respect. BURN wants to establish a legitimate, radical opposition in America at a time the country is sleepwalking towards the right. And we admire what you've done setting up a functional de facto government in Lebanon. You are our model for what the Black Muslim community can accomplish in America. Social justice and services but always a hand on the sword, or should I say AK-47?"

Shehabi's face flushed with pride. "It's true we have had a great success despite the recent war with Israeli. And yet the news is filled with stories about the democratic movements sweeping the region but we were there first. Why are we not as celebrated as those in Cairo's Tahir Square? Or Tunisia? Or Libya? We are, as you say in the American movies, the good guys wearing white hats."

Salaam watched Shehabi smoke. Kelly had told him that Intelligence reports estimated Iranian aid to Hezbollah had been cut to about $50 million a year because despite the rise in oil prices, Iran's economy was a disaster. Moreover, much of that aid was in military equipment rather than cash and the cash they got was mostly Supernotes. Of course, Shehabi got as much bang for the buck as he could. Shuqueiri had confessed that Shehabi was the mastermind behind the airplane bombing at LaGuardia, and that one of Shehabi's men had been the courier who handed the $1 million in Supernotes to Shuqueiri that fateful day in New York.

Shehabi brushed an imaginary piece of lint off his soccer jersey. "Say I bring your offer to the Iranians? What makes you think they'll approve it?"

"Oh, they'll approve it. They're being squeezed by economic sanctions. They see protestors across the Gulf and North Africa being treated like heroes while they are demonized for putting down their own Green Revolution. And I'm sure that Stuxnet worm cooked up the by Americans and the Israelis that took out their reactor really burns. Think of BURN as their Stuxnet worm."

Shehabi was finally starting to smile. Even the harelip couldn't hide that. "But still, there's the element of trust," said Shehabi.

"Got that covered. Before we do this deal we're gonna give the Iranians a gift. Just a little something from the two of us that will let them know I'm for real and you're more valuable than ever to them."

Shehabi smoked in silence and then finally said, "Tell me more."

Salaam felt something sinewy rub against his leg. He looked down and saw the cat. He picked it up. It purred.

Salaam told Shehabi the plan.

-:::::-

Less than one hour after Israeli Intelligence observed Shareef Salaam leaving the Khalidi Booksellers escorted by two of Shehabi's guards, Mia Kelly knew about it. The information went first to Tel Aviv since the Mossad agents were on site and saw it go down. Then, the facts flew by secure satellite connection from Tel Aviv to Mia Kelly in New York. Mia contacted the British Ambassador in Tehran who, without asking too many questions, was making the embassy's secure phone lines available to the Americans for the operation as needed. A British diplomat — a senior British intelligence agent posing as a Deputy Cultural Affairs Officer — called Farragut at the Laleh and invited him to the British Embassy for tea and to discuss giving a lecture for the culture-starved expatriate community. An hour later Farragut, deep in the bowels of the British Embassy off Ferdowsi Avenue, took the call on a secure line and his cup of Earl Grey with lemon, no sugar.

"Three hours ago in Beirut, Salaam's Mossad shadow saw him signal that Shehabi bought the plan so we're good to go for now," said Mia.

"What was the signal?" asked Farragut.

"Salaam, per instructions, coughed twice, and in plain view. Really, John. Relax. It was affirmative. Shehabi bought Salaam's goods. We're on. Repeat. We are on."

Farragut coughed himself and sipped his tea, savoring the soothing liquid. The odious Tehran pollution was bothering his throat and he knew, despite his still healthy appearance, that the cancer had knocked his immune system for a loop. But he wasn't worried so much about his health as about Salaam's enthusiasm for the mission. Salaam was so damn smart and he had heart. Farragut still wasn't copacetic just because Salaam gave the signal.

"You still there, John?"

"Yes."

"Good. I just wanted to say congratulations. I hear your thing went well."

By "your thing" Farragut knew Mia meant the assassination of Sepanlou. She had an annoying way of using euphemisms for the ugly parts of the operation. Maybe it was her Catholic guilt.

Farragut said, "Yes. Thank you."

"What about London? Are you ready for your little mini-break?"

By which she meant executing the deal for the antiquity that would force the printing of Iranian Supernotes and had necessitated the killing of Sepanlou in the first place.

"All the preparations are in place. I'm ready as soon as Azadi infiltrates the Press. It shouldn't be long now, not with Sepanlou out of the picture but until then all I can do on this end is wait for Azadi."

"The waiting is the hardest part."

By which he knew Mia meant, finally, exactly what she had said.

CHAPTER THIRTY

FOUR DAYS AFTER Farragut had assassinated Farhad Sepanlou, three days after Salaam had entered Beirut, Azadi sat surrounded by the solitude in his apartment, reading a letter to his father.

"Dear Father," he read aloud in English because it wasn't often he heard English anymore. "This letter must remain in Tehran but it comes from my heart. I miss you terribly. I have never felt more alone and afraid. I want my father to sit me down on his knee and tell me that it is going to be all right. Do you remember how you used to do that for me when I was a boy? I used to think you were weak because you cared so deeply. I used to feel embarrassed when you cried. You cried when mother left you. You cried when the nightmares of torture tore you from sleep. You cried when you found out I was a criminal. You cried when I told you I was leaving for Tehran. I now realize that a strong man cries because he does not fear being afraid. I am afraid all the time. But I cannot cry."

Azadi swallowed some Johnnie Black from the open bottle on the desk. He picked up the pages of the letter and felt the paper with his fingers, as if the sentiments could penetrate his skin.

The feel makes it real, Kelly had said. *The stiffness, the crackle of the paper.*

And as it was with currency, so it was with Azadi's emotions. If he wrote his feelings down on paper, then he could be sure they were what he really felt. The feel made it real.

The phone rang. It had to be Babajan again, probably on his cellphone and on his way over. Azadi didn't have an answering machine but he could imagine the message that Babajan would leave. *Omar, you lazy bastard! Where the hell are you? Where is my goddamn car? I'm going to fire you when I find you!*

Azadi had said he was taking Babajan's car to drop off the newly printed menus at the restaurant owned by the Finance Minister's son. He had said nothing about returning the car and leaving for the day. Babajan would be in a foul mood when he arrived. Azadi stared at the Scotch. He had drunk just enough to back up the bullshit story.

The phone stopped ringing after 14 rings.

Babajan is not your friend; he is your boss, Ishmael, the cabbie, had advised Azadi. *You would never admit to him your deepest, darkest secret. Better he catches you in the act because of your stupidity, much the way the Treasury Agents caught you because of your stupidity. You're sensational at stupidity, aren't you, Omar?*

Azadi had to stage stupidity but the letter to his father wasn't part of it. He carried the letter to his bathroom and tore it into thin strips. He dropped the strips into the toilet and flushed the remains of the letter into the Tehran sewer system.

Azadi walked into his bedroom and pulled the mattress off the bed, revealing a hairline rip in the box-spring underneath. He plunged his hand through the rip and pulled out the two partially engraved currency plates, bound in bubble wrap, one for printing the backs and the other for printing the fronts of 2011 issue $100 bills. Azadi pulled out a magnifying lens and a burin, both stolen from Babajan's shop two weeks previously.

Azadi reentered his living room and sat at his desk. He turned on the powerful lamp and pulled a piece of fine linen from the desk. He placed the linen on the desktop and rested the printing plate for the front of the bill on top of the linen. The back printing plate he put in the drawer of the desk to be discovered later.

Azadi began to work. It felt good to look through the ten-power magnifying glass and cut lines into steel with the burin, lines no deeper than a human hair.

He lost track of time as he cut. Even the sound of a cab door slamming outside on the street below did not break his concentration.

Next Babajan was banging away at the door and bellowing his name. "Omar! Open the door. I know you are in there! I saw my car out front! You are fired! Do you hear? Fired!"

It was time to get caught in the act right according to plan.

"Mr. Babajan? Just a minute, I will be right there."

But Babajan couldn't wait a minute and barged through the door which, according to plan, had not been locked. Azadi, according to plan, tried not to look too obvious as he shoved the front plate in the desk with the back plate and slammed the drawer shut. The bottle of Johnnie Black fell off the table from the impact of the drawer and smashed into many pieces. This had not been part of the plan but it was a nice touch because it drew Babajan's attention to the desk and away from his groveling employee begging for forgiveness. Babajan was no longer interested in why Azadi had failed to return to work with his car. That was, as Azadi kept repeating, all part of a simple misunderstanding. Hadn't Babajan loaned him his car overnight several times when Azadi was going to deliver more booze in the morning? Well, yes, he had, but Azadi hadn't said anything about booze. Yes, he had, pleaded Azadi.

And then Azadi raced off to his room to bring back the new case of Johnnie Black. Meanwhile, Babajan was free to set his broad ass down on the desk and notice the burin and magnifying glass that had been stolen from his printing shop. And as Babajan's anger increased, he noticed the partially closed desk drawer and the two steel plates glinting within it.

Babajan opened the drawer and pulled out the plates. Azadi arrived with the box of Scotch and pulled out a bottle.

Azadi need not have bothered with the Scotch. It wasn't the warm amber of Johnnie Black but the cold silver of steel that calmed Babajan's soul that night.

-:::::-

Azadi confessed in a cheap pizza joint that lay just around the corner. For the first time that Azadi could recall, a bracing sobriety seemed to have overcome Babajan.

"Were you a counterfeiter back in America?" asked Babajan, picking the olives off his slice and popping them into his mouth.

Crooks recruit other crooks, not choirboys, Kelly had told him.

"I was one of the best," replied Azadi, relieved not to have to lie.

"Were you ever caught?"

"If I had been, they wouldn't have let me come here, would they?"

"And what do you plan to do with the plates, Omar?"

"I plan to finish them and then, perhaps sell them."

Babajan nodded and narrowed his eyes, deep in thought. The completeness of his transformation, as well as its suddenness, scared Azadi.

"Are you going to tell anyone about me?" whispered Azadi, staring into his tea.

Ishmael had said: *He will boast of you to his Uncle Farja. Tell him that you are a specialist in the injection of ink onto engraved plates, an essential skill in the art of printing money. He will also mention to his Uncle Farjad that you let slip, quite innocently by way of coming clean to your new boss and best friend, that you were a counterfeiter back in the States.*

"Whom would I tell?" smiled Babajan, licking grease off his lips.

Babajan shook Azadi's hand. It was all a misunderstanding and all was forgiven. If Azadi wanted to supplement his wages by printing a little money on the side, well, it was not Babajan's business now, was it? And thanks so much for buying him dinner.

Babajan drove home with the case of Johnnie Black in the trunk of his car. Azadi walked the five minutes back to his apartment while keeping an eye open for his liaison but Ishmael was nowhere to be seen.

CHAPTER THIRTY-ONE

AZADI WORKED hard all through the next week. Babajan stayed drunk and seemed delighted to let him run things. Sometimes he shot Azadi a funny look that seemed to acknowledge their little secret about the currency plates. Or was that just the booze and all in Azadi's head?

Azadi went home at night and engraved the Supernote plates. Babajan had not taken back the magnifying glass or the burin. Had he forgotten or had he become a co-conspirator? Had he talked to his Uncle Farjad? Had the vacancy at the Press promised by Ishmael been secured?

A few nights after the Babajan incident, Azadi received a telephone call from Mojgan, the female bureaucrat with the plain face from the Ministry of the Interior. She asked how he was doing. He said fine. She asked if he needed anything. He said no. The conversation lagged and she invited him over the following week for a delicious plate of her *khoresht*, just as she had promised him, remember? He didn't. There was a long pause.

"Mr. Azadi, I have a joke. Would you like to hear it?"

"Sure."

"An evil man dies and journeys to the gates of hell. The gate-keeper tells him he must choose between the American sector and the Iranian sector. In the American sector, he is told, they pour hot tar down your throat once a month. In the Iranian sector, they pour hot tar down your throat three times a week. The evil man laughs and obviously picks the more lenient American sector. At the end of the first month, his throat scalded, the Americans give him a vacation and he visits some fervent nationalists who have chosen the Iranian sector. He notices that they are all fine, singing and dancing and acting like they have spent a month in paradise. He asks them why they are unhurt and they tell him that choosing the American sector was a mistake because Americans are so efficient. In the Iranian sector, one day they had plenty of tar but no one found the funnel. The next day they found the funnel but no one delivered the tar. And finally, when they had both the tar and the funnel, the administrator for torture had gone home for the day."

Almost all the Iranians you will meet will be warm, considerate, passionate people that will want to befriend you, Kelly had said. *Except for the ones that will want to betray you.*

Mojgan was still giggling like a schoolgirl when Azadi politely told her he'd call next week, next week for sure, and hung up the phone.

-:::::-

"Are you a faggot, Omar?" Babajan asked him as they closed up the shop on Thursday evening. It was a week since Babajan had "outed" Azadi as a counterfeiter, eleven days since the death of Sepanlou, though Azadi didn't know this since no one had informed him of that man's demise.

"Well, I love all mankind so I guess, yes, I'm a faggot," said Azadi, biting down on his anger and playing along.

Babajan tittered. "Okay. I just ask because a good-looking guy like you never talks about girls."

"I haven't met any girls to talk about. Know any?"

Babajan put his arm around Azadi and breathed Johnnie Black into his face. "Tomorrow, you and I will go to Shemiran, to the museums, and look at the pretty girls. The pretty girls hang out in the museums in the winter. In the summer, they walk the trails in the Alborz Mountains. Winter or summer, I know where to find the sexy girls."

"But isn't tomorrow Friday? The Sabbath?" said Azadi.

Babajan shrugged as if what he was about to say was as obvious as the sun rising in the morning. "Yes. But the Sabbath is the sexiest time to be a man in Iran."

-:::::-

That night, Azadi watched a movie at the cinema, one of his agreed upon rendezvous points with Ishmael. The cheapie gore-fest about suicide bombers had been replaced by a cheapie gore-fest about the Iran-Iraq war. After the movie he waited for Ishmael because he figured the cabbie would want an update on how things were progressing with Babajan and might swing by the cinema. He had not seen the man for a week.

Sometimes we'll set a meeting up, sometimes, I'll surprise you, Ishmael had said. *If I don't come it may mean nothing or it may mean they're watching or it may mean I'm dead.*

Ishmael never came. Azadi rode home in a cab driven by an old Afghan refugee who had lost an ear in the war against the Soviets and talked Azadi's ear off with plans to breed poodles with Labradors.

"Labradoodles are very popular in America. You would not believe how popular, my sources tell me," concluded the Afghan with the seriousness of a spy relating a state secret. "So that makes me think they will be popular here, too. You Iranians love all things American. Well, except for their government. Have you ever been to America?"

So now it was *you* Iranians. Well, when in Rome…or Tehran…whatever…

Azadi said, "I have never been to America. It's an evil land of infidels and whores."

That shut the veteran up.

Azadi slept poorly that night, tossing and turning and dreaming about acting in high school plays that he'd never acted in but forgetting his lines nonetheless.

The next day was Friday and Babajan met Azadi at the entrance to the White Palace. Babajan was sober. He wore a suit that was the color of an eggplant. He threw a meaty arm around Azadi and pulled him so close that Azadi could count his nose hairs.

"Omar, my friend. Are you ready to have some fun?"

Truth be told, Azadi was struggling not to. He had not slept well. He had not heard from Ishmael. He wondered what the hell was going on and why he was wasting his time with the brain-dead Babajan.

They walked by a big pair of bronze boots standing at the White Palace entrance. Babajan explained that the White Palace had been one of the Shah's residences. The American puppet master who pulled the Shah's strings had commissioned a massive self-portrait sculpture to stand here but it was defaced soon after the Revolution.

"What do the American cowboys say?" asked Babajan, quickly answering his own question and stealing the punch line. "He died with his boots on?" It was going to be a very long day.

-:::::-

The museum was overheated. The exhibits were dull, mostly expensive, tacky furniture and hideous paintings. Yet it wasn't the Shah's bad taste but Babajan's taste for teenagers that defined this excursion. Young girls were everywhere, their lithe bodies bursting out against tight jeans and short, colorful coats in contrast to the all-concealing *chadors*. They flirted with their heavily made-up eyes across the long hallways and cavernous rooms with an equal number of teenage boys. The teenage boys played it cool and closed ranks in their packs, feigning to ignore the girls but stealing glances over their shoulders.

Babajan stared openly at the young people, getting off on the mating rituals and the danger. The atmosphere of frivolity contrasted with Azadi's own sense of lingering unease; he imagined the *Komite* storming in any second, guns drawn, arresting the whole museum for crimes committed against the Islamic Republic.

"All these pretty girls and you can't seem to smile, my friend," said Babajan, picking up on Azadi's tension. "I know just the thing to help you relax."

Babajan and Azadi left the museum and walked across the manicured lawns to a tea garden situated in the heart of the grounds. They spread out on carpet-covered bench as Babajan explained to Azadi how to smoke a hookah. Azadi feigned ignorance but in fact the hookah was nothing more than a sort of big bong, with its long, flexible pipe attached to a container of water. Babajan placed a mild, apple-flavored tobacco in each of their pipes and then fit a small, hot coal over the tobacco.

"Now just inhale through here," said Babajan, holding up the mouthpiece to demonstrate as if Azadi was some kind of idiot who would inhale through his own thumb. "The water filters and cools the smoke. Do you understand?"

"I think I do," said Azadi. "Let me see if I've got it right."

Azadi inhaled deeply, pulling the smoke through the cool water and up into his lungs. He savored the smoke and the mild buzz in his brain. It wasn't killer dope but it wasn't bad. After 30 seconds, Azadi exhaled the smoke into Babajan's face.

"Omar!" exclaimed Babajan with a big smile. "Where did you learn to suck on a pipe like that? Perhaps girls aren't what you are interested in after all!"

Babajan gestured obscenely. Even though the innuendo wasn't funny, Azadi smiled and took another hit. He reclined further on his bench and started to relax. His nerves had gotten the best of him.

The *Komite* wasn't after him. Everything was going according to plan and soon he would be leaving Tehran a rich man.

A waitress arrived with tea. Babajan, inhaling more smoke, reached up for his cup. Whether Babajan knocked the teacup or the waitress dropped it, Azadi couldn't say because he wasn't really watching. In either case, the cup fell onto Babajan's lap, soaking his crotch in hot tea. Babajan screamed in pain. Azadi saw Babajan shoot to his feet and swing his hand back and above his head, threatening to hit the waitress and hit her hard.

"Stupid cow," shouted Babajan. "Look at what you've done!"

Azadi jolted upright, the mild narcotic effect of the tobacco fell away from his consciousness like the scarf from the head of the waitress as she leapt backward. He grabbed Babajan's hand before it could strike the woman and yanked it behind Babajan's back, holding him at bay. Azadi had reacted so fast to Babajan's threat of violence that it took another few seconds for him to register that the waitress, begging for forgiveness and pulling her head scarf back in place, was the most beautiful woman he had ever seen.

-:::::-

Azadi and Parisa Halajeh ate lunch together in a poor Iranian imitation of McDonald's called Super MacBurger. Less than an hour before Babajan had threatened to call the manager of the tea garden and have her fired. Parisa had told him not to bother because she was quitting. She had marched out of the tea garden, scarf-covered head held high. Azadi had ignored Babajan's pleas to let her go. Instead, he had followed her, catching up to her outside as a cold rain began to fall. It had been necessary for him to reach out and put a hand on her shoulder — gently, not as a threat – to get her to stop. She had reeled around and admonished him not to touch her. He had agreed that he had been wrong to do so; in that moment he would have agreed to confess all his crimes to this paradigm of Persian beauty.

Parisa's café-au-lait skin was molded across high cheekbones. She was tall, almost as tall as he was, but as slim as a ballerina. He imagined that her legs, sadly hidden under her long coat, were toned and tanned. Her hair was thick and black with bronze highlights. Azadi, with the eye for detail that was his particular gift, recognized her as an Iranian Audrey Hepburn from "Breakfast at Tiffany's."

"Would you like to get lunch?" he'd asked, hungry for her company rather than food.

She had laughed at his question. She told him that she found his directness dangerous but refreshing. Didn't he know that an unmarried man and woman could not be seen socializing? Azadi had replied that he didn't care. She considered this and asked him if he cared for cheeseburgers. He said he loved them but realized for the first time in his life that the word "love" was to be used with the utmost precision from here on out.

So they sat in Super MacBurger eating and talking. He told her his life story, leaving out the incriminating parts but embellishing the good stuff. She didn't interrupt him and she didn't seem to want to tell him her story. After a few minutes, she told him she recognized him from all the media coverage and said that anything else she needed to know about him she could find out in the papers. They both laughed and he realized that he had indeed been talking almost non-stop. That wasn't like him but he felt like an entirely different person around her. The cheeseburger tasted like an ordinary cheeseburger. The French fries tasted like ordinary French fries. But something extraordinary was happening; Azadi felt it in his marrow as sure as one feels lightning in the air seconds before it strikes.

A neon sign behind the counter reminded the patrons to respect Islamic Moral Values. Portraits of various spiritual leaders looked down on the diners. There were more teenagers here, flirting by subterfuge under the scowling *mullahs* and neon warnings, acting the way normal kids act the world over. Parisa picked up on it and offered Azadi a generous smile.

"There is revolution in the air, isn't there?"

Azadi nodded and devoured her beauty along with the last of his cheeseburger. Revolution? Yes. But for Azadi, the revolution was not political but personal.

Omar Azadi was falling in love.

CHAPTER THIRTY-TWO

POLICE INSPECTOR Kamran Hadian loved to listen to his son Ahmad recite the Quran. The meaning of the words themselves did not inspire him. Hadian was a mediocre Muslim in practice, an agnostic at home, an atheist at heart. No, Hadian loved to listen to Ahmad recite the Quran because his son sang the words in an ethereal falsetto, as beautiful as a nightingale. That was the secret to memorizing the Quran: sing it. Muhammad himself had said to melodiously recite the Quran was the best way to learn it. And when Ahmad attached his lovely voice to the words of Allah and his messenger Muhammad, Hadian felt infused by the rare light of divine inspiration, not to mention the cheap kick of fatherly pride.

Father and son were sitting on a bench in Laleh Park on a drizzly December afternoon. As Ahmad's voice lifted into the leaden sky, Hadian thought back to a day more than 30 years earlier, a cool wet December day very much like this one. He remembered a massive demonstration at Tehran University just a few blocks away. He was a student at the University then but completely apolitical. The communists, the nationalists, the religious fanatics had all come to recruit him but once they sniffed around his dorm room they were discouraged by his large collection of Beatles albums and "The Incredible Hulk" comic books.

All this suited Hadian fine. He loved his country and detested the Shah, but he was no revolutionary. He was an observer who was content watching the wheels go round as his hero, John Lennon, had sung; and that was all he intended to do that fateful December day a quarter of a century ago.

He couldn't recall what the demonstration had been about. There were so many in those early days of the revolution. But he could remember gunfire and a boy in his comparative literature class lying in a pool of his own blood. He remembered running east with two boys from his organic chemistry class, the sound of gunfire small and sharp like firecrackers in the distance. He remembered an Army truck rumbling past as the classmates hopped a fence and found themselves in an alley. He remembered the two other boys had bolted in opposite directions and disappeared before he could figure out which one to follow. He remembered he had heard a tank approach as soldiers were yelling. He had felt an unbearable tightness grip his chest, as if the Incredible Hulk were squeezing him in his giant green hands.

He remembered he had felt like he was going to die.

He remembered the girl darting from the doorway of the apartment building. He remembered her pushing him inside and the two of them collapsing in the doorway as a soldier from the street lobbed a grenade into the alley. He remembered the grenade exploding and his heart racing and clutching the girl as if she were a blanket and he were a child awakened by the monster under the bed in the middle of the night. He remembered crying then laughing with the girl in perfect unison. He remembered kissing her and tasting garlic on her lips and thinking garlic had never tasted so sweet. He remembered the terror in his heart turning into love. He remembered realizing without a shred of his usual self-doubt that Allah or some other great unseen force in the universe had put this girl on earth to be his guardian angel, his soul mate, his best friend, his lover, his wife –

"Poppa, are you okay?"

Hadian's memories crawled back under the carpet of consciousness. His eyes focused and he saw Ahmad standing before him.

"What did you say?"

"You were staring off into space, like you were dreaming with your eyes open."

Hadian smiled and stroked his beardless chin. "I was just sitting here watching the wheels go round and round."

Ahmad made a face. John Lennon again. He had long ago accepted that his father was a Beatles fanatic. He liked them, too, although he didn't get to listen to them much. His father kept his albums hidden in a secret opening beneath the kitchen floor so that the police could not confiscate them. He thought it funny that his father should have to do this since he was a policeman, too.

"What did you think of my recitation?"

Hadian stood and wrapped an arm around his son's shoulders. "I think you have conquered the Quran like Darius conquered the Egyptians. And for that, you deserve a reward."

Hadian's gaze traveled around the park. He was a superb observer, the best detective on the Tehran police force, and his unprepossessing appearance allowed him to see things that most detectives missed. He observed the park was empty. The bad weather had kept most people indoors.

Hadian saw his opportunity. He pulled a CD out of his coat pocket and held it close to his body. It was John Lennon's "Imagine."

Ahmad smiled when he saw the gift. "Thank you, poppa."

"You're welcome. I think it's his best solo album."

Ahmad knew the album well. His father had a vinyl disc copy stashed beneath the kitchen and played it every year around this time on the anniversary of John Lennon's death. Ahmad reached for the CD but Hadian stuffed it back in his coat pocket. "I'll hold on to it until we get home."

Ahmad frowned but did not protest. Hadian had gotten the CD from a pimp in exchange for not busting his top girl, a beauty from Esfahan who had been servicing a Korean electronics CEO at the

Laleh Hotel. A moral digression on Hadian's part perhaps, but great art demanded great sacrifices.

Hadian took his son by the hand and checked his watch in one motion. "Look at the time. Your mother will already have dinner waiting."

"But your promised me a kebab."

"So I did. Oh, well, we'll just tell your mother you have a stomach ache."

Hadian didn't mind lying. He loved his wife but she was a dreadful cook.

Hadian and Ahmad walked south towards the Tehran University campus and stopped at an excellent kebab stand on Engelab Boulevard, the huge east-west artery that cut through the heart of central Tehran. Hadian bought Ahmad a lamb kebab, then bought one for himself because it smelled so succulent. No matter. He'd eat his wife's dinner even if it was awful and he was stuffed.

The sun broke through the clouds. Father and son ate their kebabs while walking back to their apartment. Hadian felt joy in his heart. The simple pleasures were most important. A tasty kebab. A beloved son. Ahmad had been an unexpected blessing late in life long after Hadian and his wife had been told by countless doctors that they could never conceive.

Hadian began to whistle "*Beautiful Boy*," and Ahmad began to sing the lyrics, surprising Hadian who hadn't realized Ahmad knew them.

They turned off Hafez Avenue and stopped in front of their apartment building, where they lived in a two bedroom flat on the ground floor. Hadian opened the door and Ahmad dug into his father's coat pocket and grabbed the CD. As they walked inside the flat they continued to sing Lennon's lullaby to his son, Hadian letting his son's magical voice prop up his middling croaking.

Hadian immediately stopped singing as soon as he saw Colonel Tabriz standing in the foyer, his eyes black as two pools of oil in the desert. He had a cherry drink with crushed ice in his hand. Laden,

Hadian's wife, the girl who had saved his life so many years ago in the alley, stood behind Tabriz, a tight smile plastered on her round face.

Laden said, "Ahmad, why don't you go to your room?"

Ahmad was flushed, his cheeks as red as the cherry drink in Tabriz's glass. He was on such a high that he did not think twice about flashing the CD that Hadian had given him.

"But, mama, I haven't showed you the present that poppa–"

Laden stepped forward and flicked Ahmad's ear as if she were shooting a marble. Ahmad vanished like a vapor.

Laden said, "Colonel Tabriz, is there anything more I can get you?"

Tabriz smiled beneath his thick black mustache. "No, thank you."

Laden disappeared towards the kitchen to tend to the duck stew burning on the stove.

Hadian had not moved a muscle since entering his home. He stared at Tabriz's mustache and thought how feeble his own looked in comparison. Tabriz fixed him with a long stare.

"Black market imperialist music? Kamran Hadian, if you were not the best detective in the Tehran police department I think I would behead you."

Sour smoke drifted in from the kitchen. Hadian smelled burning duck. "I apologize, Colonel. I realize my digression is serious. A crime, in fact."

Hadian bowed by way of an apology. If Tabriz had an ax, he could have lopped off his head right there. "Your singing voice is the real crime. Tell me, where did your boy's talent come from?"

Hadian straightened himself. Tabriz was smiling again beneath that bushy mustache. "His mother sings like a bird but his taste in music is all his father's fault. Please, sit."

Hadian gestured towards the adjoining living room. Tabriz stood his ground. "I haven't the time and neither do you. The Ministry of Intelligence requires your expertise in a matter of national security."

Tabriz held out the cherry drink as if it were bugged with a remote transmitter. He was a man who was used to having doors opened for him and underlings around to anticipate his needs.

Hadian took the glass – the ice clinking as Hadian tried to control the shaking of his hand — and put it on a table standing 17 centimeters to Tabriz's left. Next he closed the sliding doors, sealing off Tabriz and himself in the foyer. When Tabriz was satisfied that Hadian had created an atmosphere of suitable privacy, he spoke.

"Nine days ago, a Lebanese patrol boat engaged two Israeli commandos in the waters off Beirut. One Israeli was killed. The other captured and released to Hezbollah's custody. Most unusual this prisoner. A black Jew. Some sort of African immigrant sympathetic to the Zionist cause. Hezbollah interrogated him, employing their usual methods, but the man revealed only scant details of his mission. It may be nothing – perhaps a decoy, but that is for you to find out."

Hadian stroked his chin as he tried to decode what he had been told. "Usual methods" meant torture. "Scant details" meant "more than I am willing to tell you." As usual, the Ministry of Intelligence, or VEVAK, was short on information, but Hadian knew the name was a misnomer. The government bureau was, in fact, less about intelligence and more about brute force. They were the revolutionary equivalent of the Shah's SAVAK. Their assassins were behind the deaths of dozens of journalists and political dissidents. Hadian loathed them. Tabriz, Hadian's old boss in the National Police, of which the Tehran Police Department was the largest segment, had tried to recruit Hadian to the Ministry of Intelligence when the boss himself had decided to go over. But, sensing a softness in Hadian's political convictions, he had rescinded the offer. Hadian had celebrated this rejection by making love to Laden all night long. However, Tabriz still called on Hadian to assist the Ministry whenever his detective skills were deemed essential to Iran's national security. This, to Hadian's displeasure, was one of those times.

"What were these 'scant details,' if I may be so bold in asking, sir?"

"The Israeli spoke of an American. When pressed, he revealed, in English, that the mission was about 'dead presidents.'"

Hadian searched Tabriz's face for more information but the man's expression was utterly indifferent. He spoke the words in English, as Tabriz had done.

"Dead presidents?"

Tabriz nodded. His eyes were blank.

Hadian resumed speaking in Farsi.

"An assassination, perhaps. The Israelis have planted an American assassin in the Middle East. But if he's in Lebanon, why assume our president is the target?"

"Because the president is visiting there next month. Moreover, the Ministry has intercepted communications from several dissident groups that the President of the Islamic Republic is a target. As you well know, many of our countrymen feel the president has not acted swiftly enough on promised reforms. They would not be averse to seeing him replaced by whatever means necessary. As you also well know, the United States has an interest in seeing this regime collapse so the US can continue their imperialistic plundering of the Middle East. Rest assured, security around the president has been increased appropriately."

Hadian licked his lips. He suddenly felt an overwhelming thirst. The lamb kebab he had eaten earlier was salty and he had neglected to buy a beverage…

"Colonel Tabriz, what exactly would you like me to do with this information?"

"I would like you to question recently arrived foreigners in Tehran, paying particular attention to Americans and those who fit an assassin's profile. It is possible that the attempt may take place here in the city. It is also possible that there may be several assassins working together to ensure success. The Ministry has some experience in these matters."

A greater understatement was never spoken, thought Hadian.

"Colonel, with all due respect, you do not give me very much to work with."

"You have worked with much less. That is your special gift, Hadian, is it not?"

Tabriz gave Hadian another smile beneath his mustache. He moved towards the front door and waited for Hadian to open it. Tabriz then disappeared into the evening.

Hadian closed the door. The smell of scorched duck filled the apartment. He turned and saw Laden waiting for him in the foyer. Her round face did not wear worry well, crinkling in strange places and bloating in others. She was no beauty, he knew, even back when she had saved his life in that alley so many years ago. But no other woman could love him as unconditionally as she did. He was going to work for murderers because he had no choice. Despite his country's terrible flaws, he loved Iran nearly as much as his family. And Laden understood this and forgave him without as much as a word.

He took her in his arms and kissed her, and his thirst disappeared in the salty tears streaming down her cheeks.

-::::-

At approximately the same time the Iranian police officer was kissing his wife, Farragut was finishing up his lecture at the British Embassy with a direct quote from Lord Curzon's conclusion to *Persia and Persian Question.*

"The Persian character has ever been fertile in device and indifferent to suffering," read Farragut aloud. "And in the field of judicial executions it has found ample scope for the exercise of both attainments. Up till quite a recent period, well within the borders of the present reign, condemned criminals have been crucified, blown from guns, buried alive, impaled, shod like horses, torn asunder by being bound to the heads of two trees bent together and then allowed to spring back to their natural position, converted into human torches, flayed while living."

Farragut closed the book, looked up at his audience and said, "In conclusion, as this paragraph so clearly demonstrates, Curzon was too twisted by Victorian English prejudices to be anything but the most unreliable reporter of nineteenth century Persia. Anyone beg to differ?"

"Excuse me, Professor Farragut."

Farragut nodded at Ingrid who was raising her hand like the polite girl at boarding school she had once been. "Yes, Frau Mader. You have a question?"

"Just one. Will you join me for dinner tonight?"

Farragut laughed and snapped the book shut. "It would be my pleasure," he said.

There was no reason to be discrete. Ingrid was the only audience member left in the handsome, book-lined library of the British embassy that smelled of lemon wood polish. Farragut didn't take the lack of interest in his lecture personally. The event had been sparsely attended in the first place, the audience consisting of four bored, expatriate housewives who had begged off after an hour of Farragut's pointed refutation of Curzon's imperialist, anti-Persian attitudes. They, after all, had a more pressing engagement: a bridge game.

"Was I that boring?" asked Farragut as Ingrid helped him collect his books. "That's the problem with the world today. People would rather watch television than read a book."

She shut him up with a kiss on the mouth. Then she pulled back.

"I love when you get all grumpy. It's very sexy."

They had dinner in his room at the Laleh. Room service hamburgers. Ingrid smuggled in a bottle of fine German Riesling that was unfortunately a bad match for the burgers — too fruity. But Farragut didn't mind. The fact that Ingrid was a good match for him was much more important. And after they had made love, deep in the fog of the hours before dawn, he held her in his arms and felt her heart beating in her chest and the lovely curve of her back and the salty taste of her mouth. She was so damn alive. At that moment, he thought of asking her to join him in London. The thought of a few days alone with her in his favorite city made his stomach go light with excitement. But then he remembered he didn't know when exactly he would be going to London. Or when Azadi would infiltrate the Press and print the counterfeit money that would make the trip to London possible. All Farragut could do was wait and play the part of the visiting professor. But the thing with Ingrid was beginning to feel less like acting and more like the most wonderful reality he'd ever experienced.

CHAPTER THIRTY-THREE

AZADI STOOD before the Emam Khomeini Mosque in the center of the Tehran bazaar, searching for Parisa. Why she had picked this place to meet, he didn't know. So many of the faithful were buzzing about, some using the mosque, others passing through on their way to the bazaar, that he wondered how he would ever find her in the crush of humanity.

"Omar. Over here."

Azadi turned and there Parisa was. She was observing *hijab*, covering herself from view. But her tea garden uniform of a brown coat and black scarf had been replaced. She now wore an elegant, multi-colored coat. It flashed in the winter sun like a peacock's feathers. A scarf the color of fine claret covered her head and shoulders. He walked up to her and was about to kiss her (albeit chastely on the cheek) when she waved her hands in front of him and stepped back.

"No. Please don't touch me. It wouldn't be proper."

"I'm sorry. I was just trying to be nice," said Azadi, hating himself for sounding like a schoolboy playing spin-the-bottle with the eighth grade prom queen.

"Do you have to *try* to be nice, Omar? It doesn't come naturally to you?"

Azadi fumbled for a response. He didn't know how to read Parisa. But there was that smile again and he realized that she was kidding.

"So, what do you want to do today?" he asked.

"Today? Today we go to the mosque and pray."

And before he could object, Parisa dove into a dark river of chador-covered women entering the mosque. Azadi found a corresponding pack of men and, for the first time since he had been in the Islamic Republic of Iran, Omar Azadi fulfilled this most basic act of Islam.

A gigantic dome rose to the heavens in the middle of mosque. The dome amplified the sound of the large crowd and distorted it. Azadi looked in vain for Parisa, trying to see beyond the white curtain that separated the sexes in the mosque. Then he looked around at his fellow Muslims and was surprised by the variety he found. Some of the men wore stylish shirts and hid their eyes behind sunglasses. Other men wore traditional robes and their eyes flashed with the peculiar fervor of fanatics. Young men and old, prosperous and poor, prayed together.

Azadi knelt barefoot, prostrate on the floor, hands on his knees, nose and palms to the ground. And then he rose to the sitting position. And then he went back down again. And it was strange because he had not been in a mosque since he was eighteen but a serene sense of peace and contentment came over him. Maybe it was the solidarity of being surrounded by so many of faith. And maybe it was his infatuation for a woman that he hardly knew. Or maybe it really was a connection to God in all his glory and greatness.

The intensity of emotion he had felt in the mosque confused him. When he met Parisa outside afterwards, he felt the sensation of weightlessness and vulnerability to emotions he couldn't control.

"How was it? Was it not incredible?" she asked behind a smile bordering on beatific.

He gave the question more consideration than he should have and chose his words carefully, even though they had been words suggested to him by Kelly for just such an occasion.

"Look. I don't mean to offend you or anything," he said, coughing into his hand to telegraph his discomfort at the subject. "It's just that I have my own set of beliefs."

"I understand. Religion is a personal and private matter. It is not a competitive sport, although many in Iran see it that way."

Azadi nodded, contemplating the aptness of this analogy. Then she blew him away with the outrageousness of her next statement.

"Let's get married," she said.

Azadi stared at Parisa but she was straight-faced. Was she being funny? Was she insane? She handed him a gold wedding band. He noticed that she had slipped one on already, probably in the mosque. She definitely hadn't been wearing one earlier.

"You're serious?"

"Yes."

"But I hardly know you."

"Put it on. If anyone asks, and the rings should guarantee that they don't, we are a married couple. As I told you before, an unmarried couple cannot be seen walking together."

Azadi nodded and put on the ring. It was impulsive. It was crazy. He loved it.

-:::::-

"The bazaar is the beating heart of the Iranian capital," Parisa had explained as they walked down corridors crammed with copper pots, carpets spices, and fruit. They stopped in front of a vendor wearing a skullcap. He was haggling over the price of an intricately detailed rug with an obese man in a brown robe. Parisa's voice was low and for Azadi only.

"The merchants in the bazaar remain a pillar of support for the Islamic regime. They tend to be much more conservative than the average Iranian."

"People with money tend to be conservative," offered Azadi, though he could think of plenty of examples in LA where that wasn't the case.

Parisa flashed a playful smile. "Oh? And are you conservative, Omar?"

"If I had money I might be."

"Then I guess I'm lucky you're just a poor printer." She flashed him another smile, but this one was sexier and more ironic.

He laughed and said, "You never know. I might win the lottery someday."

"Sorry. Iran doesn't have a lottery."

No, Azadi thought, *but it has a US government printing press. And once we find it and blow it up, I'm in for ten million bucks.*

"I wish it did have a lottery," Parisa continued, her voice wistful as she watched the carpet merchant and his customer haggle. "I don't know any other way a university dropout like me can make enough money to get out of this country."

A darkness descended over Parisa's lovely features and she walked away from the stall. Azadi followed her, concerned. For the past hour Parisa's mood had been buoyant as she talked about movies (she loved the comedies of Pedro Almodovar and Judd Apatow, all of which she had seen courtesy of a friend who was a *filmi* – someone who rented black market DVD's). Her enthusiasm for these forbidden films had been so great that she didn't try to hide it, even as they strolled within earshot of men in frayed fatigues: the religious militia, the *Basij*.

"I hadn't realized that you went to college," observed Azadi, taking her arm and leading her back into the throng of shoppers.

"I was a performing arts major. An actress. I left with a year still to go for my degree."

He sensed sadness in her voice that he hadn't heard before. He squeezed her arm. "That's three years more than me. And there's no law that says you can't go back."

"I can't afford it. My parents divorced and there wasn't enough money to continue school."

The pain smoldering in Parisa's coal black eyes moved Azadi deeply. He barely knew her and yet she felt as familiar as the late afternoon breeze that kicked in like clockwork off the ocean in Marina Del Rey. That breeze. It would whip over the city west to east, lifting the wind chimes in his beachfront condo and creating intricate music from the interplay of metal and air that always made him feel at home. That's how he felt now with Parisa. Like he was home. He wanted to cherish her, protect her. Yes, he barely knew her but he felt like he'd known her all his life and that, in fact, his life — his *new* life — depended on keeping her close forever.

"I want to know everything about you," he whispered, surreptitiously squeezing her hand under the folds of her *chador*.

Parisa returned the squeeze and turned to face him. "Well, my dear *husband*, I must confess that the truth about me would only disappoint."

"I doubt that."

"It's true. A woman's personality, like her body, is best kept under wraps and left to the imagination. Women must learn to wear an emotional *chador*, as well as a physical one."

Her beauty made his heart beat faster. "I'm a printer, Parisa, not a poet. I don't have much of an imagination but I know quality when I see it. And what I see in you is something special. You shine."

"You are very sweet, my *husband*. But what is shining, is the gold."

They had stopped in front of a gold merchant's stall. The merchant, an elderly man with an eye patch, had just sold a bracelet the size of a Buick to an African in a dashiki.

"I would like to buy a gold chain for my husband," Parisa said to the merchant. "Price is no object."

The merchant beamed and waved a finger for her to wait while he picked out several chains from underneath the glass display case. Azadi rubbed his temples.

"Parisa. What are you doing?"

"It's like I said. I'm buying you a gold chain."

"But it's expensive and you just lost your job."

"My father left me some money when he died. Not much. Not enough to return to school. But enough to buy a bauble or two."

"I didn't know he had died. I'm sorry. And I'm also sorry but I can't accept such a generous gift from a woman I've just met."

He regretted the gaffe immediately. Parisa covered for him like a pro. "Just met? What a terrible thing for a husband to say to his wife," Parisa turned from Azadi to the merchant, who was holding up several gold chains. "Isn't that a terrible thing for a husband to say to his wife?"

The merchant vigorously nodded his agreement. Yes, terrible. He smelled a sale.

Despite Azadi's protests Parisa bought him a handsome gold chain that must have cost her plenty, although she wouldn't let him hear how much. When she slipped the chain around Azadi's neck she whispered, "The chain belongs to you but you belong to me." And he did, no doubt about it. No woman, let alone one that really couldn't afford it, had ever bought him such a nice gift.

He had miles of gold chains back home but Kelly, thinking he would appear too ostentatious, had told him not to bring them. And, of course, she had ordered him to steer clear of women. But that was the past. Here, in the present, there was only this one gold chain and this one woman. Parisa. The hell with Kelly.

"I think I could fall for a woman like you," confided Azadi as he and Parisa walked past a bored looking *Basiji* and out of the bazaar.

Parisa didn't say anything. She seemed finally happy to trust the silence and let their emotions fill in the blanks. They stopped outside the Golestan Palace. Intricate, colorful decorative patterns swarmed across the entire façade like the images in a child's kaleidoscope. The patterns made Azadi think of all the work he had put into engraving the Supernote plates. Where could this relationship with Parisa really go? Honestly, what was he doing?

Parisa said, "There was a monarch who lived in this palace who had over 200 wives."

"One is enough if it's the right one," said Azadi squeezing her hand but wanting to make love to her right there.

"Things are happening very fast between us, Omar."

She looked at him with some trepidation. And of course she was right. He had just met her. Kelly had warned him not to get involved and she was right, too. It was too risky. He was ready to break it off right there but Parisa glanced around to make sure nobody was looking and when she was sure nobody was she leaned over and kissed him on the lips and he was a goner.

-:::::-

"Perhaps there is something we can do," she whispered to him. "Something so that we can explore this relationship at a quicker, dare I say, more American, pace."

-:::::-

The next day he called the Interior Ministry. He called Mojgan, the female bureaucrat who had given him her card. He was at work but he made the call on a payphone a few blocks from Babajan's shop because he didn't want him snooping around. Mojgan got right on the line, her voice as chipper and expectant as a schoolgirl's.

"It's so good to talk to you again, Mr. Azadi. All of us at the Interior Ministry have been wondering about you. How have you been?"

"I've been very well, Mojgan" replied Azadi. "Look, let me tell you why I've called —"

"That is not necessary, I already know. You have finally accepted my offer for some home-cooked *khoresht fesenjaan.*"

"Excuse me, what?"

"That chicken dish? We ate it that first day in the cafeteria at the Interior Ministry?"

Azadi didn't like the happy lilt in Mojgan's voice. Poor, plain-faced Mojgan. He'd forgotten about her offer of dinner and her obvious crush on him. He didn't mean to be an asshole to her but he really had to get back to work and move this along.

"Mojgan, the reason I'm calling is not about your *khoresht*, it's about *sigheh*."

Now it was Azadi who listened to a long pause. "*Sigheh*?" croaked Mojgan.

"Am I pronouncing it right? *Sigheh*?" Another long pause. "Mojgan? Are you there?"

"Yes. *Sigheh*. Temporary marriage. What would you like to know about *sigheh*?"

"I've met someone. I'd like to know how I go about marrying her temporarily and whether you can help me."

The longest pause of the conversation followed. When Mojgan finally spoke, her voice was thin and strained. "I can help you, Mr. Azadi. And who will you be temporarily marrying?"

CHAPTER THIRTY-FOUR

OMAR AZADI temporarily married Parisa Halajeh two days later. The Interior Ministry speeded up the paperwork and helped push it through the appropriate religious authorities. While much of the world, and certainly the Sunni sect of Islam, looked down on temporary marriage as a barbaric custom peculiar to the more backward Shiite Muslims, the *mullahs* in Iran were more than happy to oblige their newest citizen who was both a minor celebrity and public relations poster boy. Temporary marriage had existed since the time of Muhammad and had been used primarily by pilgrims, for pilgrims who traveled had sexual needs. And though some Iranian clerics and many citizens considered *sigheh* nothing more than legalized prostitution, more powerful and practical heads did not concur. After all, a restless, young, chronically unemployed population meant often had to put off permanent marriage until they could afford it.

The marriage, as specified by Shiite tradition, had to be for a specific period of time, anywhere from a few minutes to 99 years. Azadi and Parisa chose to be married for six weeks. After that time, by mutual consent, they could agree to renew their contract or break it off. They also agreed that no money or dowry of any kind had to exchange hands. Virgins were supposed to get written permission from their fathers but Parisa's father was dead and she had no living male relatives so there was no family member that had to consent. Parisa's mother did not have the right to give consent and she chose not to attend, for she lived in Kuwait with her sister and her sister's husband and did not feel up to the trip. Azadi, friendless and without family, felt no compunction to invite anyone.

And of course, he didn't invite Ishmael. First, he hadn't seen the man in over a week and he didn't even know his real name, let alone how to get in touch with him. Second, if the cabbie knew that Azadi was seeing someone, much less married, there'd be hell to pay. In light of this Azadi had already laid down the law with Parisa. He would never go to her place. They always had to meet at his. He wanted this relationship to be as discrete as possible. He couldn't tell her the real reason for this. That he was a US spy sent to destroy an important piece of government property and was under surveillance by his spymasters. So he blamed it on his sense of decorum. He was new to this country and wanted to fit in. Flaunting his union with a young, beautiful Iranian woman would not endear him to his new countrymen, even if that union was now technically legal.

Tradition decreed that Parisa, as a previously unmarried woman, be a virgin on the day of her marriage but the reality of modern day Iran dictated that she only had to pretend to be one. She didn't have to pretend on their wedding night. No, Azadi thought she was a fine lover, not the best he'd ever had but then he'd had many, some quite professional. What Parisa lacked in experience and technique, she made up for in stamina, effort, and loveliness.

Four nights passed in rapid succession. They made love; they slept; they made love again. They tried to sleep and wound up talking. Well, Parisa talked. About religion. About the status of women in Iran. About American movies. About American music. About wanting to live in America someday. Azadi just nodded warned her that his room was probably bugged, as was the telephone. She'd laughed and told him that if the Islamic Republic of

Iran had nothing better to do than take offense at the musings of a 23-year-old unemployed waitress who had dropped out of college, well, things might be more dire than they appeared.

"Where did all this Scotch and caviar come from, my pet?" she whispered to him on their honeymoon night, crouched naked in his closet and looking wide-eyed at his stash of luxury.

"I'm a smuggler. A black market man, my sweet Parisa," he whispered in her ear while cupping her smooth buttocks in his callused hands. "You talk about getting rid of the system but I actually do something about it. I'm rotting it from the inside out."

And then on their fourth night of temporary wedded bliss, while he was pre-occupied with opening up another tin of caviar, he heard singing – rapping actually – in uncertain English. He turned around and saw her dancing naked in the center of the room as dawn leaked through the bedroom window. She had found his iPod.

Azadi watched his beloved rapping and strutting along to the late, great Tupac's "All Eyez on Me." There was something so playful and sexy about it despite her awful voice. He grew hard in front of her. She noticed and smiled. Then she pulled off the headphones and took the caviar from him and spooned some into his mouth.

"Black market American music?" she laughed. "You really are a subversive!"

Azadi shrugged. If the Iranians had his room bugged, the cat was already out of the bag and there was nothing he could do about it now. "Rap is the music of the oppressed in America," he said with a mouth full of caviar. "Am I a subversive in Iran if I listen to music that comments on the corruption of the godless capitalist society?"

Shit. I sound like some geek on National Public Radio, he thought. But Parisa didn't seem to mind. She gave him a kiss and led him back to bed.

"I love American music, too. I learned English listening to the Britney Spears. My parents were horrified."

"Listening to crap like Britney Spears? I'm not surprised."

"What? No. It wasn't the quality of the music but the fact that it was forbidden —"

He kissed her on the mouth and shut her up. She kissed him and demanded that he make love to her. So he made love to her and after the sex, she talked about how Iran would always be weak because half its people, its female population, lived in abject slavery. Yeah, right, he'd laugh. No one was twisting her arm to make love and drink Scotch and spoon yet more precious caviar onto that sharp tongue of hers. A slave, indeed!

But after Parisa would fall asleep, Azadi would lie awake and try to rationalize his actions even as doubt and uncertainty flashed through his brain. Yes, maybe he'd been reckless with this marriage but...fuck it. He deserved some fringe benefits. He was putting his ass on the line for America with this mission. Remember THE MISSION? Where the fuck was Ishmael anyway? When was the so-called liaison going to get him into the Press anyway? Fuck the Press. Fuck the mission. Fuck Ishmael. I like fucking Parisa and I deserve fucking Parisa. No, not fucking. With Parisa, I make love because I'm falling in love, even while this mission falls off a cliff.

CHAPTER THIRTY-FIVE

JASHNI, A.K.A Ishmael, would not have agreed with Azadi's negative assessment. From where he sat two weeks after cutting off contact, undercover in the front of his cab but also at the nexus of the three Americans responsible for the mission, he felt quite confident. Sepanlou had been taken out of the equation, rather too theatrically for Jashni's taste, but thoroughly none the less. Farragut had proven that he possessed the necessary *sang-froid* and the recruitment of the German Ambassador's wife had been an inspired touch, too. Further afield but just as importantly, Israeli intelligence, with which Jashni was in daily contact, had confirmed the arrival of Salaam in Beirut and his meeting with that Hezbollah butcher, Hasan Shehabi. Two brave sons of Zion had been lost getting Salaam into Beirut, true, but that was a small price to pay for luring that twisted-mouthed murderer into the trap.

And then there was Omar Azadi, no doubt sweating out the seemingly random disappearance of his guide and good friend, Ishmael the cabbie. But being a solitary foot soldier, Jashni had been forced to focus his limited time but boundless energy to the task of trailing the idiot Babajan. He had observed the nephew journeying to his Uncle Farjad's office no less than three times in the days following Azadi's revelation of his criminal past. Information was being relayed, decisions being made. Jashni assumed that Farjad wouldn't commit to replacing Sepanlou with Azadi unless he had checked the American out thoroughly. For that, the Revolutionary Guards would probably turn to the professional agents of the Ministry of Intelligence, VEVAK, or so Jashni thought. Even a seasoned Mossad man like Jashni was never quite sure who was responsible for what in the labyrinth that was the Iranian police state.

The Iranians would be trailing Azadi, staying very close. They knew the Iranian-American was a crook but they had to make sure he was just crooked enough to betray America but not so crooked as to betray Iran. It was a fine line and Jashni had no idea how the Iranians made that decision, but he knew they had to make it soon. A Mossad tap on Professor Ardabili's phone had confirmed it. On the day of Sepanlou's assassination, quite coincidentally, the Iranian government had decided to buy the stolen bull's head that Farragut had so graciously volunteered to retrieve from England. That would mean the Iranians needed counterfeit cash. That would mean after Sepanlou's demise that they needed someone to print the counterfeit cash. That would mean they needed Azadi. It was going to happen. It was only a matter of time.

-:::::-

Jashni pulled up the to the trendy hair salon frequented by wealthy Iranians and foreigners. His fare was a faded beauty wearing too much make-up and an elegant coat trimmed with gold thread. He thanked her profusely when she paid him in dollars. That was her way of thanking him for making such good time but also to show him that she moved in circles that he could only dream about. But Jashni rather liked the life of a cab driver. Make your own hours, not tied to a desk, plenty of scenery and interesting people watching. He drove around for the rest of the afternoon and picked up a few more fares. At 7:32 that night, he decided it was time to re-establish contact and relieve Omar Azadi of his insecurity.

Jashni pulled up to the cinema, an agreed upon meeting point for that day, albeit agreed upon more than two weeks ago. Azadi was the first person out of the theater, as he had been told to be, so that he could flag the first cab. He flung open the door and settled into his seat, slamming the door shut. He glared at Jashni as the cab pulled into the street.

"Ishmael, you motherfucker. Where the fuck have you been?"

Jashni smiled at Azadi in the rear view mirror. "Milan, for the men's summer collections. I've decided to chuck this life and become a runway model."

"Is that a joke? Because I don't feel like fucking laughing after you've had me cooling my heels for two fucking weeks."

"Relax, Omar," said Jashni, taking note of a green Citroen in their rear view mirror. It had been following them since the cinema. "I'm just a cab driver engaged for a ride. We are strangers. We might talk about the movie you have just seen. There is no reason in either the fiction or the fact for you to lose your cool. I told you that I might cut off contact at times. You must get used to it. If I had not cut you off, the Iranians would have watched me watching you. We can't have watchers watching the watchers now, can we?"

Jashni turned on a side street and then another one. The Citroen was still in sight, following their route. If they stopped his cab, Jashni could always argue he wasn't trying to shake them, he was finding a shortcut around the traffic. It would be impossible to disprove.

"Listen to me carefully, Omar. The wheels have been set in motion and your services are now required at the Press. But the Revolutionary Guards are not going to allow you into their inner sanctum until they feel absolutely confident about who you are."

"When will that be?"

"Never, actually. They will increase their surveillance of you after you have been allowed into the Press. But they need to recruit you very soon. It is a question of hours. Tomorrow, probably. The day after tomorrow at the outside. Are you ready?"

Azadi could feel his bowels quiver with anxiety. "Yeah. We're ready."

"It's not "*we*" that have to do this. *You* will be alone in that Press. I will be around but I may not be close for long periods. *You* will be on your own."

The prick, thought Azadi. *Doesn't he realize that I've been looking over my shoulder and flying solo my whole life?* But the thought of how Parisa fit into the scheme was something that bothered him. If the Iranians were watching him, they were watching her. Then again, the government had allowed him to marry so maybe it didn't matter. What would he tell her? Nothing. Which is what he would tell Ishmael about Parisa. It was none of his business.

"Now, remember the caviar," said Jashni as he pulled up to Azadi's apartment.

"I'll remember. But I still think it's a mistake to try to slip it past on the first day."

"If the caviar doesn't work, we'll have to improvise a new way to get the explosives into the Press," said Jashni, watching the blue Renault drive past. "So we have to know as soon as possible what we're dealing with. We talked about this. Remember?"

The green Citroen was approaching from the other end of the street. Azadi didn't notice the driver of the Citroen looking at him as it drove past but Jashni did.

"I remember," said Azadi. "I remember everything."

"Aren't you forgetting something," said Jashni after Azadi had already exited the cab and was turning to walk to the front door of his apartment building.

Azadi turned around. "Forgetting what?"

Jashni held out his palm. "My fare."

Azadi had indeed forgotten to pay the cab fare but since when had he ever paid it? The cabbie signaled with a flash of his eyes that "they were watching." So Azadi paid the fare to pay heed to the fiction. The cab drove away and Azadi was alone. As he stuffed his wallet back in his pocket, he appreciated Ishmael's professionalism.

What he didn't appreciate, however, was that the cabbie had stiffed him on the change.

-:::::-

Parisa was waiting for him in the apartment. She was sprawled out on the bed in her underwear, listening to Kanye West on his iPod and reading a reformist paper. He sat beside her, kissed her, and pulled the earphones from her head.

"I think, after tonight, we should give each other a little space," he said.

She shrugged. He continued. "It's not that I'm not having an amazing time. I am. But I'm going to be very busy at work for the next week and I could use some sleep for a change."

She started dressing. "That's fine. I like to keep it fresh." She wriggled into her tight jeans. Her ass looked so perfect in them it took Azadi's breath away. "But it seems like something else is on your mind."

"It's nothing, really," he lied. "I'm not used to be being married and I need some space."

"Yes, you said that. Space. What do you mean by space?"

I mean I'm going to be working at the Supernote Press to strike back at the country you can't stand, dear Parisa, Azadi imagined saying. *Space means I'm radioactive to you. Do not get within a hundred miles of me or you will be sucked into my vortex of deceit and bullshit.*

Azadi kissed Parisa on the forehead. "I just need a few days by myself. Let's have dinner next Wednesday and you'll stay for a few more days."

"Okay," she said, pulling on a long coat to cover the tight jeans.

"This isn't goodbye for good, you know?"

She laughed and shoved her hair underneath her headscarf. "I think I can survive a few days without you, Omar Azadi. You are not that irresistible."

But the desperate way Parisa kissed him goodbye exposed her lie. He offered to call her a cab but she refused. He fingered the gold chain around his neck, the gift she had given him, as he watched her from his window, walking to the bus stop, past the watchers and the watchers of the watchers, under a crescent moon that any other night he would've thought meant good luck.

CHAPTER THIRTY-SIX

THE NEXT MORNING Azadi was finishing up his morning tea but was already dressed. The sharp knocks summoning him to answer his door had a military precision. Azadi took a deep breath to calm himself and opened the door.

"Omar Azadi, I am General Farjad of the Revolutionary Guards. You will please come with us this instant."

General Farjad looked nothing like his nephew Babajan. He was tall and thin with a full head of gray hair and a well-trimmed beard. His black eyes flashed a sober, sharp intelligence. Like the two men at his side, he wore fatigues and a sidearm.

"Who are you people?" asked Azadi in Farsi, keeping the door held wide open.

Farjad and the two men with machine guns didn't wait to be asked in. They pushed past Azadi into the apartment. Azadi kept his eyes on Farjad.

"I have to go to work. If there is a problem perhaps my friends in the Ministry —"

"I am the uncle of your employer, Babajan," said Farjad in Farsi, as if this explained everything.

Azadi closed the door. "I'll come. Is it okay if I use the bathroom first?"

Farjad nodded. "I think you had better. We will be taking a very long drive."

Azadi walked to the bathroom. Farjad signaled to one of the soldiers to follow. Azadi entered the bathroom and closed the door on the soldier's face. He pulled his underwear down and urinated, making sure to shoot into the toilet water so that the racket would let them know that he was really urinating. When he had relieved himself, he removed the small 1.75-ounce tin of caviar from his front pocket where he had put it that morning in anticipation that they would come. He transferred the tin to his crotch and secured it by pulling up his underwear. It looked like he was hung like a horse. He rinsed his hands and exited the bathroom.

Farjad signaled one of the soldiers. The soldier frisked Azadi from his ankles to his neck, his fingers running over every part of his body, except, of course, for his crotch – a place where no man is comfortable frisking another, especially in a homophobic, fundamentalist Muslim theocracy. Satisfied, the soldier turned to Farjad and nodded.

Farjad said, "The plates, Mr. Azadi. Where are they?"

"Plates?" replied Azadi, furrowing his brow in a bad approximation of befuddlement.

"Please. My nephew saw you with the printing plates for American counterfeit currency. I would like to examine them. Please."

Azadi stared at the soldiers with the AK-47's. "In the bedroom. In my mattress."

Farjad nodded at the two soldiers. They marched into Azadi's bedroom. Azadi stared at his shoes. They needed a shine. Farjad stared at Azadi. The two soldiers returned. One handed Farjad the plates and Azadi watched Farjad examine them. The general removed an eyepiece from his breast pocket and examined the plates for several minutes, then handed the plates to one of the soldiers, telling him to return the plates to where he found them.

"Nice work," Farjad told Azadi, doling out a smile.

They asked him to close his eyes and then they blindfolded him. They insisted it was for his benefit. They led him outside to the street and secured him in the back seat of a car that was parked just outside his apartment. The car smelled like stale Turkish cigarettes. Azadi could feel the anemic winter sun shining on his face. It was morning; the sun rises in the east so he thought that they must have been driving east. But then, after a few minutes, he was aware of the car turning right and then left and then left again and then he wasn't sure of the direction. Then he had the sensation of going down a ramp and a darker darkness descending on his blindfolded eyes. They were probably in an underground parking garage. The sound of the car's brakes echoed as if indoors.

They kept his blindfold on as they helped him into the back seat of another car. This car smelled like coffee. He couldn't hear anyone sipping coffee and no one had offered him any. Maybe someone had spilled coffee on the seats the day before. Or a week before. They drove for another half-hour. No, closer to 20 minutes. He heard traffic noise. He thought he heard a plane overhead. No one in the car talked. Someone smoked. No one offered him a cigarette. He again had the sensation of driving down into an underground garage. They helped him into the back of a truck. It must have been a truck because he had to step up to get into it. He heard two doors slam, like the doors at the back of a truck. He sat not on a car seat but what felt like a stretcher. He smelled rubbing alcohol and cotton and…vomit? Yes, the faint but unmistakable smell of vomit.

They drove in silence for 609 seconds (Azadi counted), or roughly ten minutes. Then he heard a siren start up. The siren definitely came from their vehicle. They drove with the siren for a long time. His best guess was for 30 minutes. Then it was switched off for…his best guess was for twelve minutes. All the while, they twisted and turned in the city streets but his sense of direction failed him. He heard horns honking. Cars accelerating. He felt a little sick. He dozed for an indeterminate amount of time. He woke up when someone nudged him in the ribs.

"You were snoring," said one of the soldiers sitting next to him.

"Where are we?" said Azadi.

"We are there," said Farjad from the somewhere in front of him.

They helped him out of the vehicle and walked him through what sounded like an underground parking garage. He could again hear the echo of brakes. They stopped and got onto an elevator. They insisted that he put in wax earplugs. They put the plugs in his ears. He lost most of his hearing. He had the sensation of moving up in the elevator.

The elevator stopped. They exited. He sensed they were walking him through a large room. He smelled disinfectant. He heard the murmur of people but could not distinguish individual voices. By adjusting his head he was able to peek under his blindfold as the person passed by. He noticed the man's white doctor's coat and the stitching on his breast: Gheyam Hospital.

Gheyam Hospital. The best hospital in Tehran. He had been born in Gheyam Hospital. The thought occurred to him: if he screwed this up, he was going to die in Gheyam Hospital, too.

They led him forward. He sensed doors closing. They began to ascend in the elevator.

They removed his blindfold and yanked out his earplugs. He saw the two soldiers were looking at General Farjad for their cue. Farjad stared at Azadi and threw out his left arm so suddenly that Azadi thought he was trying to hit him. But that was not the case. He yanked his arm back and clamped his hand over his chest in a theatrical demonstration of wounded pride.

"I apologize for the inconvenience. But what we're asking you to do is serious business."

"What do you want me to do? Tell me. I have a right to know."

Don't be a pushover, Kelly had said. *They will know at that point that you are a crook. Show them that you are also tough. They do not respect weakness.*

"You will understand soon enough," said Farjad behind a tight-lipped smile.

One of the soldiers started to put back Azadi's blindfold but Farjad shook his head "no." Azadi noticed that the blindfold was actually a gauze bandage. He must've looked like a patient and that was why he had attracted no attention while being moved through the hospital.

They arrived at the fifth floor. They exited the elevator and walked in silence down the clean, quiet corridor. Azadi could hear the hum of fluorescent lights but little else. Azadi couldn't see into the rooms but the subdued shuffle of the doctors and nurses suggested that the patients in this part of the building were very sick. They stopped at a room. The two men with AK-47's stood outside while Farjad took Azadi's elbow and led him inside.

Azadi smelled it before he saw it. He rammed his eyelids shut so that he wouldn't have to see it. He was afraid to open his eyes because of that smell.

He smelled burned flesh. He fought the urge to vomit. He heard the sounds of medical monitoring equipment, and then the mournful voice of General Farjad.

"This is Farhad Sepanlou. He was a magnificent printer, a hero and a true friend to the Islamic Revolution. He was my friend, too. He will not live much longer because I have told the doctors not to treat him aggressively. Do honor to his memory, Mr. Azadi."

Azadi realized this was "the vacancy" at the Press Ishmael had talked about. He couldn't hold his breath any longer. He breathed in deep and then, gasping for air, opened his eyes.

He saw what was left of Sepanlou. His predecessor was unconscious, breathing through a respirator. His body was swollen like a sponge left in a bucket of rusty water. His skin, although technically it was whatever existed below the skin for his skin was burned away, was mottled brown, red, and white and covered with some sort of shiny, translucent.

"No more games," said Farjad. "Normally, I would have put back on your blindfold and driven around some more because I have to trust you and I don't trust you yet. But I can see you are a good man. I can see that I should trust you. So, okay, no more games."

They left the room. Azadi couldn't flush the smell of scorched flesh from his nostrils, even as they got back onto the elevator and descended back down. No one talked.

They exited the elevator and walked down a long corridor on the first floor level. Azadi noticed that the patients in this area were young children. Some children sat in wheelchairs; others lay on gurneys. Some walked, pushing their IV drips on wheeled racks. Male nurses attended most of the children who all had the dull, drugged look of the terminally ill. Some children were bald. Azadi realized they were walking through a children's cancer ward.

A sympathetic human shield will protect the Press, Kelly had told him.

And then he knew it for sure. They weren't here for Sepanlou at all. Sepanlou was just foreplay. They were *there*. The Press was in Gheyam Hospital.

CHAPTER THIRTY-SEVEN

AT THE END of the cancer ward, they arrived at a heavy steel door marked "Security." Two other armed men in fatigues, AK-47's slung behind their backs, were standing outside the door. These guards remained outside while the other men entered a large room. Several video monitor screens revealing scratchy black and white images were built into a console of fake-looking wood. The far wall was a large, steel panel. An armed guard stood by an ancient water cooler, coaxing the water to drip into his chipped coffee mug by kicking the cooler at the base. It took several seconds for him to turn around and notice his visitors. When he did, he saluted sharply and removed a key from his pocket. He stuck the key into a slot by the steel panel wall. The doors opened, revealing a large elevator.

Azadi's mouth was dry but he didn't ask for water. He followed his guards and Farjad into the elevator. The doors closed on them and the elevator descended. No one talked. By his estimation, they had descended for two minutes. They were deep below the earth.

The elevator stopped. The doors opened on another armed guard. Azadi looked beyond him at the steel-paneled corridor stretching about 70 yards. At the other end stood two more armed guards. And just behind the guards loomed another massive steel door.

Azadi, Farjad, and his guards walked towards the door.

"We are 200 feet below the hospital," said Farjad. "This facility was built as an emergency command post in 1981, the second year of the war with Iraq. It is impenetrable to electronic eavesdropping, poison gas, and can withstand a direct strike by a cruise missile or an American bunker-busting bomb. We have high hopes for our work here. You should be proud to be a part of it."

Azadi was already thinking ahead, not to creating the counterfeit but to how he would escape from this catacomb. Two hundred feet underground? A hospital filled with armed guards and angry civilians? They hadn't trained for this. *Relax*, he told himself. *Those Delta Force boys back at Fort Bragg are total professionals. They'll know what to do once I relay the details of the layout to Ishmael. Relax... relax... It's ShowTime...*

They arrived at the massive door. Azadi stood stiffly, Farjad at his side, with one guard down the far end of the corridor and four guards with guns right in front of his face. Azadi was the only man without a gun. So why were they running a metal detector over him alone?

The metal detector screeched as it passed his crotch. The guard with the metal detector stepped back for his comrade to point his gun at Azadi. The two guards that had escorted Azadi from his apartment grabbed him from opposite ends and drove him to the floor. Azadi hit the polished steel hard. He felt his arms yanked behind his back. He felt a hand reach into his pants and grab his crotch. He heard Farjad's voice. It must have been Farjad's hand groping his balls.

"Idiot! Do you have a gun down there?"

They yanked him to his feet, his arms still behind his back. He saw Farjad's face staring at the tin of caviar in his hand. Then he turned his withering gaze upon the soldier who had frisked Azadi back at the apartment.

The two guards at the door had their guns trained on Azadi but their show of force lacked conviction, for they both stifled smiles. Azadi knew he wasn't going to get shot, at least not right away. He found his courage and spit out the response Kelly had coached him to say.

"It's only caviar. When you came for me I was on my way out to bring it to a friend and I forgot I had it and…you take it instead. Please. Take it as a gift from a grateful citizen."

Farjad waved the tin in front of Azadi's face and said, "You are in the habit of leaving your apartment with caviar stuffed down your pants?"

"Yes. I mean, no. I mean in the off-chance that I was stopped and searched, I thought it would elude detection."

"Evidently, you're right," said Farjad, glaring at the soldier who had searched Azadi in his apartment. Farjad turned his attention back to the caviar tin. "This is black market caviar?"

"Please. It is for all of you," pleaded Azadi, ignoring the question.

Azadi swallowed hard. Kelly was right. The Iranians knew about the black market booze. They knew about the counterfeit plates. They knew it all and they still wanted him. A little black market caviar wasn't going to sour the deal. It did, in fact, seal it.

Farjad found his smile so quickly, it was startling. He pocketed the caviar to the forced laughter and envious looks of the uniformed enlisted men.

"Okay. Thank you." Farjad said. "I do not care for caviar but my wife is another matter. With this gift, you will have made her very happy. If you bring the guards more through your connections, you will make everyone happy."

The guards opened the steel door by twisting a large wheel mounted on its side. It was very low tech, like something out of World War II submarine. The door swung open. The guards remained outside while Azadi and Farjad walked inside. The door slammed shut behind them. They stood on a platform 20 feet above the press floor. Like a climber who has reached the top of a difficult ascent, Azadi relished the vista below him.

He saw the intaglio press, the size of a school bus, sitting in a room the size of a large movie theater. Paper feeders snaked around the room, past mountains of currency paper and shelves of printing supplies. But this was more than a printing facility. Azadi recognized a comprehensive machine shop for fabricating printing sheets set up in the far end of the room.

Farjad led him down the steps towards the floor.

"We have a fully independent facility," bragged Farjad. "We moved the entire operation from Lebanon in pieces and then had it reassembled here. Gheyam Hospital was my idea."

"An excellent idea," said Azadi. "Americans are loath to attack civilian facilities."

"Yes. That is correct. But then, you are American and would know such things." Farjad flashed Azadi a sideways smile. Azadi quelled his disquiet by asking a question.

"How did you get all this equipment down here without attracting attention?"

"A discontinued line of the metro passes by here," said Farjad. "It was my idea to build an auxiliary tunnel branching from that line. That discontinued tunnel runs underneath a warehouse just two blocks from here. We bought the warehouse and built a freight elevator. That is how we have been able to stock the facility without drawing attention to ourselves." Farjad pointed to a massive steel door, twenty feet high and wide, against the far wall.

"That door leads to the underground tunnel?" asked Azadi.

"Ingenious, isn't it? Lucky for us the metro has been so slow in being completed. The Revolutionary Guards are more efficient than the bungling bureaucrats in the government."

But Azadi had no time for discourses on politics or urban planning. He was thinking the Delta Force boys back at Fort Bragg would find that tunnel very useful indeed. It would make a perfect escape route out of the Press. Azadi, for the first time since he had "volunteered" for the mission, felt that maybe, just maybe, this crazy plan could actually work.

They continued walking by a large piece of equipment that Azadi didn't recognize. Six Revolutionary Guards, all armed, were stacking jerry cans of gasoline against a wall nearby.

"What's that, General?" asked Azadi.

"A gas-powered generator. We can print money even if the city's electrical grid is compromised due to war or sabotage. Luckily gasoline, unlike caviar, is not a luxury in Iran."

"Nor, it appears, are armed guards.

Farjad laughed. "We need you to produce $12 million in $100 dollar notes. Sepanlou has prepared sufficient printing sheets for that purpose –"

"There have been upgraded security measures," said Azadi, cutting off Farjad.

Azadi was sticking to the script. He was setting the bait, just as Kelly had told him to do.

Farjad stroked his chin and looked at Azadi in amusement. He was not a man who was used to having his words cut off.

"We are aware the Americans have taken new precautions against counterfeiters," said Farjad. "But we feel the quality of our bills will be sufficient at this time."

"What about for the future? I can do better. I can beat their countermeasures," said Azadi. "Trust me."

"Mr. Azadi, we know you are a man of rare skill and dedication," said Farjad. "The plates you have been engraving, we want to encourage you to finish them. As you can see, we have everything you will need to not only print new currency but fabricate new printing sheets. Mr. Sepanlou, like yourself, was a talented machinist as well as a printer. But first, the $12 million must be printed."

They stopped by the Press. Azadi couldn't take his eyes off of the magnificent machine. It shined like a new dime. Sepanlou had cared for his baby well.

"May I ask what the $12 million will be used for, General Farjad?"

"The money will buy a rare Persian antiquity stolen from our country. A home coming of sorts. Like your own. Any more questions?"

Azadi had a lot of questions, number one being how he would ever get out of this place alive, but he kept his fear under wraps and hoped his eyes flashed a touch of fanaticism.

"Just one. What do I tell my employer, Mr. Babajan?"

"What do you mean?"

"Well, I take it that from this moment on I'm officially working for the State?"

Farjad slowly shook his head as if Azadi had rice pudding for brains. "No, Mr. Azadi. From this moment on you are working for God."

CHAPTER THIRTY-EIGHT

THREE HOURS AFTER completing his first day, Azadi was riding in Jashni's cab giving a complete account of the Supernote operation including a map of the pressroom he sketched on the way.

"Very nice work," said the cabbie, glancing at the map.

"Funny. That's exactly what General Farjad told me," said Azadi, exiting the cab.

An hour after dropping off Azadi, Jashni picked up Farragut at his hotel. As they drove around the city, Jashni repeated the details to Farragut and gave him Azadi's map. Farragut absorbed the facts and found he had a grudging respect for Azadi's gifts of observation.

"Azadi has an excellent eye for details," said Farragut.

"He's a counterfeiter," replied Jashni. "It comes natural to him."

"So does fear. He emphasized this discontinued tunnel that connects to the metro could be a possible point of entrance for Special Forces, as well as an escape route."

Jashni shrugged. The Israeli made light of everything but not the fact that the Americans were on a suicide mission. He had comrades who'd served in similar situations and the topic was sacred to him. He changed the subject.

"Notice they have stocked the room with a full machine shop and gas generator. If the rest of the Iranian economy were as efficient as this terrorist operation, the *mullahs* wouldn't need to print counterfeit in the first place."

"The gas canisters are good news," said Farragut, noting their location on the map. "When the Press blows, it'll blow hot. Plenty of collateral damage. Not counting us, of course."

Farragut's flip manner offended Jashni. He'd seen the destruction created by suicide bombers in Israel and knew that "collateral damage" was a poisonous euphemism for human casualties. He was no fan of Azadi's, but he respected the courage it took to do this job. Farragut had terminal cancer; he had nothing to lose.

"I wonder if we'll need more C4?" said Farragut, scanning the map. "If we really want to ensure that the entire Press infrastructure is destroyed we —

"Tell me, Professor, are you an explosives expert?" interjected Jashni.

"No, but I'm the son of an oil man. I've seen more than my share of refinery fires."

"And my father grew oranges on a kibbutz but that doesn't make me a glass of orange juice. Perhaps you should leave the details of blowing the Press to the experts and concern yourself with how you are going to take out the numerous armed guards?"

Farragut could see the fire in Jashni's eyes and knew he had crossed the line. Farragut let it go. He had enough to do without speculating about Shareef Salaam's demolition responsibilities.

Back in New York, Mia Kelly and Doug Alson didn't have that luxury.

-:::::-

Mia and Alson were working in a windowless office in the FBI's New York field office when Farragut telephoned from the secure line in the British Embassy to let them know Azadi had infiltrated the Press and the mission was moving forward on schedule.

After hanging up with Farragut, Mia pulled a bottle of 18 year-old single malt and two tulip-shaped glasses from the drawer of her borrowed desk. Then she poured two fingers into each glass.

"What's wrong, Mia?" asked Alson. "You look sad but the news is all good."

"Yes. Of course it is. I'm just tired." She didn't tell him she had a feeling that the news was *too* good; that the sky was due to fall. Yes, Azadi had penetrated the Press. Yes, Salaam had penetrated Hezbollah. Yes, Israeli and CIA intelligence confirmed that he was en route to the Beqaa Valley for training. Yes, yes, yes. But it was the job that Salaam was training to do that had Mia drinking more and sleeping less than she should.

The job would be a staged armored truck heist, due to take place in Baltimore in three weeks. Salaam, Hasan Shehabi, and a small cadre of Hezbollah guerillas would hijack an armored truck carrying Crane currency paper from Crane's offices in Massachusetts to the Bureau of Engraving and Printing in Washington. The heist would take place at a service station when the armored truck stopped for gas. And although Mia and Alson would be watching every step of the way, she could think of a million things that could go wrong. But what choice did she have? To win Hezbollah's trust Salaam had to give them something. And a daring hijacking by Hezbollah on US soil was more than something. That was Christmas in July.

Alson stared at Mia, who was lost in thought, staring at her Scotch glass as if it were the Holy Grail. He hoisted his glass in a toast. "To you, Mia. You were right all along. The Iranians hid the Press under a human shield. All this cloak and dagger bullshit was the only way to go."

They drank. Mia had assured Alson that single malt tasted better in a tulip-shaped glass. She was as right about that as she had been about the Supernote Press.

They kept the bottle on the table and went over the logistics of the Baltimore heist, details they had gone over countless times but you could never be too careful. One hour and 2/3 a bottle of Scotch later, Alson staggered to his feet and put on his coat.

"Where are you going, Doug?" Mia asked, looking fresh as a daisy, or was it a tulip?

Alson giggled. He was drunk and tired and happy and he had waited his whole life for that set-up line, the one they fed the Super Bowl MVP, or was it the Supernote MVP? The one you said when life was going your way and only getting better.

"I'm going to Disneyland," said Alson. And with that he was out the door.

CHAPTER THIRTY-NINE

DISNEYLAND FOR TERRORISTS. That's what Salaam called the Beqaa Valley. It was where Hezbollah trained its soldiers in camps scattered throughout the length of the 75-mile long plain. Guns grew as readily as grass in the Mediterranean climate, and there were plenty of places to blow things up with impunity.

Three days after getting the okay from Shehabi's superiors to steal two truckloads of Crane currency paper right in the heart of America, Salaam and Shehabi embarked on a journey to a Hezbollah training camp outside the city of Baalbek, 55 miles northeast of Beirut. Shehabi drove a gleaming new black Land Cruiser and Salaam sat in the cushy passenger seat. The Beqaa Valley reminded Salaam of the San Joaquin Valley in California. Cypress trees grew in abundance, as did potatoes, tomatoes, beets, and grapes. Salaam saw frowning, sunburned farmers in white shirts and dark pants herding flocks of recalcitrant sheep and goats. He also saw a few sullen Lebanese soldiers standing around at a checkpoint, their camouflage hats pulled low over their bushy black eyebrows. They looked as threatening as a high school chess club killing time in study hall.

During the ride Salaam and Shehabi did not speak much. Shehabi cranked the stereo, an old Paula Abdul CD where the former cheerleader was rapping in her cutesy pie voice about how opposites attract. The coldhearted murderer of dozens of Israeli soldiers and civilians beat out sang along in an atonal alto that approximated the sound of a crow being pulled against its will through the bell of a trumpet.

Salaam sighed. He believed in God. He believed in a Paradise where believers will experience pleasure for all eternity. He believed in a Hell where those who do not repent will suffer for all eternity. He did not believe he had done anything to merit the Hell on earth of sitting in a car with an armed Hezbollah guerilla that had a passion for singing bad pop songs.

When the song ended Shehabi stopped singing and turned to Salaam. "Paula Abdul is part Lebanese. Did you know that?"

"No."

"You like Paul Abdul, no?"

"No."

The next song came on and Shehabi went back to sadistically singing along with Paula. Salaam watched the scenery pass. He recalled sitting in the car with Alson on the drive to Fort Bragg and being forced to listen to the Fed's rendition of Brooks and Dunne. Alson would no doubt be enjoying Salaam's current musical predicament. He wasn't there, of course, but his sentries were. The Israelis, on behalf of the Americans, had been watching Salaam's ass since he had arrived in Lebanon. He could feel their gaze stick to him like a cold sweat. Sometimes he didn't see them but he knew they were watching. Other times they made it obvious. It was agreed they would wear blue bandanas as a signal to Salaam he was not alone. When he and Shehabi stopped for gas before departing Beirut, Salaam noticed a man filling up his bike tires at the air pump wearing a blue bandana over his curly blond head. About three miles back they had passed two hitchhikers, a young man and woman wearing identical blue bandanas knotted around their necks.

Salaam was relieved that Shehabi was too preoccupied by his vocal endeavors to pick them up.

After about two hours they pulled into Baalbek, driving under a black banner with red and white lettering proclaiming, "Al Hussein is the Leader of Freedom in the Whole World." The sign was written in English and was signed "Hezbollah," so Salaam figured it was for the tourists. Not so the Hezbollah poster looming over a bus stop. It announced in Arabic that Hezbollah was the Party of God, and featured portraits of a glowering Ayatollah Khomeini on the left and a chubby-cheeked Hassan Nasrallah, the Hezbollah political leader, on the right. In between them, four Hezbollah soldiers, guns held high, scampered towards a fireball in the distance, meeting their martyrdom at the hands of the Zionist invaders.

"Hezbollah has its center of operations here in Baalbek," Shehabi said, pointing out the yellow and green Hezbollah flag flapping above a café whose only patron was a Dalmatian nibbling its paws under an outdoor table.

"You don't say?" said Salaam, in reply to the obvious.

They cruised past a farmer's market downtown. Salaam noticed that despite the overflowing stalls the people looked poor and hungry. Tattered clothes hung on scrawny frames. Tired eyes watched the exorbitant new SUV pass by and Salaam felt a pang of guilt: this car cost more than two dozen families could make in a year. Shehabi seemed moved by the people, too. He stopped the car, rolled down his window, and whistled to a weathered gypsy begging by a tomato stand. The man crept over on arthritic feet. His left eye was a milky white orb and his beige linen shirt smelled of mutton. Shehabi opened his wallet, pulled out a $100 bill, pressed it into the man's withered hand, and told him in Arabic to "go with God." Then Shehabi kissed the man's soiled, crooked knuckles. The stunned beggar bowed like an acolyte and crept back to his post by the tomato stand. Shehabi put the Land Cruiser in gear and they drove west.

They said nothing. Shehabi's gesture had moved Salaam. He believed now that Shehabi loved these people, loved them without prejudice and sentimentality. True, Shehabi was a murderer but so technically was Salaam. For a majestic moment Salaam contemplated abandoning the mission and joining the Hezbollah cause. But then he thought of his family, of Billie who he had let down and Gary whom he was determined to lift up. No, Salaam had a job to do. The $100 bill Shehabi had given to the beggar reminded him of that.

-:::::-

They were waiting for them as the Land Cruiser parked next to a concrete barracks five miles west of Baalbek. They were waiting in the front yard where the main crop was dust and a rusted Volvo sat on cinder blocks. A mangy German Shepherd lay in the doorway of the barracks and scratched his ear. They all were wearing the Hezbollah uniform: combat boots, olive fatigue pants, black sweaters and berets. Two of them were kicking a soccer ball back and forth between them. One was reading a copy of Paris *Match*. The last one was cleaning his gun with a piece of yellow chamois.

Shehabi jumped out of the Land Cruiser and greeted his comrades. The two soccer players and the literary lion dropped what they were doing and took turns embracing their chief. The gun nut flashed a shy smile and squirted oil in the breech of his AK-47.

Salaam stumbled out of the car. His legs were numb from sitting. Shehabi spoke English and introduced him to the crew.

"This is Shareef Salaam, our distinguished American friend. He will be training you to strike a blow against our eternal enemy, the United States."

Shehabi applauded. No one else did.

Salaam said, "All thanks be to Allah, the Lord of all mankind and all that exists."

No one said anything. The German Shepherd pissed on the Volvo.

-:::::-

That night Salaam was joined in his prayers by three of the four gue-rillas. They set up their prayer rugs on a grassy bluff and faced Mecca while a blood red sun dropped behind the Lebanon Mountains to the west. Afterwards, they relaxed and talked. The two soccer players were brothers, Hafez and Rafik. They were from Tripoli. Hafez, 25, wanted to be a doctor. Rafik, 23, wanted to be a lawyer. They had both gone to Jinan University in their hometown to join Hezbollah soon after graduating. Their father was a half-Palestinian architect who had made a lot of money from the Beirut reconstruction. He gave most of what he had to the Hezbollah cause, including his two sons. They spoke excellent English and loved sports, especially basketball. They asked Salaam if he knew Kobe Bryant and told him he looked like a shorter version of Celtics legend Bill Russell, which Salaam took as compliment.

The third soldier to pray with them was named Fady. He was the one reading Paris *Match* when Salaam arrived. Fady had been edu-cated at the Sorbonne and spoke French as well as English. He was 35 and divorced. His ex-wife and child lived in Paris. He said she had run off with a French soap opera star who was rich and beauti-ful and – oh, by the way – a woman. He said he couldn't blame her. Fady had been a journalist before joining Hezbollah, but a freelance assignment in Israel for *Le Monde* had made him see the evil inher-ent in Zionism. He had traded in his PowerBook for a Kalashnikov and never looked back.

That night they ate dinner in the barracks. When Salaam and the other three entered, the fourth guerilla, Youssef, was polishing gre-nades at the dinner table. He used the same yellow chamois cloth he had used on his gun. Fady had told Salaam that Youssef didn't talk much. He was 30 and from Baalbek. His father was dead and his mother sold sugar beets in town. He was a crackerjack shot and would sometimes hunt rabbits for their dinner. He had, in fact, shot one this very afternoon.

Shehabi love to cook and made an excellent rabbit stew in red wine sauce that everyone devoured. Fady, who was plump, patted his paunch and told Shehabi he made the best *civet de lapin* this side of Arpege. Salaam had never eaten at the famous Paris restaurant but he had to agree. He was surprised to see Shehabi blush. The Hezbollah leader seemed most at ease with his men. Salaam could understand why. They were intelligent and committed, compassionate and sophisticated.

It was too bad Salaam had to betray them.

-:::::-

They slept in the barracks. There were no rooms. There was no privacy. It was just one big space with a kitchen, a dining area, and cots. Two portable toilets out back were their big luxury. They did all of their training outside while a crisp morning breeze bent the grass and the afternoon sun baked their skin. Salaam taught them the lessons he could teach them. He didn't have to teach them about courage or stealth or marksmanship or that death in battle would bring them to the gates of Paradise. They had learned all that in the Hezbollah indoctrination camps. No, Salaam's job was to teach them how to steal paper.

It was a perfect little diamond of a job. There was an armored truck leaving the Crane and Company factory in Dalton, Massachusetts, in three weeks. Its destination was the Washington, DC, branch of the Bureau of Engraving and Printing. The truck would be loaded with 40 packing skids. Each skid contained 10,000 sheets of US currency paper, and there were 32 notes per sheet, with embedded security features to print new issue $100 bills. Salaam had done the calculations and Shehabi's jaw had dropped: the truck was hauling enough paper to print $1.28 billion in funny money.

Why steal US currency paper? Because this paper would keep Iran's Supernotes worthy of the name. The paper would include the latest security measures. When Shehabi played coy Salaam had told him he knew all about the Supernote Press. The story – concocted by Mia Kelly, of course — was that Kareem Shuqueiri had told Salaam about Iran's dirty little secret in exchange for protection while at TI. Salaam was looking for a score and Shuqueiri was looking to make friends. There was a pecking order in prison and sand nigger terrorists who had killed innocent women and children ranked half a notch below child molesters. Salaam had done a lot to improve the lives of the prisoners, regardless of race or religion. If he put a leash on the wolves, they would stay leashed. Shuqueiri was only too happy to play *quid pro quo*. It was better than playing hide the salami in the shower with the Aryan Brotherhood.

Even after Salaam's escape alibi cleared, Shehabi had not gone to the Hezbollah leadership with the plan. He knew that the powers that be would be too cautious to approve the operation. They would argue that Hezbollah had no business operating on US soil. The La Guardia plane bombing had eliminated an Israeli warmonger but had also focused too much attention on Hezbollah. With the Middle East in turmoil and Hezbollah's sponsor, Syria, struggling to contain its own restless population, things were just too unsettled. Some accused Shehabi, accurately it turned out, of being a loose cannon, carrying out the operation without express approval. Shehabi was another Bin Laden and look what had finally happened to him. There would be nowhere to run. Yes, others in the leadership were more sympathetic to Shehabi's daring and happy to see the war taken to the American soil. But Shehabi realized he could not directly win Hezbollah backing for such an audacious attack.

Instead, he went directly to a sympathetic ear in Iran. General Farjad of the Revolutionary Guards was fighting his own battles against the forces of moderation in the Islamic Republic. Farjad had enough rank to say "yes" but enough trepidation to realize that the less the *mullahs* knew of the plan, the better. At least until the paper was delivered. Both Shehabi and Farjad agreed that only at that point could they marshal support from their superiors.

Salaam, for his part, played the frosty pro to perfection. He explained to the men that an armored truck was at its most vulnerable when it was stopped. Problem was, the truck hauling the paper was not scheduled to stop during its seven-hour trip from Dalton to DC except, of course, for gas. This was standard operating procedure. Salaam had told Shehabi he knew this because he had a friend in Terminal Island who had a half- brother who worked for Speed Armored Transport Services, the company contracted to transport the paper to DC. The guy had been with the company 15 years and was still hauling cash from Piggly Wiggly's instead of chatting about his golf game in the boardroom, where he expected to be. In return for a small percentage of the take he had given Salaam all the information: itinerary, truck specs, what kind of guns the guards would be carrying and how they were trained to respond in case of a robbery.

It wasn't a hard sell. Salaam provided all the details. All the details, that is, except the one Kelly and Alson wouldn't allow him to provide, that the heist was a hoax.

But Salaam prepared Shehabi and his men as if the heist were as real as the fear that grasped their guts when they contemplated how hard it would be to pull off. He told them they would have to hit the truck when it stopped for gas in Baltimore and Salaam showed them how it would work. He taught them about plastic explosives. Hezbollah had plenty of Semtex, the Czech-made equivalent of C4. Salaam would do the demolition work but he wanted everyone to understand how hairy this stuff was. He explained how explosive material undergoes a rapid chemical reaction when triggered by the detonator. He explained that in the chemical reaction compounds break down to form various gases, mostly nitrogen and carbon oxides. He explained that in an explosion the gases expand rapidly at about 26,400 feet per second. He explained that at this expansion rate, it was impossible to outrun the explosion like in all those bad action movies they had seen. He explained they would be blowing the doors off a gasoline vehicle, so the threat of fire was real.

Shehabi and Salaam drove into town and overpaid some farmers for their oldest, most useless trucks. They bought six of them. For two days, they choreographed their moves around the rusting hulks. On the third day, they started to blow them up. Blow them up real good. Salaam felt some of that "burn the flag and pass the ammunition" nihilism he had grooved on back in the good old-bad days. The guerillas watched the trucks burn with the same open-mouthed smiles that Americans reserve for their Fourth of July fireworks displays. It was fun. It felt like kids play-acting terrorists.

But in two weeks, when the heist went down, Salaam was going to play the biggest part of his life. And this time he'd have an audience of Kelly, Alson and God knows how many armed federal officers watching his every move. His would be a complicated role, dense and deceptive, with more layers than the mammoth onions Shehabi bought at the market and crafted into a rustic stew for his brave little platoon. Salaam had to keep the twists and turns from getting tangled in his mind. He ran them over in his head at night after his evening prayers. He had to play one role for the Lebanese, another for the Americans, and one for himself. This last role only he knew about. Well, God did, too, but He wasn't telling anyone now, was He?

Neither would Salaam.

CHAPTER FORTY

BILLIE HASTINGS STARED at the bunions on the old woman's feet and thought about death. She thought about the old woman succumbing to a paralyzing stroke, spittle dribbling down her desiccated lips, the same lips that had so far ordered Billie to fetch seventeen pairs of shoes in the last hour. Then Billie thought about her own death, which could not come soon enough now that she was selling women's shoes at Nordstrom in Seattle, Washington.

Billie slid a pair of tasseled Bruno Magli 'Freesia' loafers over the old woman's bunions.

"How do they feel, ma'am?"

The old woman stood up and frowned tightly. She had enough plastic surgery done to her face to finance a Porsche.

"Oh, dear, they're rather tight around the toes, aren't they?"

Billie kneeled and pressed down on the mule's toes.

"Actually, you have plenty of room, ma'am."

"Hmm. Maybe you should show them to me in size eight?"

"Of course, ma'am, I'll be right back."

Billie got into the stock room fast before more fantasies of death by designer shoes could dominate her thoughts.

"Hey, Billie, how are you doing today?"

It was the new guy, Walter. He was beefy with a florid face and a sandy crew cut. He had started in men's shoes the week after Billie. He didn't seem to know too much about shoes – Billie had had to explain to him the difference between a loafer and a slip-on – but he was tall and good at reaching the top shelves without a footstool. He was friendly and always asked Billie how she was doing in a forced casual way that left Billie no doubt that he was FBI sent to spy on her.

Billie said, "I'm doing great, Walter. How are you doing?"

"Oh, you know. Working hard, hardly working."

Walter laughed as if this was the first, not the four hundredth time, he had replied with that line. His eyes closed as he laughed and his face turned the color of cooked beets.

"Yeah. We all working for The Man now, ain't we?" Billie said with a playful trace of a black accent.

"Yes. We certainly are. Yes indeed."

Walter had a big smile plastered on his face, but his eyes betrayed fear that Billie had him marked for what he really was. Billie enjoyed that fear. It had the effect of brightening her day.

"Hey, Walter, would you grab me a pair of those Bruno Magli 'Freesia' loafers in a size eight?"

Walter lifted a box off the shelf and handed it to Billie. The box contained Stuart Weitzman boots in a size six. Walter didn't notice but Billie did. Good enough for government work, thought Billie.

Billie returned to where the old woman was sitting, hoping to get a rise out of her with the wrong pair of shoes but the woman had disappeared. Billie glanced around the sales floor but didn't see her. The rich bitch had split after all Billie's hard work.

Then Billie saw a tall black man dressed in a red plaid shirt and jeans staring at her from the escalator. He wore a yellow baseball cap with the words "Garden State Steel" embroidered above the brim. The man turned his head as Billie made eye contact. He wandered off towards men's sleepwear.

Billie's stomach bounced. The tall man looked like her father but it couldn't be him, could it? He had escaped from prison more than six weeks ago and he would never be so reckless to show up here at her place of work. Or would he? She breathed deep and tried not to faint. Better to focus on work. She dropped to her knees and began to gather up the shoes the old woman had been trying on.

"You okay? You look white as a ghost. Er, I mean…"

It was Walter. He kneeled down next to Billie.

"That's okay, Walter. I'm just feeling a little under the weather. Gary picked up a cold in daycare and you know how it is with kids."

"Sure, sure. How's he doing? The little guy misses the sunshine of LA, I'll bet?"

Billie had never told Walter that she had moved to Seattle from LA but she didn't want to go there right now.

"Yes, he does. But he loves his Aunt Lucille's cooking. And his Uncle Jim has promised to take him to a couple Mariner games so he's adjusting pretty well."

"Great, great. You're lucky you can rely on your family."

Walter crawled over to a pair of shoes. He grunted; his girth made it difficult to move around on all fours. Billie wondered if he envied the two Feds who got to sit on their asses in a Ford Taurus and stake out her apartment in Capitol Hill. They seemed to do nothing more strenuous than eat donuts and drink coffee for hours on end. Plus they didn't seem to care whether she knew they were there or not. But poor flabby Walter, he had to put on this act of being a shoe salesman while he spied on her. She imagined him drawing the short straw in the squad room and the other Feds teasing him as if he were a misfit eighth grader who had lost at spin the bottle and had to kiss an ugly girl.

"Walter, you really don't have to help."

"No problemo," gasped Walter, still on his knees as he put the shoes in the wrong box.

"Those are the boots. They go in that box. The pumps, the ones with the pointy toes, go in the other box."

"Got it. Boots in there. Pumps in here."

Walter packed the shoes in their proper boxes. He stacked all the boxes on top of each other and lifted them as he staggered to his feet.

"Thanks, Walter. You're a dear." Billie meant it, too.

"No problemo," wheezed Walter as he carried the shoeboxes back to the stock room.

Billie was kneeling on the floor. Her knees ached. She hated this job. She wanted to quit but was trapped by her responsibility to Gary. She imagined herself as old as the old woman she'd just been slaving over, except poor and arthritic and bitter beyond the blues.

"Excuse me, miss. But can I give you a hand up?"

Billie saw a pair of old work boots. She looked up into the face of the tall black man she had seen by the escalator. No, the man wasn't her father but there was something familiar about him, something in the eyes. He had a box of women's shoes cradled in his left arm. He offered Billie his right hand. Billie took it and the tall black man helped her to her feet.

Billie said, "Thank you."

"You're welcome."

His skin was dark and his eyes were weary and wise with a tinge of yellow rheum the color of his baseball cap. His hands were big, meaty, callused mitts. They were working man's hands and Billie understood immediately that they were like her father's hands, toughened by years of hard prison labor and incessant wringing.

The tall man said, "I bought these shoes for my wife and they don't fit and I'd like to return them."

The tall man offered Billie the shoebox. Billie noticed he did not wear a wedding band.

"Sure. If you have the receipt I'll credit you. As long as it's been less than thirty days from the time of purchase."

The tall man glanced uneasily at the stock room as if he expected Walter to come charging out. He whispered, "I was in the joint with your father. Open the box and check the left shoe. Don't let anyone see you, especially that Fed."

And with that the tall man turned and walked away.

Billie was so astonished that she barely remembered seeing the tall man get on the escalator and disappear into the ether as if he never existed. She looked around the shoe department and saw customers and salespeople moving as if in slow motion. No one was looking at her. She was just another pretty black salesgirl in a twill jacket and pants set holding a box of shoes. She looked at the stock room and did not see Walter the Fed crouched in the doorway, his service revolver pointed in her direction, his flat Midwestern voice ordering her to drop the shoebox and put her hands over her head. She tucked the shoebox under her right arm and walked towards the employees' restroom. Her legs felt numb. When she reached the restroom she entered and locked the door and put the shoebox on the washbasin.

She looked at her reflection in the mirror. She realized for the first time what people had always told her. She looked like her mother. Her eyes were puffy from lack of sleep, and the stress of the last few weeks had begun to hollow out her cheeks and plant gray hairs at her temples.

Did mommy look like this because of daddy? She thought. *Did his selfishness sap her beauty like a hummingbird sucks nectar from a flower?*

A hummingbird. That's what she felt like was fluttering inside her chest as she opened the shoebox. Inside was an elegant pair of women's ankle boots. They were calfskin with two-inch stacked heels. Billie vaguely remembered selling a pair last week but she could not remember to whom. She picked up the right boot and examined it. It was unspectacular. She picked up the left boot and examined it as well. She felt something jammed down into the toe and extracted several sheets of paper folded up together. She unfolded them. She recognized her father's handwriting. She began to read. Her heart slammed against her ribs as she realized that from this moment on her expectation of how her life was going to play out was as meaningless as a raindrop in the ocean.

CHAPTER FORTY-ONE

BEFORE ALEXANDER the Great reduced it to ruin, all visitors to Persepolis, once the crown jewel of the Achaemenian Empire, had to pass through The Gate of All Nations. Built by Xerxes I in the 5th Century B.C, the gate's high ceiling and mud brick walls had been lost to the ages. In 330 BC, Alexander had sacked Persepolis, stolen its royal treasure, and ordered his troops to destroy most of its buildings and structures. Only two of the gate's four columns remained, rising like giant asparagus stalks above the Marv Dasht plain. Two Assyrianized man-bulls carved from stone still flanked the east doorway, while a colossal pair of conventional stone bulls guarded the west doorway. One of these conventional bulls was missing its face; the other was missing its head. A trilingual inscription engraved above each of the four bulls implored those who passed through the gate to respect other peoples' cultures.

Farragut sat in a fold-up canvas chair at the entrance to the west doorway and sketched the headless bull. It was the wrong season so there were just a handful of tourists milling about and they were lost amongst the massive scale of the complex. That was fine with Farragut. He cherished the peace and quiet after the hectic pace of Tehran and he was happy to revisit Persepolis. To Farragut, the true culture of Iran, of Persia, was right here. It was easy to convince himself that he had come to this country not as a killer but to return one of its ancient treasures, the missing bull's head, to its rightful owners – the people of Iran.

So there he sat, projecting the image he wanted to project, that of a middle-aged American academic in a floppy sun hat and ancient tweed jacket, sketching pictures of artifacts he had loved ever since his youth in the land of the Persian tribes.

Farragut removed his tweed, tossing it over the back of the canvas chair. He wiped sweat from his brow and then pulled off his wrinkled, white Brooks Brothers button-down shirt. He now wore only a faded T-shirt from The Rolling Stones' 1982 "Tattoo You" concert tour. The T-shirt was almost as old as the ruins but it was an unseasonably warm winter day and Farragut was feeling the change in climate and, though he pushed it out of his tumor-wracked mind, the effects of the cancer.

All Farragut's fantasies of being an innocent academic ended when he spotted Ali Ardabili struggling up the monumental staircase to greet him. His friend carried a black briefcase that looked heavy enough to disengage his arm from his shoulder socket. Ardabili staggered over and placed the briefcase next to Farragut's chair. He looked nervous and wasted no time.

"Here is a sample, John. Half a million dollars, non-consecutive serial numbers."

The tourists had moved on to the Palace of Darius to the south of the *apadana*. Farragut and Ardabili were alone. Farragut opened the briefcase and surveyed the counterfeit. He grabbed a tight stack of $100 bills and rifled through them. Azadi had done good work. The detail work was sublime. Perfect. But the notes had been artificially weathered so they didn't look too perfect.

"I'm no expert," lied Farragut. "But these look like the real deal. And the balance of the funds?"

"Will be ready in time for your trip. Shipped through diplomatic pouch. Funny. I never realized how much mass $12 million really has until I saw how little can be carried in a suitcase."

Farragut placed the sample bills back in the suitcase with the others and shut it tight. Then he gave Ardabili a warm smile and pointed to the headless bull. "Look. He's been standing without a head just because some English lord got it into his head that Persia was his personal Home Depot. But thanks to you, the head is coming home."

Farragut and Ardabili were both startled when they heard a voice behind them.

"Magnificent. Just magnificent."

Police Inspector Kamran Hadian was standing a few yards to the west of Farragut and Ardabili. Unlike the latter, he had seemed to appear out of nowhere. His white shirt was open at the collar and an expensive black Canon camera hung around his neck. His son, Ahmad, was standing next to him. He wore a red T-shirt with a smiling frog on it, and a joyous expression from having been plucked out of school by his father to take this trip.

Hadian took a picture of the Gate of Xerxes. Ahmad dashed forward as if shot out of a cannon and tried to climb the headless bull.

Hadian said, "Ahmad, please. You're spoiling Professor Farragut's tableau of the Gate of Xerxes."

Farragut stared at Hadian and wondered how this stranger knew his name. Ardabili's gaze drifted to the suitcase full of counterfeit money sitting next to Farragut.

Hadian took a few tentative steps towards Farragut. He stopped when he saw the sketches in Farragut's open sketchbook. "Oh, my. I knew of your reputation as a scholar, Professor. But I had no idea you were such a talented artist."

Hadian was standing over Farragut, who was still sitting in his chair. Farragut felt very small indeed. He stood up and was pleased to see he towered a good half foot above this mousy, unprepossessing man who nevertheless had a clever cast to his eyes.

"I'm sorry. I don't think we've met. You're…?"

Hadian thrust out his hand to shake by way of an apology. "Inspector Kamran Hadian. I'm with the Tehran Police Department.

And that young man over there is my son, Ahmad, with…well, with me. Anyway, I had heard that you and Professor Ardabili were here doing research and since it's imperative we talk, I took the opportunity to come down here to do a little sightseeing."

Farragut shook Hadian's hand. He was not nervous. He had been in countless covert situations while with the Agency and was used to subtle – and not so subtle – interrogations.

"It must be important, Inspector. Tehran is over 400 miles away."

"Important? Yes, I suppose so. But not as important as cherishing the relics of Iran's glorious past." Hadian took some pictures of Ahmad, who struck muscleman poses like a pint-sized Schwarzenegger beneath the headless bull.

Ardabili, annoyed by the boldness this minor civil servant, cut Hadian a withering look. "Inspector, can this wait? Professor Farragut and I are engaged in state business."

"What a coincidence," said Hadian, still snapping away at his clowning son. "So am I."

Farragut put a hand on his friend's shoulder. "It's okay, Ali. I'll talk to the inspector."

Hadian stopped taking pictures. He looked at Ardabili with a thrilled expression. "Perhaps, Professor Ardabili, you can talk to my son? What a privilege – no, what an *honor* for him to have a guided tour of Persepolis from the man who has so beautifully written about it?"

Ardabili knew it was more an order than a request. "It would be my pleasure, Inspector."

Ardabili walked over to Ahmad, said a few words to him in Farsi, then the two of them headed off towards the *apadana*.

"Persepolis," said Hadian, gesturing towards the ruins. "Is it not inspiring? Shaken by earthquakes, looted by scoundrels – my country remains resilient against those forces that wish to destroy it, even to this day."

Hadian stuck his face behind his camera and began to take more pictures. Farragut could not help but hear the tacit accusation in Hadian's remark.

"What is it that you wish to know, Inspector?"

"Tell me," said Hadian, continuing to take pictures. "How did a man born and raised in Iran become a world-class biathlete?"

"For a few years before high school my father sent me to boarding school in Switzerland. That's where I learned to ski and shoot."

"My goodness. Why Switzerland?"

"Because he felt this country was no place to raise a child. Plus he thought getting away from home, from my mother and him, would do me good."

Hadian stopped taking pictures. "I cannot imagine a father who would not want to be with his son. Ahmad and I are inseparable. He is practically my twin. Well, a shorter, younger twin who eats too many sweets. But I think you understand me, yes?"

Farragut nodded. "He seems like a very nice boy."

Hadian produced an apologetic smile. "You are very kind. Now. The biathlon. One must be both expert marksman and skier, yes?"

"That's right. I still ski but I am out of practice with a gun."

"Oh, yes. I am, too. I just use this to crack nuts."

Hadian pulled aside the right half of his sport coat to reveal a holstered pistol. Farragut made it as a Glock 25 .380 auto. He could not tell if the gesture was a threat on Hadian's part or just a joke. Sometimes in Iran it was the same thing.

Farragut said, "They must have some big nuts in Iran."

Hadian laughed. He let his sport coat cover up his gun. Farragut checked his watch. "Now is there anything else, Inspector? I have to drive back to Shiraz and catch my return flight to Tehran this afternoon."

"Just one more thing. A matter of small importance, but it did pique my interest..."

Hadian dug into his left coat pocket. He produced a small notepad. He flipped through some pages and squinted at them. He flashed Farragut another apologetic smile, then patted his coat until he located a pair of steel-frame reading glasses in his right inside pocket. He put on the glasses and read his notes.

"Ah, here it is. Our records show you spent two nights at the Laleh Hotel, then checked into the Heydam Hotel for one night, then checked back into the Laleh the following night."

They know I was at the Heydam the morning Sepanlou died, thought Farragut. *Well, so were a lot of other people. It means nothing.*

"That's correct," said Farragut.

"May I ask why you chose to change hotels?"

"I found that the accommodations at the Laleh were not suitable for my needs that night."

"Really? But the Laleh has the finest accommodations in the city."

Farragut shrugged. He focused on keeping his voice as uninflected as possible.

"For my needs the accommodations were not suitable."

Farragut offered nothing more. He stared at Hadian. The inspector's irises loomed as big as figs behind the magnifying lenses of his glasses. He seemed to realize how ridiculous he must have looked and plucked the glasses off his nose, burying them back into his coat pocket.

"Well, that's it then, Professor. You don't mind if I take the opportunity to play tourist, do you?"

"No. It's a free country, isn't it?"

A bad joke on Farragut's part. Hadian did not seem to notice. He lifted his camera to his face and took more pictures of the ruins.

"You know, Professor, one thing the Heydam has over the Laleh is a wonderful view onto *Be'sat* Park. Indeed, the Heydam offers a wonderful view from which to shoot the president."

Farragut felt a tremor of fear shoot through his body. He touched his throat. It was all he could do to keep the tremor out of his voice. "Shoot the president? I don't understand."

Hadian kneeled and took some low angle shots of the bulls. "The President of Iran will be laying a wreath in the park to honor a friend of the state who was killed there. A propane tank explosion. Perhaps you heard it that morning?"

Farragut felt goose bumps rise on his arms. He glanced down and saw a sharp rock as big as a brick at his feet. He looked up and saw that there was no one else within sight of him and Hadian. "I did hear it. I was there that night, as your records already show."

Farragut reached down and picked up the rock. Hadian continued to snap pictures, kneeling on the ground, his back to Farragut.

"Yes, of course. But the point is, a man looking down from the Heydam Hotel – a man looking down from your very room, in fact – would have perfect vantage point to shoot the president when he lays that wreath."

Farragut could hear his pulse pounding in his ears. It beat out a frantic rhythm for the cyclonic rush of thoughts swirling through his mind.

Does he suspect I killed Sepanlou? Maybe. But he seems more concerned I plan to assassinate the president. Either way he's suspicious and could jeopardize the mission. I could bash his brains in with this rock. Nobody would know. I could kill him and carry his body to my car. I could bury the body in the plain or leave it by the road and make it look like a robbery. I would tell Ali he knew about the counterfeit money, that our careers would be ruined. Ali would be sick but he'd go along with it. But what about the boy? What would I do with Ahmad? I am here because Yasir died, because I wanted to prevent the death of more children. Can I kill one child in order to save many?

"Did you hear me, Professor? Don't you think that room in the Heydam would make an excellent place to shoot the president?"

Farragut squeezed the rock in his hand. He inched closer to Hadian. He saw a bald spot nestled in the back of Hadian's head. The flesh looked waxy and fragile, like parchment paper.

"Excuse me, Inspector. But I don't like what you're implying."

Hadian wheeled around. He held up his camera. "My English. I forget the word. Shoot? How do you say it? Photo?"

Hadian pantomimed taking pictures, wagging his finger over the shutter release button. The realization hit Farragut like an exhilarating desert breeze.

"Photograph? You mean shoot pictures of the president laying the wreath?"

Hadian flashed a big smile. "Yes! That is exactly what I mean. Photograph the president laying the wreath." Hadian got to his feet. "I thought I might get a room at the Heydam myself. I'm a big... photobug, yes? That's how you say it in English? Photobug?"

Farragut nodded. "That's how you say it in English."

Hadian beamed. "Excellent. Well, I should catch up to Ahmad. By the way, Professor, is that your jacket?" Hadian was pointing to Farragut's old tweed hanging over his canvas chair.

"Yes, it is my jacket. Why?"

Hadian picked up the jacket and admired it. Or perhaps, thought Farragut, he was checking it for a concealed weapon.

"Harris tweed. The finest craftsmanship," he said. "A little tatty, this one, but it will last forever, like the Gate of All Nations. Perhaps you should put the jacket on now, yes?

Hadian handed the jacket to Farragut. Farragut placed it back over the canvas chair.

"No, thank you. I'm rather hot."

"But your arms are covered with goose bumps," said Hadian, pointing at Farragut's forearms. "I thought you must be cold. Or perhaps you're nervous?"

Farragut stared at the goose bumps that were still covering both his forearms. How had the cop noticed them when he seemed so pre-occupied with the jacket? Farragut calmly grabbed his white button-down and slid it on over his T-shirt, leaving it open at the front.

"No. I'm not nervous, Inspector. Must be heat rash. But thank you for noticing."

The men stood staring at each other smiling pleasantly. After a few moments, Hadian said, "I notice you're a Rolling Stones fan."

Hadian pointed at the cartoon lips and tongue decorating Farragut's T-shirt front.

Farragut smiled. "Greatest rock band in the world. Ever."

Hadian shrugged and said, "Yes, well, perhaps the greatest if one does not include The Beatles. Anyway, thank you for being most cooperative."

Hadian offered his hand to shake. Farragut became aware he was still holding the rock in his right hand. He was going to drop it but the sound of it hitting the ground would, to his mind, be too conspicuous. Instead, he transferred it to his left hand and shook Hadian's hand with his right. Hadian did not remark upon it, though Farragut felt he wanted to. Farragut knew it was time to pull the old bait and switch.

"I'm not sure I was as cooperative as you give me credit for, Inspector. You see, I never answered your question as to why I stayed at the Heydam that night."

Farragut released Hadian's hand. Hadian continued to smile pleasantly. "But of course you did. You said it was not suitable to your needs."

"But I never told you what those needs were."

Hadian folded his hands over his belt buckle and rocked on his heels like a man waiting for a bus to arrive.

Farragut said, "I was meeting a woman. The type of woman who would not want to be seen with me in the Laleh amongst the businessmen and diplomats."

Hadian puckered his lips and looked past Farragut to the emptiness of the plain. "What was this woman's name, Professor?"

Farragut had withheld the information at first because he knew that if he gave it too soon it would seem too easy, too much like the sordid alibi that, of course, it was. And as he betrayed his lover's trust, Farragut noticed that this little detective with his cartoonish glasses and notepad was not writing any of it down. He just watched the horizon over Farragut's shoulder, watched the place where the light blue sky disappeared into the sandy dry earth, the place where Alexander the Great's troops had come from over 2,000 years earlier on their terrible quest to conquer everything in their path.

CHAPTER FORTY-TWO

ADIAN HAD HEARD that Ingrid Mader, the ambassador's wife, was an art lover, but he found it impossible to love anything, much less look at, the vulgar spatterings of paint on canvas hanging on the bone-white walls of the German ambassador's residence. One masterpiece looked like a vat of pig's blood had been emptied upon a plate of scrambled eggs. Another brought to mind a broken chandelier wedged inside some unsuspecting animal's colon. Hadian distracted himself by reviewing in his mind the previous day's interview with Professor Farragut at Persepolis.

Hadian had prepared himself for the interview by visiting the Khavaran Public Library and reading several of Farragut's articles and books. He discovered that the professor wrote in an accessible style about a variety of interesting topics. A history of the *Daria-e Nur*, the "Sea of Light," a 182-carat diamond brought back from New Delhi by Nader Shah in the 18th century, was quite entertaining. But what intrigued Hadian even more was Professor Farragut's monograph on the murderous cult of the Ismailites, also known as the Assassins, a splinter group that emerged from a schism in the Shiite community. Feared by Muslims and Christians alike, they defended their limited numbers by attacking their enemies' most prominent men, despite the protection that might surround them.

The Assassins were daring and dangerous. They killed out of political and religious conviction. They were what Inspector Kamran Hadian suspected Professor John Farragut himself might very well be.

The professor had answered all his questions, that much was true. But still Hadian sensed he was holding something back. The propane explosion in the square had been ruled an accident and surely Farragut had nothing to do with that. Those types of catastrophes happened every day in Tehran, where public safety inspectors were all on the take. No, Hadian realized it was the professor's extraordinary composure under questioning that triggered his suspicion. He seemed too calm, too collected for someone confronted with the accusation of being a potential assassin. Then again, perhaps the professor felt more apprehension than he displayed. The rock in his right hand, the one he had shifted to his left when they shook hands, seemed an interesting detail. Maybe the rock meant nothing; or maybe Farragut had intended to use it for some sinister purpose. He had many more suspicious foreigners to interview but would keep a close eye on the professor —

"Inspector Hadian? I'm Ingrid Mader. Sorry to have kept you waiting."

Hadian looked up to see a stunning, slender woman with radiant green eyes advancing on him. She spoke English. Her smile was dazzling and as Hadian stood he felt self-conscious about his own horsy teeth showing through his lopsided grin.

"My pleasure, Frau Mader. It gave me time to enjoy your outstanding art collection."

Hadian gave a shallow bow. Frau Mader glowed. "If you like the paintings, Inspector, I would be more than happy to give you a tour of the residence. Treasures fill every room, rest assured."

"Your invitation is too generous. Regrettably, I am somewhat pressed for time and would like to conduct the interview now, if that were possible."

"Unfortunately, the ambassador is held up in traffic and may not arrive for another hour."

"It is not necessary for your husband to join us. The questions I have to ask are for you alone. They are of a most delicate nature."

Ingrid flashed a mischievous smile. "I'm intrigued. 'Most delicate' is usually my husband's domain. Please, sit…"

Hadian resumed his perch on the hard wooden chair. Ingrid sat on the plush plum-colored couch opposite him. Her skirt rose up when she crossed her legs and it was all Hadian could do not to gawk. He busied himself by digging in his pocket for his notebook and pencil. He wanted to put on his glasses but felt self-conscious. Besides, he realized that under present circumstances it was probably best for him – and Frau Mader — if he kept his vision fuzzy.

"Please tell me," began Hadian. "What is the nature of your relationship with John Farragut?"

"He's my lover. And a terrific one at that."

Hadian did not mean to do it. It was a reflexive action — and one that he could have avoided if he could have prepared himself for the ambassador's wife's direct response — but on the mention of the word "lover" Hadian pressed so hard on his pencil that it snapped in two.

Ingrid said, "Oh my. It appears your pencil is inadequate. May I offer you a pen?"

Hadian offered her a meek grimace. Ingrid stood, crossed to a well-polished walnut desk, picked a ballpoint pen out of a drawer, and returned it to Hadian.

"Thank you, Frau Mader. Now the reason I am asking such personal questions is that I fear John Farragut may be…how do I say this? Using you."

Ingrid laughed. "Please, Inspector. I can assure you that the relationship between John Farragut and me is 100 percent consensual."

Not surprising, thought Hadian, *considering your husband is a homosexual.* Both the Tehran Police Department and the Ministry of Information had extensive files on the German ambassador's sexual liaisons. Hadian had seen the files, and after seeing the majestic

Ingrid Mader, he thought he'd never understand anything about the sexual proclivities of westerners.

"Have you known Professor Farragut long, Frau Mader?"

"No. Just a few weeks actually."

Hadian referred to his notes. "If you don't mind me asking, were you with John Farragut on the night of the third in the Heydam Hotel?"

"Yes."

Hadian felt the blood rush to his cheeks. A powerful urge to walk to the nearest wall and bang his head against it overcame him. Luckily he controlled that urge.

"May I ask what you did that night?"

"We made love until about 1:00 a.m. Then we slept and I went home about 4:30 a.m."

"Did Professor Farragut insist on privacy? Did he request you leave?"

"No. Of course not."

"Then why did you leave?"

"Because I like to be home when the children wake up."

As if on cue, an infantile braying exploded from the adjoining room. Hadian became aware that two tow-headed twins, a boy and a girl, were now entering the sitting room. The boy scrambled on all fours like a donkey while his sister rode on his back and whipped his head with a soggy piece of red string licorice.

Ingrid leapt to her feet and clasped her hands together, beaming as if her offspring had just performed Bach's Goldberg variations blindfolded on the harpsichord.

"Here are my little darlings!"

The donkey emitted a piercing shriek. The cowgirl slapped him in the face with the licorice and jumped into her mother's arms.

"Inspector, this is my daughter, Francesca, and that creature down there is my son, Rolf."

Hadian rose to his feet and repeated the same shallow bow he had given to Ingrid. Francesca returned the gesture by clutching her mother and sucking her thumb. Rolf displayed greater social sophistication by nipping at Hadian's heels and barking like a rabid Rottweiler.

Ingrid said in English, "Rolf, stop that please. The inspector is not a fire hydrant."

Young Rolf took a kick in the rear from Ingrid and scampered up onto the couch.

Ingrid sat down on the couch, still clutching her daughter. "They have too much imagination. I fear they get it from me."

Hadian smiled tightly. "Frau Mader, thank you for your cooperation. I believe we are done here."

Hadian deposited his notebook and the pen in his coat pocket. He knew he would get nothing more of value from the ambassador's wife. Besides, the image of her coddling her plump, blonde children beneath the harrowing paintings on the walls created in Hadian the powerful sensation that he would, in the next few moments, have to vomit. He bowed to Ingrid again and moved towards the entrance hall and the marvelous sanctuary of the front door.

"Inspector, please tell me — is Professor Farragut in some kind of trouble?"

"No. This is merely a routine inquiry into the events surrounding the recent propane tank explosion in downtown Tehran." *Or rather,* thought Hadian, *that is what I'm telling you. You may no longer think your Professor Farragut is such a terrific lover if you knew he was possibly scoping out a place to assassinate the President of Iran.*

"Oh, yes. I heard the explosion. It woke John and me up."

Hadian stopped at the front door. He stroked his frail little bush of a mustache and stared at the diamond-shaped black and white tiles on the entranceway floor.

"You were still in bed with Professor Farragut at the time of the explosion?"

"Yes. Why?"

Hadian looked into Ingrid's eyes. "Because the explosion happened at approximately 5:05 a.m. During the *adhan*. If I recall you told me you had left the hotel room at 4:30 a.m."

Hadian watched Ingrid flash a smile of beautiful white teeth without missing a beat.

"You know," she said. "I may have left later than 4:30 a.m. I seem to remember the explosion waking us up and me hurrying home to be with my children. I was afraid the blast might have been some sort of terrorist act. You never know these days, do you?"

"No. You never know these days."

"Yes. I'm sure I arrived home later. Probably around 6:00 a.m."

"And your husband will, of course, verify the time of your arrival?"

"Of course. And so will the security detail assigned to the residence."

"Excellent. I can check with them now."

"Unfortunately, Horst was on duty that morning. He is off today. Peter is on."

"Well surely they keep time logs."

"Inspector, I'm sure you can appreciate that with the fluid arrangement of my marriage to the ambassador the security detail does not find it prudent to keep written records of every time we pop in and out the door."

Hadian sighed. The donkey boy brayed in the sitting room and something heavy crashed to the floor in there. Hadian hoped it was one of the paintings.

"Oh, dear. I best check on the children. Good day, Inspector. I will tell the ambassador to expect you to call on him."

And with that Ingrid dashed back into the sitting room.

Hadian let himself out.

-:::::-

That night at dinner, while Hadian hacked his way through his wife's impenetrable lamb roast, he thought again about his visit to the ambassador's wife. Ingrid Mader was a beautiful, brilliant woman, there was no doubt about that. What was doubtful was her story. Maybe she really had been in bed with Farragut when the propane tank exploded. Hadian knew that eyewitnesses to crimes rarely accurately assessed at what time they happened. Then again, the propane tank explosion was not a crime. True, two men had died, a kebab vendor and an unemployed printer. But there was nothing suspicious about their deaths, and they seemed unlikely targets even if there was. Hadian would check with the ambassador and the security detail about Frau Mader's claim to have arrived home at 6:00 a.m., but he already knew they would back up her claim. That was fine. He had more suspects to interview and had to report on his progress to Colonel Tabriz soon. He looked forward to the day he would be done with this assignment and could return to his regular cases for the police department. That day could not come soon enough.

"Hopefully sooner than I can cut through this roast," Hadian mumbled.

"What was that, dear?" Laden said, looking up at him from across the table.

"Nothing," Hadian replied. He stuck a forkful of dried animal leather into his mouth and smiled at his wife.

CHAPTER FORTY-THREE

ARRAGUT EASED HIS body into the bathtub of his suite at London's Dorchester Hotel. The water was hot but the Bombay Martini he sipped was ice cold.

It had been a good day. That morning he had purchased the counterfeit bull's head from the counterfeit Lord Owen for $12 million in counterfeit $100 bills. The transaction had occurred at the Iranian embassy with the Iranian ambassador present but not the real Lord Owen nor the real bull's head, both of which remained at the actual aristocrat's Sussex estate. Owen, who had served with distinction in military intelligence, had no problem giving his blessing to the subterfuge and knew not to ask too many questions. Whether the Iranian ambassador knew that bogus bills were being used to buy a priceless Persian artifact Farragut wasn't sure. He was sure, however, that the ambassador had no idea that Lord Owen's sales agent was, in fact, Billy Joe Sniffen, an undercover CIA agent from Dogtown, Mississippi, with an ear for aristocratic English accents. Farragut was also certain that the ambassador had no clue that the bull's head being purchased had been carved by a specialist in the CIA's Directorate of Science and Technology and had 20 pounds of C4 explosive plus detonators packed into a special cavity. The Iranians were shipping it via diplomatic pouch to Tehran, with express instructions that it was not to be examined by anyone except Professor Farragut upon his return.

Farragut sipped the last of his martini and thought about the mission. He knew Salaam and his Hezbollah operatives were already en route to Baltimore via a Saudi Arabian freighter, *Riad El Solh*. They planned to hijack the Crane paper in five days' time on a Saturday. Farragut worshipped precision, and although Mia and Doug Alson had worked out the hijacking in exhaustive detail, he tried to imagine all the things that could go wrong. His head spun and he dozed off.

Farragut awoke when he heard the gentle click of the bathroom door being opened. His eyelids lifted and he watched Ingrid enter the bathroom. Her hair was up and she wore a thick robe. When she lifted it off her delicate frame Farragut saw she was naked. She dropped the robe to the floor and for a moment Farragut just stared at her standing in a shroud of steam. He never tired of looking at her. The humidity flushed her cheeks and the added color made her look younger. Across her middle she carried a tiny roll of fat. It was barely a belly, the price she paid for bearing two children, and its appearance on so youthful-looking a woman stirred Farragut's passion in a profound way he found impossible to articulate.

Ingrid said, "Sorry I'm late. The lines at the Tate were impossible and you know what the traffic is like at this hour."

Ingrid lowered herself into the tub. She turned her back to Farragut and he opened his legs so she could sit against his chest. It was a snug fit. Farragut dipped a washcloth into the water and used it to massage the nape of Ingrid's neck.

"If you want I can fix you a drink. I already had my martini, but there's Champagne in the ice bucket."

Ingrid glanced at the two glasses and the silver Champagne bucket on the wash basin. An open bottle of Dom Perignon was sitting inside, waiting wistfully for a celebration.

"No. Thank you."

Farragut could feel she was preoccupied. Usually when he massaged her neck like this, at that soft spot beneath the base of the skull and above the right ear, she groaned in ecstasy. Now she made no sound, just swiped desultorily at the bubbles on top of the water.

Ingrid said, "A police inspector came to see me the other day. He asked about our relationship. I told him the truth. That we were lovers."

Farragut reached for the olive in his Martini glass and popped it in his mouth, chewing as he said, "Sorry about that. He questioned me about that propane tank explosion near the hotel. I explained that I was otherwise indisposed that morning. I figured he would be discreet."

"I lied for you, John. I told him I was in bed with you when the explosion happened. I told him you had nothing to do with it. You did have nothing to do with it, right?"

"Of course not. I'm just a boring, old college professor."

Farragut reached for her breasts. Her hands intercepted his.

"Boring is the last thing you are."

Ingrid stepped out of the bath. To Farragut's disappointment she put her robe back on. She crossed to the bathroom window and looked out at the rain starting to soak the city below. In Hyde Park, she watched people lifting their umbrellas against the wind, their faces turned aside as raindrops smacked against their skin. She felt their coldness and wanted to climb back inside the warm bath; but in some inexplicable way the man sitting inside the tub, her lover, a stranger really, chilled her more than the pitiful creatures battling the elements outside in the night.

She turned from the window to face him. "John, whatever it is you're up to, I can help. I want to help."

A closed-lip smile spread across Farragut's face. It was meant to show affection but could easily have been interpreted as condescending. "You want to help me? Then pour me a glass of Champagne."

Ingrid padded over to the wash basin and poured two glasses of Champagne. One she handed to Farragut, the other she carried over to the window, where she again stared at the storm.

"What's bothering you, Ingrid?"

Ingrid watched traffic swirl around Hyde Park Corner. In the Park, a gust of wind carried off a young woman's umbrella and she unlocked herself from her male companion's grasp and chased it, laughing as she splashed through puddles. She had always loved London, rain or shine. She took a sip of Champagne.

"My grandfather was in the *Luftwaffe* during the war. I wonder, would he have risked his life to destroy this city if he knew, years later, his granddaughter would be drinking Champagne in the English rain?"

"He would if he believed in what he was doing."

"What he was doing was killing innocent women and children."

Farragut sighed. "No. What he was doing was fighting a war. He was an airman, a soldier. He was doing his job. There are times when killing is the right thing to do."

Farragut stared at the back of her neck. Its gentle curve aroused him. He wanted to make love to her and she wanted to root around in his secrets. She knew nothing of his true purpose in Iran, of course, and even if she did he had no fear that she would ever betray him. But Farragut was a professional and he would not betray the mission. For a fleeting moment, he thought he might even kill her if she did know. But then Ingrid turned to look at him, and the tears in her eyes and the words she spoke made him mortified that he had ever thought such a thing at all.

"When does a man say 'enough,' John? When does he say 'I will kill no more, I will do everything in my power to preserve life rather than take it, because killing is never the right thing to do?'"

She was crying now. Farragut pulled himself out of the tub and strode to her. He embraced her. He was unclothed and she was in her robe; but he felt that she was the exposed one until she spoke again.

"I'm sorry you're so sick, John. Because I think I could fall in love with you. Or at least, the man I know you could be if we had more time together."

Farragut shuddered as if shot. He had not told Ingrid of his illness. He stepped back from her and searched for his robe but he had left it in the other room. He pulled a towel off the rack and wrapped it around his waist, relieved to be rescued from his nakedness. Ingrid didn't seem to notice. She had stopped crying but not prying.

"I know about the tumor, John. And I know about your first career before you became a college professor. Did you think I wouldn't check up on you? My sister's ex-husband was a chief director of the BND. I'm closer to him than I am to her. He made some inquiries for me. Just as you made inquiries about me before you came to Iran."

Farragut rubbed his face, contemplating the error in judgment he and Mia had made in picking Ingrid for his alibi. They needed her pedigree and had accepted the risks. The BND was the German Secret Service, and he and Mia had known Ingrid's sister, Lita, was married to a former director. But their acrimonious divorce and Ingrid's falling out with Lita had made the Americans confident that she had little, if no, contact with the BND. As ambassador to Iran, Ingrid's husband had friends in all the German ministries, but it seemed unlikely Ingrid would call on her husband to use his sources to investigate the background of her new lover, which was, in any case, impeccable. It also seemed unlikely, now that Farragut thought about it, that Ingrid could compromise the mission, even with what she did know about him. She certainly wouldn't tell the Iranians that he had once been a spy, and he doubted the BND knew the full extent of the work he did for the CIA. No, the more he thought about it, the more Farragut felt Ingrid wasn't an error in judgment after all.

Farragut folded his arms across his chest. "What do you want me to say, Ingrid? Do you want me to tell you everything about me? I can't do that."

"I want you to tell me that what we have is not a lie."

She looked at him without rancor. He met her gaze. "What we have is not a lie."

To prove his point he touched her face and brushed the back of his fingers against her cheekbone. He kissed her on the lips. She allowed it but did not kiss him back.

"Men. If they knew what it felt like to have a child grow inside them they wouldn't be so eager to kill for a cause."

Farragut kissed her on the lips again.

Ingrid said, "I'm going to call my kids."

She turned her back on him and left the bathroom. He picked up the glass of Champagne and drained it. In the reception room, he could hear Ingrid talking on the phone to her children in German. Beyond the bathroom window he could hear the rain was coming down even harder now.

CHAPTER FORTY-FOUR

THE ARMORED International Navistar left the loading dock at Crane and Company's offices in Dalton, Massachusetts, at 8:03 a.m. Besides the 40 packing skids of US currency paper, four human beings were along for the ride. They were all undercover FBI agents wearing the drab gray uniform of Speed Armored Transport Services. Two of them sat in the front seat behind the bulletproof windshield, one driving and one, literally, riding shotgun. Two others sat in back with the paper. All the men had volunteered for this job. They knew they were going to be robbed by six individuals at a gas station off route I-95 in Baltimore. They knew that dozens of Federal Agents from the Treasury Department and the FBI were controlling the robbery and would be staking out the gas station as well as the escape route to the Port of Baltimore. The men were armed with 12 gauge shotguns and .357 pistols, but were under orders not to resist the robbery unless fired upon by the robbers. The men had been assured that this would not happen. As brave and practical souls with an indefatigable faith in the primacy of the Bureau among law enforcement agencies, they were, to a man, relaxed.

-:::::-

Three hundred and fifty miles to the south at a Shell service station in southeast Baltimore, Salaam was watching a young boy about the same age as his grandson Gary eat a giant Hershey's bar as he sat in the backseat of his mother's battered Honda Accord. The kid nibbled on the candy bar lengthwise like an ear of corn. The kid succeeded in attaching most of the melting chocolate to his face. The kid smiled at Salaam, in on the joke, and Salaam smiled back. The kid's mother, who was filling up the car, noticed the conspiratorial grin pass between her son and the black man in the olive parka cleaning the blackened windows of his white Chevy van on the other side of the pump island. She shot Salaam a nasty look, hung up the nozzle, climbed into her car, and drove off with her chocolate covered kid.

The mother and son reminded Salaam of Billie and Gary. They were nearly 3,000 miles away in Seattle but Salaam felt closer to them than he had in years. Although he had dangerous work to do before he would ever hope to see them again, the thought of being reunited with his family invigorated Salaam. He dipped the squeegee into the basin and vigorously rubbed it against the van's front windshield in time to the Barry White song playing over the station's PA. Shehabi and his men had remained in the van while Salaam cleaned the windows since, in this day and age, five Arab guys walking around together in even the most innocent setting could arouse suspicion.

Salaam was glad to get out of the van. Shehabi had been smoking his beloved Cuban cigars incessantly since they had sailed from Beirut. The smoke made Salaam sick to his stomach. But it was a small price to pay. Shehabi's habit would come in handy, although only Salaam knew how.

Salaam finished the windshield. He pulled up the sleeve of his parka and checked his cheap Timex watch. It was 1:47 p.m. The armored truck would be here in four hours. Salaam glanced around. His prison vision, sharpened by years of protecting his ass, was acute. Across the street was a lot filled with container trucks. No doubt FBI and Treasury Agents sat in those trucks and monitored the Shell station. Mia Kelly and Doug Alson may have been inside one of those trucks, or they may have been coordinating last minute details at the Port. Salaam looked up the street. The homeless brother in the old army jacket, the one pushing a grocery cart full of bottles and cans, he was probably a Fed. Ditto for the grease jockey in the station's garage, banging away at a Camaro's engine block like it was a drum.

With the fine-tuned instinct of a predatory animal, Salaam sensed the gaze of others was not upon him. This was his moment. He undid the latch of his watch so it was barely hanging on his wrist. He turned to the squeegee basin. It was a black plastic square attached to the motor oil shelf between the pumps. It had an opening twice as big as a mail slot into which you put the sponge end of the squeegee. The inside of the basin was hidden from view. As Salaam put the squeegee back into the basin he made sure his watch slipped off and sunk into the water.

"Damn," said Salaam, just in case anyone was listening. He stuck both his hands inside the basin slot to retrieve his watch in the grimy water. As he did so his hands were invisible for a few precious moments. In this time Salaam slid his left hand under the right sleeve of his parka. He felt a solid object attached to his right forearm by electrician's tape. The object featured a plastic substance linked to a small metal tube by red wires. The wires were connected to a Timex watch face identical to the one Salaam had dropped in the water. The object was the length of a letter envelope and weighed half a pound. Salaam slipped the object off his arm and pressed it against the top rim of the basin, where it adhered out of view eight inches above the waterline. Salaam then dipped both hands into the dingy water. He found his watch and pulled it out of the basin, muttering curses. The whole process took less than five seconds.

Salaam put the wet watch back on his wrist. It was still ticking. He walked over to the station's convenient mart. He bought six Almond Joy bars from the cashier. The cashier had raging acne, a silver stud in his right nostril, and a tattoo on his neck that read, "Ramona." Salaam figured he wasn't a Fed but you never knew.

After buying the candy Salaam crossed back to the van, opened the passenger side door, and climbed in. The air inside the van was thick with cigar smoke. Salaam coughed and handed Shehabi, behind the wheel, an Almond Joy.

"Here. Eat this instead of smoking that cancer stick."

Shehabi puffed on his Cuban and stared at the candy bar. "I don't like almonds. How about a Mounds bar?"

"I mean it, Hasan. You smoke during the job and it could set off the gas."

"Don't worry about the gas. Worry about doing your job."

Salaam didn't press the point. He turned and saw the other crew members bunched up in the back of the van. The brothers, Hafez and Rafik, were looking out the darkened windows at the service station imaging themselves standing out there with submachine guns pointed at the armored truck. Fady, the fat one, stared at the candy bars in Salaam's hands. Youssef, the quiet one, dozed.

Salaam said, "You boys hungry?"

The brothers replied in the affirmative. Fady blinked as if holding back tears. Youssef didn't bother to wake up. Salaam distributed the candy bars. He gave two extra ones to Fady because Shehabi had refused his and Youssef had started to snore. Salaam crawled into the back of the van and tugged on Youssef's arm. "Wake up Sleeping Beauty."

Youssef opened his eyes. He had a dopey smile on his face and white spittle at the corners of his mouth.

Salaam checked his cheap Timex watch. "Let's synchronize watches. I've got 1400 hours in five, four, three, two, one, mark."

The five Lebanese synchronized their watches, each identical to the one on Salaam's wrist. They were water resistant with luminescent hands. Salaam had purchased seven of them at a department store in Beirut just before their departure. He didn't tell Shehabi, or anyone else for that matter, about the extra watch ticking away inside the squeegee basin.

"What now, chief?" Salaam asked Shehabi.

Shehabi exhaled an indigo plume of carcinogens. "We go back to the lot, check the other vehicles, and wait."

Shehabi put the truck in drive and they pulled out of the service station. They drove a mile through the concrete wasteland that was southeast Baltimore and pulled into an abandoned lot where ash-colored slush covered the asphalt in grimy patches. Shehabi parked in between an identical white van and a 24-foot diesel box truck. The day before, Salaam had stolen the truck from a Mia Kelly-approved depot just outside the Port of Baltimore. It had a valid Maryland Port Authority decal on its windshield, essential if the robbers were going to be able to load their cargo and sail back to the Middle East. Salaam had rented the two vans from a Hertz Rent-A-Car, using the Maryland driver's license he had lifted from a simi-lar-looking African American male in crowded Baltimore Harbor. The man – an undercover Treasury Agent posing as a tourist — was too busy listening to a street musician play "Bewitched, Bothered, and Bewildered" on his alto sax to notice Salaam picking his pocket, just as the Asian kid behind the Hertz counter was too bored to notice that Salaam did not look exactly like the picture on his driver's license. Then again, the kid probably thought all blacks looked alike. As he waited in the van with the Lebanese terrorists, that thought – that all blacks looked alike – brought a smile to Salaam's lips.

You bet your ass they do, he thought. *You bet your sweet ass.*

-:::::-

"Look at that ass," Special Agent Trent Hurley said, admiring the swell of a slender blonde's buttocks in her tight jeans. "You could eat lunch off that ass; then eat her buns for dessert."

As much as he was tempted to check out the girl's glutes, Special Agent Max Voelker kept his gaze focused on the front door of a weathered Victorian house painted brown with yellow trim. Colored balloons had been taped around the doorframe and a sign painted in green tinsel proclaimed "Happy Birthday, Gary!" Voelker and Hurley were sitting in a silver Ford Taurus parked just east of Broadway in Seattle's Capitol Hill neighborhood. Students from nearby Seattle University, musicians, gays, and young families filled its tree-lined streets. There were excellent coffee shops, even by Seattle's high standards, and Hurley and Voelker had begun experimenting with more exotic brews than the average FBI agent would dare drink in the office.

"Here come two more," said Voelker, sipping his Jamaican Blue. He picked up a pair of binoculars and watched a black woman and her young son approach the front door of the house. The boy held a present wrapped with a bow. The woman wore a traditional African Sa Shu dress and headwrap. The bulky, brightly-colored dress and headwrap were similar to those worn by the nine other black women who had already entered the house with their sons. Unlike their mothers' colorful garb, the boys all wore black suits, white shirts, and black bow ties.

Hurley and Voelker watched the woman ring the bell. After a moment the door opened and Billie Hastings met her guests with a big smile. Gary, the birthday boy, stood shyly behind his mother, picking his nose. In contrast to their guests, Billie and Gary were dressed in cotton sweaters, jeans, and sneakers. Almost immediately another mother and child arrived, also bearing a gift. She, too, wore a traditional African dress and headwrap; her son wore the little black tux. The women greeted each other like long lost sisters, hugging and laughing. Through the open door Voelker could see more women and children, attired in like fashion, eating birthday cake. Billie let her guests enter her home, then closed the door behind her.

Hurley said, "How many is that now?"

Voelker put down his binoculars. He wrote something down on a clipboard. "Besides Hastings and her son, we got eleven moms and eleven kids. All boys."

"Why do the women dress like that?"

"Like what?"

"You know, with those big, fucking parachute dresses. I mean, you can't see any T and A. And that headwear. You can't see their hair."

"They dress like that to celebrate their African roots. Walt Pietrowski says they're members of the Muslim Women's League. Seattle chapter."

"How does Pietrowski know that?"

"Hastings told him. I thought you knew. He's working with her in the women's shoe department at Nordstrom. She has no idea he's a Fed. They've become friends. They chat."

Hurley laughed. "Pietrowski selling women's shoes. That's priceless."

"Hey, he gets a 30 percent discount on all merchandise. His wife's never been happier."

Voelker saw another black woman and her son approach the front door. They were dressed like the others. "It's an even dozen," he said, writing on his clipboard.

"They all look alike to me," said Hurley, polishing off his Sumatran bold. "Black as java. Say, I'm up for a fresh cup. How about you?"

Their operations room was a container truck parked in a crowded depot across the street from the Shell station. *(You might want to note geographic location, as just changed from Seattle.)* The forty-foot steel container had the words "Musso Brothers Dairy" painted in red script across its length. The container held not butter, cheese, and eggs, but computers, phones, and video monitors — not to mention two dozen special agents from both the FBI and Treasury. Mia Kelly and Doug Alson sat in front of the communications console and watched ten monitors showing various angles of the Shell station. It was 5:15 p.m. and the armored truck had radioed in that they were running a bit late. They had hit traffic outside Philadelphia and expected to re-fuel sometime before six. All the Feds could do was sit and watch and wait.

"There's Salaam," Alson said. He pointed at one of the monitors. It showed a white Chevy Astro van with darkened windows pulling into the deserted station. The van had circled the station a half-dozen times. Now it pulled up to the pump island closest to the garage. The driver's side door opened and Salaam got out. He made a show of checking the tires.

"What's he doing?" asked Alson.

"Checking the tires," replied Mia.

"No shit. Thanks for enlightening me."

"He's probably getting nervous," said Mia. "They were expecting the armored truck 30 minutes ago. We have no way to tell him about the delay."

Alson said, "I don't see why he's that worried. We're guaranteeing them clear passage to the Port. What's the difference to him if it goes down at five o'clock or an hour later?"

Mia shrugged. "He's there with a bunch of antsy terrorists. The sooner it's over with, the better."

Mia's explanation was reasonable but bothered Alson. Something didn't feel right. He was about to say this when the monitors showed the armored truck pulling into the Shell station.

Mia said, "Here we go."

CHAPTER FORTY-FIVE

SALAAM, KNEELING by the left front tire of the white van, saw the armored truck enter the Shell station. He glanced at his Timex watch. The time was 6:07 p.m. The armored truck was supposed to have arrived between 5:30 and 5:45.

Salaam knew that the heist would still go down as planned and the Feds had it all covered. The escape ship, the *Riad El Solh*, was waiting in the Port and would continue to wait as long as it took for the robbers to get the paper out of the truck and burn rubber to Dundalk Marine Terminal. Twenty minutes, two hours – what did it matter to Kelly as long as all the pieces were in place? What Kelly didn't know, however, was that there was one piece in place that only Salaam knew about. And it was ticking away inside the squeegee basin just a few feet away from where he was kneeling.

Salaam watched the armored truck park at the diesel fuel pump 20 yards away. Two guards exited the cab from the passenger side door. The first guard jogged to the station's convenient mart. He handed a credit card to the cashier then hustled back towards the restroom. The second guard grabbed a hose from the pump and began to fill the truck with diesel fuel. That meant that there were still two guards inside the truck. They would be sitting in the cab, not in the cargo area, as previously agreed upon.

The driver's side window rolled down and Salaam saw Hafez staring at him. He wore the same shit-scared expression as Rafik wore in the passenger seat. Salaam tried to reassure them with his best avuncular smile but he was scared, too.

Salaam glanced around the perimeter of the Shell station. The station squatted in the heart of the Canton industrial area of southeast Baltimore. Mia had chosen this spot for its desolation, isolation, and access to the port. There was no traffic on the pothole-infested streets. The only pedestrian was a black rat scurrying across the street towards the truck depot where, Salaam knew, the Feds were watching him.

Salaam was about to check his watch again when the reason for his impatience cruised into the station. It was another white Chevy Astro van, identical to the one that Salaam, Hafez, and Rafik had arrived in. The second white van parked next to the armored truck. Salaam felt fear shoot up from his balls to his brain. It was about to go down.

Salaam saw the dual rear doors of the second white van fly open. Youssef and Fady slipped out, wearing green olive parkas identical to Salaam's. Youssef sprinted to the front of the armored truck. Fady ambled over to the guard at the pump. Just as they had trained to do in the Beqaa Valley, they concealed their Uzi 9mm machine pistols until the last moment. Fady showed his gun to the guard at the pump and apologetically asked him to please remove his .357 from his holster and lay face first on the ground, which the guard did. While this was happening Youssef drew his Uzi and barked orders at the two guards in the truck's cab.

The guards exited with their hands over their heads. Youssef took it upon himself to disarm them, then ordered them to lie down in the same prone position. The guard at the pump, expedited things by placing his right foot in the small of their backs and gave them both a shove. One of the guards hit the ground mouth first and

Salaam heard a sickening *crack* as the pavement knocked out the man's two front teeth.

Salaam's first instinct was to make sure the guard was all right but he had a job to do. He knocked on the door of the first white van. Hafez and Rafik jumped out and raced towards the convenience mart. While Fady and Youssef bound the guards' arms with plastic restraints, the brothers took care of the cashier in the market and the guard in the restroom. Youssef and Fady marched their prisoners to the convenience mart, the injured guard staggering as he fought passing out. These three guards were locked inside the bathroom along with the cashier and the fourth guard. This all took about two minutes.

As soon as the guards were out of the way Salaam opened the rear doors of the first white van and removed a small black duffel bag. While he was doing this, the second white van slammed into reverse and roared backwards from the armored truck, parking next to the first white van. Shehabi exited the cab of the second white van. He smoked his cigar. His eyes sparkled with mischief; he was having fun.

Shehabi said, "My men did well, did they not? The guards didn't resist."

Because they were told not to resist, you ignorant pinhead, Salaam wanted to say. Instead he said, "Youssef got too rough. Knocked a guard's teeth out. You promised me your men would not use unnecessary force."

Shehabi shrugged. "A little violence lets them know we're for real."

And fifty Feds racing across the street with guns blazing will let you know what's real, thought Salaam. But again he kept his thoughts to himself.

Salaam said, "Let's get to it."

With the guards and the cashier locked in the restroom, the four men left the convenient mart and took up positions around the perimeter of the Shell station, keeping a lookout for any approaching traffic and obeying Salaam's orders to stay away from the blast area.

Salaam lugged the duffel bag over to the far southeast corner of the Shell station, as far from the gas pumps as possible. He unzipped the duffel bag and removed two one pound bricks of Semtex plastic explosive with digital timers already attached. As Salaam checked the gear, Shehabi got behind the wheel of the armored truck and backed it towards where Salaam was waiting. The guards had been instructed to leave the keys in the ignition, which they had, but Shehabi was confused when he exited the truck.

"I still don't understand why we don't take the paper out through the bulkhead door."

Shehabi was referring to the locked walk-thru door in the zinc-alloy steel bulkhead separating the cab from the cargo area. Salaam explained to Shehabi what he had already explained to him during their training in Lebanon. Shehabi had had a few too many glasses of Chateau Masur that night and Salaam had not encouraged him to keep his wits about him. As far as Salaam was concerned, the less Shehabi knew about detonation, the better.

"One. The bulkhead door has electric solenoid lock controls. Only one of the guards knows the combination and he has orders not to tell anyone," said Salaam, as he attached one of the Semtex bricks to the stress point between the 4-point dead bolts on the rear cargo doors. "Two, we don't have time to press each of the guards to find out which one knows the combination. Three, there's not enough room in the cab to blow off that door without blowing up the entire truck. And four, even if we could blow the door off the bulkhead, the opening's too narrow for the six of us to remove the packing skids before the cops get here."

Salaam attached the second Semtex brick over the external electrical solenoid lock in the center of the rear cargo doors. That's what made this job such a bitch. The cargo doors were locked from within by the 4-point deadbolts and from outside by the external solenoid lock. Even if you could get inside the cargo area through the bulkhead and open the deadbolts, the combination on the external solenoid lock was known only by the head of security at Crane and Company in Massachusetts and security personnel at the Bureau of

Engraving and Printing in Washington. None of the guards knew its combination; they couldn't exit or enter the truck through the cargo doors until arrival at the BEP. No one could. Unless, of course, you had a few bricks of plastic explosive on hand to blow the bastard out of Baltimore.

"That's it," said Salaam, setting the digital timers on the electrical blasting caps to one minute. While the two Semtex bricks would not explode at exactly the same moment, it would appear like they did. The delay interval, the time in milliseconds between successively detonated charges, would be minimal.

Salaam and Shehabi dashed away from the truck and crouched behind a trash dumpster 75 feet away.

As the seconds counted down Salaam watched a shiny, brown cockroach crawl out of a rusty crack in the dumpster and scurry away. The bug was a foot beyond the dumpster in open ground when a gigantic concussive force swept it away into the night. Salaam heard a sharp *bang* inside an enormous *boom*. The smell of cordite pounded the air and Salaam felt a pain in his right leg. At first he thought he was hit by debris, but when he checked his thigh he saw Shehabi's left hand gripping it so tightly that the veins on the back of his hand protruded like worms. Salaam gently removed Shehabi's hand from his leg and stood up to observe the truck.

He liked what he saw. The two pounds of Semtex had been more than enough to blow the cargo doors clean off the truck. The rear frame of the truck had sustained major damage, with jagged pieces of steel jutting here and there. The packing skids were visible inside the cargo hold and did not look to have been compromised by the detonation.

Armored debris had scattered around the Shell station but there was no fire. Semtex, like other plastic explosives, was not highly flammable. However, Salaam had warned his team that the threat of an explosion from static electricity reacting with gasoline vapors was real, if remote. He was pleased to see that they had all pulled on rubber work gloves as they descended upon the truck to begin unloading the paper.

"*Incroyable*," said Fady, lapsing into French as he stared at the destruction. The others looked equally impressed.

Salaam pointed to his watch. "We've got 15 minutes, 20 tops. The guards have to call in to their company to confirm they've fueled up and are on their way. When they don't, the cops will be called in to check up."

This wasn't true but Salaam didn't want things to slow down. Luckily, the men followed their training flawlessly. Youssef and Fady backed up the two white vans towards the rear of the armored truck. Salaam and Shehabi put on rubber work gloves and helped the others load one of the vans with currency paper. This took five minutes. After the first van was loaded, Shehabi got behind the wheel and Youssef and Fady climbed in the cab. The three of them sped off to the abandoned lot, where they were to start unloading the paper into the 24-foot diesel box truck.

Salaam stayed behind with Hafez and Rafik. The plan called for them to finish loading the second van, it being felt that if the authorities caught them in the act, at least one of the vans with paper would have a shot at getting to the Port. After loading their van, Salaam and the brothers would proceed to the abandoned lot to unload their cargo with the help of the others into the box truck. The entire team would then travel in the box truck to the Port. The switch from the vans to the box truck was necessary in case someone had witnessed the heist and told the authorities to be on the lookout for the vans. Also, unlike the vans, the truck could hold the full cargo of currency paper and had the Maryland Port Authority decal on the windshield that they needed to get into the Port.

As Salaam, Hafez, and Rafik loaded the rest of the paper from the armored truck into the van, Salaam realized they were in trouble. Without the three other guerillas to help, it would take them at least 10 minutes, maybe more, to do the job. The armored truck's late arrival had screwed up Salaam's plans. His gaze settled on the squeegee basin 50 yards away. Hafez and Rafik had their backs turned while loading a skid into the van. It was time to make his play.

Standing on the armored truck's tailgate, Salaam located a jagged piece of steel on the rear doorframe where a latch had been. He lowered his left hand and made a fist, engorging the veins of his lower arm with blood. Next he removed his work gloves to wipe sweat from his brow. As he did this he made a show of losing his balance and fell towards the doorframe, brushing the back of his left hand across the jagged edge.

Salaam said, "Ahhh."

By the time Hafez and Rafik had turned around, Salaam was clutching his bloody hand. The brothers had already had a rough day and were hanging on by a thread. The sight of Salaam bleeding profusely from what looked like his nearly severed extremity didn't help matters.

"What happened?" croaked Rafik.

"Cut myself on that damn door frame," said Salaam through clenched teeth. "Finish packing up. I'm gonna check out the market. I think I noticed a first aid kit in there earlier."

Hafez and Rafik exchanged a look. "Maybe we should all just head back now?" said Hafez nervously.

"Not until I treat this wound. This place is filthy and I can't risk the infection. Besides, with this hand, I'm not going to be much help loading those skids."

Salaam stepped off the tailgate. He jammed his wounded hand into a pocket of his parka. As Salaam hustled towards the convenient mart, Hafez and Rafik looked like two kids left alone at summer camp for the first time.

Salaam entered the convenient mart. He found the first aid kit between the diarrhea medication and the toilet paper in the middle aisle. He didn't have time to treat his injury so he stuck the kit inside his parka for later use. His hand was still bleeding but it didn't hurt. He knew from his time spent working in the prison infirmary that the human hand contained many surface veins that were non-essential. He had seen many cons at Terminal Island self-inflict superficial injuries like this to get out of work details. The wounds bled, but weren't serious.

Salaam strode towards the rear door of the convenience mart. He could hear the guards and the cashier talking inside the locked restroom. He stopped outside the door and waited. They were talking too low for him to make out what they were saying. He looked up and saw the surveillance camera watching him. He knocked on the door of the restroom.

"You all okay in there?" he asked.

There was a silence, then a muffled reply that one of the guards was in pain from hitting his mouth on the pavement. Salaam said nothing; he just waited. In a moment he heard the explosion from outside and felt the convenience mart shake like jelly.

Salaam exited through the rear door and dashed across the back corner of the Shell station lot. Fire filled the sky, lighting Salaam's way. He climbed over the concrete wall and entered into the back alley. He found the storm drain cover that Dexter had loosened earlier. He lifted the cover and dropped down into the sewer.

In the sewer, Salaam used the flashlight he had concealed inside his parka. He had splashed forward ten yards when he heard another explosion. He stopped and watched a wedge of white light slice through the drain grill above. He guessed that a second pump island had been set off by the first detonation. He prayed that Hafez and Rafik were all right, then resumed sloshing through the muck, and even though he was knee deep in shit he thought to himself that freedom had never smelled so sweet.

-:::::-

When the bomb planted by Salaam in the squeegee basin exploded, Hafez and Rafik were lifting a skid of paper inside the armored truck's cargo hold. Luckily, as the flammable gasoline vapors in the fuel tanks were set off by the first blast, the thick skin of zinc-alloy steel that covered the truck provided a fire shield as flames shot 100 feet into the air.

Rafik and Hafez felt the fierce heat rush into the open cargo hold. After a visual scan of the Shell station, the brothers realized that one of the pump islands had exploded. Instinct took over. They exited the cargo hold and slammed shut the van's dual rear doors. They had not gotten all the paper out of the armored truck, but in light of present circumstances Allah would certainly forgive them. They hoped Hasan Shehabi would, too.

Rafik had just taken the wheel and Hafez had sat his terrified ass in the passenger seat when the second pump island exploded. Self-preservation instinct kicked in. Rafik maneuvered the van out of the inferno and towards the rendezvous faster than Hafez could bark out the directions: *East on Keith Avenue! North on Broening Highway!* The landscape rocketed past, a nondescript gray fuzz. They heard distant police and fire sirens. They were terrified but focused. It wasn't until they were pulling into the abandoned lot where Shehabi, Youssef, and Fady were waiting when both brothers realized simultaneously that they had left Salaam back at the Shell station.

Hafez burst into tears and Rafik howled.

The rest was mercifully a blur. Shehabi quieted Rafik with a hard slap to the face; this also quelled Hafez's crying when he realized he didn't care for a similar remedy. Explanations were given, excuses made. Salaam was on his own — running, dead, or captured. Shehabi accepted it stoically. If Salaam were alive, he wouldn't talk; Shehabi was sure of this. And if Salaam were dead, well, it was a great honor to abandon your mortal flesh in the enemy's backyard, the better to remind him that hate has no boundaries.

Youssef and Fady had finished loading the rest of the paper into the box truck by the time Shehabi had calmed Hafez and Rafik. Shehabi assigned Fady the task of driving the box truck to the Port. With his green eyes and auburn hair he could have passed for a fifth generation Irish American from nearby Pigtown. The others hid in back with the paper. The vans were abandoned in the lot as the box truck pulled out and the robbers started the hazardous trip towards the Port of Baltimore and, ultimately, hopefully, God willingly — Lebanon.

CHAPTER FORTY-SIX

THE EXPLOSIONS across the street were caught on tape by the surveillance cameras but caught the Feds off-guard. The cameras first recorded Salaam injuring himself in the armored truck and entering the convenience mart to get a first aid kit. The Treasury Agent assigned to the monitor showing the back hallway saw Salaam waiting outside the restroom, but he turned his attention away during the first detonation; he did not see Salaam exit the building and slip into the alley. Like everyone else in the command post, he joined the frenzied discussion concerning what had happened and how to proceed with the operation. By the time he thought to glance back at his monitor, Salaam was long gone.

To this point, Mia was pleased with how the operation was going. Alson was more skeptical. He was concerned about the use of explosives in close proximity to unstable gasoline vapors. Mia had assured Alson that the pumps were lined with an aluminum mesh used by the military to reduce the risk of accidental gasoline initiations. Alson, however, had served in the Navy and knew these liners were not full proof. His worst fears had now been realized.

After the first explosion, Alson immediately wanted to send in his men to arrest Rafik and Hafez and to rescue the undercover FBI agents locked in the restroom. Mia argued against it. The entire mission would have to be aborted; not just the heist but the plan to get the Press in Iran. She also felt that the men in the restroom were not in immediate danger from the fire, an opinion she abandoned when the second pump island exploded. She then made the decision to send in the 12 FBI agents from the Hostage Rescue Team who were hidden in the warehouse adjacent to the Shell station. By this time Rafik and Hafez had fled and she could send in HRT without jeopardizing the operation.

Two tanker trucks filled with firefighting foam – on standby in case of this emergency — left the command post depot. They rumbled across the street to the Shell station while Mia barked into her radio and told HRT to rescue the Feds. Everyone assumed Salaam was still in the convenience mart and could be transported to the Port to meet up with the guerillas; that is, until Alson checked the monitors and realized that Salaam was nowhere to be seen.

"Salaam's gone, Mia."

Mia was listening on the radio to the HRT squad leader confirm that the four guards and the cashier were safe and accounted for. She wasn't going to panic, not with a container truck full of male Feds watching her every move. She spoke calmly into her radio.

"HRT, this is command. Have you located Salaam?"

"Negative," the HRT leader's voice came over her radio. "We've checked the store and back rooms. They're clean."

Mia turned to the other Feds in the command post. "Did anyone see Salaam get in the second van?"

A few Feds shook their heads. Some grunted in the negative. Some did nothing.

Mia pulled the radio to her lips.

"Street, this is command. Does anyone see the truck?"

There was some static and a voice over the radio.

"Command, this is Burton at rendezvous. The truck loaded and left three minutes ago."

"What was the headcount?"

They listened to some static as Burton conferred with one of his men.

"Command, I can confirm that five men are en route to the Port."

"Is Salaam one of them?"

"We can't confirm or deny that. All the men wore their parka hoods up to cover their faces. We can only confirm that at least five guerillas are on the truck."

Alson mumbled an expletive. Mia squeezed her radio. It looked like her hand would break before the contraption did.

"Street, this is command. Can anyone give me a visual on the truck?"

Another voice came over Mia's radio.

"Command, this is Welch. The truck just passed intersection of Willow Spring and Dunhill. ETA at Dundalk approximately two minutes."

She contemplated this news. The robbers were apparently on their way to Dundalk Marine Terminal as originally planned; however, nobody knew for certain if Salaam was with them, and all evidence pointed to the conclusion that he was not.

She turned to Alson. She didn't even ask the question before Alson answered it.

"Let's take them down at the Port, Mia. Cut our losses."

Mia clenched her jaw. "Salaam and the paper are essential to the mission. If we take out Shehabi and his men, we lose everything we put in place in Tehran."

"If we don't take them down we lose everything. Period. Salaam set us up. I'll bet you my pension that he set off a bomb to distract us. Fucker's probably half way to Havana by now."

"We don't know until the bomb squad does a post-op analysis. Salaam might show at the Port. Maybe after the second van abandoned him he decided to get there on his own. Remember, we've got his family under glass."

"Fuck Salaam. We can take down five terrorists. Their organization blew up a plane and killed two-dozen people. Every American taxpayer will feel their hard earned cash is doing more than subsidizing the US body count in Afghanistan."

"I could care less about a PR opportunity for the Department of Homeland Security. I care about the Islamic Republic of Iran using counterfeit cash to fund terrorism worldwide and maybe, just maybe, buy a nuclear warhead. The Press is a lot bigger than Shehabi and his men."

"Dammit, Mia! Shehabi and his men are murderers. So's Salaam for that matter. We'll put out a BOLO and stick his face at the top of the Ten Most Wanted List. He won't be able to scratch his ass for fear a cop's gonna crawl out of it."

The thought of a "Be on the Lookout" alert distributed to every law enforcement organization in the country did not reassure Mia. It had been her idea to spring Salaam from prison. It would be the end of her career, even if they caught Salaam. No. She had lost her child, her marriage, and her sense of blessed invincibility in the last few dreadful years. She wasn't going to lose the mission. Not yet.

"Let's go to Dundalk. If Salaam's not with them, I'll make the call then."

"Shit," groaned Alson. But it was Mia's call to make.

CHAPTER FORTY-SEVEN

S ALAAM EMERGED from a storm drain ten blocks away from the Shell station. Dexter had marked the underside of the manhole cover with yellow paint. As Salaam crawled out of the drain he felt a powerful hand grab his arm and pull him to his feet.

Dexter smiled and said, "What's up, Doc?"

The two old friends embraced. Dexter Opie had called Salaam "Doc" ever since they had met in the library of Terminal Island 12 years before. Salaam had been re-reading Dostoyevsky's "The Brothers Karamazov" and Dexter was studying a correspondence manual for becoming a long distance trucker. Dexter had remarked on the thickness of Salaam's book and suggested that Dostoyevsky should be renamed "Door-stop-evsky." The cons struck up a friendship that had lasted even after Dexter won his parole and moved across the country to New Jersey, where he got a job driving a big rig for Garden State Steel.

Salaam choked back tears. The relief of seeing a familiar face for the first time in months overwhelmed him.

"LTD. You are a sight for sore eyes."

Salaam's nickname for Dexter was LTD, which stood for Long Tall Dexter. This was also the nickname of the great tenor sax player,

Dexter Gordon, whose masterful ballad playing had kept Salaam sane during some very dark days in the joint.

Dexter put one of his big hands on Salaam's shoulder. "Told you we'd make it, Doc."

Sirens rose in the distance. Dexter maneuvered Salaam towards the yellow Garden State Steel tractor-trailer parked a few feet away. He got behind the wheel and Salaam slid into the sleeping compartment behind the cab. Dexter had custom built a small, concealed section beneath the sleeping compartment floor. Salaam would be safe here in the event the Feds stopped them on the way to the Port. Dexter had secured Salaam passage on a Nigerian freighter, *Nnamdi Azikiwe*, bound for Lagos later that night. Salaam's first-rate fake passport and visa — courtesy of a forger friend from his prison days — would get him into the country. Once in Nigeria, a Muslim cleric named Dalhatu Ibrahim, who Salaam had started a correspondence with while still incarcerated, would provide sanctuary. At least long enough for Salaam to put the next phase of his plan into effect.

Before Salaam crawled into the narrow space and pulled the trap door over himself, he asked the questions he had been meaning to ask all along.

"Hey, LTD, you did get the note to Billie, right?"

"Yes. They had a Fed watching her but I put it in the boot and delivered it just like you told me to."

"And Gary?"

"She and the boy are grand, Doc. Now shut your ass back there and let me drive."

-:::::-

Vance Llewellyn was drunk and pissed off. He had been a long-shoreman for the Oriole Stevedore Company for just nine months and already he was out on his ass. Perkins, the operations manager, had just canned him for drinking on the job again.

Llewellyn took another gulp of Wild Turkey. Yes, he had to admit it: he had a drinking problem. But wouldn't you drink if the whore you had married had left you for another man, and a nigger no less?!

The spade's name was Malcolm, as in Motherfucking Malcolm. He was a big, handsome spook, a former three-sport star from DeMatha Catholic, who had ripped up his knee and lost out on that scholarship to the University of Maryland. Llewellyn had read about him in the sports pages of the Baltimore *Sun*. He'd felt bad for him when it happened – hey, Llewellyn *loved* the Terps – and even liked the guy when he'd first met Malcolm on his first night tending bar down at their local watering hole Clancy's. What Llewellyn didn't like was the way his wife flirted with Malcolm and kept insisting on going back even though she always called Clancy's a dump. Well, it was a dump. And she was whore. Turned out she started up with Malcolm the next day.

Three months later the bitch, who had bankrupted him by getting pregnant three times (didn't she swear she was on the pill?) and spending his money like he was Fort fucking Knox, had moved in with Motherfucking Malcolm and filed for divorce.

The bitch had ruined him. The bitch and her jigaboo boyfriend.

Llewellyn was yanked from his bourbon daze by the blare of truck horn. He looked up and saw a yellow tractor-trailer stopped in the road behind him. The headlight beams blinded him. Llewellyn managed to lurch out of the way and let the truck pass.

Llewellyn watched the truck park next to the Pier 11 warehouse. He watched a man climb down from the cab. He saw the man's parka was olive. He saw the bandage on the man's hand was white.

He saw the color of the man's skin was black.

As the truck drove off, Llewellyn saw another color: red. The color of his rage. Vance Llewellyn, possible father of that bitch's children, and the sap cuckolded by a black tailback with a bum knee, was out of a job and out of luck but not out of options.

When all else failed, he could still kick some black ass.

-:::::-

Special Agent Ben Tucker killed time by leaning against a forklift and trying not to look like he was a Treasury Agent in disguise as a longshoreman. He polished off the java in his purple Baltimore Ravens thermos mug and decided to stroll over to the Pier 11 warehouse and get a refill. It was a quiet night at the terminal, just a single ship loading off the pier, and he saw only one longshoreman as he strolled over to the warehouse. The man was obviously drunk, cursing to himself and holding a bottle of bourbon. Tucker saw the drunk stumble out of the way of a large yellow truck like an ostrich on ice skates. Stupid fuck. He was going to get himself killed. Tucker decided to help the bastard when he saw the black guy in the parka exit the big rig.

Tucker's balls bounced off his work boots. It was Salaam.

Tucker pulled the radio to his mouth so fast he almost bashed in his front teeth.

"Command, this is CNX. I've got Salaam in my sights. He must've took a wrong turn."

Mia Kelly's voice blitzed over his radio as hard and bright as a .38 slug.

"CNX, maintain visual contact. Backup is on the way."

No sooner did Tucker retreat behind a shipping container so he could keep an eye on Salaam then he saw the drunk longshoreman charge the terrorist.

"Oh shit," thought Tucker, contemplating his options. "This is not good."

-:::::-

The black Ford Tacoma sped northwest on Broening Highway from Dundalk to CNX. Only two miles of port separated the two terminals. Alson kept his size 14 Florsheim loafer planted on the accelerator. Mia sat next to him and finished up a phone call with the Director of Port Security. She snapped her clamshell cellphone shut and stuck it in her jacket pocket.

"DPS confirms that Shehabi and his men entered Dundalk and loaded their cargo on the *Riad El Solh*. He says there's only one ship scheduled to depart tonight from CNX. That's the *Nnamdi Azikiwe*, leaving for Lagos, Nigeria, from Pier 11 in 20 minutes. She's loaded down with a cargo of steel and coal."

"And Shareef Salaam. Unless we get there in time," added Alson. He leaned on the horn and blasted past a Hyundai that was clogging up the fast lane. The noise of the engine and the horn almost drowned out Tucker's voice over the radio.

"Command, this is CNX. Salaam is being assaulted by a third party. Advise, over."

Alson responded by pressing his foot harder down on the accelerator.

Mia said into her radio, "CNX, Can you positively identify the third party?"

"Negative. I think it's a shitfaced longshoreman, over."

Mia rolled her eyes. Alson kept his on the road.

"A minute away, Mia. Want to notify the port police?"

She shook her head. The Director of Port Security was the only POB law enforcement officer privy to all that was going on. She had her own men in place and hadn't wanted some overzealous dock cops to blow the show.

Mia said into her radio, "CNX, hold your position. Backup is almost there, over."

The voice coming back over the radio sounded shrill.

"Command, this guy is beating the shit out of Salaam with a bottle."

"Serves the motherfucker right," mumbled Alson.

Mia had always been a control freak. Straight A's at Choate and Dartmouth. A Rhodes scholarship and a 40-mile a week running habit that, in her forties, was turning her knees into chalk dust. She had a perfectionist's faults – a propensity to judge quickly and trust slowly – but also the virtues: competence, dedication, and an unflagging determination to do the job herself so as to ensure it be done right; or if she failed, at least she'd know who to blame.

Mia said into her radio, "CNX, hold your position. I repeat, hold your position. Copy, over."

Alson flashed his I.D. to the guard as they drove into the CNX terminal.

Mia waited for Tucker's confirmation over the radio but there was only silence.

CHAPTER FORTY-EIGHT

BEN TUCKER HAD watched the lush trying to crack open Salaam's head like it was a Chesapeake Bay blue crab. It was like he had something personal against Salaam, like he'd fucked his mother or fondled his kid. Whatever it was, it was getting out of hand. And Tucker's orders be damned, he was going in before Salaam got killed. Let Kelly chew his ass out later.

Tucker moved away from the container he was hiding behind and pulled out his gun. He walked forward and aimed at the drunk.

"Treasury Department! Drop the bottle and lay face first on the ground!"

Salaam swiveled his neck and stared in dazed amazement at the man with a gun. The drunk apparently didn't hear Tucker because he continued to batter Salaam.

"Fucking great," Tucker said to himself.

-:::::-

Salaam wanted to pass out. The angry man straddling his chest made it hard to breathe. The bottle swung by the angry man made it hard to think. The bottle was going to break. Salaam knew he would die.

Salaam tried to think of chemical equations but the periodic table of elements, once as familiar to him as his own skin, proved elusive.

Salaam heard a voice identify itself as a Treasury Agent. Salaam turned his head and saw the man with the gun. He was about to connect it with The Mission but another bottle blow knocked the connection out of his head.

Salaam's central nervous system exploded. He knew the bottle had broken because he felt shivers of glass prick his flesh.

Salaam felt the angry man's weight shift on top of him. He heard a scream. He felt something warm splash on his face. Blood. But it wasn't *his* blood. His broken consciousness somehow understood this.

Salaam heard a *thump*. The Treasury Agent with the gun was suddenly lying next to him. His eyes were open but not looking at anything. His neck looked red and raw like steak tartar. A crimson pool pulsed from beneath it.

Salaam looked up. He saw the angry man on top of him raise the broken bottle above his head to gain leverage for the killer blow.

Salaam closed his eyes. He thought about Billie and Gary. He thought about Victoria, his dear wife, who would surely be waiting for him in heaven. That is, if Salaam made it to heaven after the hell he had put her through.

Salaam heard a *pop*. Then he heard another *pop*.

Salaam opened his eyes. He looked up. The weight on his chest was gone. The angry man with the bottle was gone. He saw thick clouds covering the moon.

A face blocked his view of the moon. It was a pretty face, Mia Kelly's face. Her jaw was clenched.

Two strong arms lifted Salaam to a standing position. He sucked in air. He smelled after-shave. Old Spice. The crap that had polluted his nostrils on those long drives with Alson in North Carolina and Fort Bragg.

Alson said, "In the fucking car. Now."

Alson march stepped Salaam to the black Tacoma. Before Alson shoved him in the back seat, Salaam saw Mia standing over the bodies of the angry man and the Treasury Agent with the steak tartar neck. She had her big black gun clutched in her tiny white hand.

Alson stood outside the car. He clamped a hand on Salaam's shoulder to hold him upright and dabbed at the wounds on Salaam's face with a towel.

"Nice work, Professor. Thanks to you, we've got one dead Treasury Agent and one dead, drunk dipshit. Personally, I could care less about the dipshit. But the Fed, well, for that I'd like to see you get the chair. Or at least a needle in your arm."

Salaam wanted to explain that he had not killed anyone but he knew his excuses meant nothing at this point.

"Looks like your nose is broken. Does this hurt?"

Alson pressed his thumb into the bridge of Salaam's nose. The pain blasted through his body. He wanted to scream but found the fortitude to just grit his teeth.

Alson chuckled. "Tough guy. Your cuts are superficial. Babe Ruth back there had too much bourbon in his blood to swing straight. Here, asswipe. Clean yourself the fuck up."

Alson tossed the towel in Salaam's face. He entered the Tacoma through the driver's side door and got behind the wheel.

Mia climbed into the back seat with Salaam. She shut the door and the Tacoma moved forward. It drove out of the CNX terminal then headed southeast back to Dundalk.

Mia stared straight ahead, not looking at Salaam. "You're getting on the other boat."

Salaam dabbed the blood trickling from his busted nose. "Shehabi might kill me."

"You can take your chances with Shehabi. Or with me."

She showed Salaam her gun. Her eyes were as black as the gunmetal.

Mia and Salaam said nothing for a while. Alson drove while he spoke on his cellphone. He hung up and glanced at Mia in the rear view mirror.

"Everything's kosher in Seattle. Gary, Jr.'s having a birthday party and he and mom have been inside all day. The Bureau boys are on them like stink on shit." Alson caught Salaam's eyes in the mirror. "I had you pegged wrong. I thought you gave a fuck about your family. But you were gonna bolt and leave them to the wolves. You're a hell of a role model."

Salaam gazed at the gauze on his cut hand. He thought about how things had gone terribly wrong. He knew it had been a risk to try to escape from the same port as Shehabi and his men, but he felt the risk was worth it. The Port of Baltimore was huge, a small city really, and it offered his best chance to escape the country. A flight out would have been impossible and the more time he spent hiding in the US the better the odds he would have been captured. But now he *was* captured and he had no idea how Mia Kelly was going to play her next move.

Mia stared out the window at the graceless scenery. Finally she said, "I don't want you to explain anything. I think you set us up. I can't prove it until we do a chemical analysis of what set off those gas pumps, but that's going to take time, time I don't have. If you were setting us up, then you were also setting up Shehabi. Either you can talk your way out of it with him or you can't. Personally, I hope you do. I hope you convince him that things got screwed up at the Shell station, that a spark or static electricity or the force of blowing the doors off the truck triggered the gas pumps to blow. If you can do that, then you can finish this job. If you don't finish the job, if Shehabi kills you or you run when you get back in the Middle East, then make no mistake about it, you will ruin the lives of your daughter and grandson. The IRS will hound them and you will be given highly publicized credit for the murder of those two dead men back there at the other terminal. Your loved ones will be tainted by association and fucked for life. I will personally see to it."

Alson drove the Tacoma right down to the pier where the *Riad El Solh* was still loading. Neither Mia nor Alson made a move, so Salaam opened the door himself and exited the vehicle. His broken nose throbbed but the cool night air filled his lungs and he began to feel almost normal. Normal for a man about to walk the plank.

Salaam checked the pockets of his parka. His hand found the first aid kit. Good. He would need it for the cuts on his face. He dug into another pocket and located his forged papers. He would need them to show that he was on the ship's manifest. He was good to go.

Alson and Mia watched Salaam as he boarded the boat. They kept watching for another hour until the boat finished loading and pulled away from the pier, its heavy horn cutting through the fog like a sledgehammer.

Alson turned to face Mia. She looked so drawn and tired and deeply disappointed that he felt something he had never felt for a woman before, including his two ex-wives, tenderness.

"We can still board the ship and make the arrests, Mia. At least that way we got something to show for all our hard work. Otherwise, we got zilch. Shehabi's not stupid. Odds are he'll kill Salaam and dump his body overboard half-way across the Atlantic."

"Maybe. Or maybe he believes Salaam's story and it goes down like we planned." Mia shrugged. She was not usually a shrugger but a shrug seemed the only appropriate gesture given the circumstances. "Either way," she added. "Salaam's a dead man."

Alson put the Tacoma in gear and they drove back to Washington in silence.

-:::::-

The cabin was drafty. There was an open porthole that let in the thick ocean air. A couple of cots with frayed yellow sheets flanked a steel night table. It wasn't the Queen Mary.

Salaam stood in the middle of the room and shivered. Shehabi straddled a chair in front of him. He sucked on his cigar and contemplated the bullshit that Salaam had shoveled out of his mouth. The other guerillas had been excused to kill time in another part of the ship.

"An accident? You tell me it was an accident?"

They'd been over it and over it but they were going over it again.

"Look. I've been telling you since Baalbek that gasoline vapors are unstable. Any number of things could have set off those pumps. The initial blast. Static electricity. A spark from your cigar."

"Or a change of heart by a traitor?"

"If were trying to betray you, what am I doing here? And what are you doing with 30 skids of US currency paper, thanks to me? If I were a traitor, I'd be long gone and you'd be arrested or dead."

Shehabi flicked some ash on the floor. "I don't trust you, but what I think is not important now. I've already radioed ahead to Tehran. They are pleased by the outcome of our mission. They've authorized the printing of $50 million in counterfeit to finance our joint operations in America."

Shehabi lifted himself off the chair. He walked towards Salaam and studied his face. He took another puff and blew a smoke ring into Salaam's broken beak.

"But just in case you get an overwhelming urge to borrow a lifeboat and take a premature leave, Youssef will watch you for the rest of the trip."

Shehabi opened the cabin door. Youssef was waiting outside. He stepped inside the cabin. Salaam could see the Uzi bulge beneath his parka.

Shehabi left and closed the door behind him. Youssef's expression would not have been inappropriate for a baked potato, except the potato might appear more animated.

It was going to be a long trip back to Beirut.

CHAPTER FORTY-NINE

AZADI SAT HUNCHED over a desk in his apartment, engraving the new currency plates. He was unaware that at roughly that very hour, he had a co-conspirator named Shareef Salaam who was escaping by sea, bearing the Crane currency paper for which Azadi's plates were intended. Azadi knew only his piece of the puzzle. That was the plan and the plan, as far as he knew, was proceeding as perfectly as his engraving of the plates. After nearly five hours of focused labor, Azadi cut the "t" at the end of the word "Trust." *In God We Trust? No*, he thought. *Trust Omar Azadi to engrave the finest counterfeit currency plates in all God's creation.*

"*Dead Presidents in black and green. Dead Presidents mean the money ain't clean,*" he sang, giddy with a sense of accomplishment.

Azadi wrapped the plates in linen and hid them in his mattress. He thought of opening up a tin of caviar to celebrate but decided against it. He would need all the caviar for the guards over the next few days.

But it was too early to celebrate anyway. The plates were just one part of the plan. The devil was in the details. In fact, the production process of the new bills was so complex and the layers of security features so great that even the U.S. government hadn't gotten it right. In 2010, they had completed a run of 1.1.billion of the new bills. Almost 30% of the run had been unusable because of a creasing problem in which paper folds over during production, revealing a blank, unlinked portion of the bill face. At a printing cost of 12 cents per bill, the taxpayers would be on the hook for some $120 million of very expensive shredded paper.

Good enough for fucking government work, thought Azadi. The great irony was he had drilled with the equipment courtesy of Alson and Kelly and knew the procedure perfectly. But of course, printing perfect bills were not part of the plan. Not at all.

General Farjad had told Azadi to telephone when he had completed the plates. He answered the phone on the first ring.

"This is Farjad."

"General, this is Omar. The new plates are completed."

"Excellent. It is convenient that you should call now, Omar, because I have just received some most interesting news that concerns you."

Farjad didn't volunteer the information. He made Azadi ask for it. "May I ask what that news is, General?"

"We will be needing you to print more money. The order is for $50 million."

Azadi felt a surge of excitement. He didn't know all the details but he knew this $50 million order was a result of Kelly and Alson's plan. "When do you need me to start, General?"

"We will put your new plates to work immediately. A meeting with the man who has requested the money is planned for ten days' time. We would like to have the money ready by then."

Azadi followed the script the Feds had written for him. "Unfortunately, that's not possible. The new issue $100 bills must be printed on special currency paper. The paper contains security features that I can't replicate. I suggest we continue printing older issue bills until —"

"You will have the new currency paper in a few days, well before the meeting," cut-in Farjad with a cockiness in his voice.

Azadi's heart raced with excitement. Back in the States, Kelly had promised him the delivery of the Crane paper at just the right time. The plan was proceeding perfectly.

"If that is the case, I will begin creating the printing sheets from the plates tomorrow, General."

"Of course you will, Omar. That is what we expect of you."

Azadi heard Farjad's hang-up *click*.

Azadi thought of writing a letter to his father back in the States, a letter he would never send. He comforted himself with the thought that his father would soon profit handsomely from his heroism. And then his thoughts drifted to his darling wife Parisa. He had not seen her since he took the Press as a mistress almost ten days ago. Putting her out of his mind had been the only way to do the job without cracking up. But the job was done and Parisa was only a phone call away. He picked up the phone again.

"Come over," he said without giving his name.

"I will," she said.

-:::::-

Parisa lay at Azadi's side, snoozing after the sex. He lay awake, running his finger up and down her toned thigh, still glistening from exertion. He drank in the sight of her, finally turning away when he felt almost satiated by her perfection. There was only the here and now. There was only this bed and this woman. He kept telling himself that as his eyes closed and sleep came and the trickle of fear that always flowed through his subconscious swelled into a raging river.

A nightmare. He was outside himself now, watching himself. Not in the apartment now, no. He was watching as he and faceless Delta Force grunts fought their way out of the Press. They were down too deep, there were too many faceless Revolutionary Guards with guns. Bullets flew everywhere. A bullet flew into his mouth and buzzed like a bee; he tasted blood.

His body grew rigid with fear. He remained like that for a while, until Parisa stirred and snapped him out of it. She touched his mouth and the spell of immobility was broken.

"Oh, my sweetheart, you have bitten your lip."

Azadi ran his fingers over his lip and realized she was right; it was bleeding.

Parisa kissed him. "My dearest, darling. What is the matter?"

"I had a bad dream," he said, sitting up.

"What were you dreaming about?"

Death. His death. Her death, too, he realized. Because once the mission went down, whether he lived or died, Parisa would be implicated. Farjad and the Revolutionary Guards would make Parisa pay for his betrayal. But he couldn't tell Parisa that. He looked at her and nearly gasped. He wanted to fuse with her, become one with her, to obliterate any trace of himself.

Clarity. He loved her. This *was* love, deep, profound, and unconditional. But he realized to say it now, to her face, was to pass the point of no return. He knew, as surely as he knew his own heart, that if he admitted that love to her right now, the mission was over. How could he risk his life when he wanted to spend the rest of his life with this woman?

And then, as if she were reading his mind, Parisa said, "I love you, Omar."

He kissed her and said nothing. She smiled and offered to cook him dinner. She was going to make him a delicious *dolmeh-yeh felfel*, peppers filled with ground meat, rice, and herbs.

Parisa dressed and went out to shop, promising to return in an hour. After she left, Azadi went to his desk and began to write down the words that he could not say to her. Writing the truth down on paper confirmed it in his heart. He wrote down the truth about everything. It felt good to come clean. After he was done, he held the letter in his hands and crinkled the paper and it was like touching his own soul. The feel made it real.

Azadi hid the letter in his mattress with the plates. He lay on the bed, waiting for Parisa. He put on his iPod and listened to the rapper

Jay-Z spout off about money, guns, whores, and hatred. For the first time in his memory, he couldn't relate to the aggressive music and angry lyrics. He himself had run out of rage. He felt, for the first time in his life, truly at peace.

CHAPTER FIFTY

"YOU DON'T LOOK well, John," Ingrid said to Farragut across the candles and crystal. "Perhaps we should call it a night?"

Farragut and Ingrid had secured a table at Tehran's smartest Indian restaurant. Normally, Farragut loved to indulge in a good meal but not tonight. His stomach was tied in knots, thanks to Shareef Salaam.

Hours earlier Farragut had been resting in his hotel room when he received a phone message requesting he attend a cocktail party at the British embassy. Farragut knew this was a coded message from Mia Kelly to contact her immediately.

At the embassy Farragut was ushered into the ambassador's office. There he used the ambassador's secure line to call Mia at her office in Washington. She told him about the Baltimore debacle and Salaam's possible treachery. She was having serious second thoughts about allowing Salaam to return to the Middle East, and gave Farragut the option of standing down the mission. He could head home ASAP. Jashni would be given orders to terminate Azadi. Mossad agents would do the same to Salaam upon his arrival in Lebanon if, of course, Shehabi didn't terminate him first.

Farragut was stunned by the news. Not that Salaam had tried to pull a fast one; Farragut supposed he would have tried the same thing in Salaam's position. No, what really shocked Farragut was the realization that the mission hung on such a thin thread. And what shocked him even more was how much he cared that the thread didn't snap before his health did.

He was dying now, really dying. Earlier that week he had suffered a crippling migraine, his worse yet. He had also experienced double vision when trying to read at night. If he had not been a forthright individual or a superb athlete — one attuned to the potencies and imperfections of his body — he could have attributed the symptoms to exhaustion or stress. But Farragut was under no illusions that the tumor was getting better. It had begun its inexorable destruction of his vitality. He only hoped he could resist it long enough to fulfill his mission and perish with an elegant sense of completion.

The alternative? Go back to Dartmouth and teach preppies about the Peloponnesian War. No way. He was fighting his own war now. That, he realized to his surprise, was what he was now living for and, ultimately, dying for.

But the news about Salaam made Farragut realize how little control he really had over how events played out. He had told Mia that he wanted to continue with the mission, that it was worth waiting to see if Salaam showed in Beirut before deciding to pull the plug. She had agreed. *Reluctantly*, he thought, *and for good reason.* Salaam, Azadi, even Jashni could fail to perform their assigned tasks, either through willfulness or incompetence. Farragut could die before all the pieces were in place. And Mia could, of course, stand down the mission if she decided it was no longer worth the risk. She wanted the Press, but she lived in a sea of shifting political tides and would do anything to advance – or save — her career.

Farragut pushed away his plate. He had barely touched his tandoori chicken. It was time to call it a night. Farragut felt as terrible as he no doubt looked.

"Shall I call you tomorrow?" he said, signaling the waiter for the check and signaling Ingrid that they would not be spending the night together.

"If you're up to it," she said, preoccupied with the contents of her purse and avoiding looking him in the eyes.

They left the restaurant together. Farragut saw Ingrid off in a cab. He received nothing more than a parting peck on the cheek. He walked the short distance to the National Museum, pulling his collar up against the cold night and thinking of the frosty wedge of formality that had come between them since London.

She's pulling away from me, he thought. *She knows about the tumor, she knows that I am CIA. I am a dead man, either way, and she is pulling away.*

The National Museum sat just north of the bazaar, situated amongst a cluster of museums on Eman Khomeini Avenue. Farragut walked up the steps to the building. The sight of the elegant, red brick façade never failed to thrill him. It was more than 35 meters high and 50 meters wide. The French architect, Andre Godard, had designed it to mimic the Arch of Chosroes, entrance to the famous palace of the Sasanian Empire at Ctesiphon. Farragut appreciated the harmony between the Bastan's structure and the treasures held within. Such care and consideration for aesthetic principles were rare in the modern metropolis of Tehran.

Farragut knocked at the entranceway. Reza, the elderly security guard at the front desk, shuffled over on arthritic knees and unlocked the door. It was not uncommon for Farragut to work late at night in the office he kept at the museum; the security guard would suspect nothing. Farragut gave Reza a doggie bag of his tandoori chicken and the man's bright smile indicated the gesture was appreciated.

"Professor Farragut, you look so tired," he said, sniffing his chicken. "Perhaps you should sleep rather than work so late tonight."

"I'll sleep when I'm dead, Reza. Besides, night is the quietest time to work."

Farragut drifted like a ghost through the dark, empty exhibit halls. Here were displayed artifacts of a glorious, varied, and violent past. Pottery molded by men more than 3000 years before Muhammad. Bronze Age cudgels and maceheads. Gilded bowls and swords from the Achaemenid period when the Persian dynasty was first established around 550 B.C. But as he walked to his office Farragut barely paid attention to these priceless treasures from the past. He was too preoccupied with perilous events in the future.

Farragut now knew, thanks to Azadi's maps and descriptions, the level and quality of security at the Supernote Press. He would need to perform at his peak skill level. The Press was located beneath Gheyam Hospital and Farragut planned to use this to his advantage. A cancer-stricken professor would have a perfect excuse to be there on the day the raid went down.

Farragut reached a storage room on the basement level. The only sounds this deep down were his own footsteps. The only light in the corridor came from a naked, flickering 60-watt bulb. He caught a glimpse of his reflection in the glass window of the door. The flesh of his once handsome face was becoming sallow over sunken cheeks. Dark shadows fell in the crevices beneath his eyes. The tumor reigned triumphant at last. Was it just, well, luck, that his decline had seemed to accelerate in order to bolster the alibi he would soon need? Farragut didn't know whether he had subconsciously let himself go. He was not an expert in those things. His area of expertise lay inside the room.

Farragut opened the door and entered the room. He locked the door behind him and turned on the light. The room served as a work studio for the museum and contained everything anyone would need to perform detailed restoration of artifacts: work lights, tools, chemicals, and plenty of space.

Farragut saw the unopened crate containing the bull's head. Markings on the crate in both English and Farsi indicated the diplomatic status of the cargo.

Farragut produced a crow bar from a tool bench on the near wall. He jammed it into the still unbroken seals holding the crate together, for according to his instructions, it had not been touched since arriving in Tehran. Once the seals were broken, Farragut jimmied the crow bar into the crate's seams. He felt flush from the stuffy air and his own exertions but the sides of the crate gave way and the bull's head inside was revealed.

Farragut selected a chisel style, steel rock hammer for the next part of the procedure. He ran his free hand over the back of the bull's head and found the slightly raised, hairline fissure. The untrained eye would see the detail as erosion if it noticed it at all. With the precision of a diamond cutter, Farragut wedged the tip of the rock hammer into the fissure. He drove it deeper into the stone with a few taps of his finger. Then he twisted the head of the hammer to the side.

By design, the bull's head cleaved neatly in two. Each half contained a cavity. Packed into the larger cavity were 20 pounds of high-grade C4 plastic explosives. Packed into the smaller cavity was a steel, shockproof square box holding 10 detonators.

Farragut removed a black duffel bag from a utility closet. Inside the larger duffel was smaller duffel. Farragut placed the box of detonators inside the smaller duffel bag. He packed the bricks of C4 into the larger duffel bag. The packing took less than a minute. Next Farragut fitted the two halves of the bull's head together, joining them with an archaeologist's liquid adhesive. He finished up by applying a restorative, color-matched paste along the almost invisible hairline fracture. Farragut took a workman's pride in the fact that when the paste had dried a half-hour later there was no sign of the split. The technicians back at the Agency couldn't have done it better. The bull's head appeared beat up and weathered as befitted an authentic antiquity. It certainly did not appear to have been a vessel for smuggling explosives.

Farragut strained to carry the duffel bags through the museum to the front entrance. Reza, the security guard, who had often seen Farragut leaving the building with suitcases and duffels (filled with the professor's prodigious paperwork, he assumed) gave a wave goodnight and thanked Farragut for the delicious tandoori chicken. He repeated that Farragut looked like he needed a good night's rest.

It was past midnight. Farragut hit the street and flagged a cab. Jashni arrived seconds later as planned. Farragut climbed into the cab, shoving the duffel bags beside him on the seat.

"There's been a development," said Farragut. Then he told Jashni everything that Mia had told him about Baltimore and Salaam. Jashni nodded and clucked his tongue against his buckteeth. Farragut may as well have been telling him a recipe for marinara sauce. *Just another day at the office for him*, thought Farragut. Jashni was Mossad and used to plans going to hell. Farragut for the first time felt grateful to have the man's cool-headed experience on his side.

"How was London?" asked Jashni as he pulled away from the curb.

"Great," replied Farragut, relieved to not be talking about Salaam anymore.

"Indeed. I hear the restaurants now rival Paris though I haven't been in a while. By the way, you look awful. I hope it was something you ate and not the other thing."

The other thing, as Jashni so delicately put it. The tumor. Jashni knew about Farragut's health; Mia had seen fit to disclose it to the Israelis. Still, Farragut didn't want to get into it.

"The C4 and detonators are here," said Farragut, patting the duffel bags. "I'll leave the bags with you. Get them to Azadi as soon as possible."

"In the morning," said Jashni. They drove in silence the remainder of the ride to the Laleh.

CHAPTER FIFTY-ONE

PARISA KISSED Azadi awake and he greeted the morning with a moan. They had shared a bottle of Johnnie Black over Parisa's disastrous attempt at cooking *dolmeh-yeh felfel*. Azadi's mouth tasted like pond scum. He opened his eyes and saw Parisa was already dressed.

"I've got to go, my love," she said.

Azadi sat up in bed and grabbed his head. It throbbed.

"Where are you going?"

"I've got a job interview."

She kissed him again and left. He checked his watch on the side table. 8:05 a.m.

Shit. Ishmael was coming by at 8:00 a.m. to hand off the explosives.

Azadi leaped out of bed. He yanked on jeans and a T-shirt. He looked around for his sneakers but couldn't find them. He vaguely remembered Parisa doing a sexy, Scotch-induced striptease for him sometime after midnight, wearing only his Nikes and the teeny thong he'd bought her on the black market.

What had he been thinking? Rather, he hadn't been thinking. He'd forgotten the mission and now he risked fucking everything up.

That's when Azadi heard Parisa's angry voice arguing with someone on the street below. He dashed to the open window and looked down onto the street.

He saw a cab parked at the curb and Parisa standing beside it. She was scolding the cabbie over his refusal to drive her to her destination.

Azadi knew the cab was meant for him, not her. Ishmael was there to hand off the explosives and detonators. And although Azadi knew that the cabbie would be furious that he had violated Kelly's mandate to not fraternize with the enemy, his fear for Parisa's safety overpowered his fear for his own.

Azadi stuck his head out the window and yelled, "Parisa! I'm coming down!"

It was a stupid thing to do but love makes you stupid, not to mention too much Scotch and too little sleep. Azadi saw Ishmael stick his head out the cab's window and stare up at him. The cabbie made the connection: Azadi and Parisa were together.

Now Azadi had to get to her before Ishmael did.

Azadi bolted out of his apartment. He sprinted down the stairs and emerged barefoot onto the street.

But it was too late. The cab was careening around the corner, taking Parisa away into the Tehran traffic.

-:::::-

She was beautiful. Jashni could appreciate that. What he couldn't appreciate was that Azadi might have compromised the mission, even for a face as bewitching as this girl's.

"You and your husband are newlyweds?" asked Jashni with a simpleton's smile as he steered past a stalled Toyota pick-up. "I can tell by the glow."

The woman wasn't glowing. *Glowering* was a more accurate description. Jashni expected her to be angry since he had initially refused to pick her up. Well, he was angry, too. Azadi had been instructed not to date any women. But it was clear this woman was his lover as soon as he called down to her from his apartment window. Now Jashni was whisking her away to establish the depth of their relationship. How had she met Azadi? Had he given her that ring on her finger? How long had they been together? And most importantly, what did she know of the mission, if anything? All important questions, but ones Jashni could not risk asking outright.

"You can tell me," continued Jashni. "I want to hear how you met. I am a romantic myself. I love women so much that I have been married five times."

Jashni snorted like a constipated chimp. Perhaps by playing the fool he could get this woman to let down her guard. But the woman just stared out the window and said nothing.

"Your husband looks familiar. Is he on the TV? I know I have seen his face before."

His questioning continued for another 20 minutes, as did her silence. He dropped her at Mellat Park, near the state broadcasting offices, as she had requested. He drove to the end of the block and double-parked his cab, watching the woman in his side-view mirror.

Two minutes later Jashni watched as a black Mercedes sedan slowed at the entrance of the park. He watched General Farjad exit the sedan and greet the woman who had left Azadi's apartment. He watched the woman and the general enter the park together. Jashni felt like someone had kicked him in the head. What did these two people, one Azadi's lover, the other Azadi's employer, have to talk about?

But then Jashni was only pretending to be a fool and could hazard a good guess.

CHAPTER FIFTY-TWO

PARISA AND GENERAL Farjad strolled in Mellat Park. Normally, a married man like Farjad would not walk in public with another man's wife, even if she were only another man's temporary wife. But save for the squirrels, the park was empty this cold morning. Nobody would see them. And of course, generals in the Revolutionary Guards could get away with things other men couldn't.

Parisa said, "Azadi has told me nothing. He has never revealed to me any reasons for his return to Iran, other than what was reported in the media."

"I find that hard to believe," countered Farjad. "In the heat of passion, a man will reveal almost anything."

They had been going on like this for ten minutes. Parisa did not feel like answering any more questions, especially after the cabbie had barraged her with so many on the ride over.

"I've made myself available to him as you requested, but don't blame me if he's not much for pillow talk."

She immediately regretted her insolence. Farjad stopped dead in his tracks, forcing her to do the same.

"If I were not a gentleman I would kill you right now for being disrespectful. Remember, you came to us. You asked us to make things easier for your brother. All we asked for in return was that you meet Azadi. Talk to him and get him to tell you things. We gave you the temporary marriage so you could sleep with him without shame. But I want information and you give me insolence. Now I will have to consider rescinding our agreement. And then it will be your brother who suffers, not you."

Parisa's blood boiled when she thought of her brother. All he had done was organize an anti-clerical protest and print a satirical news-letter. For that he was sentenced to life in a cell the size of a broom closet. Since she had accepted their assignment, they had increased her brother's rations and taken him out of solitary. That was true. But it was also true that Omar Azadi was clean as far as she knew. What she didn't know was how to make Farjad believe it.

"I have tried to draw out Azadi politically and personally. I have never heard him speak out against the government or suggest that he has deceitful motives for being here. He is a printer, plain and simple. I believe him. So why won't you believe me?"

"Have you fallen in love with this man?"

She was covered head to foot in coats and scarves and shoes and, yes, a thong her lover had given her. But she felt naked because Farjad had found a way to peer into her heart.

"Of course not," she lied.

"I have heard your voice on the tapes made from the conversations in his apartment. You sound like you love him."

"I am an actress, General. That is why you thought I would be perfect for this part. I am also a patriot."

"I have seen surveillance photos of you with him. You smile in his presence. You laugh like a woman in love. You look at him like you love him."

She could feel her future and her brother's future slipping further away, like a rope being yanked through her hands and burning her skin raw.

"I do not love him. You must believe me."

"As you said yourself, you're an actress. A professional liar. Why should I continue to coddle your baby brother when you treat my request for information so contemptuously?"

Parisa tried to feel dead to Farjad's threat. Perhaps her brother's death was preferable to the life of a prisoner? But she realized that was a rationalization born of fear and fatigue. To stop fighting for her family was to dishonor Allah. It was not written in the Quran but in the marrow of her bones.

"Please forgive me, General. I did not mean to talk in such a manner. I will continue to try to find out what I can about Azadi. You can depend on me."

"It is Azadi that all of Iran must depend upon. If he is as pure as you say, then I am overjoyed. But I cannot deny my doubts."

Parisa bowed her head, staring at the cracks in the concrete path. She did not say anything more and neither did Farjad. When Parisa lifted her head, Farjad was gone. The park was empty, save for a squirrel making a mysterious clicking sound in the tree above her. She stared at the squirrel and envied his life, one so far removed from the world of men, of generals and jails and sisters who became whores so their brothers could live. And then the squirrel shoved a nut into his mouth and grew as silent as her.

CHAPTER FIFTY-THREE

FARRAGUT EXITED the Laleh Hotel and walked to the end of the block where Jashni's cab was waiting. He thought the Mossad agent looked tense, no small feat when you look like a chipmunk.

"I have some bad news," said Jashni, pulling into traffic.

Farragut listened as Jashni explained in detail the Azadi/Parisa/Farjad situation. Farragut said nothing in reply at the conclusion of Jashni's report, so Jashni continued talking.

"I should have spotted the woman earlier," admitted Jashni, honking his horn at a pedestrian crossing the street. "But I've been giving Azadi a wide berth. The Iranians are watching him now, and it would not do for them to notice me watching him. A few of my men are keeping an eye on him, but the surveillance hasn't been constant."

Finally Farragut spoke. "This is the first time you've noticed the girl?"

"Yes. I suspect Azadi avoided suspicion by never meeting at her place. He's clever enough to know that we'd be curious if he spent the night elsewhere. I was there to deliver the explosives. It was pure luck that I saw them together."

"Did you give Azadi the explosives?"

"There was no time. They're still in the trunk. I will give them to Azadi tonight."

"Where's Azadi now?"

"At the Press. Creating the printing sheets from the currency plates."

"Take me to Azadi's. I'm going to toss his place."

"I have already taken the liberty of searching Azadi's apartment. Like you, I suspected that he might have left incriminating evidence there. Something that this woman could have latched onto whether he had told her anything or not."

Farragut could barely conceal the fury in his voice. "You were way out of line to do that without consulting me."

"A window of opportunity opened after I dropped off the girl. And you looked so, well, *unwell* last night that I felt it prudent not to trouble you."

Farragut's exasperation with Jashni made his heart beat faster, pumping blood into the tumor. His head pounded. He rubbed his temples with his thumbs to squelch his pain and anger.

"I found something," continued Jashni, reaching into his pocket and pulling out a piece of paper. "Something that makes me think Azadi has said nothing to this girl, though his silence is something he has obviously struggled with."

Jashni handed Farragut the letter he had pulled from Azadi's mattress. Farragut began to read it, finding the contents so fascinating that he momentarily forgot about the pain in his head and the pain in the ass driving the cab.

-:::::-

While Farragut and Jashni were driving around one part of Tehran, Azadi and a contingent of Revolutionary Guards were zigzagging around another. Farjad, though not along for this ride, still insisted on taking precautions. He still believed somebody may have been following Azadi, though Parisa had given him no proof of that.

The long, circuitous drive gave Azadi ample time to reflect on his spectacular fuck-up that morning. He had failed to pick up the explosives while allowing Ishmael to pick up Parisa. He should have told Ishmael about Parisa but fear had prevented him. Now that the cabbie knew, he feared even more what Ishmael would do to her.

Azadi took a deep, calming breath. *Keep it together*, he thought. *You haven't done anything wrong.* The more he considered that, the more he believed it. He had told Parisa nothing and she knew nothing. Surely, Ishmael would see this. Yes, he'd be upset at Azadi for this breach of confidence, but he would see Parisa was harmless. To put Ishmael's mind at ease, Azadi would promise not to see Parisa until after the mission was complete. Ishmael could put him under 24-hour surveillance if he didn't trust him. Azadi practiced in his mind how he would plead his case as the car careened around corners and ran red lights.

An hour later, Azadi and his guards arrived at Gheyam Hospital. They walked openly through the patient wards towards the seventies style security office. They rode down the elevator and marched down the corridor towards the vault door at the entrance of the Press. The guards at the vault door kept their guns on Azadi as they searched him. He was clean. Then they searched the duffel bag he carried, although it, like Azadi, had already been searched by the guards who had picked him up at his apartment. They found the same thing in the duffel bag that the other guards had, two printing plates wrapped in linen and four 1.75 ounce tins of fine, Iranian caviar.

"A gift for my friends," said Azadi to the guards. "We have much work to do over the next few days and I thank you for your dedication and commitment."

Azadi's friends opened the vault door along with the first tin of caviar.

Azadi had lied about many things but not about the amount of work that lay ahead. Before he could even begin printing Supernotes, he had to create the printing sheets that would run through the Press. Fabricating these sheets from the steel engraved plates would take days and tax his technical expertise but everything he needed was at the Press. The powerful industrial oven, sensitive measuring devices, and machine tools were in excellent working order. He noted an ample supply of the proper plastic, metals, inks, and dies. He couldn't wait to get started. Anything to take his mind off Parisa and what Ishmael may have done to her.

-:::::-

The first stage of creating the printing sheets involved transferring the engraved design details from the steel plates to plastic. Azadi placed a special sheet of plastic over both the front and back plates. Capable of withstanding the punishing printing process, this durable polymer was the same type used by the Bureau of Printing and Engraving in DC. The plastic was available on the black market for a price but Farjad had proudly told Azadi that the Iranians manufactured it themselves. After all, he had further boasted, we are now a nuclear power as well. Azadi wedged each plastic-covered plate between heavy metal paddles and slid both combinations into the oven set for 250 degrees Fahrenheit. He would cook them for half an hour, allowing the heat to transfer the engraved details from the steel plates to the warm plastic.

While the plates cooked Azadi invited the guards from the vault door to leave their post and join him and the others in the pressroom. They shared the remaining three tins of caviar. The men talked of soccer. They talked of sex. They talked of money problems and the latest Lexus SUV. Azadi made conversation but his thoughts were elsewhere.

Ishmael wouldn't hurt Parisa, would he? He would question her and find out that she is my beloved wife. The cabbie may be a bastard but he's not a barbarian.

The timer on the oven rang. Azadi removed the two engraved plate/plastic sheet combinations. He peeled the plastic sheets off the steel plates. His eyes confirmed that the details of the new issue $100 bill, both front and back, had been set into their respective plastic sheets. Azadi tested the two plastic sheets with an engraver's measure, making sure the depth of the design impressions in the plastic sheets matched that of the engraved steel plates. They did. They were perfect plastic copies of the steel plates.

Parisa's face is perfection, her heart a thing of beauty. If Ishmael dares lay a hand on her, I will kill him. I promise I will kill him.

Azadi repeated the plastic sheet making procedure throughout the day, creating a total of 64 plastic sheets marked by the design of the new issue $100 bill, 32 identical fronts and 32 identical backs. Since the fronts and backs of US currency are always printed separately, Azadi then created two master plastic sheets by joining the 32 fronts into one plastic sheet and the 32 backs into another. Azadi calculated that with the Press running at full speed, he would be able to print approximately $6,000,000 of perfect $100 bills per hour.

I would rather be penniless and live in poverty than see Parisa harmed in any way.

It was late. The guards were restless and Azadi found himself yawning despite the knot of tension in his stomach. He had to conserve his strength and stamina. He had completed the plastic printing sheets but it was only the first step. He would need to spend another few days refining them before they would be ready for the Press. But now it was time to go home and find out if he was still married or a widower.

CHAPTER FIFTY-FOUR

AZADI FOLLOWED the routine. He had the guards drop him off downtown at his favorite movie theater. He tried to concentrate on the film. It was an Iranian-made flick about the American occupation of Iraq. In the film, some Iranian pilgrims arrived at an Iraqi Shiite holy city and uncovered a prostitution ring being run by American soldiers. Azadi barely paid attention to the plight of the women in the movie; the only woman he cared about was Parisa.

When the movie ended, Azadi walked to the corner. Ishmael's cab appeared within 10 seconds. Azadi opened the rear door and climbed in. His hands were shaking and he was sweating, although it was a cold evening. Ishmael didn't greet him or look at him. Azadi stared out the window as they drove down a deserted street. The shops were shuttered and there were no streetlights or pedestrians on the sidewalks. The cab pulled up to the curb. *Here it comes,* Azadi thought.

But what came wasn't an *it*. It was a *he*.

"Who the fuck are you?" asked Azadi, as a gaunt, blond man wearing a tweed coat opened the cab door and sat in the back beside him. The man slammed the door shut. He did not make eye contact with Azadi. He did not appear to have heard the question.

The cab began to move down the quiet streets. Azadi stared at the blond man. His skin was gray, the same color as his unblinking eyes. He looked sick.

Azadi leaned forward towards the front seat. "Ishmael, who the fuck is this guy?"

The cabbie didn't answer but the blond man did, although not in reply to Azadi's question. "You fucked up. You fucked up big time."

Azadi noted that the man had a killer's voice. Frozen steel. Before stepping in the cab Azadi had been so worried over Parisa's fate that it had not occurred to him that his own life might be in danger. But now he was sure: this was a hit and he was a dead man. His feelings were confirmed when the blond man reached into the breast pocket of his tweed coat. *A gun*, thought Azadi. *He's got a gun —*

Before the killer could pull out the gun, Azadi jumped at him.

The blond man pulled a letter from his pocket with one hand and punched Azadi in the gut with the other. The air exploded from Azadi's lungs. He saw stars. He keeled over, landing face down on the floor of the cab. Amidst dry heaves, he heard the blond man tell the cabbie to drive out of the center of the city.

-:::::-

While Azadi was incapacitated, Farragut reread the letter Jashni had found in Azadi's apartment. The words confirmed that the mission was in jeopardy. Jashni was of a like mind. Before picking up Azadi they had discussed their options. They could tell Mia about Azadi's "wife." They could tell her Parisa was a spy for the Revolutionary Guards, that it was only a matter of time before Azadi told her everything. Yes, they could tell Mia the truth and let her make the call. She was, after all, in charge of the operation.

Or they could handle it on their own. Farragut knew that Salaam's near escape in Baltimore had rocked Mia's boat. She was one bit of bad news away from standing down the operation. Both men agreed that Azadi's infatuation with Parisa would certainly qualify as bad news. So they had decided to take matters into their own hands and come up with a plan. Besides, what Mia didn't know wouldn't hurt her. To the contrary, their lives were the ones at risk if the Parisa situation weren't dealt with firmly. They were in agreement about that.

What had surprised Farragut was Jashni. He hadn't realized how important the mission was to the Mossad agent. The man was an Israeli; there was no shortage of plots and intrigue in the region to keep him busy until he retired to a kibbutz or got killed in the line of duty. But Jashni had been as willing as Farragut to go behind Mia's back for several reasons, Farragut conjectured. First, Jashni knew this job was *The Job*, the one that got a street named after you in Jerusalem and a permanent seat in the Knesset. Also, as an Iranian Jew, Jashni wanted to stick it to the Islamic Republic. But Farragut didn't care what Jashni's motives were, as long as he wanted to continue with the mission. For the first time since his arrival in Iran, he felt like he and Jashni were, if not comrades, at least on the same page.

Farragut watched Azadi pull himself up off the floor of the cab and sit back in his seat. His face was pale. Snot dribbled from his nose and lint from the floor had stuck to his beard.

Farragut figured now was as good a time as any. He started to read the letter aloud.

"*Dear Parisa. If you are reading this, it means that I am already dead. I will not have had told you before this that I love you. I feared saying those words would have made it impossible for me to do what I had to do. So let me assure you of that now. I love you. I love you completely and deeply and unconditionally. You have made me feel part of something deeper and more important than my own life...*"

Farragut paused. He had not meant to, but something in Azadi's words got to him. He had read the letter a dozen times. And this part, the part about love bringing Azadi a feeling of connection to something bigger than his own life, made Farragut reflect on his own loveless existence. But now was not the time to show weakness. He continued to read the letter aloud.

"'...And because you made me feel this way, I feel that you deserve to know the truth about what I am doing in Iran. I have left you some money as I feel that if things had worked out differently, we would be man and wife for eternity, rather than a moment. Money is a poor substitute for my own life, for the time we should but won't be together, but it is all I have to give to you. And money is the reason that I am here.'"

Azadi rested his head against the window. His vision was clearing and he was certain that resistance was futile.

Farragut said, "The letter continues with you describing in detail the classified nature of what you are doing in Iran. Then you name a bank account in the Caymans where this woman can access the money that we paid to you. You conclude with a torrent of romantic platitudes and adolescent proclamations of eternal devotion."

Farragut crumpled up the letter and handed it to Jashni. Jashni stuffed it into the cab's ashtray and torched it with his cigarette lighter. Azadi watched the letter burn.

"That letter is none of your damn business," said Azadi.

"Tell me everything you've told the girl about the mission."

"I've told her nothing. That was the point of the letter. I wanted her to know everything after it went down, after I was dead."

"Why?"

"Because I love her."

"And why else?"

"And because the letter would protect her. It could prove she knew nothing. Because why else would I be writing her that letter and telling her everything? I thought, after it all went down, she could show it to General Farjad."

Jashni chuckled from the front seat. "Omar, you *putz*. Parisa *works* for General Farjad."

Azadi didn't know what to say so he didn't say anything. He balled his hands into fists. The thought of knocking out the cabbie's buckteeth almost gave him a hard on.

Farragut said, "Parisa is a spy. She works for General Farjad."

"Farjad was the one that sent her to fuck you," Jashni added.

Azadi felt the blood rush to his face. "You're a fucking liar."

Azadi lunged for the back of Jashni's head. Farragut yanked Azadi back into his seat, his fingers clamping down on Azadi's throat. Azadi gasped for air. His lips began to turn blue. Just before he was going to pass out, Farragut let go. He let Azadi suck in wind for a minute, then handed him a cellphone.

"Call Parisa. Ask to meet her at Mellat Park because you have something important to tell her. Walk her up that stairway to the lake. It will be secluded at this time of night and allow me to keep an eye on you. When you meet tell her that you can never see her again. When she asks why, tell her because you have lied to her. Tell her that you want to see other people, that you're not a one-woman guy. In light of your romantic history, that's probably the most honest thing you'll ever tell her. Tell Parisa that you can no longer live a lie and stay married to her. She will be suspicious. She may act like she is hurt. It will be an act. Like your marital situation is an act. Like your whole reason for coming to Iran is an act."

Azadi stared at the cellphone in his hand. "Why do I have to see her in person? Why can't I break it off over the phone?"

"Because you love this woman. A coward breaks up with his beloved over the phone. You're not a coward."

"You seem pretty sure about that."

"If you were a coward, you wouldn't be here."

Azadi wiped his nose on his sleeve. He didn't think he was crying. It was probably snot from when this psycho tried to strangle him, but he wasn't sure. He wasn't sure about anything.

Azadi said, "Parisa loves me and you're a goddamn liar. So's the SOB in the front seat. You both can both burn in hell before I make that call."

Ishmael laughed. "Give him the photos I shot this morning."

The blond man dropped some photos in Azadi's lap. They were photos of Parisa and Farjad taken in a park. Ishmael had obviously taken the photos at an awkward angle while concealing his digital camera. Parisa's head was sometimes bowed as Farjad scolded her, and the photos didn't capture the detailed beauty in her face. But details were, as Azadi often told himself, the lifeblood of a counter-feiter. And there were enough details in the photos to convince him, even as his sight grew blurry with tears, that Parisa was as phony as a $3 bill.

CHAPTER FIFTY-FIVE

IT WAS JUST past one in the morning of a long day. Farragut, Jashni, and Azadi sat in the cab. It was parked on the eastern side of a normally busy thoroughfare, the *Vali-ye-Asr*. At this late hour there was no traffic. Mellat Park sat on the western side of the street across from the cab. The park was dark and deserted, as were the embassies and businesses of this fashionable North Tehran neighborhood.

The three men waited. Jashni hummed a Brahms concerto. Farragut drummed his long fingers against his increasingly bony thigh. Azadi fingered the gold chain around his neck, the gift from Parisa on their first date. He thought about her exquisite face. He thought about the way she pressed her ass against his crotch under the covers. He thought about how she made him laugh and how she sometimes hiccupped when she kissed him and how she had made this miserable time of his life worth living.

"There she is," said Jashni, as Parisa appeared from the shadows across the street. The three men watched her walk towards the British Airways office.

Farragut said, "Remember. You take a walk. You break it off with her. You keep it short. One of us will follow you to make sure you do it right."

Azadi opened the door and exited the cab.

She is the most beautiful woman I have ever seen, thought Azadi as he walked up to Parisa. *And I loved her. How could she do this to me? Did she really do this to me?*

She flashed him a smile as she noticed his approach.

-:::::-

Farragut and Jashni stared through the windshield at the scene playing out up the street. The lovers were face-to-face.

"Azadi's doing fine," said Jashni.

Farragut said nothing. Unlike Azadi he wasn't doing fine. He was sick to his stomach and his head hurt, and it had nothing to do with the tumor.

"We're right to do this," whispered Jashni, more to himself than to Farragut.

Jashni started the cab's engine. Farragut watched through the windshield as Azadi took Parisa's hand, checked for traffic, and stepped off the curb.

Jashni steered the cab into the street. Through the windshield, they watched Parisa grab Azadi's ass. A reckless gesture, especially for an Iranian woman in Tehran, but she was feeling safe.

Jashni jammed his foot on the accelerator, aiming the car towards Azadi and Parisa, who were in the middle of the deserted road. Farragut swallowed hard. He despised himself. *I deserve the tumor,* he thought. *What kept it so long?*

Jashni kept his foot on the accelerator. The engine roared. The cab picked up speed. Through the windshield Farragut saw Azadi and Parisa react to the approaching vehicle.

Jashni swung the wheel to avoid Azadi. The cab slammed into Parisa at 40 m.p.h. The impact shattered her pelvis and ruptured her spleen. She flew 50 feet through the air. Her neck broke and her skull cracked open upon hitting the street.

Jashni braked hard. The tires screeched and left 12 feet of rubber on the pavement.

Out in the street Azadi was howling. He skittered along the pavement to where Parisa lay broken in a pool of blood. He cradled Parisa in his arms. Her head hung at a weird angle because of her fractured neck. He propped up her head with one of his hands. He did his best to make her look normal, to make her look alive, but he couldn't. His howling downshifted into sobbing. He ran his hand through her hair. The collision had knocked off her headscarf. Death made decorum difficult in the Islamic Republic of Iran.

Farragut jumped out of the cab. He ran to Azadi, his expensive Tim Little shoes clacking on the street, echoing obscenely in the empty night.

Azadi convulsed. He bawled. He lost it. He didn't care. Fuck it. He pulled Parisa close. He let his tears mix with her blood. He kissed her dead lips. He ignored the blood and brains sticking to his fingers. He ignored her floppy neck.

He ignored Farragut shouting in his ear to get into the car.

He ignored Farragut pulling on his shoulders.

He couldn't ignore the blow to the back of his head that sent him into unconsciousness.

CHAPTER FIFTY-SIX

JASHNI PARKED THE cab in an alley behind Azadi's building. Three feral cats made a meal out of some rancid lamb stew that had dripped out of a cracked garbage can. There was no moon and the street lamp at the end of the alley was broken. It was a good place to disappear in the dark.

Jashni and Farragut sat in the front seat of the cab. Azadi slept in the back. Farragut's blow had knocked him out, which was just as well. Farragut and Jashni were supposed to be the professionals. It would not help for Azadi to hear them argue.

"It was the right thing to do," said Jashni. He found a toothpick on the dash and scooped lint out from underneath his fingernails.

Farragut shook his head. They had both agreed on the best method to deal with Parisa, but her death had disturbed him nonetheless. Farragut had killed before but it was Azadi's overwhelming grief that really got to him. It brought back that Christmas Day years ago when the State Troopers had knocked on the door of the house in Rye. *We have some bad news*, they said. Then they told him about the accident that killed his mother. They left out the part about her decapitation as she rocketed through the windshield. They left out the part about how the force of the crash ripped off her blouse and bra and deposited her half-naked in a snow bank, her breasts as stiff as icicles when the ambulance arrived. *She died instantly*, they said. *She didn't feel pain.*

"We could have let her live," Farragut said.

"No. We could not let her live. We discussed this. She couldn't be trusted. And if she lived, Azadi couldn't be trusted. We did what was best for the mission."

Farragut watched the cats at the garbage can fight over their putrid meal. "Did we? I wonder if we can trust Azadi after what we have done."

"Azadi is getting paid a fortune to do what we tell him. He's a thief and money is what motivates him. If he grows a conscience, which he won't, he'll do nothing because now he knows we'll deal with him in the harshest terms. Besides, he can't go to Farjad and confess we killed Parisa. He would be implicating himself in the plot. The man's a fool, but not when it comes to self-preservation."

Farragut nodded. That had been the reasoning: not only to kill Parisa, but also to do it in front of Azadi. He had to understand who was calling the shots. It was Hardball 101. But what had seemed clear to Farragut hours ago now seemed like a miscalculation. Killing Parisa was not only risky; it was morally repugnant. Normally Farragut did not suffer from self-doubt, but the tumor was apparently destroying his resolve along with his body.

"Hit and runs are very common in Tehran," said Jashni for the sixth time that night. "Farjad will not suspect a thing."

Jashni exited the cab. He opened the trunk and pulled out the duffel bags containing the C4 and the detonators. Farragut got out of the cab and opened the rear door. Azadi was still passed out. Farragut pulled him into a sitting position. Jashni's eyes opened.

"Come on," said Farragut. He helped Azadi out of the cab. Azadi was covered by Parisa's blood. He'd gotten it all over the sleeves of his jacket when he'd cradled her corpse.

"Get cleaned up," said Jashni, dropping the duffel bags at Azadi's feet.

Farragut helped Azadi out of his jacket. The blood had soaked through to the sleeves of Azadi's cotton shirt. Farragut removed his tweed coat and handed it to Azadi. "Put this on. It will cover the blood on your sleeves."

Azadi just stood there, his eyes blank, so Farragut dressed him in the tweed. It fit Azadi better than it did Farragut, who had lost weight. It concealed the blood on his shirtsleeves. No one would suspect a thing if they saw Azadi in the hall as he returned to his apartment.

Farragut tossed Azadi's bloody jacket to Jashni. Jashni folded it up and hid it under the spare tire in the trunk for disposal later. He lit a foul Turkish cigarette and watched the cats eat.

Farragut handed the duffel bags to Azadi. "These are the explosives and the detonators."

Azadi's eyes looked less glassy now. The cold, night air, and seriousness of the situation were knocking some sense into him. He took the duffel bags from Farragut. Farragut was tempted to help Azadi carry the bags up to his apartment but he had taken too many risks already tonight. He had broken the wall of compartmentalization and committed murder. Still he needed Azadi to understand that they were connected through a shared purpose, a shared humanity, and a shared sense of grief.

Farragut said to Azadi, "This might not mean anything to you but I hope it will. In ancient times, King Darius commanded an elite corps of soldiers, the Ten Thousand Immortals. They were so called because when one of the Immortals died, they were immediately replaced. In this way the corps strength never fell below ten thousand. But Darius never told the people that he replaced the dead Immortals with other men. He told them that the Immortals could not die, that way the people would always feel safe and protected. And the people understood the value of this social contract, so when an Immortal did die, the grieving family would simply pretend his replacement was their son."

Farragut paused, hoping his words would make Azadi understand that Parisa's death was unavoidable. "They did this because it was necessary. Because lying about the living was easier than be-lieving in the dead."

Azadi stared at his feet. He wanted to cry tears of rage but he was cried out.

"Omar, you must understand. We did not kill her."

A tremor shot through Azadi's body. It was the first time Farragut, still nameless to him, had used Azadi's name and the intimacy un-nerved him. But what unnerved him even more was Farragut's assertion that he had not killed Parisa. He stared at Farragut uncomprehending.

"The Iranians killed her, Omar. When Farjad put the squeeze on her, she was as good as dead. And the only way to give her death any meaning, is to finish this thing."

Azadi glanced at the cabbie, who was hiding behind a curtain of filthy smoke. Azadi could not work up the righteous rage to counter Farragut's rationalizations. He could only look in those dead, gray eyes and tell him the truth.

"You're obviously an educated man. And you obviously know I'm not. But I know something you don't. I know it takes more courage to live as a man than to die as a martyr."

Azadi turned and walked to the alley entrance of the apartment building. Farragut watched him disappear inside, than he sat in the back of the cab, slamming the door shut.

Jashni took a last drag on his cigarette. He flicked the burning stub at the hungry cats. He hit one in the ass and it howled. The cats scattered. Jashni grinned and got in the cab.

-:::::-

Jashni drove past Gheyam Hospital on the way back to Farragut's hotel. It was not the fastest route he could have taken. Although he never said it outright, he hoped Farragut got the message: the mission is all that matters.

But Farragut wasn't looking at the hospital. He was looking into his past. He flashed on a jumble of images. The images, as if seen first through a kaleidoscope, coalesced and became clear in his consciousness.

His father's frown. His mother's grave. Yasir unexpectedly hugging him at LaGuardia before boarding his plane. Sepanlou's face smiling through the sniper's scope. Mia in a Hanover hotel room telling him there would be "no extraction." Ingrid in a London hotel room watching the rain fall on Park Lane. Parisa bleeding in Azadi's arms. He heard Ingrid ask with tears in her eyes, *"When does a man say 'enough,' John. When does he say I will kill no more?"*

Thinking about all these things was painful but also a relief. He had felt so much guilt and doubt and disgust but had fought mightily to keep it all in check. Now the dam holding back his feelings had broken, broken as surely as Parisa's neck had broken.

Farragut thought about Azadi's letter to Parisa. Its ashes were still in the ashtray of the cab. The letter was gone but the words were lodged in his memory. And in Azadi's declarations of love and sacrifice, Farragut began to see the method and manner of his own salvation.

Farragut made a momentous decision, one that would allow him to be true to his country and true to his conscience. His decision would affect everything. Its implications were literally life and death and would reverberate from Tehran to Tel Aviv to Washington.

In the front seat, behind the wheel, Jashni had no idea that the game was no longer the same. Farragut would never tell him. Unlike the decision to murder Parisa, he knew that Jashni would never agree with what he had decided to do. He would have to find out after the fact.

The time was just past 7:00 a.m. when Jashni dropped Farragut at the Laleh. Farragut felt relieved at his momentous decision and exhausted from the night's exertions. He crawled into bed and fell into a deep sleep, his first in many months.

Elsewhere in the city, other men were waking up and getting ready for work.

CHAPTER FIFTY-SEVEN

INSPECTOR KAMRAN Hadian arrived at the precinct that morning, punctually, at 8:00 a.m. Coffee cup in hand, he walked through the squad room, exchanging "good mornings" with those officers already busy with work. He sat down on his uncomfortable government-issue chair, placing his weathered briefcase upon his tatty wood desk. He opened the briefcase and pulled out some files he had taken home the night before. The files concerned his top priority case. Five prostitutes had been murdered in the last four months, at least five that the police knew about. All had been strangled and sexually assaulted post-mortem, their bodies dumped near Mehrabad airport. Violent crimes such as this, though still rare in Iran, were on the rise. The reformers believed the root causes were economic malaise and political oppression. The conservatives believed the root causes were godlessness and decadent western influences. Hadian believed he would rather have root canal than waste one more minute on unimportant cases while the killer of these women, whatever his political bent, was running around free.

Hadian closed the file and pulled free a call reminder sheet taped over the photo of his wife that stood on his desk. Colonel Tabriz had called twice since 6 a.m. Clearly, the Ministry of Intelligence was dead serious about the "Dead Presidents" case. Hadian did not share Tabriz's enthusiasm. He thought the odds of a foreign assassin infiltrating Iran were miniscule, though they dwarfed the odds of his actually arresting the man should he exist.

The phone rang. Hadian answered, already knowing who was calling. "Colonel Tabriz, how can I serve you this morning?"

Tabriz got right to it. "I have seen your latest report on the matter I requested you look into. I asked you to look into Americans who might fit an assassin's profile. The source said he remembered an American mentioning 'Dead Presidents.' But I am disturbed to see that you have gone beyond the parameters of my initial request. I see from looking at your report that you have interviewed Canadian, British, Irish, and South African citizens as well as a New Zealander."

Azadi had seen this coming. "Colonel, you mentioned the source was a black Israeli officer with African origins. Correct?"

"Yes."

"Then English is not his native tongue. It is my experience that someone who is not a native English speaker may assume another English speaker is American without correctly placing the accent. For example, would you be able to distinguish the accent of a Canadian from Toronto from that of an American from Milwaukee?"

"I would not."

"How about an Irishman from Belfast and a South African from Cape Town?"

"No."

"Neither would I. Thus, I have expanded my search to include all native English speaking people in Tehran who may, even remotely, fit an assassin's profile."

"Good work. But our president leaves for Lebanon next week. If there is to be an assassination attempt, it may come before he departs. We have not ruled out that Lebanon is a decoy story and Tehran is where they will actually strike."

"I will work faster, Colonel."

Hadian heard the dial tone sting in his ear as Tabriz hung up. He glanced at the crime scene photos of the murdered prostitutes.

The case was an abomination but it would have to wait. He closed the folders. He looked at his wife's photo. Plain, decent Laden. He loved her so.

Hadian's deputy, Moshen, arrived with a manila folder. Moshen knew his boss disdained computers and preferred to hold reports in his hands rather than view them on a screen. It was old-fashioned and superstitious but Hadian's tactile senses were fine-tuned and no one could dispute he got results.

"Good morning," said Moshen, handing him the folder. "No murdered prostitutes last night."

Moshen sat on the edge of the desk while Hadian opened the overnight mortality report. Hadian kept abreast of every suspected criminal death in the capital, whether he personally investigated it or not. Even with his additional responsibilities, he was not one to break from routine.

Scanning the report, Hadian was thankful that it had been a quiet night. In South Tehran, two husbands had murdered their wives in domestic disturbance incidents. Both men were in custody and had confessed. In central Tehran, a jeweler had shot a prowler who had broken into his shop. The dead thief had a past record of burglary and had served time. The jeweler was not charged. In North Tehran, a car had struck dead a young woman, one of an epidemic that had been plaguing the city. It was a hit and run, assailant unknown. The ID in her wallet identified the victim as Parisa Halajeh Azadi. She had recently been married in a *sigheh* ceremony. Like many newlyweds, she carried proof of her marriage on her person as defense against intrusive religious police. The marriage certificate was included in the report. So was the fact that her husband had not yet been informed of her death. Her husband's name was Omar Azadi. Moshen had scrawled Azadi's address in the margin of the report.

Hadian read the name and address aloud. He had seen that name before, though he couldn't quite place it. "Moshen?"

Moshen had been staring at the framed photo of Hadian's wife and thinking that love was truly blind. "Sir?"

"Would you now please bring me the *coonee* file?"

"Right here, Sir. You're not the only cop in Tehran with ESP."

Moshen smiled as he handed Hadian the "Dead Presidents" file. Hadian had used the slang term for a man who enjoyed receiving anal sex: *coonee*. That's how he referred to the "Dead Presidents" file with his deputy. He was not normally vulgar but he felt like the work on the American assassin was a waste of time and that he was literally "taking it" from Tabriz in agreeing to this assignment. The slang term also protected the privacy of the case, as Moshen was the only other officer who knew its true nature. Any other officers in the room would assume that their best inspector was working on a case involving sodomy, still a major crime in the Islamic Republic.

As Hadian scanned the file he quickly found what he was looking for. A man named Omar Azadi was on the list of Americans recently arrived in Iran. The address matched that of the husband of the deceased Parisa Azadi. This man was probably the same Azadi married to the woman who had been killed in the hit-and-run. A strange coincidence, but then meeting your future wife on the day she saved your life, as Hadian had, was a strange coincidence, too.

Moshen had included several news clippings about Azadi's return to Iran along with a copy of his passport photo. Hadian had not yet interviewed Azad, since the Ministry of Intelligence had already vetted Azadi before allowing him into Iran. But Hadian was meticulous and knew he would have to interview Azadi soon, just as the man would have to be told of his wife's death even sooner. And because Hadian loved his wife, and because Azadi had lost a wife and did not yet know it, Hadian decided he would be the one to inform him. He could do it with more tact than any other man in the office could. At the same time, he could record an interview with Azadi on the "Dead Presidents" case. He didn't have much to ask Azadi regarding assassination but Hadian had promised Tabriz he would be thorough. Police Inspector Kamran Hadian was many things but he was not a liar. At that point, he had no reason to believe that Omar Azadi was a liar, either.

-:::::-

Hadian arrived at Azadi's apartment just after 9:15 that morning. It was Friday, the day of rest. Hadian rang the bell repeatedly but Azadi did not answer. He knocked on the door, not too loudly in respect to the neighbors. Azadi still did not answer. Hadian pressed his ear to the door and heard running water. Perhaps the man was taking a bath and couldn't hear? Hadian waited for the sound of running water to subside and then knocked again.

The door opened and Hadian found himself facing a handsome, muscular man wearing what looked to be an expensive silk kimono. Azadi had thick black hair and piercing green eyes. A closer look revealed his eyes were bloodshot and he looked like he hadn't slept. Had an argument driven his wife from the home and up to the neighborhood where she died? Had he been up all night worrying about her?

"Omar Azadi?"

"Yes."

"I am Chief Inspector Kamran Hadian from the Tehran Police Department."

Azadi nodded and gestured inside. Hadian entered the small apartment as Azadi closed the door behind him. "Perhaps you would like to sit down, Mr. Azadi? I'm afraid I have some bad news."

Azadi said, "I know why you're here. If you wait a minute, I'll make this easy for you."

Azadi walked across the living room towards his bedroom. Hadian decided against reaching out and pulling him back. "Actually, Mr. Azadi, if you'll just let me speak…"

But Azadi had disappeared into his bedroom. Hadian stood awkwardly in the middle of the living room and glanced around. The place was untidy; clothes were strewn about on the furniture. A pair of Nike sneakers sat on the coffee table along with what looked like a skinned cat on a plate but he suspected was really day old pasta. No comfy pillows on the couch. Just clutter and chaos. The room did not reveal a woman's presence. Women added creature comforts and small touches to transform a dwelling into a home. This was not a home. Parisa Azadi had not spent much time here. Well, they had not been married long. It had been one of those medieval temporary marriages. Azadi was still practically a bachelor.

Azadi returned with a small black tablet, about the size of a cigarette pack, and offered it to Hadian.

"What is this?" asked Hadian.

"That's the reason you're here, right?" said Azadi. "It's my iPod. It's loaded with black market American music. Mostly rap. Sixty-four Gigabytes. That's all of it."

Hadian, surprised, took the iPod. Although he had seen young people handling them before, he himself had never seen one up close, especially one that looked like it cost more than he would make in a dozen life times. He stared at it as if it were as indecipherable as the Dead Sea Scrolls.

"I broke the law, Inspector. The possession of black market music is a crime. The neighbors complained when I played the music too loud through my external speakers. They called you, right?"

Hadian shook his head. This misunderstanding was making an awkward situation worse. "No. But you are correct about the illegality of the music."

"Inspector, perhaps if you accept the iPod this situation can be forgotten? It is a collector's edition. Very valuable."

The Tehran police department was notoriously corrupt but Hadian had never accepted a bribe and wasn't going to start now. However, in light of the more serious business at hand he decided to take Azadi up on his offer. The device was criminal evidence, after all, and he would give the iPod to Ahmad as a gift to assist him in his musical education. He would have it appraised and if it was as valuable as Azadi said it was, well, that would more than *pay* for Ahmad's musical education along with a nice little nest egg after he graduated. Hadian felt a pang of guilt when he thought of an old Iranian proverb: "*When the cat and mouse agree, the grocer is ruined.*" But with the amount of time he was spending on the "Dead Presidents" investigation, he was not feeling particularly sympathetic to the state or the grocer for that matter.

"I'll take the iPod with me for your own protection. Now please sit and I will tell you the reason that I am here."

Azadi sat on the couch. Hadian sat in a reclining chair opposite him and tried to get comfortable. "The police found a woman's body on *Vali-ye-Asr* last night. We believe the woman was the victim of a hit-and-run. He papers identified her as Parisa Azadi."

Azadi did not react with surprise or pain. In Hadian's experience, some people were like that.

"I am sorry for your loss, Mr. Azadi."

"Parisa lived in that neighborhood, but are you sure it's her?"

"We are almost certain but we request that you identify her body at the morgue. I have written the address down here on the back of my card."

Hadian handed Azadi his card. "This was vehicular homicide. It may have been an accident that your wife was hit, but it was a crime for the driver to leave the scene. Such incidents are quite common in our capital. We rarely apprehend the perpetrators. But a detective will be assigned to the case."

Azadi bowed his head. "She should have spent the night with me but I told her to leave. I've been busy at work and I needed some time to myself. She was probably out walking. She loved walking at night."

Azadi buried his face in his hands and began to cry. Hadian could now see this man loved his wife just as he, Hadian, loved his wife. Hadian didn't want to stare at Azadi; it felt impolite. So he gazed around the room at the clutter and clothes tossed about the furniture. *Jeans and jackets and sneakers. Expensive. Perhaps the man had money in America.*

Hadian's eyes played over a tweed jacket tossed over the back of the couch. *An old frayed tweed. Not exactly the style one would expect in a man who wore a gold chain and a silk kimono. More like a college professor's tweed.*

The memory of seeing that tweed struck Hadian hard and fast.

That is Professor John Farragut's tweed. Definitely. The same color, the same elbows in need of patching and the same Harris Tweed label on the inside right pocket. I remember seeing it flung over the profes-

sor's chair weeks ago in at the Gate of All Nations. What is Professor Farragut's tweed doing in Omar Azadi's apartment?

As Azadi continued to cry, Hadian thought how to steer the interview around to "Dead Presidents." He hadn't thought a formal interrogation was going to be necessary but the appearance of Farragut's jacket changed that. But if Azadi was indeed connected somehow to Professor Farragut, that wasn't a crime, just a coincidence. By the time Azadi stopped crying, Hadian had figured out a plan.

"Mr. Azadi, sometimes it is helpful to talk to someone who has experienced a similar loss. I know an American like you. He lost his mother in a car accident. Perhaps you would like to talk to him? I can call you later with his number if you like?""

They walked to the door together. Hadian had done a background check on Farragut that revealed his mother had died in a car crash after leaving Iran. Hadian had not thought much of it then but he knew that he could use it now. It was a calculated risk, but one worth taking.

"An American?" asked Azadi, opening the door for Hadian.

"Born in Iran but American. Perhaps you have already met? There are not many Americans in Iran. Professor John Farragut?"

Azadi shook his head. His eyes showed no recognition of the name.

Hadian glanced at Farragut's tweed coat on the couch. Then back again to Azadi's face. Still nothing. No reaction.

Hadian made a decision. Yes, he could confront Azadi with the fact that Farragut's coat was in his apartment, but he couldn't prove it *was* Farragut's coat. No, better to wait. He would not flush his quarry. He would try to get more definitive proof of the connection between John Farragut and Omar Azadi.

"Again, I am sorry for your loss, Mr. Azadi. Goodbye."

Hadian left Azadi's apartment, taking the iPod with him. He was tempted to stop at home, knowing how much Ahmad would enjoy this new toy and its booty of black market music, but duty called. As he drove to his next destination the Tehran traffic gave him time to reflect on the "Dead Presidents" case. He didn't consider Azadi a strong suspect because he didn't fit an assassin's profile. According to Azadi's sheet in the "Dead Presidents" file, he was printer who worked at Babajan's Print Shop. He had never done military service nor been arrested for any crime. But Azadi's denial of knowing Farragut, combined with his possession of Farragut's jacket, had piqued Hadian's interest. He hoped to glean something pertinent about Azadi from his employer. If he found nothing at least he would have the satisfaction of being thorough.

It wasn't until he reached the door of the Babajan Print Shop that Hadian realized it was Friday and the shop was, of course, closed. Luckily, Hadian noticed a man through the window, sleeping in a cot jammed against the far wall. Hadian knocked on the door and after several minutes, the man roused himself and answered. The smell of cheap, Georgian wine stung Hadian's nostrils as Babajan welcomed him inside. The sight of the printer's obese body – for he answered the door naked – offended Hadian's eyes.

The interview didn't last long. Babajan had the attention span of a slug and was unable to coherently answer questions. He managed to curse Omar Azadi to the high heavens for leaving his business to wither on the vine and die. It seemed that Babajan was broke and had been evicted from his apartment for not paying his rent and was forced to live in his shop. He had little to say about Azadi's past whereabouts and habits. He knew nothing about the man's friendship with any American, blond or otherwise. He did admit that Azadi was a brilliant printer and begged Hadian to talk to him and convince him to come back to work with his dear friend Babajan.

"Where is Azadi working now?" asked Hadian, keeping his eyes on his notepad and off Babajan's sweaty belly.

"Ask my uncle, General Farjad of the Revolutionary Guards," sputtered Babajan. "That traitorous whore Azadi works for him." With that Babajan raced for the bathroom and concluded the interview by vomiting in the sink.

Hadian left the shop, more unnerved by the news that Azadi had connections to the guardians of the Islamic Revolution than he was by Babajan's inebriated condition. If the dreaded Revolutionary Guards were involved in this case, he wished that he himself were not. He drove slowly back to the precinct, in no hurry to take the next steps he knew he must take.

CHAPTER FIFTY-EIGHT

AZADI LAY DOWN on his bed after Inspector Hadian left. His brain was fried. Though it had been a rough night and a tough morning, he felt good about how he'd handled the inspector.

Azadi heard the cold, winter wind whistling outside the window. He shivered. The heat wasn't working in the apartment. He spotted the blond American's tweed hanging on a chair and contemplated wearing it outside. No. The thing was threadbare and not his style. He opened the trash bag and stuffed the tweed in there with the garbage. *The man who killed Parisa wore this rag*, he thought.

Azadi pulled a leather Versace jacket from his closet and put it on. Then he grabbed the trash and headed out to the street. The frigid wind slapped at his cheeks and played havoc with his hair. Friday traffic was light, people were sleeping in for the weekend. The few pedestrians he passed on the sidewalk seemed happier than usual. Days off did that for most people. But he still had a lot of work to do.

Azadi tossed the trash bag in the dumpster behind a butcher shop a few blocks away. He walked a few more blocks down a tree-lined, trendy shopping street and entered a coffee shop he frequented. "Cozy Corner" was no Starbucks but it attracted its share of rich housewives and spoiled teenagers. Sure enough, the place was packed and some of the women were beautiful. Normally, Azadi would have scoped the place but this day was nowhere near normal.

Parisa. Dead. God Dammit.

He drank four double espressos. He congratulated himself for how he'd handled the cop. Giving up the iPod had been an inspired touch. Deflecting suspicion from one crime by confessing to another was old school. He'd known plenty of drug dealers, counterfeiters, and car thieves who'd done just that — pleaded out to misdemeanors and gotten away with felonies. He'd never had a chance to try it himself; well, not until Mia Kelly knocked down his door and offered him this damn deal.

Azadi hadn't gotten around to buying a cellphone so he used the café's public phone to call Farjad's home. The General was having breakfast with his family but he took the call. Azadi told him about Parisa's death. Farjad sounded shocked. He told Azadi that he didn't even know he was married. He offered to help with the funeral arrangements. Azadi had to take a deep breath to keep calm, to keep from expressing his hatred for this liar, this monster who was truly responsible for Parisa's murder. He told Farjad no thank you, he could handle the funeral and needed to take the day off from that "special project" to take care of it all. Farjad said yes, of course, take the day. But you must get the work done on time, the important work that you promised us, Omar. Azadi said he would get it done and hung up.

Azadi rested his head against the wall, feeling out of whack from too much caffeine and too little sleep. On the phone, Farjad had given no inkling that he knew Parisa, let alone that he was using her to spy on him. But Azadi knew that it was just that, an act. Just like Parisa's love for him had only been an act. Just like his allegiance to Farjad was an act.

Azadi fingered the gold chain around his neck, the one that Parisa had given him as a gift on their first date. The chain seemed to constrict and strangle him by its own volition. His breath came to him in short, sharp bursts. His palms felt sweaty against the walls and began to slide. He lost his balance. He fell to the floor in a heap.

He was a coward. He was so scared. He sat there on the floor with all the customers looking at him and he wet himself.

He bolted to his feet and ran the hell out of there.

Azadi wandered the Tehran streets, hands in pockets, not making eye contact. The cold wind was accompanied by steady drizzle. Cooking smoke and car exhaust hung down at eye level like wet ghosts. More people were up and on the street now. Crowds jostled him, people sneezing and coughing in the dank winter air, their expectorate soiling the sidewalk.

Walking the rain-swept city streets, Azadi felt his own death shadowing him. He felt a desperate need to go home. Not home to apartment in North Tehran. Not home to America. But home to his Creator.

He found himself standing outside a mosque.

-:::::-

In the mosque, Azadi went through the motions of prayer.

"God is great," he said.

He placed his right hand over his left below the navel. He looked down at the ground. "Glory to You, Oh Allah, and Yours is the Praise," he said.

He continued praying, hearing himself saying the words, "Ruler on the Day of Reckoning. You alone do we worship, and You alone do we ask for help. Guide us on the straight path, the path of those who have received Your grace; not the path of those who have brought down wrath, nor of those who wander astray."

He dropped his hands to his sides, bent at the waist, back parallel to the ground, looking at his feet and continued praying. He continued praying as he lowered himself to his knees and placed his nose and palms to the ground.

"God is great," he said.

Azadi continued the ritualized movement. He continued saying prayers. He was not devout, never had been, but he was desperately trying to open himself up to the infinite possibility of Allah. He was in despair and he had heard that despairing souls often found God just when they needed Him most. He needed Him now.

Azadi knew what it took to create a perfect counterfeit bill. But what he really wanted was God to show him a perfect logic as to why he should go on with this mission. He knew the Quran provided the logic by which to live a righteous life. That's why he was here. This was his last chance before he jumped off into the abyss. So his mouth said the words and his body went through the movements of a Muslim at prayer.

Azadi saw men praying all around him. He envied their belief in a moral universe and a beneficent God. If God would let him believe it, he would do something in return. Maybe he'd sell out the Americans and confess to Farjad. Then the Revolutionary Guards would arrest Ishmael and the blond American and keep printing their money until their Islamic Revolution spread throughout the Globe. That's what Allah wanted, right? If Allah showed himself to him right then he'd do it. He'd rat out his people. *Come on God. Show me a sign and I'll drop a dime.*

The men praying around him seemed ecstatic. Ten million joints, 100 million lines of coke, and one billion orgasms could not have made them any more ecstatic than they seemed at that moment. He wanted to feel like they felt. He wanted to believe like they believed.

He tried to reconcile the idea of murder and being a Muslim. He knew that Islam was a religion of peace, dignity, and order. Islam meant "peace" in Arabic. He had never been devout but his counterfeiter's mind didn't easily forget details. He could quote dozens of passages from the Quran, some he'd only heard once many years ago, passages that emphatically stated the moral, majestic, peaceful vision of Allah as told to his last and final prophet Muhammad.

"Do not kill or take human life, which God has declared to be sacred," he remembered reading. Was it al-Anaam 1:51? All he was sure of was that the blond man and Ishmael had killed Parisa. She

was sacred to him and to God, and for that they must be punished. But they were not the only ones responsible for her death. He blamed Farjad, too. Farjad had forced her to betray him, and in doing so had sealed her fate.

"God is great," he said.

Azadi's mouth said one thing, but his mind thought another. He was remembering September 11, 2001. He had argued with his father, goading him, insisting that the tragedy proved once and for all that there was no God and, if there was, Islam was the worst way to worship Him. It was the continuation of an old argument, for Azadi detested how his father had suffered so much himself yet refused to blame Allah. But the foundations of his father's belief had proved much stronger than the steel of the World Trade Center. Against Azadi's onslaught, his father hadn't even attempted a reasoned defense of Islam. The old man didn't try to explain that what was done in the name of Allah that day was an anathema. His father merely said, after much quiet deliberation, that Allah was love.

Allah was love.

Azadi put on his shoes and left the mosque. He walked through the cold drizzle as it swelled into a frigid downpour yet he felt warmed by the gold chain around his neck. The gold was glowing with the life force that had once been Parisa. It was not strangling him now. It was caressing him like a lover's touch. He interpreted this as irrefutable proof that Parisa had really loved him. He knew that he had loved her, loved her still. The photos he had seen of her and the accusations they had made no longer meant anything. They had mattered to him before but all that mattered now was the perfect appreciation of the love they had shared.

Azadi knew he might be crazy but he didn't feel crazy. He felt exhilarated. This was the sign from God.

A great burden had been lifted. She really had loved him. He had the motivation to go on thanks to the sign from God.

He was going to complete the mission. Destroying the Press would punish Farjad.

And on the day of the mission, when he had fulfilled his duties and he and the blond man would be in close proximity at the Press, Azadi would shoot the man dead. Kill him in cold blood as Parisa had been killed in cold blood.

Destroy the Press. Kill the blond American. Do them both.

Azadi reasoned that if he could kill the blond American before the Special Forces arrived, he would blame it on the Iranian guards and try to escape according to plan. If the Special Forces caught him killing the blond American, he would accept his fate like a man. The American soldiers would shoot him dead but it did not matter. Live or die, all that mattered was revenge. Azadi's only regret was that he would not get a chance to kill Ishmael, too.

-:::::-

Azadi walked all the way to the morgue, arriving an hour later. A detective sent over by Inspector Hadian had been waiting for him since the morning. The detective didn't seem fazed by the delay; he had happily passed the time playing chess with the coroner. The detective wore a black suit and the coroner a white robe. They looked like opposing chess pieces.

Parisa's body lay in a room that smelled like chemicals that preserve the dead. There were 10 autopsy tables flanked by trays of scalpels and saws. The craftsman in Azadi took an interest in the technical side of other peoples' workspaces. The husband in him wanted to think about anything else but the lump under the opaque plastic sheet that they had led him to.

Azadi stared at Parisa's face as the coroner drew back the plastic sheet. He was shocked to see how dramatically death had drained away her beauty. But this wasn't his Parisa; Parisa lived in the chain around his neck, communicating to his heart. It sounded crazy but it wasn't.

He nodded his head to the detective. Yes, that was her. Azadi squeezed out a tear but he felt as cold and hard inside as the shiny steel table his dead wife's body lay upon.

At the funeral home a few blocks from the morgue, Azadi arranged for Parisa to have a proper Islamic burial the next day. He spared no expense; it was going to cost him a fortune.

The day after the funeral he would go back to the Press and start working on another.

CHAPTER FIFTY-NINE

HADIAN AND COLONEL Tabriz met in the bazaar. Living in the Islamic Republic had made Hadian paranoid and he preferred to confront the official from the Ministry of Intelligence in a public place, despite the fact that Tabriz had personally brought him on to the "Dead Presidents" case. They stopped at a vendor selling fresh *ranginak*, a pastry made with dates and walnuts. Tabriz bought two and gave one to Hadian. Hadian's stomach was churning from nerves and he wasn't hungry, but he knew better than to refuse the Tabriz. As they walked away from the vendor and back into the crowd, Hadian got to it.

"It is possible, Colonel, that Omar Azadi and John Farragut are involved in a conspiracy."

Tabriz took a bite of his *ranginak* and chewed. "What type of conspiracy?"

"According to his past employer, Naghmen Babajan, Azadi now works for the Revolutionary Guards, for a General Farjad. Doing what? I don't know. I do know that Farragut, out of all the men I have interviewed, best fits an assassin's profile. He has the marksman's skills and the right nationality. He also has a distinctive tweed jacket that I saw in Azadi's apartment, though Azadi denies knowing

Farragut's name. But perhaps he was never told the name? Azadi may be the link between the Revolutionary Guards and Farragut. He is compartmentalized, kept in the dark about Farragut's identity, for security. Your own operatives follow similar procedures, correct?"

"They do," said Tabriz, polishing off his pastry. "But what are the two Americans, in your opinion, conspiring to do?"

"Our president, despite being loved by the masses, has his enemies," said Hadian carefully. "He has become a visible symbol of our nation, unafraid to speak truth to the west and take provocative stands. There are those in the traditional, established power centers, the oil ministry, the army and yes, the Revolutionary Guards, who may think he is pushing too hard too fast. Then there is an element of jealousy because of the way he dominates the national debate. I believe it's possible that the Revolutionary Guards has contracted a foreign assassin to kill the president and thus preserve their position as the standard bearers of the revolution."

Tabriz tossed away the paper wrapper his *ranginak* had come in, obviously not fearing that Hadian would cite him for littering. "You are saying that the threat to our president comes not from the outside but from within?"

"It is a theory but one I wish to pursue further."

Tabriz laughed. "My dear Kamran, your mind is like this bazaar. A maze running in every direction but leading nowhere."

Hadian felt a flash of anger. "It leads to a dead president, Colonel. *Our* dead president."

Tabriz made no attempt to hide his dubious expression. "Are you going to eat that?" he asked, pointing to Hadian's untouched *ranginak*.

Hadian handed his pastry to Tabriz. Tabriz devoured it in two bites. "Come. Walk me to my car. We can talk in private there."

They exited the bazaar and approached Molavi Avenue to the south. When they reached Tabriz's car Hadian noticed it was parked illegally. Tabriz sat in the driver's seat and Hadian in the passenger seat. Tabriz turned on the car radio. Persian pop wailed from the speakers. Tabriz was making sure the discussion could not be heard by anyone passing by on the street.

"What proof, besides the word of a dissolute drunk, do you have that Azadi is connected to the Revolutionary Guards?"

Hadian was going to ask how Tabriz knew Babajan was a drunk, but thought better of it. "No proof. Just my instincts. I believe that the Revolutionary Guards were watching Azadi, making sure he was loyal to their cause. They were using Parisa Halajeh as a spy. How else to explain the *sigeh* ceremony that allowed Azadi to marry a woman whose brother is a known political dissident? They controlled her, used her brother's plight against her. How do you explain that it normally takes weeks, if not months, for a *sigeh* license to be pushed through the system yet Azadi received his in days? Higher powers had to intervene. And except for the Guardian Council and the Supreme Leader, there is no higher power than the Revolutionary Guards."

Tabriz remained expressionless. Hadian wasn't sure if he was considering what Hadian had just told him or if the overproduced pop song blasting from the radio had deafened him.

"My dear Hadian, what I'm about to tell you is to be held in the utmost confidence. And the only reason that I am telling you is so you don't embarrass yourself. Or worse, get yourself thrown in jail if you pursue this line of investigation. Do you understand?"

Hadian nodded. Tabriz's dark gaze smothered him like a moonless night. "Our government, under the direction of the Revolutionary Guards, operates a secret press to print high-quality US counterfeit currency."

"I have heard rumors," Hadian said with a shrug, hoping the casualness of his lie would encourage Tabriz to relax and tell him more.

"It is a testament to the stupidity of the Americans and the shrewdness of the revolutionary regime that we've been able to hold on to the Press," continued Tabriz. "The CIA gave it to the Shah so he could finance his regime. After the revolution it remained in Tehran, then was moved for security purposes to Lebanon, then the Beqaa Valley, where the Syrians protected it. With America's recent aggression in this region and Israel's regrettable eagerness to strike into Lebanon and Syria, the decision was made to the move the Press back to Tehran. Now General Farjad oversees the security and operation of the Press. Knowledge of its existence, location, and operation was supposed to be limited to a chosen few."

Hadian heard the bitterness in Tabriz's voice. He guessed that Tabriz was not one of the "chosen few" and resented it. "But you found out that exact location, Colonel?"

Tabriz could not suppress a mischievous smile. "Yes. The Ministry of Intelligence is, after all, the organization that should be in charge of such things. We are professionals, not paramilitaries. And yes, despite the Revolutionary Guards attempts at keeping the location secret, we have known for some time that the Press is under Gheyam Hospital."

Hadian nodded but did not otherwise show his gratitude for being let in on the state secret. He knew Tabriz was taking a big risk by telling him this.

"Thank you for your candor, Colonel. But this information doesn't explain the mysterious connection between Azadi and Farragut."

"I am getting to that. The ministry may not control the Press but we keep an eye on its operations. On *all* operations within Iran's borders. We know Azadi is the head printer at the Press. Recently Professor Farragut purchased a valuable antiquity for our country using counterfeit cash printed by Azadi. So you see, the Press connects them. Perhaps Farragut left his jacket in Azadi's apartment while picking up the buy money?"

"Perhaps you are right, Colonel. But then why did Azadi not know Professor Farragut's name when I mentioned it to him?"

"Perhaps because Professor Farragut is a respected academic with a sterling reputation. He may have used an alias to protect his identity."

Hadian turned off the radio. He wanted no distractions for what he had to say next. "You say Professor Farragut has a sterling reputation. But he used his lover, the wife of the German Ambassador, to provide him with an alibi for the Be'sat Park explosion."

Tabriz flinched as if shot. "You talked to the German Ambassador's wife about Farragut? Idiot! Why would you do such a thing?"

Tabriz's strident tone made the hair stand up on the back of Hadian's neck. "Because you hired me for my investigative skills and she is where the investigation led." Hadian licked his lips, buying time to gather his courage. "But this discussion isn't about her. It's about Professor Farragut. I believe he's a liar, just as I feel that Omar Azadi *was not lying* when he said he didn't know Farragut. What or how that relates to this investigation, that I still don't know. But I intend to find out."

Tabriz stared out the windshield at the traffic-clogged street. He had hired Hadian for his instincts, not his impudence, but as Tabriz knew from their previous collaborations you paid for the former with the latter.

"My dear Hadian," said Tabriz in a low voice. "As always I respect your dedication and thoroughness. However, I am sure that you can pursue your investigation without embarrassing the wife of a respected German diplomat. I don't have to remind you that Germany is one of Iran's best friends in Europe, if not *the* best friend. We desperately need their capital investment in our country, not to mention their influence with the United Nations and the International Atomic Energy Agency. Now you have other names on your list. Focus on them. Forget about Farragut and Azadi. And never dare bother the German Ambassador's wife again."

Tabriz gestured towards the passenger side door. Hadian exited the car but held the door open so as to make his final plea before Tabriz could drive off. "Please understand, Colonel. The investigation flows where it must. Like water, it will find its own path."

"And you, Chief Inspector, shall find yourself walking a path to early retirement should you not heed my advice."

Tabriz leaned across the seat and slammed the passenger door shut himself, putting an exclamation point on his threat, though it had been delivered in a voice even sweeter than the *ranginak* he had devoured earlier.

Hadian watched Tabriz drive away. He couldn't wait to go home, to kiss Laleh and hug Ahmad and put the stresses of the day behind him.

His cellphone rang. It was a patrolman informing him that yet another prostitute's mutilated body had been discovered near the airport. This woman had no ministries or religious paramilitaries to protect her. She was not the beautiful wife of a diplomat. She was not a distinguished academic or state-supported counterfeiter. She was nothing in the eyes of the Islamic Republic except an embarrassment and a nuisance and a whore.

Hadian got in his car, pulled an illegal U-turn and drove towards the crime scene, vowing to do the unheralded but necessary work of avenging poor women without friends in high places, women without friends anywhere at all.

CHAPTER SIXTY

SPECIAL AGENT TRENT Hurley sipped his third cup of Yemen Mocha Sanani and tried not to fall asleep. The coffee was strong. The cute Goth girl waitress at the coffee shop had promised that it would keep him awake all night. Hurley had been back twice for refills, not only to keep the caffeine in his system, but also to take another gander at the butterfly tattoo above the Goth girl's tight little ass. *Sweet*, he thought, *very sweet*. Even sweeter than the Yemen Mocha Sanani, with its earthy tones and subtle chocolate finish.

Hurley yawned. It was hot and stuffy in the car. The heat was blasting but he was too lazy to turn it down. Besides, it was fucking freezing outside. Another cold, wet winter night in Seattle. What a surprise. He glanced over at his partner, Special Agent Max Voelker. Voelker was snoring with his mouth open and Hurley could smell the green curry chicken on his breath. They'd both ordered it for dinner. Takeout for the stakeout. Too spicy for Hurley's taste, but he was sick of cheeseburgers and fries. Stakeouts always packed on the pounds.

Hurley took another sip of coffee. He glanced through the windshield at Billie Hastings's house. It was still there. And, as usual, nothing was happening. A week had passed since Gary Jr.'s birthday party. The guests had left — all those black mamas with their colorful robes and big head scarves, and the little boys in their natty tuxedos – and since then nothing. Hastings and her kid hadn't been outside the house since the party. Apparently the kid had a bad cold and his mother was staying home from work to care for him. She'd gotten only two phone calls in that time. A wrong number asking for someone named Howie and an unsolicited call from a carpet cleaning company. The boys in the sound van had picked up nothing interesting on their audio surveillance equipment, with the exception that Ms. Hastings liked to watch a soap opera where the handsome town stud turned out to be a transsexual serial killer.

Hurley polished off his coffee. He was contemplating heading back to the coffee shop for some tattoo gazing and a blueberry muffin when he felt his intestines buckle. A bubble of hot gas shot through his gut and exploded into the van with a resounding *phhhttt!*

Maybe it was the smell. Maybe it was its sound. Whatever it was, it woke Voelker up.

"Jesus," said Voelker.

Hurley bent over and grabbed his belly. "Max, I gotta go."

"No shit," said Voelker. He laughed at his pun.

"I'm serious, Max. I got the runs. The coffee and the curry, I'm –"

Another titanic fart cut off Hurley's words. He pushed open the passenger side door.

Voelker said, "Where're you going?"

"I gotta take a dump!"

"Hang on, partner. Our relief will be here in an hour."

"Fuck that," said Hurley as he bolted out of the car. On the sidewalk he debated his options. He could make a run to the coffee shop down the street but jogging the three blocks would surely open the floodgates prematurely. Even if he made it he'd have to negotiate with the Goth girl for the restroom key. He doubled over as another methane tremor assaulted his innards. Screw it. He had to move *now*. From weeks of observation he knew the half dozen immediate homes were all empty, their owners not yet returned from negotiating the Seattle rush hour traffic. He had only one choice.

Hurley lumbered up Billie Hastings' front walk, cupping his belly like a pregnant woman. Despite the cool, night air he broke out in a sweat from the effort of holding in his bowels. He rang the doorbell repeatedly, pounding the button with the heel of his palm.

After a few seconds the door opened. An attractive African American woman greeted Hurley. She wore blue jeans, a black cashmere sweater, and a brow knit in surprise.

"Can I help you?"

Hurley managed to pull one hand from his belly and flash his badge. "Special Agent Trent Hurley. FBI. According to federal law an agent may requisition a suspect's place of residence should an emergency –"

Hurley felt an avalanche of coffee and curry rumble inside him. The explanation would have to wait. He brushed past the woman and sprinted through the entrance hall. Entering the living room he saw a small, mocha colored boy in a green Seattle Supersonics sweatshirt. Hurley glanced around the living room, desperately trying to ascertain where to run next. The boy seemed to instinctively understand what Hurley wanted. He pointed towards a hallway. Hurley dashed towards it. He tried the first door he saw and hit the jackpot.

Hurley had his pants to his knees before his ass hit the toilet seat. Sitting there, finally at peace, his gaze moved around the bathroom and settled on some family pictures hanging near the sink. One picture showed Billie and Gary posing with Mickey Mouse at Disney World. Another showed Gary dressed in his pajamas sitting next to a Christmas tree surrounded by unopened presents. A third showed Billie and Gary in bathing suits, building a sandcastle on the beach north of the Santa Monica Pier. Hurley could not help but notice they were an attractive, loving family. He smiled. Then he frowned as a troubling thought began to gnaw at him.

"Mister, you okay?"

Hurley saw the boy in the green Supersonics sweatshirt standing in the doorway. In his haste to get to the toilet Hurley had forgotten to shut the bathroom door. The boy's mother appeared and without looking at Hurley she pulled her son away and gently closed the door, leaving Hurley alone with his pants down around his ankles and his spirits lower than that.

No. Hurley was not okay. But it wasn't this invasion of privacy that had him down. It was the pictures on the wall; or rather, what the pictures confirmed.

The woman and boy in the house were not the woman and boy in the pictures.

Billie and Gary Hastings had disappeared.

CHAPTER SIXTY-ONE

"**HER NAME IS** Helen Uwanda. She's the same height and weight as Billie Hastings, give or take a couple pounds. Her son, Jaffar, looks a lot like Gary, Jr. if you're not looking too hard."

Farragut listened to Mia Kelly say these words over the secure telephone line at the British embassy in Tehran. He was alone in the room. A portrait of the British Prime Minister smiled down on him. Framed photos of the ambassador with various Iranian leaders flanked the phone, as if they were trying to listen in on the conversation.

"John, are you still there?"

Mia was calling from Frank Finley's office at the Treasury Department in Washington DC. The Deputy Director of the Secret Service had a secure phone and was listening in on the conversation, as was Doug Alson. Farragut listened to Finley's raspy breathing over the phone line. Farragut had met him a couple of times. The man smoked like a broken diesel engine and looked like Ichabod Crane on a hunger strike. If he wasn't careful he'd get in his lungs what Farragut had in his head.

"I'm still here, Mia. Tell me more."

"Not much to tell. Uwanda is a member of the Muslim Women's League in Seattle. Big African American contingent. She's a model citizen. No priors. She and her son switched places with Hastings and Gary, Jr. during his birthday party. Seems the agents watching the house got confused and didn't realize Salaam's family slipped out with the other guests. They'd exchanged clothes with Uwanda and her boy and surveillance didn't pick up on it."

Alson cut in aggressively. "I'd like to add this switch had obviously been planned for months. Salaam must have set it up through his contacts in the Muslim community. The female guests all wore concealing African clothing. The boys wore identical tuxedos. On top of that, the party broke up at the end of the agents' 12-hour shift. Hastings knew that surveillance would be at its most vulnerable. It's not an excuse, but the men watching her were at a disadvantage."

Finley cleared his throat and spoke for the first time since the call had been made. "You're right, Doug. It's not an excuse."

Farragut could imagine Alson's meaty face turning the color of pulverized veal.

Mia said, "Long story short, John, we're in trouble. Salaam got on that boat but he can't be trusted. He'll try to join his family, wherever they are. If Shehabi doesn't kill him during the sea voyage we should assume Salaam will try to escape once he's back in Beirut. The Israelis will do their best to watch him but Shehabi will undoubtedly keep Salaam on a tight leash. If they get a clear shot the Israelis will attempt to terminate Salaam, but only if he's not surrounded by Shehabi's goons. They don't want a shootout with Hezbollah, especially on Lebanese soil. If Shehabi and Salaam show up in Tehran as planned, then it's up to you to take them down. Azadi, too. No loose ends, remember?"

It took Farragut a few seconds to process what Mia had just said. The tumor was partially to blame. Its incessant growth was starting to impair his powers of concentration. But Farragut also was not sure he had heard Mia right because what she said sounded so wrong.

"Are you suggesting we stand down the operation?"

"I'm not suggesting it. I'm ordering it." Mia had pounced on this last too quickly, anticipating Farragut's resistance. When he didn't say anything right away, she softened her tone. "John, Salaam is no good. He presents too much of a risk. Now we've all discussed it here and no one wants another Operation Eagle Claw. We have to stand down the operation."

Mia reference to Operation Eagle Claw, the failed attempt to rescue the hostages from the US embassy in 1980, infuriated Farragut. Eagle Claw had been a PR disaster, but this was not some massive military mission. This was a small-scale covert job that was publicity proof. If it succeeded the Iranians would not want to admit they were vulnerable. If it failed they would not want to admit the existence of the Press. The US would never make it public. Azadi and Salaam were expendable and Farragut was terminal. Jashni was an Israeli and knew that if his country kept expecting Uncle Sam's aid in the Middle East he'd better not utter a peep.

"We've come this far, Mia. We don't need Salaam. Azadi and I can finish the job with some modifications in the original plan."

"John, with all due respect, you're being too optimistic. Salaam's part is integral; without him, the plan collapses. You'll be lucky to take care of your end on your own. Plus, neither you nor Azadi have enough demolition experience. No. It's over."

Farragut knew from the resignation in Mia's voice that the decision had been made over her head. What Finley said next confirmed it.

"Professor Farragut, your country thanks you for your extraordinary bravery and sacrifice. Rest assured that the full financial amount promised you for your work, despite it not reaching the conclusion we all hoped for, will be paid in full."

Mia still had some pull. She got Finley and Alson out of the room and explained herself personally to Farragut. She talked about her disappointment that things had not worked out as planned. She talked about her struggle to convince the Supernote Committee that she could find another man to take Salaam's place, but the Baltimore fiasco had doomed that idea before she could make her pitch. She talked about her respect for Farragut and how she would never have attempted to put together a job like this without his participation. She talked about spending time together — his remaining time together — upon his return to the US. She would take a vacation. They could go away. Aspen for some skiing. Maybe Napa. She had an uncle who owned a small vineyard. They could drink wine and share some laughs. Maybe even... you know, for old time's sake. If he was feeling up to it, of course. She could make his last days good days. No, *great* days.

While Mia talked Farragut let his mind wander. He wasn't going back home, that was for sure. He didn't have the heart to tell Mia there was nothing left for him there. In fact, the more she talked about their friendship, the more he thought about Ingrid. He needed her now, needed her desperately in a way that terrified him. He only hoped that he hadn't let things deteriorate between them beyond the point of return.

CHAPTER SIXTY-TWO

THREE DAYS AFTER leaving Baltimore the *Riad El Solh* was 50 nautical miles southwest of Bermuda. At noon a Sikorsky S-92 helicopter owned by the same Saudi Arabian shipping company that owned the *Riad El Solh* landed on the deck. Six men with papers identifying themselves as members of the ship's crew boarded the helicopter, along with a cargo of 30 packing skids of US currency paper. The helicopter flew to Bermuda International Airport and landed next to a Gulfstream 550 that displayed the same corporate logo as the *Riad El Solh* and the helicopter. The six passengers disembarked the Sikorsky, two immediately boarding the G550 and four waiting until they had transferred the currency paper to the plane's cargo compartment. If someone had been watching they would have noticed that the two passengers who immediately boarded the plane were a tall, black man with a bandaged hand and a younger man with a harelip. They also would also have noticed that the younger man had a gun bulge beneath his jacket. But nobody was watching. The airport manager had been paid a substantial sum to ensure that this flight was treated as nothing more than a routine executive jet departure.

Once all the passengers were on board they settled into the luxurious cabin. This was the chairman of the shipping company's personal plane, and no expense had been spared to make it as comfortable as his 12-bedroom palace in Riyadh. The cabin featured calfskin leather seats, framed artwork by LeRoy Neiman, and a full bar stocked with a panoply of 30-year-old single malt Scotch whiskeys (the chairman, a good Muslim, never drank in his own country where alcohol was banned, but international air travel was another matter). The flight crew consisted of two former Saudi Arabian Air Force colonels. The regular flight attendant, a 20 year-old Indonesian beauty queen, had been left home due to the sensitive nature of the passengers' business and the chairman's desire to have her entertain him at his penthouse apartment in Jidda.

As the plane taxied on the runway, the captain informed the passengers that they would be flying non-stop to Beirut. The G550's range was 6,700 nautical miles, well beyond the 4,700 nautical miles to the Lebanese Capitol. The passengers settled into their seats and adjusted their seat belts. Salaam, sitting across from Fady, noticed he was having trouble with his. The strap was jammed inside the buckle mechanism, preventing Fady from adjusting the belt to fit his paunch. Salaam watched Fady put his Uzi on the floor and attack the buckle with both hands.

The gun, thought Salaam. *I have to get my hands on his gun.*

"Let me help, Fady."

Salaam undid his belt. He took a step towards Fady before Shehabi appeared out of nowhere and blocked his way. "I'll help him. You sit."

The look in Shehabi's eyes and the Uzi in his hands left Salaam no choice but to do as he was told. He sat back down and buckled up. Shehabi switched seats with Fady, who joined Hafez, Rafik, and Youssef in the middle of the cabin.

Salaam stared out the window as the engines kicked to life and the G550 zipped down the runway, taking off into partly cloudy skies. He nervously tapped his feet as the plane pulled out over the Atlantic. He didn't mind flying but he hated takeoffs and landings. And he especially hated takeoffs and landings when he had a suspicious Hezbollah terrorist sitting across from him with a loaded sub-machine gun on his lap.

Salaam watched the clouds fall away beneath the plane as it climbed to its initial cruise altitude of 41,000 feet. He prayed the flight would be as uneventful as the sea voyage had been. The weather had been calm and the days had passed predictably, ebbing and flowing to the steady rhythm of the swell beneath the boat. During the entire voyage Salaam hadn't had a minute alone. Shehabi had confined him to his cabin and assigned one of his men to watch him at all times. They seemed embarrassed to have to do this; the men liked Salaam and apparently didn't share their leader's suspicion that he had sabotaged the Baltimore heist. So they kept him under guard and tried to show they were still on his side. Rafik taught Salaam how to play *basra*, a Middle Eastern card game. Hafez told Salaam stories that he had memorized as a boy from *The Arabian Nights*. Fady described in loving detail the best meals he had eaten in Paris (the Bresse Chicken Cooked in a Pig's Bladder, with Albufera Sauce and Stewed Vegetables at Alain Ducasse won top honors). Youssef polished his gun and allowed Salaam to pepper him with questions about his personal life, none of which he answered. Whether this was through indifference or ignorance Salaam wasn't sure.

Shehabi, for his part, had steered clear of Salaam. They didn't talk after the initial interrogation. That was fine with Salaam. He had nothing more to say to the man. He had not expected to see Shehabi ever again after they had parted ways at the Shell station. It was just bad luck that some drunken asshole had tried to crack open his head back in Baltimore. Otherwise, Salaam would be in Lagos, Nigeria, reunited with his daughter and grandson.

His family. The thought of them kept Salaam going. God willing, they were out of the US by now. Dexter had handled all their documentation himself. The man drove a big rig for his current gig, but in his day he'd been the best forger in the business. Passports, drivers' licenses, social security cards — LTD did them all. The man had thumbs as thick as bratwurst but as nimble as eels. Salaam promised himself to pay his old friend back as soon as he could give Shehabi the slip. And make no mistake: he *would* give him the slip. He just had to find an opening, which wasn't going to be easy because Shehabi wasn't going to let him out of his sight.

Salaam's broken nose began to hurt and he took one of the Valium that Hafez had secured for him from the *Riad El Sohl's* medical officer. He closed his eyes and the next thing he knew the captain was announcing the plane's descent into Beirut. The G550 touched down so smoothly that Salaam didn't have time to worry about crashing.

"Welcome home, Sleeping Beauty," lisped Shehabi. Salaam could have done without the man's smug smile but Shehabi had the gun and Salaam didn't.

The plane taxied to a stop at the far end of the airport. Rafik and Hafez stayed behind to supervise the shipment of paper, which was being flown from Beirut to Tehran via Iran Air. Salaam, Shehabi, Fady, and Youssef disembarked and climbed into a waiting silver Mercedes van. The driver was a Hezbollah guerilla who Salaam recognized as one of the thugs that had guarded him that first day at the safe house. Salaam assumed that's where they were going now. Tomorrow he and Shehabi were scheduled to fly from Beirut to Tehran, where they would meet Shehabi's patrons and discuss their plans to wreak international terrorism together. Today was supposed to be a day of rest.

But rest was the furthest thing from Salaam's mind. How could he relax when the next few hours were so crucial? If he were going to make his move, he'd have to do it in Beirut, before he got on that plane to Iran. He assumed Kelly had discovered that his family had fled surveillance. She had nothing on him anymore and would have put out the word to take him down. If he showed up in Iran, he was a dead man, plain and simple.

So Salaam sat in the van and thought about escape. Squeezed between Fady's gut and Youssef's gun it was stressful, to say the least. To relieve the pressure he stole glances out the window. Beirut was bustling, and it was impossible to reconcile his uncertain fate with the determined displays of *joie de vivre* put on by the city's inhabitants. The rain that had fallen for the past week had halted. The reluctant winter sun broke through the clouds by noon and pushed the temperature into the seventies. The cafes were filled with effervescent people imbibing effervescent drinks, toasting this early glimpse of spring with Champagne and beer. On the Corniche, the long seaside promenade, slim girls in tank tops worked on their tans before the inevitable gray curtain of winter descended again. The haggling in the Souk el Barghout was fierce: the inclement weather had bottled up the bargaining instincts of merchants and shoppers alike, and now they embraced the chaos of commerce as if the sun's visitation shed a new light on hidden deals and crooked business practices.

Salaam observed all of this, as the driver had taken a circuitous route, driving north from the airport and hugging the coastline around the harbor before heading back south through the heart of the city. This type of roundabout itinerary was standard operating procedure for paranoid Hezbollah drivers. Salaam thought nothing of it, even when the van bypassed the safe house in central Beirut and traveled into the slums south of the city.

Salaam observed that even by Middle East standards the neighborhoods were exceedingly bleak and for good reason. They functioned as *de facto* Palestinian refugee camps, filled with wide-eyed disenfranchised boys who had never seen their putative homeland and weathered women old before their time who never expected to see it again.

Salaam still expected that the van would make a U-turn and head back towards the safe house. He was not prepared when it parked in front of a dilapidated tenement building.

Shehabi turned around to face him from the front seat. "Get out of the van."

Salaam looked past Fady to the building. Anti-Israeli graffiti was spray-painted in Arabic on either side of the main doorway. A couple of nut brown kids with curly hair and skinny limbs passed a deflated basketball back and forth through the grubby front yard.

Salaam felt his innards twist. "What's going on?"

Shehabi said something in Lebanese to Fady and Youssef. Fady exited the van and Youssef nudged Salaam with his Uzi. "Out," said Youssef.

It was the longest sentence Salaam had ever heard Youssef utter. No wait – it was the *only* sentence he had ever heard Youssef utter.

Salaam exited the van. The two kids stopped passing the basketball long enough to stare at him. Shehabi got out of the van, too. He took Salaam by the arm and walked him towards the building entrance. Fady and Youssef followed behind.

Salaam smelled wood smoke and shit as they entered the building. Trash filled the hallway. Salaam saw soiled diapers scattered across the cracked linoleum floor. He heard a baby crying somewhere above them, its shrieks echoing in the open elevator shaft.

They walked to the fire stairs at the end of the hall. Youssef pushed Salaam through the door. Shehabi led the way down the stairwell, which had the same noxious odor as the hallway, only more intense due to the lack of ventilation.

As they descended the stairs Salaam felt strangely at peace. He had no doubt he was going to die. There was no escape. It was one unarmed man against three armed soldiers. He recalled that the Mexican Mafia cats in Terminal Island called this the *paseo*, the "walk of death." It was a one-way walk. Always.

But Salaam was cool with it. The important thing was his family was free. Billie had been able to withdraw $250,000 from the first $5 million payment to Salaam for agreeing to do the mission. Salaam had insisted on this five-percent "good faith" payment to his family before he left for Lebanon and Kelly had consented. It wasn't that much money to the government, especially in light of how much the Supernote Press was costing the US taxpayer, but to a single mother with a young son to raise and a father in prison, it was a lifesaver. Salaam had directed Billie not to spend the money until she was out of the country. She was stubborn but she wasn't stupid. That money would buy her and Gary, Jr. a better life in the place they were heading.

They reached the basement level of the stairwell. Shehabi went through the door first, followed by Salaam, then Fady and Youssef. They entered into a dark corridor lit by a single overhead light bulb. Shehabi led them towards a black void in the distance. Their boots kicked up dust from the floor. The air was dry and hot. Salaam caught glimpses of little gray lizards scampering across the concrete walls as Shehabi marched him towards the room that he was sure would be the place of his execution.

Salaam wondered how the Hezbollah leader would explain his death to his patrons in Iran. He wouldn't come out and say he killed Salaam because he suspected him of treachery. He couldn't prove a thing. No, he'd probably claim it was an accident. *The old man was tired from all the traveling and slipped and hit his head on the street. We burned the esteemed martyr's corporeal vessel and scattered the ashes in the Mediterranean, per his request.* Or maybe he'd say Salaam had fled once they got back to Beirut. *Your holiness, the American, felt he had done enough for our cause. He had been imprisoned for so long that he didn't want to risk capture at the hands of Satan's infidels. This was his last jihad. Allah be praised!*

Whatever Shehabi told the Iranians, Salaam wondered if they would buy it. They clearly held Salaam in higher esteem than Shehabi did. Otherwise they would have ordered Shehabi to kill him on the boat. But Salaam had delivered the paper as promised – albeit with a hitch or two. He was also a devout Muslim and an enemy of the US government. The currency paper would go a long way towards funding terrorism across the globe, and the Islamic Republic of Iran could certainly see the strategic and political benefits that would accrue from the participation of an American citizen in their war against democracy and freedom. Yes, the more Salaam thought about it the more he realized that if Shehabi killed him, the Iranians might do the same to Shehabi. He only hoped Shehabi would come to the same conclusion before he decided to put a bullet in the back of Salaam's head.

They stopped at the end of the hallway. A rusted iron door blocked their path. The doorknob was missing and hundreds of little dents covered the lower half. Shehabi kicked open the door, adding another dent.

A hot stink hit them. The stench of piss, shit, puke, sweat, and blood stuck to the air like it had hooks. It wasn't the stink of life so much as the stink of what flowed out of the body after life had left. Salaam's knees buckled and he tried to vomit, but he hadn't eaten anything since they got off the boat and nothing came up. Fady, who had gorged on caviar and Cointreau from the G550's galley, projectile puked on the wall, drowning a lizard in the process.

Youssef and Shehabi grabbed Salaam's armpits and carried him into the basement room. The door closed behind them. Fady stayed in the hall, retching like a man possessed.

Salaam's eyes took a few seconds to adjust to the darkness. The windows near the ceiling were boarded up. The light that managed to penetrate through the cracks attached to the shapes of machinery and men like film on a dead fish.

Salaam saw a Hezbollah guerilla dressed in fatigues. He stood next to a bedspring mounted on a wooden platform. A naked man, his black skin glistening with sweat, was anchored to the bedspring, his wrists and ankles secured to the corners by leather straps. The man's nipples, penis, and throat were connected to metal clips, which in turn were connected to wires plugged into a truck battery on the wooden platform. Grotesque bruises that looked like the silhouettes of crabs covered his body. His chin rested on his chest. Puddles of human filth stagnated around the wooden platform like an obscene medieval moat.

Salaam's body shook with the effort not to pass out. Shehabi slapped his face. The blow forced Salaam to suck in a breath of putrid air. He gagged.

Shehabi said, "This man, or what's left of him, is an Israeli commando. He was captured off the coast of Beirut by Lebanese sailors soon after you came to us."

Salaam shut his eyes. He knew now that the man on the rack was Captain Regassa. How had Regassa managed to live so many weeks with so much pain? It seemed a miracle, no, a curse, that the man's life force was so resilient. Salaam prayed for tears to come, to wash away the realization that he was responsible for the wretched creature before him. But he couldn't cry. Allah was not going to let him off that easy.

"This is wrong," Salaam whispered. "Our religion preaches purity, not torture."

Shehabi stared at him, his features strangely indistinct, as if he were a watercolor portrait. "'The punishment of those who wage war against Allah and His Apostle, and strive with might and main for mischief through the land, is execution. That is their disgrace in this world, and a heavy punishment is theirs in the Hereafter.'"

Shehabi was quoting the Quran to him, a passage often used to justify Holy War. Well, Salaam knew the text better than Shehabi did. He'd stake his life on it, and Regassa's life, too.

"Fight in the cause of Allah those who fight you, but do not transgress limits, for Allah does not love transgressors,'" said Salaam. He gestured towards Regassa, barely able to choke out the words. "And this, this is a terrible transgression."

Shehabi's eyes became so black they seemed to suck the darkness out of the room. "No. A terrible transgression is Israel's illegal occupation of the West Bank and Gaza Strip. A terrible transgression is Israel forcing three million Palestinians to live in disease and poverty outside their rightful homeland. A terrible transgression is Israel sending spies like this man into Lebanon, a country it invaded and plundered for 20 years. A terrible transgression is Israel's systematic murder of thousands of Palestinian children through military attacks, economic deprivation, and the withholding of medical care. A terrible transgression is a country that claims to have been a victim of genocide inflicting a similar punishment upon a people whose only crime is to rightfully claim the land that Israel stole from them."

Shehabi barked in Lebanese to the guerilla. The man flipped a switch on the truck battery. Regassa's body jolted. His muscles moved in a fascinating mixture of spasm and release. His mouth opened wide but his scream was silent, his vocal chords paralyzed by the electrical current transmitted through the clips gripping his throat.

Salaam lunged towards the truck battery but Youssef, his quiet comrade who hunted rabbits in the tall grass of the Beqaa Valley, held him back.

Shehabi let Regassa twist in agony, then signaled the guerilla to turn off the power.

Salaam said, "You son of a bitch."

Shehabi chuckled. "Stop acting like a schoolboy. The Israelis do the same thing to us in their prisons. Even worse, because they have the technology to keep us alive longer. You just don't hear about it on '60 Minutes.' The Zionist cabal who control your media don't want you to know, and McDonald's can't sell cheeseburgers when the last image you've seen before the commercial is the rotting flesh of an Arab political prisoner. Riyadh, show him."

The guerilla that had operated the truck battery rolled up his left sleeve. He had a crude prosthesis affixed below his elbow where his forearm should have been.

Shehabi said, "From 1985 until 1999, the Israelis ran a torture center at Khiam in southern Lebanon. Men, women, children, Palestinians and Lebanese – the Israelis tortured anyone who they felt posed a threat to their occupation of my country. Riyadh was beaten so severely, they had to amputate his left arm. Then, to remind him who was in control, they left this."

The guerilla pulled up his shirt exposing his belly. In the dim light Salaam could see that a Star of David had been scorched into the skin covering his abdomen. Salaam guessed that the scar tissue indentations came from cigarette burns.

Shehabi said, "You come here to the Middle East. You say you want to be a part of our struggle. I tell you that the American prison you escaped from was a country club compared to the shit we live through every day. The shit we inherited from our parents and will leave as a legacy to our children. I want to trust you because I know you love Allah. But you're also an American and because of that I have my doubts. Yes, we have risked our lives together. We have the paper and my patrons are pleased. But before we go fly to Tehran and present ourselves as a team, I need you to prove to me that you are committed to the cause."

Shehabi gestured to the guerilla named Riyadh. The man handed Shehabi a .45 semi-automatic pistol. Shehabi offered the gun to Salaam.

"There is a single bullet in the chamber. Do God's work and put this piece of shit out of his misery."

Salaam stared at the floor. Apparently Regassa had not betrayed him. If he had Salaam would be dead by now. He wasn't even sure the man was alive enough to recognize him.

"No. I'm not a killer."

"Oh, really? So I suppose after you blew up that Federal courthouse they arrested you for being a litterbug?"

"It was an accident," said Salaam, his eyes rising to stare at Shehabi with contempt. "The charges were set to go off at 4:00 a.m. The place should have been deserted."

"But it wasn't, was it?" replied Shehabi. "Because a young US attorney was scheduled to try her first case Monday morning. But Sunday night, she was nervous and couldn't sleep. And when she crawled out of bed at 2:00 a.m., her husband knew that she was just going to the courthouse to practice her opening argument for the millionth time. The security guard liked her, so he let her into her office. And when the bomb went off, maybe she was thinking what a great future lay ahead of her. She was ready to make the world a better place. For everyone certainly, but especially for the unborn child she carried inside her." Shehabi flashed a smile so wide it looked like it would rip his harelip. "I saw the report on CNN. They can be quite melodramatic. Now, you want in...?"

Shehabi again offered the pistol. Salaam thought about taking it and using the bullet to shoot Shehabi but a weak voice in the darkness distracted him before he could grab the gun.

"Fuck you, Shehabi. You don't even have the balls to shoot me yourself."

Regassa. He was staring at the Hezbollah leader. It occurred to Salaam that the Israeli must have been mustering every last ounce of strength to hold his gaze like that.

Shehabi said, "So now you feel like talking?"

Regassa took a raspy breath. "Better than listening to that monstrosity you call a mouth."

Salaam was surprised to see Shehabi flinch. Riyadh almost jumped out of his fatigues to flip the switch on the truck battery. The stench of burnt flesh stuck in the air for half a minute after the battery was turned off.

Shehabi pressed the gun into Salaam's hand. "Kill him now."

A cough, a wheeze, and an order from Regassa. "Shehabi, you're a gutless *majbub*."

Salaam's Arabic was so-so, but he knew that *majbub* means "what is cut." From the expression on Shehabi's face Salaam guessed that the slang referred to a man's genitals, specifically Shehabi's lack of them.

Shehabi trotted over to Regassa. He pistol-whipped the Israeli's face. Regassa's nose spurted blood. His lips were so swollen that the words were almost inaudible.

"That's it, *majbub*. Do your dirty work yourself. He's not your nigger."

Nigger. It was what Salaam had called Regassa back in the Zodiac. Regassa had been insulted although Salaam had meant it as a term of solidarity. Salaam was sure that Regassa was using it that way now.

Salaam said, "Shehabi, stop. Please –"

Shehabi pistol-whipped Regassa below the waist, so hard that the clips disengaged from his cock. The Israeli vomited bloody mucous. He'd been deprived food for so long there was nothing left to regurgitate.

Shehabi said, "Who's the *majbub* now?" He had a sweat stain on the back of his shirt in the shape of California.

Regassa coughed. Salaam thought he may have been smiling, but it was hard to tell since his teeth were broken and his jaw had swollen to the size of a grapefruit. The Israeli finally managed to spit out the words. "Did anyone ever love you? Did you ever find a girl who would kiss…those cloven lips…you fucking freak?"

A muzzle flash. A gunshot echo. Tissue and brains rocketed out the back of Regassa's head and hit the floor with a wet rag slap.

Shehabi kept pulling the trigger. *Click. Click. Click. Click.* The empty gun sounded like a leaky faucet. He dropped the gun. It clanged. He thought about his first love, the redheaded Jewish girl in Oxford. Had he kissed any girls since her? He couldn't recall. He had fucked a few, for sure, but he was pretty sure he had not put his lips to theirs. Oh well…

Shehabi kicked open the door and disappeared down the hall.

No one moved for a while. Finally Riyadh shuffled his feet. He detached the clips from Regassa's body. He began to untie him from the bedspring. His prosthetic hand had trouble undoing the knots. Youssef went to help. They worked in silence.

Salaam watched the two Lebanese gently remove the dead Israeli from the rack. He watched them place Regassa on the floor and cover his body with a blanket. Salaam wondered how they could brutalize this man in life yet treat his corpse like a holy relic. Their solicitude seemed absurd. It didn't make sense. Nothing made sense anymore.

Salaam turned and walked towards the door. Youssef and Riyadh were on their hands and knees, using rags to mop up the filth. Neither tried to stop him from leaving the room.

In the hall Salaam stepped over Fady. The journalist turned terrorist was sitting with his back against the wall. He had puke crust on his shirt. His eyes were glassy.

Salaam climbed the stairs to the main floor. In the foyer, he saw a plump woman in a purple tracksuit. She was sweeping the dirty diapers into the elevator shaft. She offered Salaam a wan smile. He didn't smile back.

Upon exiting the building Salaam took a deep breath. The fresh air felt alive in his lungs. He looked up and down the street but the silver Mercedes van was gone. So were the two kids passing the basketball.

The sun was shining and sky was blue. It was a beautiful day in Beirut. Salaam was alone. No one was watching. He could walk away. He could go anywhere in the world.

But Salaam knew there was only one place to go.

CHAPTER SIXTY-THREE

A ZADI RODE TO Gheyam Hospital in an ambulance. The guards seemed nervous and drove an even more circuitous route than usual. Azadi's attempts at small talk were met with indifference. He tried to continue what had been a lively debate from the day before, whether Nicole Kidman or Halle Berry was more beautiful. The guards no longer seemed interested in such things. One guard mentioned the weather. The other talked of the traffic.

Arriving finally at the hospital, Azadi went through the long walk and elevator ride. At the entrance to the Press, he gave the two guards at the vault door two, 1.75 ounce tins of caviar, as was his custom. They were the last small tins he had.

"In a day or two, when we are finished with this job, we shall really celebrate. I have purchased a large shipment of caviar. There'll be enough for you and your families to treat yourselves for months. Or you can sell it yourselves on the black market. Whatever you like."

The guards had come to appreciate Azadi's generosity and didn't judge his supposed black market connections. But this time they thanked him with tense smiles. They were clearly on edge. When Azadi entered the pressroom, he understood why.

General Farjad stood against the far wall, inspecting five guards as they unloaded stacks of Crane currency paper from a forklift.

Azadi could feel his palms sweating. He descended the stairs and asked Bashir, a skinny, young guard, why he was filling the generator with gasoline.

"Orders from the general," said Bashir, with a nervous glance towards Farjad. "He is convinced that Zionist spies are planning an attack on our electrical grid as retaliation for our nuclear ambitions. They want to test the operation running from an independent power source."

Azadi nodded. It made no difference to him where the juice came from. Let Farjad worry about imaginary Zionist spies; it would keep his mind off the actual American spy in his midst.

Azadi joined Farjad at the far wall. The general was too busy supervising the unloading of new issue currency paper to notice him at first. Azadi inspected the rectangular skids of paper, each four feet high. He counted 30 skids and he knew from his tutorial at the Bureau of Engraving and Printing that each of the skids contained approximately 10,000 sheets of paper. Thirty-two $100 bills could be printed on each paper sheet. Azadi did the math in his head. With enough time and enough ink, he could use this paper print about $960 million in Supernotes. But his job was only to print $50 million by tomorrow.

Azadi cleared his throat and finally got Farjad's attention. "You are later than I expected," said Farjad glancing at his watch. "An update on your schedule, please."

No more "Omar, my dear friend." No more "like a son to me." Farjad, the lying murdering bastard, was all business.

"I'll complete the plates today. Tomorrow, I'll start printing," said Azadi.

"Unacceptable. I need the money sooner. Need I remind you that we lost time because of your personal obligations?"

By "personal obligations" Farjad meant Parisa's funeral. The man had balls; Azadi would give him that. "Forgive me, General. I will stay here until the job is done."

"Exactly how long will that be?"

"It will take about 16 hours to print both the fronts and backs of the bills, as you know they must be printed separately. I shall sleep a few hours in between, allowing the ink to dry. I will then need four hours to print the serial numbers. The money will be ready in 24 hours."

"You have 24 hours. No more. The man who will be receiving the money cannot afford to stay in our country much longer. There are political considerations for both him and Iran. Do you understand?"

Azadi did understand. He didn't know the details of that side of the plan but he figured whomever Mia Kelly had dropped on the Iranians had to be a real hot potato.

"You will have the money in 24 hours, General. I promise."

Farjad looked again at his watch. Then he looked around the room. Then he looked at the stacks of paper. He made a point of not looking at Azadi.

"The paper arrived this morning. Just as I promised you." Farjad held a sheet of the Crane currency paper up to the light, examining it closely. "I can see the watermark and security strip you Americans put in. Very clever."

So now it was "you Americans." Fuck Farjad. Azadi didn't want to talk shop. He wanted to kill this SOB ASAP.

"I realize we lost some time. And for that I am sorry," Azadi said, struggling to contain the bitterness in his voice. "But, well, I'm sorry you could not attend Parisa's funeral. It was very beautiful. She was very beautiful."

Farjad was still examining the paper, still not making eye contact. He was making it easy for Azadi to hate him.

"Yes. I truly would have liked to have met her."

"You would have liked her. And I'd like to thank you again for the time off."

"Don't mention it. It was the least I could do after all you've done for me."

Farjad replaced the paper sheet and marched towards the exit without saying goodbye. Azadi went back to work on the printing sheets. He was grateful for the distraction; it kept him from thinking about how much he wanted to kill Farjad. He checked the original plastic printing sheets. After soaking 20 hours in the electrically charged nickel bath, they were now covered with a layer of silver and nickel. Azadi removed the sheets from the bath and secured them on a worktable. He began by pulling the original plastic sheet free from the solidified silver-nickel combinations. The $100 note design, front and back, had now been transferred from the plastic sheets to their respective silver-nickel sheet. Azadi put the plastic sheets aside, for the silver-nickel sheets would be the ones used to print the money.

Azadi laid the two silver-nickel sheets flat in a deep, industrial sink. He removed the silver coating by scrubbing with a chemical solution that looked like the flesh of a blood orange but smelled like medicine. With all the silver removed, the next step was to grind down the printing sheets to a thickness of 3/100 of an inch. The thickness of the sheets had to be exact so that their impact with the paper in the Press would create a bill that felt real to the touch. Azadi began with the back bill sheet, reducing it on the powerful lathe, sluicing water over the metal to minimize heat from the friction as well as to wash away the ground particles.

Azadi enjoyed laboring at the lathe. He liked the solid feel of the metal and the hum of the powerful tool. The act of counterfeit creation, from steel plates through nickel printing sheets to paper currency, satisfied something deep inside of him. Just as Parisa had made him feel part of something deeper and more profound than himself, so did this act of creation. These metal sheets, the soon-to-be printed Supernotes, they were his legacy, yet they would be destroyed within a day or two. What a waste, just like Parisa's life had been such a waste.

That was as much thinking as he did. Grinding down the printing sheets required his utmost concentration and he couldn't think about other things too much.

"Dead Presidents in black and green. Dead President's means the money ain't clean," Azadi sang over the din of the lathe. By the time he had sung the song twice, he was done with the second sheet.

Azadi secured the two sheets onto a table and brushed a layer of chrome over the nickel, adding strength and durability. After ten minutes, the chrome-covered nickel printing sheets shined like the pipes of his old Harley Davidson. He hadn't thought of his Harley in months. He had sold it to a smug stockbroker from Santa Barbara. His father had often warned him that he would kill himself on that Harley someday. He'd been wrong.

Azadi had been working for several hours but he was in the zone. His final step was to shape the chrome-covered nickel sheets to fit the rounded drum of the Supernote Press. He did this by curling the printing sheets with a mechanical dowel. It only took a few minutes to complete both sheets.

He checked his watch. It was 11:41 a.m. With uncanny accuracy, Bashir sensed it was time to begin the printing. He stood from his sitting position by the generator – he hadn't moved for hours – and walked up to Azadi.

"Would you like some help now?" Bashir asked, smiling sheepishly.

Azadi wanted to tell him "no" just to hurt him. He wanted revenge now. He couldn't wait for revenge. But he was tired from his labor and he could use the help.

"Do you know what to do?" he asked Bashir.

"We use black ink for the front of the bills, green ink for the back. We print the fronts after the backs so that the portraits will stand out clearly. Finally, we print the serial numbers."

"Very good," said Azadi, truly impressed.

Bashir shyly averted his eyes. "Mr. Sepanlou taught me. He used to let me help him with his work. I hoped to learn about printing from him and one day follow in his footsteps."

Azadi thought about his predecessor, Sepanlou. He had died three days ago from his burns. Soon, when the shit went down, this poor, skinny kid Bashir would be joining his mentor in his heaven, if that is indeed where the souls who served the Islamic Republic wound up.

"Sounds like Mr. Sepanlou taught you well. Now please get me the green ink."

While Bashir went for the ink, Azadi bolted the rear sheet onto one of the Press' cylinders. At the BEP, four sheets would be bolted on the Press at a time, enough to print roughly 38 million individual notes in a day. Azadi only had one sheet for each side of the bill. Still, one sheet per side would be more than enough to print the $50 million in the available time.

Bashir arrived with the green ink. Azadi examined it carefully, stirring it with a palette. It looked as good as the US government's own, which was made from a secret formula. Farjad had been right: if the Iranians could build a nuclear power plant they could certainly analyze and recreate an ink formula. Except for the one thing about the ink he didn't want them to replicate and he wasn't going to tell them. It was that one thing the mission depended upon.

"Load the paper," he told Bashir.

With Bashir occupied, Azadi slathered the ink evenly over the back printing sheet forcing it into the detailed grooves. Then he inspected Bashir's loading of the paper. Perfect printing required the paper be lined up properly. Sepanlou had taught Bashir well. The paper looked perfectly aligned.

Azadi hit the power switch. The intaglio presses pulsed with life. He watched the machine, hypnotized by the action of the sheet-fed, high-speed, rotary presses. In the vortex, under 20 tons of pressure, the almost worthless materials of paper and ink merged to miraculously become something so much more valuable. *Each $100 bill costs approximately four cents to create*, he thought. That was the official line from the BEP. But that wasn't right. How do you measure the worth of the people who had died, who were going to die, to create these bills that were destined to be blown up tomorrow? The math to measure that hadn't yet been created. Perhaps it never would be.

Azadi checked his watch. It was almost 12:39 p.m. He eyeballed the sheets of paper shooting out from the cylinders. To the naked eye, the details of the back of the bills looked perfect as did the color and quality of the ink. He would do more thorough testing later but for now it was enough to let the machine do the work.

He would run the Press for another 8 hours, printing 2,000 sheets per hour. At 32 $100 notes per sheet that meant 64,000 notes per hour. At the end of the eight hours, he would have printed the backs of just over $50 million in counterfeit currency. Then Azadi would sleep for four hours, allowing the green ink of the back of the bills to dry. Then he would run the Press another 8 hours, printing the fronts of the bills in black ink. Then, with both the fronts and backs printed, he would finally print the serial numbers. Then he would give the money to Farjad.

Then it was out of his hands.

CHAPTER SIXTY-FOUR

THE IRAN AIR flight from Beirut to Tehran took three hours. The plane was half full and Salaam and Shehabi didn't sit together. Through his hangover haze Shehabi tried to read a dog-eared edition of *Catch-22*. Salaam stared out the window and reflected on the past 24 hours.

After witnessing Regassa's execution Salaam had walked back to the safe house. It took him a couple of hours but he was grateful for the time alone. It gave him time to think about how Regassa had saved his life. He had not betrayed Salaam. More than that, he had spared Salaam the ignominy of executing him. Salaam had entered that ghastly basement fearing it would be the place of his death. Now he was alive and all he wanted to do was die.

As he had walked the streets of the city he became determined to pay back Regassa. He could, of course, kill Shehabi but that didn't seem like enough. No, Regassa had lost his life because of the mission. Salaam would make sure that his sacrifice wasn't in vain.

He had found Shehabi back at the safe house. He was sitting behind his desk in his office, polishing off a bottle of Chateau Masur and smoking his Havana down to a nub. He did not seem surprised to see Salaam, this despite not having let him out of his sight for the past 72 hours. They did not discuss what had happened back in the basement. Shehabi made Salaam feel he could come and go as he pleased. They made small talk about the weather. Then, over a simple dinner of tabouli, they finalized plans for their presentation in Tehran. After dinner Shehabi killed another bottle of wine and passed out at his desk. Salaam said his evening prayers and spent the night tossing and turning on the cot.

Shehabi and Salaam passed easily through customs after the plane landed at Mehrabad. They each had packed only an overnight bag. Shehabi had booked them a room at an apartment hotel in North Tehran near Vanak Square. They had a day to kill in the city. Tomorrow morning they would meet Shehabi's patrons.

Exiting the airport terminal Shehabi hailed a cab. Salaam made note of the cab's license plate number. It did not correspond to the one that Kelly had made him memorize months before. The driver, an old man with a bloated paunch, did not look like the man Salaam expected to be driving the cab that he knew was waiting for him.

Shehabi helped the driver toss his bag into the trunk. He slid into the back seat and looked at Salaam still waiting at the curb. "Are you coming? I'm going to the hotel. To sleep."

Salaam shook his head. "I'm going to a mosque. To pray."

Shehabi told the cab driver the address of the hotel. He shut the door and the cab drove away.

Salaam stood at the curb. He knew the cab was coming. There was one flight out of Beirut per week. The man he was waiting for would have orders to be ready for it. The terminal entrance was crowded and Salaam didn't fear for his safety. He knew that if someone wanted to kill him, he would not do it in such a public place. He took a breath and held the smell of jet fuel inside him awhile. He released it when another cab pulled up in front of him.

Salaam checked the license number and it matched. He was surprised, however, by the physical appearance of the driver. He looked like a rodent with red hair and freckles. Salaam hadn't been expecting the Grim Reaper but still, the man looked as deadly as a sock puppet.

Salaam tossed his luggage into the back seat. He got in and closed the door. The cabbie had made no effort to help him. In fact he acted as if Salaam weren't even in his cab. He stared straight ahead through the windshield.

Salaam said, "Take me to the Masjed-e Emam Khomeini."

The cab pulled into traffic. The cabbie finally looked into the rear view mirror.

"You want to go to a mosque? Tell me, are you going to pray for your soul or for the souls of your family? And as long as we're on the subject of your family, you should be aware that certain parties are concerned that your daughter and grandson have abandoned their domicile and taken up residence God knows where. Well, God and you, of course."

The cab suddenly pulled up in front of the Air France terminal. A gaunt blond man with grayish skin entered the cab and sat next to Salaam. He carried no luggage. His sport coat looked too big for him and his shoulder bones protruded from his open shirt collar. Salaam noticed that the brown leather belt that held up his slacks had been fastened to the last hole.

The cab pulled away from the curb without the blond man telling it where to go. Salaam, a product of both Oakland's tough public schools and the nation's most elite universities, recognized the blond man's accent as American and well-bred.

"You're here to kill me," said Salaam.

"I'm here to ask you a question," replied the blond man.

"Here's the answer. I changed my mind. I want to go through with it."

The cabbie cackled. The blond man looked at the cabbie and he shut up fast.

"Why am I supposed to trust you?"

"If you didn't need to, I'd be dead already."

They drove in silence for several minutes. The cab approached Azadi Tower, Tehran's most famous monument. The large triumphal arch rose to the west of Tehran, a grandiose gateway to the city. It reminded Salaam of a giant tombstone. He stared at the tower and thought of Regassa and how he would never be given a proper Jewish burial. He wondered where the Lebanese would dump his body. He hoped they wouldn't burn it. He knew Jewish law prohibited cremation but he doubted whether the Lebanese knew or cared.

"Here. Take this."

Salaam turned from the window. The blond man was offering him a handkerchief. Salaam stared uncomprehending until he tasted blood. He'd been biting down so hard to keep from crying that he'd bit his lip. He took the handkerchief and dabbed his mouth. Silently he cursed himself for not allowing himself to cry. Was he ashamed? That was pride. He'd have to get over that. Shame came from pride and his pride had hurt enough people already.

Salaam said, "I love my family. But I cannot face them as a man if I do not face my obligations as a Muslim. When I got to prison, I was full of pain. But I found Allah and through Allah I found peace. Becoming a Muslim saved my life. Now I have the chance to save others."

The cabbie snorted sarcastically. "How very touching. Now let's kill him."

"Shut up and let him finish," said the blond man in a low, even voice.

Salaam stared out the window. The cab had reached downtown. Salaam saw a mural painted on the side of a building. It showed an American flag. In the blue field, human skulls had replaced stars. The red horizontal stripes were depicted as fiery lines trailing from the backs of missiles. "Down With the USA" was printed in English in the flag's center.

Salaam said, "What I saw done yesterday — done to a good man in the name of Allah — was an abomination." He turned and looked in the blond man's gray eyes. "If you want to kill me, kill me after the job. I don't care. I just care that these men are stopped. And if cutting off their cash saves even one life, then my death will have been worth it."

The blond man held his gaze. "Are you ready for tomorrow?"

Salaam nodded. Without taking his eyes off Salaam the blond man said to the cabbie, "Drop him off wherever he wants to go."

"Professor, please. That is not the course we agreed upon."

The blond man pulled a pistol from his sport coat and pressed it against the cabbie's neck. "I'm dying. I can do anything I want. Understand?"

The cabbie turned so white his freckles appeared to evaporate. The blond man seemed not the least bit self-conscious that they were traveling on a busy street. He waited for the cabbie to say, "I understand" before burying the pistol back in his sport coat.

After ten minutes the cab pulled up to the mosque at the north end of the bazaar. Salaam got out. The blond man handed him his bag. He looked ill to Salaam, but the way he handled the heavy bag told Salaam he was deceptively strong.

The blond man flashed a lopsided grin as the cab pulled away, a grin that seemed to say he was holding onto a delicious secret and too bad for the rest of the world for being in the dark.

Salaam entered the mosque and prayed.

CHAPTER SIXTY-FIVE

THE BEDROOM CURTAINS were drawn tight against the night. Farragut could barely make out Ingrid's face even though she was lying in bed next to him. The clashing perfumes of sweaty sex and Ingrid's skin cream, clean like sailcloth in the sun, told him she was really there. He breathed in as deep, smelling her essence and feeding the tumor oxygen.

A strange thought hit Farragut. This is the last time I will make love before I die.

"What's that expression for orgasm again? The little death?" he whispered to Ingrid.

"*Le petit mort*," Ingrid mumbled in her flawless French. She was almost asleep but managed a wry smile. "I know you're dying but could you please try to be less morbid?"

"I thought I was being funny."

"Oh, you're just hilarious. What's next? Keeling over dead on top of me?"

Farragut squeezed her warm, round buttock by way of an answer. She attempted a laugh but it got lost in her pillow as she drifted off to sleep.

They had been drifting apart themselves. He hadn't seen her since their cordial Indian dinner a few weeks before. But with the tempestuous events of the past days – Parisa's death, Salaam's shenanigans and then his fervent promise to carry on – Farragut found himself needing to anchor himself emotionally. He had ulterior motives in seeing her, sure, but he also had a heart. If she suspected him of the former she did not let him know. When he'd phoned her that morning and asked her to spend the night with him at the Laleh, she had not hesitated in saying "yes." He'd even had a pleasant chat afterward with her husband. The ambassador had taken the phone from her and invited Farragut to spend the New Year at the family's ski chalet in the Alps. Farragut had respectfully declined.

Back in America, in just a few more hours, Mia would have to explain that her hand-picked team leader had disobeyed her direct orders and gone ahead on his own. Of course, if the mission played out perfectly, and Farragut was by no means confident it would, all might be forgiven. *Might* was the best he could hope for at this point.

When Ingrid's snoring signaled she was asleep, Farragut lifted himself out of bed and walked unsteadily towards his desk. His head was pounding with pain as he sat down and turned on the desk lamp. The light shot like a laser beam to his retinas. Gradually, his eyes adjusted. He could feel the tumor throbbing.

He looked over at Ingrid and saw that she was still asleep. Why not? To a healthy person, the light was dim and the room still very dark.

Farragut pulled a pen from the desk drawer and began to write his letter on the hotel stationary. Writing the letter only took him 20 minutes, for he had been composing it in his head since the day Parisa died. Azadi's letter to her had been Farragut's inspiration. Parisa's death had given Farragut the motivation.

After Farragut wrote the first letter, he wrote a second one for Ingrid's eyes only. He wrote the latter to explain to her why he had written the former. He put each note into a separate envelope and slipped both envelopes into her purse on the nightstand by her side of the bed. She didn't wake up when he did this.

Farragut walked back to the desk and sat at the chair.

It was time. He knew how to pace himself, how to conserve his strength and pull it out of reserve when it was most needed. Such intuition had served him well in the Olympics, skiing and shooting over many days and qualifying heats. Such intuition would serve him well now. He had just enough life left in him to do the things he would have to do and then he would be dead. His tumor-wracked brain told him this. His dying body agreed.

-:::::-

Ingrid awoke two minutes later at the sound of Farragut's body collapsing to the floor. He had dragged the desk lamp with him and the bulb had shattered, momentarily illuminating the room with a strobe-like flash.

Ingrid put a pillow under his head where he lay because he told her not to move him. She called the front desk and asked for an ambulance. They did not talk as they waited because he wanted to conserve his strength and everything he had to say was in the letters she had not yet found. The ambulance arrived 20 minutes later and took him to Gheyam Hospital, the best hospital in the city.

He had, of course, requested it.

CHAPTER SIXTY-SIX

INSPECTOR KAMRAN HADIAN looked at the South African's hands and knew the interview was a waste of time before he asked his first question. Arthritis had twisted the former army major's fingers into stiff, angry claws. Yes, the man spoke English and had a distinguished military record — as well as a less savory one as a mercenary in the waning days of apartheid— but he could not possibly be an assassin intent on killing the president. Those hands could barely hold a pen, let alone a sniper's rifle. The South African was no doubt nothing more than what he claimed, a security consultant to the Japanese engineering firm subcontracted to drill tunnels for the Tehran Metro.

Hadian left the engineering firm's elegant penthouse offices in a boxy glass tower and emerged onto the crowded Tehran sidewalk. The air was unusually crisp and cold and clean. Snowcapped mountains loomed to the north of the city, towering over the metropolis and seeming to flaunt their superiority to man-made structures.

Hadian pulled his scarf tighter around his neck, plunged his hands in his pockets, and walked back to the precinct. He hadn't taken his car because he wanted to take his time. Walking helped him to think and there was a lot to think about.

Hadian had completed his investigation of possible suspects in the "Dead Presidents" case with the interview of the South African engineer. He would report to Colonel Tabriz that, in his professional opinion, the potential American assassin of the Iranian president was not in Tehran — if he existed at all. Tabriz could believe him, his old friend who he himself called the finest police inspector in Iran. Or Tabriz could believe the word of a captured Israeli commando in Beirut, dying and delirious with fear, if he wasn't already dead, spitting out fantasies to save himself from torture. To Hadian, it was that simple.

Hadian picked up the pace and pulled his scarf tighter as the wind blew colder. His tattered, threadbare winter coat did little to keep out the chill but he couldn't afford to buy a new one, not on his meager salary. He ducked into a tea house and warmed himself over a cup of Darjeeling. The tea was very hot but so was Hadian's temper. What really bothered him, more than his failure to find a viable suspect, more than his threadbare coat and feelings of poverty, was the way Tabriz had told him to stop investigating Farragut and Azadi. Hadian detested being lied to and he felt those two Americans were lying. What they were lying about, he wasn't sure. Maybe their only connection was through the counterfeit press. That press was none of his business but it still bothered him. He was sure that Farragut's tweed coat had been in Azadi's apartment. Hadian knew there was nothing he could do about Farragut and Azadi but he still wanted to confront the professor. It was petty and unprofessional but he needed some shred of victory, some crumb of vindication, to inspire his work through the long, dreary week ahead. Last night, another dead prostitute had been found out at the airport. Hadian had no leads in that case, either. There were no fingerprints because, he assumed, the killer wore gloves. There was no semen because the killer did not rape the victims. There were no grieving relatives to help the investigation because the women were outcasts. How could Allah let such terrible things happen?

Hadian put extra sugar and milk in his tea because he was hungry and didn't want to spend money for a snack. He sipped his tea and silently scolded himself for being a failure, a poor police officer in a police state corrupted by oil riches. All he had was his family and his beliefs in Allah, in justice, in the guilt of John Farragut and Omar Azadi for…something.

Hadian walked out onto the street and the winter wind, as much as his own desire, seemed to push him in the direction of the Laleh Hotel a few blocks away. He wasn't sure Farragut was in his room but it was worth a visit.

When Hadian arrived at the Laleh, the blind night porter told him about Professor Farragut's collapse the night before. Hadian felt a tinge of pity for the professor and shame at his own pettiness. Those feelings dissipated, however, when he learned that the dying American had been taken to Gheyam Hospital.

Gheyam Hospital. The very structure that stood above the secret printing press where Omar Azadi worked.

Hadian had never run faster, even when trying to outrun bullets during his stint as a medic in the war with Iraq. Outside the hotel, he flashed his badge to steal a cab away from a Russian nuclear engineer and was on his way.

CHAPTER SIXTY-SEVEN

D R. ALI KHARRAZI, chief of oncology at Gheyam Hospital, pointed to the X-ray of Professor Farragut's brain, showing Hadian exactly where the tumor was situated.

"As you can see the tumor is quite large. And because of its position, inoperable."

Hadian had been a battlefield medic, not a doctor, but he had seen men's heads blown open and their brains spilling out. He knew how much brain a man could afford to lose and how much he couldn't. Farragut was fighting a losing battle.

"How much time does Professor Farragut have?" asked Hadian.

Kharrazi brought his elegant hands to a steeple under his strong chin.

"It is only through Allah's merciful grace that he has lived this long. But if I were to guess, I would say no more than a month, two at most."

"Does he appear lucid?"

"Yes. Very. He blacked out but that's not surprising given his condition. And given that condition, his alertness and coherence are quite remarkable."

"Excellent. Then I would like to speak to him."

Kharrazi pulled Farragut's X-ray from the light board and placed it into a manila envelope. A vestigial itch of revolutionary attitude tightened his throat. He wanted to tell the police officer to go fuck a goat. Yes, he could remember the dark days of the Shah when medicine, except for the rich, was less a priority than armaments. He had applauded the increased access to health care instituted since the Revolution. But now he believed the Islamic Republic's paranoia and dogmatic interpretation of Islam, especially as it related to women's health issues, was a disgrace. Hadian represented the system Kharrazi loathed. But Kharrazi was realist and knew he could do more good treating cancer patients from Gheyam Hospital than a prison cell.

"Professor Farragut is in room 1987," he said. "He should just be finishing his dinner."

-:::::-

Hadian smelled the night's chicken and rice dinner wafting through the hospital corridors as he exited the elevator. He entered a clean, modern wing. Televisions blared from the large, private rooms along with the humming of medical equipment. This was where the rich went to die, embraced by technology and cleanliness. Hadian noted the contrast with the wings downstairs where the poorer patients were stacked like cordwood. The failures of the state he served depressed him.

As Hadian walked down the corridor, he looked at the numbers on the doors, searching for 1987. Then he saw Ingrid Mader emerging from a room up ahead. She turned and walked down the corridor toward him. As they passed one another, she offered him a gracious smile. She looked lovely. Her skin glowed. Her health and beauty seemed an anomaly in this place.

"Good evening Inspector ... Hadian, wasn't it?"

Hadian nodded respectfully and was about to say hello but she continued on her way before he got the chance. She clearly did not want to chat. He fought the urge to turn back and watch her shapely behind disappear down the corridor.

He stopped at the room from which Ingrid Mader had come. The number on the door was 1987. Farragut's room. The door was closed. He knocked.

"Come in, Inspector. I've been expecting you," Farragut said in Farsi.

Hadian opened the door and entered. The room was white and clean. Bouquets of fresh flowers sat arrayed in every available nook and cranny. They filled the room with a sweet fragrance that mixed with the succulent odor of the chicken dinner sitting on the bedside table.

Farragut sat up in bed, propped up on pillows, looking like a wilted white rose. The color was blanched from his face and hands. His cheeks were sunken and his lips pale. Only his eyes retained the essence of the man Hadian had interrogated weeks before, shining brilliantly blue and alert.

"Hello, Professor Farragut. How are you feeling?"

Hadian took a seat by Farragut's bed. Farragut turned his head stiffly to face him.

"As Dr. Kharrazi told you downstairs, I'm dying."

"So he told you I wanted to speak?"

"As did the night porter at the Laleh. He phoned me five minutes after you left." Farragut emitted a dry, rasping cough. "Did you think I knew it was you at the door because I was psychic?"

Farragut managed a feeble laugh. He licked his pale, thin lips. Hadian saw a plastic bottle of water with a straw by the bedside and handed it to Farragut, who took it with a smile and a nod. Hadian watched him sip water.

"I think you are many things, Professor. But psychic is not one of them. Although I think you know exactly why I came to see you."

"I take it it's not to pay your last respects?"

"No. But I am sorry to hear you're dying. You have been a worthy adversary."

Farragut settled back into the pillows and said, "Is that what I am to you? An adversary?"

"You are a liar, Professor Farragut. I know that you are up to something illegal but I don't know what exactly. I do know that you know a counterfeiter named Omar Azadi, an American like you, and that you two are in business together. Do not try to deny it. I saw your tweed jacket in his apartment. I know you worked together in the past under the auspices of the Revolutionary Guards. You put together a deal and he created the cash. I know this for a fact."

Farragut took a small sip of water and handed the bottle to Hadian. "That's quite a story. If I came up with a story like that, they'd probably blame it on the brain tumor. Luckily, my mental faculties have remained sharp and I see things clearly. And you, clearly, are mistaken."

"Are you telling me you don't know a counterfeiter named Omar Azadi?"

Farragut coughed and pointed to the side table. "Would you like my dinner, Inspector? Chicken and rice. It's not bad."

"Then why are you not eating it?"

Farragut pointed to his other side table and the open 35.25-ounce tin of Sevruga caviar. "As long as I'm being consumed by cancer, I might as well eat caviar. Go on. Help yourself to some Sevruga."

"No thank you. It is rather expensive and I would not wish to —"

"— I've got more than a dozen tins under the bed. Enough to last me until the end of my days. Why not take some for your wife? My treat."

Hadian looked under Farragut's bed and saw the dozen or so 35.25-ounce tins of caviar. That amount would have cost almost more than Hadian's yearly salary. When Hadian looked back up at Farragut, he found it difficult to contain his rage.

"No thank you," said Hadian softly between clenched teeth. "It would not be proper."

Farragut smiled sheepishly and said, "Why not? Do you think I'm trying to bribe you?"

"Here's what I think. You and Azadi are conspiring to kill the president. Azadi's counterfeit money will pay for your marksmanship, courtesy of the Revolutionary Guards —"

"— Inspector, please, that's absolutely ridiculous,"

"It is the truth."

"Killing the president? How would that be possible in my state? And why would the Revolutionary Guards want him dead? The conservatives reign supreme again thanks to him. And even if rogue Guard elements, for whatever fantastic reason you've concocted, would want him dead, well, do you really think they'd hire an American assassin? You and your theories are absurd and without merit."

Hadian stiffened and bit his lip to hold his anger. "I am not your student, Professor. You need not lecture me as if I was."

Another terrible, coughing fit consumed Farragut. Hadian watched in stony silence. He didn't want to come out and tell Farragut that the Press was beneath the hospital and that Azadi worked at the Press. He didn't want to tell Farragut that he suspected this proximity aided their communication. It would be giving too much away and besides, he couldn't prove anything. Farragut was correct. The idea of the Revolutionary Guards hiring American assassins to kill the Iranian president seemed far-fetched. As for Farragut being in Gheyam Hospital? Well, he *was* dying of cancer and Gheyam Hospital was the best in city. Still, Hadian was a cop and he didn't trust coincidences. He didn't know what to say so he just stared at Farragut and hoped that by staring he could divine the man's true intention.

And then, as if by design, Farragut stopped coughing and began to confess, more to himself than to Hadian, though it was not the confession Hadian wanted to hear.

"I love this country, Inspector. I love its culture. I love its people," said Farragut. "I am as much an Iranian as an American. And I have nothing but the highest respect for Islam. It is a magnificent religion. It brought order to the chaos of the deserts, a world without water. Islamic societies fostered some of the finest minds of the time while

Europe limped through the Dark Ages. Islam's day will come again. Islam inspires so many souls all over the world. More than a billion. And young, so many of them young and uncorrupted. They will originate an Islamic renaissance. I only wish I could live to see it."

Farragut sunk into his pillows, seeming to disappear because of his diminished state. Hadian could not help feeling some pity for the American, though he didn't trust him.

"You are a good man, Professor," Hadian said. "I think in another time and place we could be friends. But let me warn you now. Whatever you are doing here will end in failure. It always does for Americans in Iran. Like when you came to rescue the hostages in 1980. You had the best troops, the best planes, the best helicopters. But someone in America forgot it was the season of sandstorms. And the best helicopter crashed into the best plane and killed the best troops. A small mistake. A cultural misunderstanding. Disaster. That is the history of the history between our two countries."

Farragut smiled. "History," said Farragut, his voice almost a whisper. "It is my greatest regret that I spent my life studying history instead of making it."

Hadian stood. He offered his hand to the dying man. They shook. Hadian noticed Farragut's grip was strong, stronger than his miserable state would seem to allow. And Farragut's eyes, which Hadian knew were blue, had become as dead as two black marbles.

Farragut grabbed the tin of Sevruga and went back to eating his precious caviar. Hadian went home to his precious wife and son, more determined than ever to keep an eye on Professor John Farragut until the man was dead and buried in the cold, hard ground.

CHAPTER SIXTY-EIGHT

THE NEXT DAY was *the* day.

Shareef Salaam awoke at dawn in his hotel in North Tehran and said his prayers. Then he took a stroll around Vanak Square to clear his head but his head was already clear, as was his conscience. He returned to his room and waited for Shehabi to collect him, reading the Quran to kill time.

Farragut slept until late morning. He drank orange juice and nibbled an almond pastry. He enjoyed the simple sweet; he was sick of caviar. He had finished all his caviar after Hadian had left, sharing the remains with the grateful hospit

al staff. The empty tins sat prominently on the windowsill. When the nurse came to check on him, he offered to throw the tins in the trash. Farragut told him not to bother. After the nurse left, Farragut collected the tins himself, put them in a carrier bag from the National Museum and dumped them in a can in the corridor reserved for bio-medical waste. Farragut returned to his bed and lay down his head. He dozed and dreamed.

Hundreds of feet below Farragut's hospital room, Azadi finished the printing. He had promised Farjad he would have the Supernotes in 24 hours. In fact, he delivered them 28 hours and 32 minutes later.

Azadi had printed 500,000 Supernotes on 15,625 sheets of 32 Supernotes each. He had cut the sheets and organized the money into units of 100 notes, with 40 units, or 4000 notes, being packaged into each brick. Now he and General Farjad examined a random sample of 100 Supernotes at the testing table. The table was similar to an X-ray board being comprised of a smooth glass surface covering a light panel. Azadi went through the litany of security features with Farjad, pointing out those that were embedded in the special Crane paper and others he had replicated through his special skill. Color-shifting ink. Security strips. Microprinting. Farjad seemed overwhelmed by the detail and slightly in awe of Azadi's expertise.

"These look excellent," said Farjad. "The details are striking. You have replicated the Ben Franklin portrait perfectly."

Azadi held one of the notes to the light and waved in front of Farjad's eyes. The faint image of Ben Franklin appeared in the blank space to the right of portrait.

"You can see the portrait watermark as it catches the light. That's perfect, too. Now feel it. Here on Franklin's right shoulder."

Farjad took and the bill and rubbed his fingertips across the portrait. "It feels... rough."

"The feel makes it real," said Azadi. "That will fool a Treasury agent every time. That texture comes from the intaglio process. You can't get that with a photocopier. You need the right press, process, and paper.

"And a printer of your expertise," said Farjad, smiling broadly at Azadi. I will admit it, Omar. Sepanlou had my complete confidence and his unfortunate accident greatly unnerved me. As for you, I had my doubts about your ability to replace him. But I am very pleased with your work. Very pleased. I have no doubt the others will be pleased as well."

The only "other" Azadi cared about was the blond American whose name he didn't know. He wasn't sure if that was who would be examining the bills. He didn't know about Shareef Salaam yet, including that he existed and was part of Mia Kelly's plan. But Azadi did know that whoever was going to be examining the bills was performing a crucial role in the mission. That was why he was pleased to see Farjad pack a random $10,000 sample into a Fox security briefcase.

"General, are you taking some bills with you?"

"Yes. The client requested to examine the bills himself."

Azadi's face flashed fear but inside he was laughing. "Do you think that is necessary?" *Damn. I should have been an actor. Sean Penn's got nothing on me.*

"Necessary? Yes. If this man is to pass this paper, he should understand all the new design details and security features for himself." Farjad gave Azadi a condescending smile and a reassuring pat on the back. "Don't worry, my friend. I'm sure he will be as impressed as I am."

"I could come along and be of assistance if you'd like?"

"That won't be necessary. My meeting is later this afternoon. Go home. Sleep. You've earned it."

"Thank you, General. I will. But don't hesitate to call me if you have any questions."

Farjad said he might. Azadi knew for certain that he would.

CHAPTER SIXTY-NINE

AT JUST PAST six that evening, Salaam finished outlining the plans for carrying out the next great terrorist attack on US soil. He spoke in the back room of the Babajan Print Shop before just two men, General Amir Farjad of Iran's Revolutionary Guards and Hasan Shehabi, representing Lebanon's faction of Hezbollah. He stood before an overhead projector on which was placed a bogus but convincing schematic diagram of a dirty bomb – a radiological dispersal device. The bomb would combine a conventional explosive material with radioactive material.

Earlier Salaam had showed many other documents, created by the CIA's Technical Services Division and delivered to Salaam weeks ago in Beirut by Mossad. The documents outlined the fictional terrorist attacks he promised he would carry out with their counterfeit cash. Included were alternative blueprints of the dirty bombs he would build, profiles of the people he had hired and would hire, account ledgers for terrorist cells he would have to pay, blast ratios, kill estimates, and projected rates of return on invested capital in three world stock markets. It was all bullshit, of course, but it was believable bullshit that he had sold with sincerity.

"In conclusion, the advantages of working with BURN are these. First, we have the people inside America right now – they *are* Americans born and bred. No immigration hassles, no risk in your people getting caught coming into our country. Second, we have the technical expertise. I can build these dirty bombs myself. Third, we can use our organization's street gang contacts to liaison with the Russian mob in New York. Through the Russians we'll purchase stolen, Soviet-era nuclear material. Preliminary talks have been held and cost estimates are outlined in Table II-A. BURN's network of sympathetic port and customs personnel, built up over years, will ensure safe passage of the material into America. After the devices are detonated, these people must be provided with new lives and secure identities — sort of our own witness protection program. The estimated figures for that part of the operation are indicated in Table II-B."

Salaam slid a meticulously prepared map of the United States on the overhead projector, outlining blast ratios and estimated casualty counts for three cities. He could feel his audience impressed by the passion and particulars of his presentation.

"Conclusion. Three dirty bombs will be detonated simultaneously. Three acts of terrorism in the three largest American cities, New York, Chicago and Los Angeles. Estimated casualties will be between eight and ten thousand dead and wounded — but the psychological and economic impact will be substantially more significant. Panic over radioactivity and evacuation procedures will paralyze these urban areas. They may be off limits for months, if not years, which will further depress the US economy. But we, as I outlined, will take the opportunity to invest a sizeable portion of the money you give us into foreign stock markets. We will short these markets, betting stocks will nosedive in the aftermath of the attack – a 100 percent certainty if 9/11 is our guide. We will thus recoup your $50 million investment tenfold, ensuring financing for future acts well into the 21st century."

Salaam turned off the overhead projector and turned on the lights. He took his place before Farjad and Shehabi, noted their intense interest and allowed himself his first smile of the day — a deal-closing smile that suppressed all emotions save for sincerity.

"BURN has the will. What we lack is the capital. Your $50 million dollars is a small price to pay for crippling the US economy and shattering the America's confidence while keeping your own hands clean. So, gentleman, do we have a deal?"

Salaam stood ramrod straight. The sounds of traffic filtered in from outside. Shehabi and Farjad sat still and took a few seconds to absorb all that Salaam was promising. Shehabi had already heard the plan in Beirut and perused the documents weeks ago. Farjad was hearing and seeing it all for the first time. His caution was keeping in character.

Farjad cleared his throat. "I think this is something we can do together, Mr. Salaam."

"I am glad you agree, General," said Salaam. "What's the next step?"

Farjad bought time by closing his eyes and nodding his head like a man in prayer, though it was politics that consumed him. He felt the plan was brilliant but he wasn't sure his superiors would see it that way. His exalted position and sterling reputation had permitted him to take things this far. To go farther, he would need to garner support at the very top. This would not be easy. Not everyone in the Islamic Republic of Iran, not even in the Revolutionary Guards, shared his revolutionary zeal. Partly this was due to the threatening presence of American troops pinching Iran between Afghanistan in the east and Iraq to the west. And out on the streets, half the population — young, educated, connected through social networks and not revolutionary Islamic teaching — protested for revolutionary rapprochement with the West and more freedom. Corrupt Arab kleptocracies were falling like dominoes but so far the Islamic Republic had held back the tide. But for how long? And would this act bring the wrath of the U.S. military directly into the Iranian heartland? Pakistan was an American ally and had nukes. And yet the Americans had flown right into Abbottatad to take down Osama. So what was the next step? Good question.

Farjad had no doubts where his own sympathies lay. He was a revolutionary and he could see that Shareef Salaam was one, too. With Shehabi's help, he might not need to concern others with this matter. Yes, perhaps he could put it all in motion himself. Once his superiors saw the results, they would give him a medal. He was sure of it.

"I asked you a question, General Farjad," said Salaam.

Farjad saw Salaam staring at him. He could feel Shehabi staring at him, too.

"I need a day," said Farjad. "Then I will get back to you with the next step. These things take time."

Salaam laughed so long that he couldn't get the words out for a while. Shehabi sensed that Salaam's laugh had very little to do with what passes for humor but he forced a smile.

"What's so funny?" said Shehabi, his face tight with tension.

Salaam turned to Shehabi and forced an even bigger smile than the terrorist. "What's so funny? Hasan, that's the same bullshit you told me that first day in Beirut. 'These things take time.' You promised Farjad had the authority to okay this deal."

Shehabi's smile melted under Farjad's furious gaze. "General Farjad *has* that authority."

"Then what's going on?" said Salaam. "What's the delay? I got you the paper. I made my presentation. Twice. I upheld my end of the deal. I don't have any more time, Hasan. I've got people waiting on tenterhooks while the American government bugs their phones, reads their mail and tracks what websites they surf. The hell with 'more time.' I need a decision now."

Shehabi's face reddened with shame. Farjad, who found it humiliating to be talked about as if he were invisible, could see he needed to be strong.

"What you need is our money," said the general with some steel in his tone. "You can't do this without money. So I will ask you to show the proper respect."

Salaam was way past intimidation. He was playing the role that he had practiced again and again with Kelly and Alson back in the states.

"Let's talk about the money, General. Did you at least bring a sample so that I know what I'm dealing with?"

"I did," said Farjad, pulling the suitcase out from underneath his chair.

"Can I see it? I would at least like to know that you are capable of making good counterfeit even if you can't make a decision."

Farjad gave Salaam a cold, hard look and opened the suitcase on the chair. With a dismissive wave, he invited Salaam to inspect the contents. He knew, thanks to his training, what to look for and how to sound authentic looking for it. His manner was more authentic than the bills he examined.

Salaam handled a random half-dozen Supernotes. He barely looked at them at first. Rather, he held the bills in his hands and rubbed them between his fingers.

"They feel good. They feel real. That embossed ink feel. The intaglio areas feel raised. And that genuine Crane paper, courtesy of me, thank you very much. Feels crisp. Yeah. They feel real. There's not a bank teller from Tehran to Tacoma who won't touch these and think they're Grade-A, USDA prime."

Neither Farjad or Shehabi knew what Grade-A, USDA prime was but they assumed it was good because Salaam was smiling.

Salaam put away six bills and pulled out another six at random. He examined each with his naked eye, holding it up to the light, checking the front and back of each bill.

"I knew some top counterfeiters in prison. They taught me how to tell quality. These bills look good, real good. The portrait mimics the watermark perfectly. Security thread in the right place. Treasury seal's a dead ringer, too. Serial number configuration – eleven numbers and letters. Got the Federal Reserve Bank indicator printed below. Lots of dudes forget that one. Not your guy. Good. You wouldn't happen to have a magnifying glass, would you?"

Farjad did have one and handed it to Salaam. Salaam examined the bills with the magnifying glass, one after another.

"Can't skimp on the little details. 'USA 100' in the lower left corner?' Check. 'The United States of America' in Franklin's coat? Check. Your engraver's damn good. He's got the microprinting down pat. And the fine line printing behind the portrait and Independence Hall looks great. Your average Joe on the street won't even notice this shit but your better class of arms dealer and money launderer will. Nice. Very nice."

Salaam put down the magnifying glass and picked up a bill. He flicked his wrist, changing the angle of the bill before the light, looking closely at the bill with his naked eye.

Farjad felt himself beginning to relax. This Salaam was an arrogant American, even if he was a devout Muslim. But Azadi's work would prove the supremacy of the Supernote and, of course, Farjad's management of the Supernote Press.

"As you can see, Mr. Salaam, our printer is a true artist." Farjad smiled smugly.

Salaam let Farjad's confidence float like a LeBron James jump shot. Then he pulled the missed shot off the rim and took the game in a different direction.

It all depended on this. Success or failure. Live or die. On this.

"Your printer is a careless fool," said Salaam.

"Excuse me? Careless? I don't understand," said Farjad, still smiling.

Salaam stuck the bill in Farjad's face. "Look at the '100' in the lower right corner. Notice anything?" He flicked the bill back and forth in front of Farjad's nose.

Farjad went cross-eye staring at the bill. "It looks fine. You yourself said so."

"It's engraved okay but not printed right. The numeral in the lower right corner's supposed to be printed with color shifting ink. It's supposed to look copper when viewed straight on but green at an angle. This one just looks copper no matter the angle."

Salaam picked up another bill and flicked it in Farjad's face. Each time the color failed to change, Salaam clucked his tongue against the roof of his mouth to show his displeasure.

Farjad pulled out a random bill and observed it himself. Then he tried it with another. And then another. Each time he changed the angle, the printed '100' failed to change color. Shehabi took a bill and tried it himself. Once was enough for him.

"How serious is this?" Shehabi said to Salaam in a very serious voice.

"Very serious. These bills might buy you a Happy Meal at McDonalds. But the juice to blow up three dirty bombs and terrorize three cities? No way. No how." Salaam turned his attention to Farjad who was still testing bills, one after the other. "General Farjad. This is a major fuck up. You know that, don't you?"

Farjad put down the bill he was testing. He had tested almost 30, pulled from random within the suitcase. They all lacked the color-shifting security feature. His face had colored, though, turning a deep red.

"I am sorry for this inconvenience," said Farjad in a flat whisper. "Our printer was new and under much pressure to perform. I assure you, this won't happen again."

"No. It won't. Because the deal is off."

Salaam made a show of packing up his many documents and photographs. Shehabi looked to Farjad who let out a laugh a few beats too late to be anything but nervous bluster.

"Off? But why?" said Farjad, his voice cracking like a teenager's.

"Because I can't trust you. You promised me you could print the money and the fact is you can't print the money."

"It's a temporary problem. I'm sure there's a solution."

Salaam shoved his presentation materials into a cheap leather briefcase he had bought back in Beirut. He locked the briefcase shut.

Here we go, baby. Fastball down the middle.

"Yeah. There might be a solution, General."

"I'm listening."

"Take me to meet your printer so I can see the operation y'all are running. If I have confidence that he's capable, we'll call this a temporary setback and continue to do business."

Farjad vigorously shook his head. "Impossible. The Press location is a state secret."

Salaam slammed his briefcase down on the table so hard that it cracked a leg. The impact of Salaam's voice was even greater.

"You talk about state secrets? I'll tell you a secret. You don't survive 20 years in a Federal prison by betraying your friends. Who do you think I am, General? Some sort of Zionist nigger spy fresh from training in the Negev? I have a history, dammit. You know my history. The whole world knows it. It's documented and checked out by your people before I got here." Salaam stabbed a long, threatening finger in Shehabi's direction though he kept his withering gaze locked on Farjad's face. "I spilled blood with your comrade Shehabi here. I put my life on the line to steal the paper that your printer played Picasso with. So don't talk to me about state secrets. Allah recognizes no *state* except the state of grace that he grants to all true believers."

For once Shehabi's harelip seemed to have gotten the better of him, for he was stammering to say something but it sounded like air escaping from a balloon. Farjad's mouth was open but no words were coming out. He had stuck his thumb between his teeth and was biting down on the end like a hungry man tearing off a piece of beef jerky.

Farjad said, "It is a matter of trust. Before I go further I must be sure…"

Salaam's voice erupted like an apocalyptic roar. The Prophet's words, straight from the Quran, cascaded down from him like boulders from the mountaintop.

"'When you have resolved upon a course of action put your trust in Allah! Allah loves those who put their trust in him! If Allah helps you, none can overcome you; but if he should forsake you, then who is it that can help you besides him? It is in Allah that the believers should put their trust! It does not befit a prophet to act dishonestly, for he who acts dishonestly shall be faced with his dishonesty on the day of resurrection! Everyone will then be paid in full what he has earned, and none shall be wronged!'"

And none shall be wronged. The words resonated like thunder within the cramped confines of the Babajan Print Shop.

Farjad and Shehabi said nothing for a few moments. They stared at their feet, cowed by Salaam's passion and authority, his use of the Prophet's words overpowering them.

Without further argument they agreed to take him to the Press.

CHAPTER SEVENTY

AZADI WAS SITTING in his living room, finishing off the last piece of an olive and garlic pizza, when the phone rang. He picked up the receiver and listened as Farjad angrily told him to be ready to meet at the Press in an hour. Farjad would send a car around in 15 minutes. When Azadi asked him what was wrong, Farjad told him to just be ready in 15 minutes and hung up.

Azadi put down the phone and belched. He walked into his bedroom and opened the closet door. He pushed away the expensive shoes he would never wear again that served only to conceal the loose boards on the closet floor. Azadi used a shoehorn to lift a loose floorboard. One by one he removed the 35.25-ounce tins of Sevruga caviar from their hiding place underneath the closet floor. He counted each tin as he removed it, pulling out 15 tins in all.

Five days ago, the day of Parisa's murder, he had evenly divided 20 pounds of C4 amongst 10 tins. Next he molded the explosive into the concealing confines of the cylindrical tins. He had hidden 10 M8 blasting caps in the remaining five tins, two caps to a tin. He had packed the blasting caps with bubble wrap bought at a local packing store, just to be sure. There was no need to take extra precautions with the C4, it could be burned with a blowtorch or shot with a rifle at pointblank range and still not go off. It was incredibly stable.

Azadi felt stable, too. He wasn't nervous. He wanted this over, come what may.

He removed the two duffel bags from the hook behind the closet door. He packed the 10 tins of C4/caviar into the larger duffel bag and the five tins of blasting caps/caviar into the smaller duffel bag.

He carried the duffel bags into the living room and sat down on the couch. Ishmael had called him yesterday and told him to call a certain number while he was waiting to be picked up for the Press. The call would be a signal to the man on the other end of the line that he was coming. He picked up the phone and called the number that he had committed it to memory.

"Hello," said the voice on the other end, answering in English.

"I'm sorry, but is this the Hussein Cab Company?" asked Azadi in Farsi.

"I'm afraid it's not. You have the wrong number," said the voice continuing in English.

Azadi's chest tightened with tension as he recognized the correct counter signal. But it was more than that. The voice on the other end of the line belonged to the blond man who had killed Parisa. He could never forget that voice. Never. But before Azadi could say anything, the man hung up and the line went dead.

If Azadi had his way, the man behind the voice would be dead soon enough, too.

-:::::-

Farragut hung up the phone by his bed and grabbed the water bottle sitting beside it. He sipped the cool, clean water – Ingrid had brought him a case of Evian – until his thirst was totally sated. He had enjoyed his final meal, a beautifully marbled, imported Porterhouse steak brought to him by Ardibili. Farragut could taste the blood of the grass-fed bovine on the back of his throat. How come the blood of dead things tasted so much like life?

Farragut didn't have a headache. He felt fine. He felt ready. His hearing was acute; he could hear the soft sobbing of the millionaire car dealer's son in the room two doors down. The boy, only fifteen, cried every night. He had a rare cancer of the retina and both eyes had been removed.

Farragut heard the heavy footsteps of the approaching male nurse out in the corridor. He reached over to his plate and took the sharp, imported Swiss steak knife, hiding it under his pillow. The knife belonged to Ardabili but Farragut doubted his friend would miss it; the curator had sworn off red meat because of his cholesterol level. The male nurse took away his plate of food and asked if he needed anything else as he walked to the door.

Farragut told him to bring a wheelchair, thank you. He was going to get some air.

-:::::-

Chief Inspector Kamran Hadian had had it up to there, thank you. He'd woken up late, missed breakfast, and been working so hard all day that he'd missed lunch, too. Fortunately, upon arriving home, he'd found his beloved wife had prepared his favorite meal. Unfortunately, she'd managed to massacre the *Maghz*, frying the lambs' brains to an inedible blackened crisp. There were no words to describe how the delicacy tasted but he tried. Hadian had never actually eaten human excrement but he could imagine it coming in a distant second to this. Laden ran off in tears, hurt by his cruel remarks.

He immediately admonished himself. It was not like him to be unkind but his hunger and frustration over dealing with Professor Farragut had blackened his mood worse than the lambs' brains. Now Laden was off in their bedroom crying. At least he thought she might be crying. He couldn't exactly hear since Ahmad was singing in English – shouting, actually – mimicking a black American's accent. It was some sort of... rap? Yes. Rap. There was no obvious musical accompaniment since Ahmad was listening with ear phones to the iPod Hadian had taken from the American Azadi. Hadian could only imagine how ugly the music would have been if he could have heard it. While only vaguely aware of the gist of the lyrics, he knew they were vulgar, decadent and threatening. What a tragedy, thought Hadian, that gangsta rap, like McDonalds, and endless hours spent "tweeting" 140 characters of banality, was this generation's idea of rebellion.

Farragut's tweed sitting there in Azadi's apartment. Both men were lying. But lying about what?

Hadian pushed at the blackened brains on his plate and thought of the tumor growing in Farragut's brain. He thought of Farragut lying there in the best hospital in Tehran, in the best wing, amongst the rich, spoiled leisure class of the Islamic Revolution. And the counterfeit press below, churning out tens of millions of dollars to support the corrupt Islamic Republic while he worried about sending Ahmad abroad for school on his meager policeman's salary.

-:::::-

Farjad and Shehabi escorted Salaam through the children's cancer ward. Salaam saw sick and dying children everywhere so it was tough not to think of Gary. But he did not think of Gary. He thought of another mother's son, Regassa. He thought of Regassa as they rode down in the elevator deep into the belly of the earth. He thought of Regassa as they walked down the seemingly endless, spit-shined corridor towards the vault door. He thought of Regassa as the guards ran the metal detectors over him, Farjad, and Shehabi. He thought of Regassa as they walked through the massive vault door and entered the pressroom. His thoughts switched from Regassa to the C4 and the detonators as he walked down to the Press that he had come all this way to destroy.

-:::::-

The C4 and the detonators were ten minutes away, packed inside caviar tins inside Azadi's apartment. The two guards who picked up Azadi to take him to the Press made no effort to open the caviar tins. They were used to Azadi's gifts of caviar and appreciated his kindness. They broke with protocol and drove a direct route to Gheyam Hospital, flashing the ambulance's lights and blasting the siren as they saw fit. The ambulance pulled up to the hospital's circular front driveway with a crescendo of screeching tires. Azadi smelled the burnt rubber from the tires and thought of his predecessor, Farhad Sepanlou, dying from his burns in the ICU upstairs.

But it wasn't the memory of Sepanlou that disturbed him most of all at that moment. No. It was the sight of the blond American who had killed Parisa. He was sitting in a wheelchair just outside the hospital entrance, his dead gray eyes scanning a copy of the English language *Tehran Times*. It was a chilly night and the man wore nothing more than expensive-looking flannel pajamas, socks, and sneakers. Even the cold air failed to redden his deathly pale cheeks. He did not look up at Azadi and his guards as they entered the building.

Azadi and his guards walked through the children's cancer ward and arrived at the first security post. Bashir, Azadi's willing protégé, was guarding the door. He warned him that General Farjad had seemed in a furious state and was accompanied by two VIP's – a Lebanese Arab and a black American. He made a perfunctory search of the duffel bags and questioned whether it would be wise to bring his black market caviar downstairs when Farjad was so angry. Azadi assured them it might assuage his anger. Bashir agreed, as Azadi knew he would. Since Bashir was nominally in command of the guard detail, he promised he would call down to the guards below and make sure Azadi got through with his gift.

Azadi and his guards silently descended in the elevator. Their heels clicked noisily on the polished floor as they walked down the long corridor. The other guards at the vault door ran their metal detectors over Azadi and his escorts. The machines blared their indignation at finding the caviar tins in Azadi's duffel bags.

"General Farjad is very angry," said one of the guards at the door. "Perhaps you should let us hold the caviar until he calms down?"

"If anything, this will make him calmer," said Azadi. "It's his wife's favorite. And today, on all days, I could use all the help I can getting back on his good side."

The guards at the vault door considered this logic. They really could go either way. But Bashir had called ahead and insisted Azadi be allowed to pass with this gift. And the guards had let Azadi through many times before with caviar. They surely appreciated his kindness and generosity in the past. Perhaps he would save some for them and not squander it all on General Farjad's fat greedy wife?

"Okay," said one of the guards, nodding at Azadi. "Go with God."

Azadi's two guards from the ambulance chose to stay with their comrades at the vault door, so Azadi walked alone through the door and into the pressroom, carrying the duffel bags containing the disguised C4 and detonators in their caviar tins.

Azadi stood at the top landing. Down below he could see the Press. Standing by the Press was General Farjad, along with an older black man and a younger Arab man. Farjad glared up at him with thinly concealed rage. The Arab man, whose face appeared wrong somehow, smoked a cigar and looked tense. The black man stared at the Press. Azadi did not know his name but he knew he was sizing it up for the kill with the explosives Azadi carried.

Azadi heard Farjad order the remaining six guards in the pressroom to leave. They marched up the stairs, squeezed past Azadi without a greeting, and headed out the door. Azadi walked down the stairs to his destiny.

-:::::-

Bashir was having a bad day. He'd was supposed to be shopping with his fiancée for engagement rings but something bad was going down below at the Press so he'd had to pull double duty guarding the upper level door. His legs ached from standing all day and his mind felt numbed by boredom. Still, he knew he shouldn't complain. He often saw the pathetic wretches with cancer just down the hall and had to admit that he had it good in comparison. And then there was the painful memory of his recently-deceased dear friend.

Bashir had loved Farhad Sepanlou like a father. The older man had taken him under his wing and taught him the secrets of becoming a master printer. He had died upstairs while the Press he loved lived downstairs, now tended to by Omar Azadi. Bashir felt sorry for Sepanlou but at least Sepanlou was in heaven and could feel no pain. He felt sorrier for Azadi, who had passed through five minutes ago on his way to face the wrath of General Farjad. But Bashir felt sorriest of all for the pitiful, wreck of a man in a wheelchair rolling up to greet him.

"Excuse me, sir," said the man in perfect Farsi. "Are you Dr. Pahani?"

The man braked unsteadily before him. Bashir noted the man's elegant accent. Imminent death cast pallor over the man's face but he was clearly not Iranian. Judging by his blond hair and blue/ gray eyes, he was probably British, American, or Scandinavian

"No, I'm not Dr. Pahani," said Bashir. The pathetic creature was clearly delirious. "And I'm sorry but you are not allowed down here. Please head back"

"They told me you were Dr. Pahani. Who are you if you are not Dr. Pahani?"

A milky froth bubbled at the corners of the man's mouth. Bashir feared he might expire on the spot.

"My name is Bashir. You can't stay here. Please move back."

The man said something Bashir couldn't make out. The invalid's head had slumped against his chest and he was mumbling. Spittle was spilling from his mouth onto his crotch. Bashir swung his AK-47 over his shoulder and bent down to hear what the man was saying.

The last thing Bashir heard was the snap of his own spine as the man's arms – so much stronger than they should have been – clamped his neck in a viselike hold and yanked it to the side. He was no longer aware of his body as his face smashed into the floor. In his remaining seconds of life, paralyzed from the neck down, Bashir thought that he was lucky to die so much faster than poor, old Sepanlou.

CHAPTER SEVENTY-ONE

FARRAGUT STOOD and pulled the dead guard's gun from his shoulder, slinging it over his own. He sat the dead upright in the wheelchair. No one else was in the corridor. No one had seen a thing. There was no blood on the floor, just a man in a wheelchair, a normal sight in a hospital should anyone be looking.

Farragut pulled the steak knife from his thigh where he had secured it with medical tape. He knocked on the door to the elevator room with his free hand.

"It's Bashir," said Farragut through the door, approximating the dead man's high-pitched voice and working class accent. It didn't have to be perfect. "Open the door."

"Why? What's wrong?" Farragut heard from behind the door.

"I've got to go to the bathroom. I need you to watch outside."

As the door opened Farragut lunged forward. He grabbed the unsuspecting guard around the neck with one hand, squeezing his voice box silent. Simultaneously with the other hand, he plunged the knife between the base of the guard's neck and his shoulder blade, severing the artery. He drove the guard back all the way across room. By the time Farragut had him pinned against the far wall, the guard had fainted from shock and was bleeding profusely from the fatal stab wound.

Farragut let the dead guard drop to the floor inside the elevator room. He ducked back outside into the corridor and wheeled Bashir into the elevator room. He closed the door behind him, locking it shut and concealing evidence of the two murders.

Farragut slung Bashir's AK-47 over his shoulder and jammed an extra ammo clip in the waist of his pajamas. It suddenly occurred to him how ridiculous he would look to the men he was about to kill, not to mention his co-conspirators. An assassin in sneakers and pajamas? He had thought of everything but not that.

He took a last drink from the water cooler because his mouth felt hot and dry though his body glistened with cold sweat. He was using up his last reserves of strength. But now he could use a gun. He didn't have to be strong anymore. Just accurate. Deadly accurate.

-:::::-

"Dead Presidents in black and green/Dead Presidents don't mean the money is clean..."

Ahmad's singsong voice was transformed into an instrument of torture as he belted out the aggressive rap lyrics. Hadian sat in the living room nursing a hunger headache. He washed two aspirin down with grape juice and prayed for the pain and the infernal singing to end soon.

Laden was no longer crying behind their bedroom door. She had grown ominously silent. He would sleep on the couch tonight.

"Dead Presidents make the world go 'round/Dead Presidents make the booty go down..."

Hadian would sleep if he could ever get that horrible song out of his head. Not only was it obnoxiously loud but it was also embarrassingly catchy. He preferred his beloved Beatles but he had to admit rap had a seductive, forbidden appeal, like a beautiful prostitute.

So many dead prostitutes left at the airport like lost luggage. So much time wasted on this damn Dead Presidents case when he could have been saving lives.

"Dead Presidents are a player's life blood/Dead Presidents make a eunuch a stud..."

That's when it began to come together. The words "Dead Presidents" playing in his mind. The words "Dead Presidents" sung by his son to music on the iPod.

The thoughts came quickly, jumbled together. It was all he could do to sort them out and give them some meaning.

"Dead Presidents" was the name of a song on the iPod he had taken from Omar Azadi's apartment. Professor Farragut's tweed was in Omar Azadi's apartment. Farragut had lied about that and lied about knowing Azadi. They worked together on a deal involving the counterfeit press under Gheyam Hospital.

Gheyam Hospital where Professor Farragut lay dying.

An Israeli soldier had set the whole thing in motion. Under torture, he had revealed something about "Dead Presidents." A plot to kill the Iranian president? Or something else...?

Hadian blasted up off the couch on ran to his son's room. He could not get there fast enough. He needed the last piece of the puzzle to be put in place.

He flung open his son's door and barged in. Ahmad was standing in front of the mirror affecting some aggressive poses and flashing what Hadian knew to be American gangster hand signs. The headphones were in Hadian's ears, the iPod in his pocket and the lyrics he sang filled the air.

"Dead Presidents are a player's life blood/Dead Presidents make a eunuch a stud..."

Hadian clamped his hands on his son's shoulders and yanked the earphones from his son's head. "'Dead Presidents?' What does it mean?" he shouted at Ahmad in English.

Ahmad, who had good English, gave his father the literal meaning of a deceased state leader. But that definition didn't fit the lyrics.

"And what else," said Hadian. "It must have another meaning."

"I'm not sure," said Ahmad, scared by his father's desperation. "Wait. I think I know. Money. 'Dead Presidents' is American slang for money."

"Money?" said Hadian.

"Money," said Ahmad. "There's the face of a president on American money. Father, where are you going?"

Hadian had run from his son's room without saying goodbye. He jumped in his car and raced back to Gheyam Hospital, hoping to stop the Americans from doing what he was now sure they had come to Iran to do all along.

CHAPTER SEVENTY-TWO

BELOW GHEYAM HOSPITAL, Azadi waited while General Farjad argued in Arabic with the man with the harelip. Azadi didn't understand Arabic but he knew that the argument was about him. He didn't pay them much attention. Besides, he was more interested in the tall black American who had accompanied the man with the harelip. He stood off to the side, seemingly bored, his eyes playing over the Press as if he were sizing up a new Mercedes in a dealer's showroom. Azadi tried to make eye contact with the man but he treated Azadi as if he were invisible.

Although he had never met nor seen the black American Azadi knew who he was. It was hard to imagine that this stranger and he shared a terrible secret that every event of their lives for the past few months had played out with the express purpose of locating them both here, together, in this place at this exact time.

Azadi heard Farjad bark something to the man with the harelip, who lit up a Cuban cigar. Then Farjad whispered something to the black American before turning his attention to Azadi.

"Omar, you're an idiot!" bellowed Farjad.

"What's the problem," said Azadi, knowing full well what the problem was.

"The money! You have made a terrible mistake with the money," screamed Farjad. He gestured to the black American, too angry to talk.

"The money's garbage, my brother," added the black American. For the first time he looked Azadi in the eyes. Azadi felt a thrill, almost like one does when making eye contact with a pretty girl from across a crowded bar.

The man with the harelip smoked his cigar and said nothing. Azadi licked his lips and played his part.

"General, what have I done wrong?"

-:::::-

"We were wrong, Colonel. 'Dead Presidents' doesn't refer to our president. It refers to the money being printed at the Supernote Press."

Hadian was driving in his car through the reliably terrible traffic, still ten minutes away from Gheyam Hospital. He was talking to Colonel Tabriz on his cell phone but it had taken too long to track him down. Tabriz, unbeknownst to Hadian, had turned off his cell phone upon arriving home. He didn't want to be disturbed because he and his wife wanted to make love in peace. By some miracle, they had the house to themselves because the children were at the movies with their friends. Tabriz was in no mood for Hadian's hunches.

"Are you sure of this?" asked Tabriz. He rolled his eyes and his wife laughed beside him in bed. She thought Hadian an annoying eccentric with an ugly wife.

"I am sure, Colonel. Dead sure."

"But what if you're wrong?"

"I am not wrong. I am going to confront Professor Farragut and he will confirm it. I would greatly appreciate your presence at his confession. This could be politically sensitive."

Tabriz thought about it a moment before he said, "I'll see you at Gheyam Hospital."

CHAPTER SEVENTY-THREE

FARRAGUT RODE DOWN on the elevator, imagining the sight that would appear when the doors opened. Azadi had estimated the corridor at 70 meters. Azadi had said two guards always stood watch at the far end of the corridor at the pressroom door. The AK-47 in his hands had an effective range of 300 meters. The gun's banana clip held 30 7.62 mm rounds of ammunition. He had taken two spare 30 round clips off the dead guards and taped them to his thigh with surgical tape he'd pilfered the night before. Ninety rounds would be plenty of ammo for the two guards at the door and the six guards, plus assorted VIP's, inside the pressroom. He would fire on automatic rather than single round just to be sure. It wouldn't be pretty. It wouldn't be sporting. This wasn't the Olympics, though this was as far as this game was going to go.

The elevator hummed as it descended. There was no elevator music to make the journey into the bowels of the earth any more pleasant. *Funny how you miss it when it's not there,* thought Farragut. He flashed back to the Muzak he had heard through the phone so many months ago back at the LaGuardia airport in New York. The day the plane exploded on the tarmac. The day Yasir died and his father did not. Karen Carpenter singing "Superstar" in her soprano…

"Don't you remember you told me you loved me, baby?/ You said you'd be coming back again this way, baby…"

The elevator stopped. Farragut aimed his gun through the doors as they opened.

The corridor was brightly lit and long. Farragut opened fire on the green fatigued figures at the far end. The noise was deafening. He emptied his clip in seconds, playing the bullets over the men at the far end like a man watering roses in the garden.

-:::::-

Moments earlier in the pressroom, Azadi had tried not to wince as General Farjad screamed in his face. At the top of his lungs he had questioned Azadi's manhood, his printing expertise, his intelligence, all while spraying Azadi with sour smelling spittle. Mercifully, the general pulled the plug on the invective long enough to let the black American explain in his mellow baritone that the counterfeit bills were useless because they lacked the color-shifting security feature. Azadi played the dupe to perfection. He furrowed his brow and bowed to Farjad.

"General, I was working fast and sometimes mistakes —"

Farjad slapped Azadi's face. It stung and Azadi was tempted to plant a left hook in his kidney but he refrained. *Be patient,* he thought. *The son-of-a-bitch will soon get his.*

He didn't have to be patient long. Farjad, Shehabi, Azadi, and Salaam all froze as they heard the fusillade of bullets in the corridor above them.

"What's that?" asked Salaam, knowing full well what it was.

With the guards dismissed to the corridor Farjad was now the only man with a gun. He pulled his 10 mm Glock 20 pistol from his holster and gestured to the three other men.

"Wait here," said Farjad, heading up the stairs to investigate the source of the shootings.

Damn straight I will, thought Azadi.

Shehabi instinctively reached for the Heckler & Koch MK23 he kept strapped to his side. He came up empty handed, as Farjad had made him disarm before entering the vault. Standard operating procedure, Farjad had said, even for our friends.

Shehabi cursed and swung his gaze around the pressroom, searching for anything he could use as a weapon, but there was nothing. He desperately dug into his pockets — hoping to find a penknife, a nail file, anything — but only came up with his Zippo lighter imprinted with the Israeli flag. A battlefield trophy, Shehabi had taken it off a dead Zionist soldier after a firefight in Iqulim al-Toufah. But now, trapped in an underground room with no weapon to defend himself, Shehabi stared at the Star of David at the center of the flag and realized for the first time how much it looked like a bulls-eye.

-:::::-

On the other side of the vault door, Farragut counted ten men tossed about in a heap. Pieces of bloody flesh and olive fatigues had splattered against the whitewashed walls and shiny steel vault door.

Farragut sprayed the mound of men with another 30 round burst, just to be sure. When the clip was empty, he removed it and rammed home his final spare clip. He took another spare clip off one of the dead guards and secured it in the waistband of his pajamas. According to Azadi, there were normally six guards beyond the door in the pressroom. Counting Farjad and Shehabi, there would be eight men beyond the doors, not including Azadi and Salaam. He would have enough bullets in any case.

He opened the vault door, his gun at the ready.

-:::::-

Farjad stepped onto the pressroom's top landing as the vault door opened. He saw the pale blond man in pajamas, an AK-47 clutched in his hands. Farjad did not fire at first because the image confused him. He was expecting Israelis or Americans in fatigues arriving in force. Why was this shell of a man in pajamas coming through the door? Before Farjad could make sense of it, Farragut pumped three bullets into his chest at close range. Farjad dropped his pistol and flew off his feet over the railing.

He was already dead when he hit the pressroom floor 20 feet below.

When Azadi, Salaam, and Shehabi saw Farjad dead they dived for cover. Azadi and Salaam stayed low and still, bellies flat on the floor, hands over their heads. Shehabi hid, crawling behind the generator amongst the extra gas cans. Realizing he still had his lit cigar in his mouth, he tossed it across the room. He didn't want to die in an explosion, remembering Salaam's warning about gasoline fumes and fire back in Baltimore. He waited for the gunfire that would signal the deaths of Azadi and Salaam. He closed his eyes and thought of Lebanon in late spring. The cedar trees rustling in a warm, Mediterranean breeze.

"Shehabi."

Shehabi opened his eyes at the sound of his name. Salaam stood above him, very much alive, holding the still-lit discarded Cuban cigar.

"This is for Regassa."

Salaam bent down and snuffed out the lit cigar on Shehabi's exposed ankle. Shehabi screamed in pain. Salaam grabbed Shehabi's leg and pulled him out from his hiding place behind the generator. He tried to stand but Salaam shoved him back down to the floor.

The first thing Shehabi saw was a gaunt blond man in blood-spattered pajamas pointing an AK-47 at him. Salaam was standing next to the blond man, who made no move to kill him. Behind them the counterfeiter, Azadi, was pulling tins of caviar from his duffel bags. He opened a tin, checking its contents, which Shehabi could see looked like plastic explosive.

Click. Shehabi looked back at the blond man with the gun when he heard the familiar sound of the AK-47 being switched from automatic to single-shot. Shehabi knew how to handle an AK-47. He had fired one many times. He had killed many Zionists. But this was a small consolation, for he now realized that he had been deceived.

Salaam was a traitor.

Shehabi switched his attention from the blond man to Salaam. His former comrade's eyes were dark and bloodshot and within them Shehabi could see no contempt, just weariness.

Shehabi said, "Fuck you."

The blond man fired and killed Shehabi with a single shot between the eyes.

CHAPTER SEVENTY-FOUR

"**W**HAT'S HAPPENED to Professor Farragut?" Hadian asked the male nurse. They were standing in Farragut's hospital room.

The male nurse shrugged. "Professor Farragut asked for a wheelchair and said he wanted to get some air. That was over an hour ago. I haven't seen him since."

Hadian knew there was just one place the professor could be: the Press. Unfortunately, Hadian had to wait for Colonel Tabriz before going further. That was the protocol.

Two minutes later the nurse left the room as Colonel Tabriz entered. A lithe, almost pretty man with a well-trimmed beard and a mole on his left cheek accompanied Tabriz. The man wore crisply pressed fatigues and a sidearm, a Glock 20.

"Inspector Hadian, this is Captain Khan of the Revolutionary Guards," said Tabriz, an even more sour expression than usual on his gloomy face. "I called him on the way over and asked him to join us. Since he is the adjunct of General Farjad and the Press is their responsibility, I thought it prudent he be here."

Hadian reluctantly shook hands with Captain Khan.

"Colonel Tabriz told me of your theory," said Captain Khan, freeing Hadian's hand.

Khan left his views of that theory to himself. Captain Ali Khan kept things close. That was why he was one of the few men that General Farjad confided in. Within the Revolutionary Guards, Khan and only Khan knew all the details of Farjad's plan for the Press and the relationship with Shareef Salaam. When the time was right and Farjad gave the word, Khan would support his superior officer all the way to the Supreme Council.

"Professor Farragut has disappeared," said Hadian. "I fear we may be too late."

Khan said nothing. Hadian continued. "Captain Khan, will you take me to the Press?"

Khan said he would do so. He was curious himself as to why General Farjad, indeed the entire security detail, had failed to answer the phones when he tried to reach them.

-:::::-

In the pressroom, Salaam expertly applied the C4 to the Press and the feeders. He had worked out the placement weeks before, gone over it in his head many times. While he worked, Farragut slung his gun around his back and helped Azadi douse the completed Supernotes with gasoline from the generator supply. Fire, not C4, would destroy the $50 million created by Azadi.

"You don't look too good," Azadi told Farragut. He still did not know the blond American's name but he felt like he knew him well. After all, he had killed Parisa.

"We'll have to destroy the printing sheets and engraved plates, too," said Farragut changing the subject.

Farragut sat on the floor, catching his breath. Azadi observed that he kept his AK-47 strapped to his body, never letting his guard down despite his obvious sickness. Azadi felt no pity, just hatred for him. The blond American was a stranger and Azadi knew nothing about him except that he had killed his beloved Parisa. For that he must die, but Azadi would have to wait until the right moment.

Hopefully that moment would happen before Special Forces came to get them out.

"I'll destroy the plates," Azadi told Farragut.

Azadi retrieved the steel engraving plates and nickel printing sheets from their storage locker then began to grind them down on the lathe. While he did this Salaam continued to plant the explosives on the Press. Farragut watched Salaam and Azadi work for a few moments while he gathered his strength. Their professionalism impressed him. He felt the urge to praise them but resisted; what would it accomplish anyway? He staggered to his feet and lit a match. He dropped the match on top of the gasoline-doused Supernotes. They burned, sending flames and clouds of black smoke into the already stuffy air.

-:::::-

Above ground, Hadian, Tabriz, and Khan arrived at the first security post just beyond the children's cancer ward.

"There should be a guard posted outside," said Khan angrily.

He tried the door but it was locked and would not open. Khan's response was to pull out his pistol and blow the lock off the door. The sound of the gunshot echoed in the corridor.

Khan pushed at the door. It wouldn't budge. Hadian and Tabriz lent their weight to the endeavor. After a collective heave the three men forced the door open.

It was not only the lock but also the two dead bodies jammed against it that had made opening the door so difficult.

Hadian's first instinct, as a former medic, was to drop to the floor and check the soldiers for vital signs. Both were dead, one of a broken neck and the other from a stab wound.

Tabriz helped Hadian to his feet and said, "My apologies, Inspector. It appears you were right after all. The Press is indeed the target."

Khan dialed the checkpoint's phone and looked up from the receiver while simultaneously pressing the elevator button.

"No answer downstairs," he said.

-:::::-

"They'll be coming soon," shouted Farragut, pointing towards the ringing phone on the wall of the pressroom. "We don't have much time."

-:::::-

Farragut watched the $50 million in counterfeit cash go up in smoke. As the flames died down he walked over to the Press where Salaam continued to work on setting the detonators.

Farragut said, "Have you ever seen what happens when gas atomizes?"

Salaam thought it an odd question to ask under the circumstances. "You mean an atomized particle explosion?"

Farragut nodded. Salaam shrugged. "Never seen one in person. But Timothy McVeigh used one to blow that federal building in Oklahoma City. He used ammonium nitrate for that one. And that plane that blew up over Long Island Sound a few years back. TWA Flight 800? Some say that was gas atomizing in the fuel tank. FAA never proved it, though."

Farragut stroked his chin. "The first time I ever saw men killed, it was due to one of those explosions. Happened at one of the refineries my dad's company ran in the south. Ten men died, they just disintegrated. No trace of them was ever found. I was there when it happened. Well, in my dad's office putting golf balls on his carpet. I went out with the fire and rescue crew. The absolute power of that explosion stunned me. Metal twisted and shorn like it was sugar candy. And human flesh? It was like the universe erased these men. They just disappeared into thin air."

Salaam set the last detonator. He turned from the Press and faced the blond man whose name he still did not know. He was staring into space, his right palm cupping his scraggly chin. He looked a far cry from the cold-blooded assassin who had executed Shehabi minutes before.

"I'm done here," said Salaam, hoping to snap the blond man out of his reverie.

Farragut looked up at Salaam, confused for a moment. Then he coughed. And coughed again. Soon he was coughing uncontrollably, the smoke from the burning Supernotes and attacking his weakened lungs without mercy. Salaam found himself patting Farragut's back as if burping a baby, trying to help this murderous stranger breathe normally again.

-:::::-

Across the pressroom Azadi turned off the lathe. The plates and sheets were now destroyed. The only sound was Farragut's coughing and the crackling of burning Supernotes. The $50 million pile of paper had been reduced to a heap of hot ash.

Azadi joined Farragut and Salaam at the Press.

"When are Special Forces coming?" asked Azadi checking his watch.

Farragut continued his coughing. Azadi turned to Salaam.

"This guy's in charge right?"

Salaam shrugged. Farragut hacked something pink and wet onto the floor.

"So," said Azadi, his voice rising despite his best efforts to sound cool and in control. "Will they be coming through the auxiliary subway tunnel or down the elevator?"

-:::::-

The elevator carrying Hadian, Tabriz and Khan descended to the pressroom level. Khan kept his sidearm ready. Hadian and Tabriz had helped themselves to the dead guards' AK-47's.

As the elevator door opened Khan rapidly fired five warning shots down the corridor.

The dead guards at the other end did not return his fire.

-:::::-

In the pressroom below, Azadi, Farragut, and Salaam heard the shots from above.

Azadi said, "That better be Special Forces."

Farragut doubled over and coughed. Salaam said nothing. He knew the gunfire wasn't from Special Forces. He had never expected the government to get him out alive. He understood he was expendable. When he had got on that plane and flown from Beirut to Tehran, made the choice not to escape, he had considered his life over. His family was now safe and financially secure. The mission, his gift to Regassa, was his last earthly responsibility. He had other debts to pay awaiting him in the afterlife but why worry about those now?

The three Americans listened to the sounds of movement upstairs beyond the locked pressroom door. They could hear running footsteps and muffled commands.

Azadi said trying to convince himself, "That has to be our guys, right?"

Azadi took a step towards the stairwell that led upstairs to the pressroom door. Farragut's hand clamped down on his shoulder and stopped him in his tracks.

"Those aren't our guys. They're Iranians."

Azadi, a growing tightness gripping his guts, turned to face Farragut. He wanted to ask Parisa's murderer, this walking corpse, a question but no words came out of his mouth. He tried to swallow but his mouth was so dry that even this simple task proved impossible.

Farragut said, "The rescue mission was a lie to get you on board. I have orders to kill you both once the explosives are set."

Upstairs beyond the door the Iranians were shouting at the grisly discovery of the dead guards. Downstairs, the Americans remained silent for several seconds.

"You have to understand," said Farragut. "The people who put together this mission don't care about us. The greater good of the country and the bureaucracies they serve is what inspires them. Men like us, we're expendable."

Farragut's words hung in the air with the remnants of the smoke from the burned bills. Salaam ambled over to the Press to double-check the detonators.

Azadi felt the blood rush to his face. He had been prepared to die but not to be betrayed when he had accepted the mission. The cops had leaned on him and offered him countless deals but he had never ratted out any of his associates. It was the code he lived by. In the eyes of the world Azadi was a crook, yes, but he didn't doubt in his heart that he was an honorable one.

"'Men like us?' I'm nothing like you. I'd never shoot my partners in the back."

Farragut gave a dry laugh. "You've been thinking of killing me since Parisa died. Don't deny it. You've been eyeballing my guns since I came down here."

The mention of Parisa infuriated Azadi. He lunged for Farragut. In an attempt to avoid Azadi, Farragut tripped and fell to the floor, losing control of his AK-47. Azadi saw the gun was free and made a move towards it. Before he knew what was happening, Salaam had passed both his arms under Azadi's armpits and pressed his hands against the back of Azadi's head, holding him in a full nelson. Azadi struggled to get free but Salaam was too strong.

Azadi said, "Let me fucking go!"

Farragut nodded at Salaam, who released Azadi. Azadi rubbed the back of his neck.

The three Americans heard shouting from the other side of the steel vault door. A reedy voice speaking English was urging the Americans to give up. Farragut didn't have to see the face on the other side of the door to know the voice belonged to Hadian.

Farragut picked himself and the AK-47 off the floor. He fired a burst at the vault door. Bullets ricocheted off the steel and whistled through the pressroom.

The voice went quiet. Farragut turned back to Azadi and Salaam. "Once they get reinforcements, they're coming through that door."

"I'm ready to set the timers on the detonators," Salaam said to Farragut.

Farragut gestured for Salaam to wait then turned to Azadi. "You think it's easy to kill a man?"

"You're not a man," said Azadi, his voice hollow. "You're a machine. Like this Press. Gears and grease and cold steel. Killing you would be no harder than emptying the trash."

Farragut nodded. The hatred in Azadi's eyes made it hard to disagree. Farragut felt no hatred himself, just a sense of completion and exhaustion. He sat on the ground, leaning on his gun. He had only one more thing to do and then it would be over.

Azadi eyed the blond man as he slumped on the ground, his grip on his gun not too steady. *Do it soon*, he thought. *Get the gun and do it soon.*

-:::::-

Ten minutes later, a backup contingent of 20 Revolutionary Guards arrived at the door outside the pressroom under Gheyam Hospital. Hadian wanted to be first through the door but Tabriz insisted that Captain Khan had that privilege since the Guards ran the Press. At that point, Khan respectfully deferred to Hadian, the lead investigator on the case. He agreed that Hadian should be the first through the door, followed by the 20 Guards, then himself and Colonel Tabriz. No one protested this arrangement, least of all Tabriz.

The men all drew their guns. Hadian pulled open the vault door and raced into the pressroom. Behind him swarmed the Guards, Khan, and Tabriz.

Hadian ran to the stairway railing. He saw three men below. He did not recognize the black man standing by the Press but he did recognize Omar Azadi and John Farragut. Azadi was pointing an AK-47 at Farragut, whose hands were raised above his head.

The black man yelled at Azadi, "Shoot him! Shoot him!"

Hadian opened his mouth to tell the Americans to give themselves up but Azadi pulled the trigger of his gun first.

A stream of bullets slammed into Farragut's chest blowing him backwards. The tumor that had taken him back to Tehran was finally dead and Farragut along with it.

CHAPTER SEVENTY-FIVE

HADIAN WAITED outside the entrance to Gheyam Hospital while the bomb squad worked in the pressroom below. Despite all that had happened, he was relatively relieved. He'd solved the case. He'd saved the Press. Just as importantly, he'd done it with a minimum of casualties. At his insistence, all the patients had been evacuated. The sickest had been transferred to nearby facilities.

The head of the bomb squad emerged through the hospital's entrance doors. He was a peevish fellow with a wax-curled moustache whose tips reminded Hadian of fuses.

"All clear?" asked Hadian.

The bomb squad leader lit a cigarette and took a drag. He exhaled a cloud of smoke that he immediately sucked back up through his nostrils. "We got all of it."

"How much?"

The bomb squad leader twitched his nose. The little waxed loops at the end of his moustache danced. "Seven, almost 8 kilograms of plastique. C4. American made stuff."

"Tell your men to keep looking."

"Why? We got all of it. The black American has been very cooperative and showed us everywhere that CIA spy forced him to put the explosives. Then, my men combed every millimeter of the Press a dozen times, just to be sure."

Hadian sniffed. "Tell your men to keep looking."

Hadian turned and walked away. He could feel the bomb squad leader's eyes drilling holes in the back of his head.

Hadian arrived at an old police truck parked at the curb. The truck bore no official markings and was painted black. Before knocking on the rear cargo doors, Hadian glanced over his shoulder. The bomb squad leader was gone, descended back down into the bowels beneath the hospital, looking for explosives. Hadian envied him. The man's job was simple compared to what Hadian had to do. Bombs don't lie. People do.

Hadian knocked and the cargo doors opened. The detective stepped inside the truck, which reeked of sweat and cigarettes. Omar Azadi and Shareef Salaam were sitting on a metal bench to the left side of the cargo hold. Azadi was checking his watch. Salaam had his eyes closed and appeared to be resting or praying, Hadian couldn't tell which. At the right side of the cargo hold, Captain Khan and Colonel Tabriz were conferring in low voices. Two Revolutionary Guards lurked behind them, armed with AK-47's and sullen expressions.

Tabriz greeted Hadian with an embarrassed look in his eyes. Hadian told Tabriz in Farsi about the bomb squad's progress. Tabriz shot a look at the Americans.

"They've told us their story," said Tabriz. "Separately and together."

"And?"

Tabriz shrugged. Hadian glanced at Khan. The captain stared through him as if Hadian were a mirror. Hadian knew it was his turn to ask the questions. He had wanted to interrogate Salaam and Azadi initially but Tabriz had suggested that Khan wanted first crack. Hadian understood that when the Revolutionary Guards wanted something, it was best to cooperate.

Hadian faced Salaam. Tabriz had briefed him about the man's identity after the Americans were taken into custody. He also knew Salaam by reputation. His escape from prison had been picked up by all the foreign news services and Hadian had no doubt that he was both brilliant and daring. But he was also a criminal. In over 20 years of police work, Hadian had never met an honest crook. Like flying pigs, the species did not exist. "Dr. Salaam, I am Inspector Kamran Hadian with the Tehran Police Department. I would like to know what you were doing in the press."

Salaam opened his eyes and glanced at Captain Khan, who shook his head.

"I'll tell you what I've already told Colonel Tabriz. I was here on official state business with the cooperation of General Farjad of the Revolutionary Guards. I'm not at liberty to discuss the details. It's a national security issue."

Hadian saw Salaam shoot another look at Khan. The Revolutionary Guards captain picked at his mole and kept his gaze hammered to a point six inches in front of his nose.

Hadian said, "Colonel, perhaps if we had more privacy?"

"Captain Khan stays," said Tabriz, looking less than thrilled.

Hadian sighed. The hierarchy of Iran's military, paramilitary, police, and security forces was understood by only a select few, but in this case a captain evidently outranked a colonel.

Hadian said, "So, Dr. Salaam, you were in the Press on official state business. Why don't you tell me what happened down there, skipping over matters of national security, of course."

"Well, I was down there doing my business when all of a sudden we hear gunshots. Next thing you know this blond guy dressed in pajamas is inside the room. He's quick on the draw, shoots Shehabi and General Farjad like they were target practice dummies. I put up my hands and tell him, 'Don't Shoot! I'm an American!' I figured he wasn't Iranian just by the look of him. So he says, 'Good to meet a fellow American. I need your help.' Then he asks me to help him plant the explosives. He said the clock was ticking and he needed extra hands."

Hadian dug into his coat pocket extract his glasses, which he put on. Then, he produced a small spiral notebook with a ballpoint pen wedged inside the coil. He opened the notebook and wrote something deliberately on the page. As he read his notes, he heard Salaam cough and Azadi shuffle his feet. *Good,* he thought, *make them sweat.* What he had written was a reminder to pick up toilet tissue and yogurt from the market but he wanted the Americans to think otherwise. After an appropriately inappropriate pause, he looked up from his notebook.

"So, Dr. Salaam, you helped Professor Farragut plant the explosives on the Press?"

"Professor who?"

"Professor John Farragut. That's the name of the American in question. You helped him plant the explosives on the Press. Correct?"

"Not at first. But the man had a gun, and as much as I hate my country I hate dying more. So I did what he told me to do."

"About how much explosive would you say the two of you attached to the Press?"

"Hey, how should I know?"

"It's a fair question, Dr. Salaam. After all, you do have some experience in these matters, if I recall correctly."

Salaam licked his lips. He shot a look at Captain Khan who betrayed no emotion.

"Like I said, I was scared and I wasn't paying attention. Off hand, I'd say 16 pounds."

"So about 8 kilograms. Of plastique?"

"C4. Yes."

"Did you attach the explosives anywhere else besides directly on the Press?"

"No."

"Did you give Professor Farragut advice on where to best plant the explosives?"

"Fuck you."

The two armed henchmen from the Revolutionary Guards rumbled forward but Khan held them back with a dismissive flick of his wrist. When Hadian looked to Tabriz for a reaction he saw him staring at his fingernails as if they were the most fascinating things he had ever seen.

Hadian said, "Excuse me, Dr. Salaam, I did not mean to suggest that you were in any way...how do you say it? *Conspiring* with Professor Farragut. I was simply curious if the professor knew about your expertise – your story has, after all, been in the news of late. And if he forced you, under great duress, of course, to assist him in ensuring that the placement of the explosives would produce the maximum destructive effect."

"I offered him nothing. The man had a plan and I did what he told me to do. If I hadn't, I wouldn't be here talking to you. I'd be in a body bag like the rest of those poor bastards down there. Besides, I tried to stop him."

"Oh?"

"Yes. I intentionally planted a brick of C4 so it wouldn't hold. When it fell off the Press, the guy, Farragut, leaned down to pick it up. That's when I jumped him. He was stronger than he looked but I managed to knock his gun out of his hands." Salaam gestured to Azadi. "My man here picked up the gun first and killed the bastard. End of story."

Salaam crossed his arms defiantly. Hadian saw Khan betray a small smile.

Azadi said, "That's right, Inspector. Everything he said I saw. The professor... what's his name again?"

"Farragut. Professor John Farragut."

"Yeah. Farragut. He came in shooting like the fucking Terminator. General Farjad and Shehabi never had a chance."

"And where were you during all this, Mr. Azadi?"

"Hiding. As soon as the bullets started flying I ducked behind the generator gas drums."

"And Professor Farragut never saw you?"

Azadi checked his watch. "I guess he was too busy setting the explosives. Did I tell you that he smuggled the C4 in caviar tins? Pretty smart, huh? This guy was good. He was shooting his gun with one hand and carried the duffel bag with the caviar tins in the other. Unbelievable. You should have seen it."

Hadian had seen the caviar tins in Farragut's room the night before. He had no proof that the caviar tins in Farragut's room weren't already filled with C4. It was possible that Farragut had done this. Still, it rankled. To conceal his irritation, he scribbled the name of his wife and son in his notebook, as well as the dates of their birthdays.

"So, Mr. Azadi, let me make sure I understand your story. Farragut smuggled in the C4 in caviar tins while shooting everyone, with the exception of you and Dr. Salaam, of course. Then, he forced Dr. Salaam to help him plant the explosives. Dr. Salaam did this, fearing for his life, until he saw an opportunity to overpower Farragut. They struggled and Farragut lost control of his gun. You claim you saw all this while hiding behind the gas drums. Is that correct?"

"I don't claim to be a hero, Inspector."

"To the contrary, Mr. Azadi. Thanks to you it appears the Press was saved. Would you please tell me the circumstances by which you killed Professor Farragut?"

"Not much to tell. When Farragut lost control of the gun, I came out of hiding and picked it up. He was begging for his life. I would have let him live but he grabbed for the gun."

Hadian felt a shudder of excitement, the same shudder of excitement he felt when hooking a sturgeon during one of his yearly fishing trips to the Caspian Sea. He planted his glasses and notebook back in his coat pocket; then leveled his gaze at Azadi.

"Yes. I saw you shoot Professor Farragut, Mr. Azadi. I caught a glimpse of it just as I was entering the Press. But please answer me this: why would the professor be begging for his life? He was already near death from cancer."

Azadi drummed his fingers on the bench, thinking. Hadian did not turn around but he knew that the eyes of Tabriz, Khan, and the gunmen were now focused on the American printer.

"I don't know why he was begging for his life. Maybe he wanted to play on my sympathy, hoping I'd drop my guard so he could get the gun. I didn't know the man."

"Oh, really? Then why did you have his tweed coat in your apartment the day I interrogated you?"

A silence filled the cargo hold. Hadian watched the muscles in Azadi's jaw quiver. The printer shot a look at Captain Khan, who nodded almost imperceptibly.

"Okay. I lied a little. I had met Farragut before," admitted Azadi with a shrug.

"Mr. Azadi. I feel you are lying quite a bit, not just a little."

"I'm telling the truth," snapped Azadi. "I knew Farragut from this one thing we did together. I printed cash that was used to buy some artifacts. He came to my apartment to pick up the funny money and left his coat by accident. He never told me his name. If you don't believe me, ask Captain Khan. I was working with the full cooperation of the Revolutionary Guards."

"So was Farragut," replied Hadian evenly. "But he's been revealed to be a spy."

Azadi shot to his feet. "Look. I'm tired of your bullshit accusations. I killed Farragut in cold blood. If that's not proof of my loyalty I don't know what is."

Before Hadian could reply Captain Khan said in Farsi, "That's enough, Inspector. These men have cooperated to my satisfaction."

"But not to mine," said Hadian, wheeling around to face Khan. "I still feel the suspects are hiding something."

"They are not suspects. They are not being charged with any crime."

"Not yet. But I intend to hold them in custody pending the conclusion of my investigation."

"You do not have that authority."

"Not as a member of the police department, no. But my services are currently on loan to the Ministry of Intelligence. By the time the *mullahs* sort out whether your agency or Colonel Tabriz's has proper authority in this matter, I shall have already completed my investigation."

Hadian and Khan glared at each other. Tabriz clapped his hands together.

"Gentleman. Please. We are all on the same side here."

There was a knocking sound from outside the truck. Khan nodded to one of the Revolutionary Guards, who opened the door. Outside the truck Hadian was stunned to see a short man sporting an English-tailored suit and a trim salt-and-pepper beard. Hadian had watched him on TV many times and knew him to be Reza Fotoohi, the Deputy Foreign Minister of Iran. The presence of this political heavyweight was enough to make Hadian's jaw drop, but what he saw next took his breath away.

The German Ambassador and his beautiful wife appeared, flanked by two members of their security detail. The ambassador was propping up his distraught spouse, tears streaming down her lovely face. In her manicured hands she clutched a letter which Hadian's detective instincts told him would soon make him want to cry, too, albeit for an entirely different reason.

CHAPTER SEVENTY-SIX

INSIDE THE POLICE truck's cargo hold, Ingrid Mader sobbed into a silk handkerchief for several minutes before attempting to read the letter aloud. Her audience consisted of Captain Khan, Colonel Tabriz, Inspector Hadian, and Deputy Foreign Minister Fotoohi. The two Revolutionary Guards had been excused. Ambassador Mader and his security detail had returned to his limousine along with Azadi and Salaam, whom Mader had invited to join him. Hadian had protested fiercely that the two Americans should remain in his custody but Minister Fotoohi had pulled rank and allowed them to leave with the German ambassador. He explained that he was present at this inquiry due to the urging of his uncle, Ayatollah Fotoohi, currently the most liberal member of the very conservative and extremely powerful Guardian Council. Ayatollah Fotoohi had lived in Germany before the revolution and had been an honored guest of the Mader family on many occasions. So, suggested the Deputy Foreign Minister in no uncertain terms, if one of the most powerful men in Iran didn't object to Ambassador Mader's graciousness towards the Americans, then perhaps a common police inspector shouldn't either? He added that what Frau

Mader was about to reveal was not for anyone's ears except the men in the cargo hold.

After folding her handkerchief and depositing it into her purse, Ingrid was composed enough to read the letter. "John Farragut left this letter in my purse last night. I did not discover it until several hours ago."

"*Dearest Ingrid,*" she began. "*If you are reading this, it means I am already dead. By now, you will have heard about the incident at Gheyam Hospital. I do not apologize for what I did but I must apologize to you. I am sorry I used you and you were caught up in my deceit. I have much hate and bitterness in my heart but your love made me feel part of something bigger and better and more profound than my own miserable soul...*"

Ingrid began to cry again. The men lowered their eyes, embarrassed, except for Hadian, who checked his watch and impatiently tapped his foot against the steel floor.

"Inspector, please..." admonished the Deputy Foreign Minister in a harsh whisper.

"Frau Mader, I beg your pardon," said Hadian through clenched teeth. "We are all sorry for your loss but we do not have much time. The investigation is still pending."

"Of course, Inspector. It is I who should apologize. I can't imagine how stressful this has been for you."

Hadian forced himself to bow politely. He tightened his buttocks in an effort to suppress the urge to rip the letter out of Ingrid's hands and read it himself.

Ingrid blew her nose and continued to read the letter. "*My darling, I wish your love had been enough to stop me from this self-destructive act. After the near death of my beloved father at the hands of terrorists, on top of my own terminal diagnosis, hatred was the only emotion I could comprehend. I hated the terrorists that killed so indiscriminately. I hated my own government that was too afraid to act, despite their declarations of the war on terror. I had served that government honorably and honestly for twenty years with the Central Intelligence Agency. That meant nothing to them. I felt betrayed, beaten down,*" *and without hope. Only through a cathartic act of revenge did I think I could feel alive. I was wrong. I was more alive with you in my dying days than I ever was before my body betrayed me..."*

Ingrid began to cry again. She dug in her purse for her handkerchief but Minister Fatoohi offered his own. She took it and dabbed her eyes. He bowed formally to her.

"I am sorry for your loss, Frau Mader. Please accept my condolences."

Minister Fatoohi turned to Tabriz, Khan, and Hadian. "Gentleman, Frau Mader was kind enough to let me read the letter when she first discovered it. It concludes with Professor Farragut's assertion that he acted alone in his plan to destroy the Press. He asks for forgiveness from his friend, Dr. Ali Ardabili, who he insists knew nothing of his deception. And although he professes no love for the government of the Islamic Republic of Iran, he declares that he still admires Iran's people and its extraordinary history. To that end, he is leaving a sizable portion of his estate to the National Museum, to be administered by Dr. Ardabili as he sees fit."

Hadian was too furious to speak without risking an outburst. He watched Ingrid pat her lovely face with the Deputy Foreign Minister's hankie.

"You were right, Inspector Hadian," said Ingrid between sniffles. "John Farragut was using me all along."

But Hadian was the one feeling used as the Deputy Foreign Minister, nephew of an *ayatollah* on the Supreme Council, escorted the German ambassador's wife out of the cargo hold, clutching her arm as if she were as fragile and precious as a Faberge egg.

-:::::-

When Ingrid and the Minister Fatoohi were gone, Hadian turned back to Colonel Tabriz.

"I have many more questions, Colonel. And I request your permission to ask them."

But it was Captain Khan who spoke before Colonel Tabriz had a chance. "Your investigation is over, Inspector. We have our man. The letter proves it. Professor Farragut was a rogue CIA agent. He was responsible for the events here. And I suggest you talk no more of the events here. The Press remains a valuable asset, thanks to the heroism of Omar Azadi and Shareef Salaam, both of whom are engaged in crucial activities to assist the Islamic Republic in its war against the imperialism of the United States of America. They were trusted by the late General Farjad and have proven that trust was warranted."

Captain Khan bowed stiffly and said, "Goodnight, gentleman."

After Khan had left, Hadian and Tabriz were alone in the back of the stuffy, dark van.

"I don't believe any of this, Colonel."

"Are you saying that the German Ambassador's wife is a liar?"

"She's cheating on her husband so she is certainly capable of duplicity."

"The ambassador is a homosexual. The Ministry has tapes to prove it. They no doubt have an arrangement. Europeans are much more lenient about these things than we are."

Tabriz's sarcastic snort failed to ameliorate Hadian's anxiety.

"Please give me more time to interrogate her."

"Absolutely not. You heard Captain Khan. Case closed."

Hadian shuddered, tamping down his anger. "I'll get the truth. She'll change her story."

Tabriz offered Hadian a fatigued smile. "My dear, Hadian. Things are changing in our country. Captain Khan and his crowd will not be in power for much longer. They may control the present but they can't control the future. Iran must prepare to rejoin the rest of the world and Germany is our largest trading partner in Europe. Politically and economically, we need them to help pave the way. And soon the United States may see us in a different light. Not as part of an axis of evil, but rather as a vast untapped market for goods and services, blessed with a young population of demographically desirable consumers. You must be patient. I believe it was your beloved Beatles who sang 'all things must pass.'" Tabriz gave Hadian a knowing wink.

The two men exited the truck. The cool, night air was a welcome change after the stuffiness of the cargo hold. Tabriz hugged Hadian and told him to take some time off. He had earned it. The Press was saved and that's all that mattered. Hadian watched as Tabriz got in his car and drove away into the night.

Despite Tabriz's encouragement Hadian did not feel like rejoicing. He went to find the ambassador's limousine, hoping for a word with Ingrid Mader in front of Azadi and Salaam. But where the limousine had been parked he found only Captain Khan milling about with a contingent of Revolutionary Guards. Hadian overheard Khan discussing plans to relocate the Press to a new, more secure location. He cleared his throat to get Khan's attention and asked him where Ambassador Mader's limousine was.

"The ambassador and his wife have left, Inspector. I suggest you do the same."

"And what about Azadi and Salaam?" asked Hadian, sensing the worst.

Khan signed a form and shielded it from Hadian's gaze as he handed it back to an aide.

"The ambassador and his wife offered to drop them off at their respective residences."

The cold air had cleared Hadian's head but he wasn't sure he had heard right.

"You let them leave?"

"The Deputy Foreign Minister insisted," replied Khan. Then he marched off, surrounded by armed Revolutionary Guards, heading back inside the hospital to secure his beloved Press.

Hadian got into his car, still stunned by what he considered a cover-up. His mood worsened as he turned the key in the ignition but couldn't get the engine of the old Paykan to turn over. It always gave him problems in cold weather. He was in no mood to bum a ride off of any of the hundred or so policemen now gathered around the hospital so he walked away, hoping to flag a cab

He found one loitering two blocks from the hospital. Despite the cab being empty the driver refused his fare, insisting he was off duty. With his buckteeth and fat cheeks, Hadian thought the cabbie looked like a chipmunk, but there was no doubt this chipmunk was as stubborn as a mule.

Hadian decided to walk home. The night air was beginning to relax him anyway. Yes, he still had questions and suspicions but the important thing was that he'd solved the case and the Press had been saved. That was more than he could say about the dead prostitutes piling up at the airport. *Don't dwell on such things*, he thought. *You have a loving wife who can't cook but to whom you owe your life. You have a wonderful son with talent and tenacity who will one day live in a better Iran than this one. You have much to feel good about, Kamran. Rejoice —*

The explosion obliterated the night's emerging calm. The concussive shock wave blasted up from below the earth and roiled the ground under Hadian's feet. At first Hadian thought it was an earthquake – the big one that everyone in Tehran waited for with abject terror — but the thought evaporated when he heard the *boom* of the muffled blast beneath his feet.

Hadian fell and hit the ground, nose in the dirt, underneath which he now knew with unerring certainty that the Supernote Press had been blown into nothingness.

-:::::-

Days later, while recovering at home from the concussion his fall had dealt him, Hadian would remember the last image he saw before passing out. The cab that had just refused him a ride disappearing into the anonymity of the city, its driver smiling so broadly that even his rodent-like features appeared, for a stolen moment, indisputably sublime.

CHAPTER SEVENTY-SEVEN

SALAAM PUMPED diesel fuel into the tank of the Catalina 400 Mark II yacht. She took 44 gallons and her 4-cylinder, 56-horsepower engine gave him the ability to cruise for hours. But this beauty was built for sailing. Her mainsail rated 400 square feet and Salaam couldn't wait to ride the wind with her. He'd grown up a poor boy on the wrong side of San Francisco Bay; he'd always dreamed of owning a boat like this. Now, here on the island of Curacao in the Netherlands Antilles more than 50 years later, he owned one.

Salaam topped off the gas tank. He'd realized he'd always associate that gasoline smell with those final minutes in the pressroom below Gheyam Hospital. He'd done exactly what Farragut had told him to. He'd gone to the gas dump used for the generator and planted 4 pounds of C4 in a half-empty, 50-gallon drum. He'd used two detonators, both set for a two hour delay, plenty of time for he and Azadi to get away.

The atomized particle explosion had also been Farragut's idea. Farragut had grown up around refineries and knew about their awesome destructive power. Salaam told himself he would have thought of it himself if he had known the Iranians kept the generator and gas down there. But he didn't know because everything had been compartmentalized. Only Farragut had seen how it all fit together. Only he was capable of changing the game and the rules on the fly.

Salaam understood how the atomized particle explosion worked. He went over it in his mind as he walked up the dock towards the harbormaster's shop to pay for the gas. It helped him not to think about how Farragut's guts had spilled onto the floor of the room after he was shot.

If a highly flammable substance is atomized or divided into very small particles, and a large amount of it is burned in a confined area, an explosion of immense destructive power is produced. The tiny droplets of gasoline burn in the air, and the hot gasses expand rapidly. If only a gallon of gasoline is atomized and ignited in a building, using a high explosive like C4, the expanding gas will push the walls of the building down and bring down the entire structure.

"That's $285 for the gas," said the harbormaster.

Salaam paid the harbormaster with a legitimate credit card assigned to his new phony identity, courtesy of Mia Kelly. He was now Horace Threewit. *Horace Threewit,* he thought, *sounds like the name of a patent attorney or a minor poet of post-modern school. Oh, well, it will have to do.*

Horace Threewit, AKA Shareef Salaam, AKA Gary Hastings strolled back to his boat and remembered how Farragut had told Salaam and Azadi he, Farragut, had to die in order for them to live. When the Iranians saw Azadi shoot the American spy before their eyes, when Salaam helped them find the C4 planted on the Press, there would be no reason for them to search the gas drums. Their guard would be down. At that point, Farragut had assured them, the Iranians would believe they had won.

Neither Salaam nor Azadi had protested Farragut's plan. It was the best chance they had to survive. And besides, if they had refused to go along with it, Farragut or the Iranians would have killed them anyway. So Azadi had taken the gun while Salaam had stood back. For the second time in less than a week, Salaam had watched another man sacrifice himself so that he, Salaam, could live. Salaam wasn't proud of it. It was just the way it was. And he felt as strongly as he had ever felt anything that God expected him to show some serious gratitude from here on out.

When Salaam returned to the boat, Billie and Gary had come up from below decks.

"Grandpa, do you want to go swimming with dolphins tomorrow?"

"Have you finished your homework?"

"Almost," said Gary, frowning. "You're a tougher teacher than I had in Seattle."

Salaam picked up his grandson and blew a raspberry into his belly button, getting a big giggle from Gary. "I'm a softie. But you're so cute I can't help spoiling you. Now go get your grandpa a glass of pineapple juice and I'll take you swimming with the dolphins today."

Salaam put down Gary and sent him off with a pat on his rump. As his grandson disappeared below decks, Salaam turned his attention to his daughter. Billie was hanging laundry to dry on the transom and seemed more relaxed than he could ever remember her.

"You wouldn't be so easy on him, daddy, if you knew he spilled chocolate milk all over your prayer rug."

"Chocolate milk? You're kidding?"

"I rinsed it in the sink with the rest of our clothes. Stain came right out. I'll hang it out to dry right here and it'll be ready by sundown." Then she added with a playful smile: "I'm watching your back, Daddy. Don't worry."

But Salaam did worry. Although the German ambassador to Iran had assured him that his government would protect Azadi and him until the United States pledged not to go after them, Salaam still did not feel safe. The US government had lied to him at least once already. But when the word came down that the Americans were "satisfied" with the end result of the mission and that Salaam and Azadi could collect their fee without fear of "interference," Salaam had flown from Cologne (where he and Azadi had been smuggled via the ambassador's private Lear jet) to Curacao. Still, Salaam prayed five times a day like the devout Muslim he was, and each time he prayed that he wasn't being naïve to believe the Americans wouldn't come for him and his family.

Billie hung the prayer rug on a laundry line she had tied beneath the boom. As she worked she sang Billie Holiday.

"Away from the city that hurts and knocks. I'm standing alone by the desolate docks. In the still and the chill of the night. I see the horizon, the great unknown. My heart has an ache, it's as heavy as stone..."

Salaam closed his eyes and breathed the scent of warm, clean clothes. He hadn't smelled that delicious scent since Terminal Island, since his job in the laundry room. The aroma always made him think of Victoria, his late wife, and he tried to remember what her face looked like, what her skin tasted like, what their life together could have been like, *should* have been like.

Salaam heard his daughter say, "I'm no Billie Holiday but I'm not that bad, am I?"

Salaam opened his eyes and turned to Billie. "No. Not at all, sweetie."

Billie laughed. "Then why are you crying, daddy?"

Salaam tasted the salt on his lips. He touched his cheeks and felt the tears. He shut his eyes to stanch their flow but it just made him cry harder. His grandson didn't even cry anymore and here he was, an old, broken down ex-con bawling like a baby.

-:::::-

Salaam met Azadi that night at the Schooner Bar in the Avila Beach Hotel, one of the better establishments on an island that catered to multi-millionaires, legit and not so legit. It was the first time the two had met since they'd left Iran to flee to Germany three months ago. Salaam had been in Curacao for almost the full three months. He had flown there as soon as he felt safe enough and could arrange for Billie and Gary to meet him. He had confirmed his money in the Caymans bank account through the branch in Curacao and was pleased to see that the account contained the full $10 million. He didn't go to the Caymans because he didn't want to be that close to the money in case *they* were staking out the bank. He had bought his yacht and looked around for Azadi – they had agreed back in Iran that this was the best place in the Caribbean to meet. Still, he hadn't seen him anywhere. He had made inquiries around town if anyone had seen a man matching Azadi's description, but no one had. Then just today he had received a message from the manager of the bank when he went in to make a withdrawal. He had been handed a note that told him to go to the Schooner Bar at 8:00 p.m. Azadi had been waiting for him at the bar. He had put on weight and his beard was growing in gray, but he looked remarkably relaxed, all things considered.

Azadi ordered a cognac and Salaam ordered a pineapple juice. The counterfeiter told Salaam he'd been traveling around and had just now decided to stop off in Curacao to close down his account. He was transferring the bulk of the funds into his father's account in Los Angeles. Azadi told Salaam he didn't want the money anyway. He'd just wind up blowing it.

They didn't speak much after that, preferring to listen to the sound of the surf and the inane chatter of the rich tourists at nearby tables. They didn't really know what to say to one another. Hell, they'd never even called each other by their first names. They didn't know each other well and what they knew about each other, they never wanted to talk about again.

Salaam said, "So. What are you up to?"

"I've been painting. Landscapes and such. I work in oils. So, painting and moving from place to place. That's about it."

"You gonna do that forever or do you have plans?"

"I wouldn't tell you if I knew and I don't know. Know what I mean?"

Salaam did and smiled. They couldn't get too close, just in case. It got quiet again.

"Want to see my boat?" asked Salaam.

"Sure."

After much arguing over who would pay the bill Azadi called for the check. When Azadi tried to pay in hundreds, the bartender pointed out the menu. Right above the mention of the service charge it said the bar did not accept $100 bills. Azadi asked why that was since the island was, after all, a center of offshore banking.

"We've had some problems with counterfeits," said the bartender. Salaam chuckled and paid with his new credit card.

-:::::-

It was just past midnight. Billie and Gary were asleep below decks. Salaam and Azadi stood on the dock admiring Salaam's yacht.

"So… what are you gonna name her?" asked Azadi.

Azadi pointed towards the boat's stern. No name had yet been painted on the hull. Salaam stroked his recently shaved face. He missed his beard.

"I was thinking *Farragut's Folly.*"

Azadi chuckled. "*Farragut's Folly.* That fits."

The men listened to the night. The soft night wind played over the water and rattled the mainstay like a snare drum. Gary had woken up down below and his mother was comforting him. Their voices were soft and almost inaudible but the boy appeared to have had a bad dream.

After a while Salaam spoke. "Why do you think he let us live, Omar?"

"No idea, Shareef."

They shook hands goodbye and never saw each other again.

EPILOGUE

ONE WEEK LATER and 1700 miles to the north, Mia Kelly met Ingrid Mader at the Museum of Natural History in New York City. Their meeting took place under the giant whale in the Hall of Ocean life. It was what Farragut had asked for so they honored his final request.

"You must be Mia," said Ingrid, hoisting herself to her feet and walking up to the slight brunette in black who had been looking around the main room like a lost tourist.

"Ingrid, it is so wonderful to finally meet you. Please, don't stand."

"Don't be ridiculous, I need the exercise. I'm as fat as a whale."

They kissed on the cheeks in the European fashion even though they didn't know one another. Mia found it awkward but Ingrid seemed to insist on this intimacy. They began to walk amongst the school kids, nannies, and teachers leading class trips.

"I suppose I should say, 'thank you,'" said Mia. "You and your husband did a wonderful thing."

"I only did what John wanted, and my husband did what I wanted. It was not a big deal."

"Yes. It was. God bless you."

Farragut had told Ingrid that Mia Kelly was earnest, devout, and direct. He had also said that she was petite and brunette and very pretty. But the woman walking beside her seemed thin and wan and very tired. The polish on her nails was chipped.

"Has it been difficult for you, Mia?"

Mia watched a little girl in a "Hello Kitty" T-shirt walk hand-in-hand with her mother. To Mia, the mother looked plump, unglamorous, and very, very happy.

"No. Just strange, really. I mean, they can't fire me for being successful. After all, the Press was destroyed. Not only has a major source of terrorist dollars dried up, but the reformers in Iran see that we are willing to go the extra mile. Our best intelligence tells us that they are emboldened and things will only get better. The Israelis are, of course, ecstatic. Their man on the ground there has nothing but positive things to report."

"But John disobeyed your direct orders when you said cease and desist. And the men who worked with him are still out there."

"The Press being destroyed is the most important thing."

"Letting these men live in peace is just as important. That's why John wanted me to meet with you. To get your word that they wouldn't be harmed."

Mia felt acute shame at that moment. The idea that this beautiful, cosmopolitan woman who had been the great love of John Farragut's life knew Mia had been capable of such abject cruelty, seemed obscene in a museum filled with children.

"They won't be touched. You have my word."

Mia noticed all the white children accompanied by black or Hispanic nannies. Where were all the mothers? Getting their hair done? Their nails manicured? She felt old and gray and desiccated next to the glamorous Ingrid Mader. The woman positively glowed with health and life and sex. Was it her or was it the little bit of John that lived on inside of her?

"So. When's the baby due?" asked Mia.

"Four months. Hopefully before my divorce is final. Oh, look, there they are."

Ingrid's husband, the German Ambassador, and their two children were by the Indian War Canoe. The little blond boy, who Ingrid said was named Rolf, had managed to scramble into the canoe and was trying to climb onto the shoulders of the Indian Chief. The ambassador was desperately trying to get his son out of the canoe but the kid was too quick and his father too dignified to discipline him in public. A security guard was simultaneously shouting into his walkie-talkie and wiping away the remains of a vanilla ice cream cone that the blond girl, who Ingrid said was named Francesca, had tossed onto the front of his shirt.

"Would you like to join us for lunch?" asked Ingrid. "My treat. The Petra Café on the fourth floor has delicious sandwiches."

"I'd better get back to the office. I've got a lot to clear off my desk."

They promised to keep in touch though Mia wasn't sure that was a promise she could keep. But the other promise she *would* keep. She would keep those men safe. She told herself that and she believed it. Or tried to.

Mia exited onto Central Park West and headed downtown. The air was balmy and smelled like damp earth and tree buds and steam from the subway below. Early spring. She didn't want to take a cab; she wanted to walk. But she really had to get back to work.

She walked the 20 blocks down to Central Park South, letting the living city surround her like a mother's womb. And then she relented to her bunions and caught a cab and headed crosstown to the East Side rather than downtown to work. On Madison Avenue she threw caution to the wind and had her hair and nails done in her favorite salon. They took her without an appointment because they had always liked her and it had been such a long time since they had last seen her. She gossiped with the stylist and the manicurist and she thought how wonderful it was to play hooky and act like a girl.

And when they asked her how her son was doing she said fine. She didn't even cry.

And by the time she was ordering her first single malt in the bar at the St. Regis at just past six, she realized that life was a very fine thing indeed.

Made in the USA
San Bernardino, CA
28 December 2018